The Hunting of Cain

THE
HUNTING
OF CAIN

A True Story of Money,
Greed and Fratricide

DAN E. MOLDEA

Atheneum New York 1983

Photographs of Tony Ridle, John Harris, William C. Dear, Larry
Momchilov, Richard Munsey and William Lewis are by Dan E. Moldea
Photograph of Rich Craven is courtesy Scottsdale Police Department.
All other photographs, with the exception of that of David Harden,
are courtesy Summit County Sheriff's Office.

LIBRARY OF CONGRESS CATALOGING IN PUBLICATION DATA

Moldea, Dan E., —
  The hunting of Cain.

  1. Murder—Ohio—Bath. 2. Victims of crimes—
Ohio—Bath. 3. Milo, Dean. 4. Crime and criminals—
Ohio—Bath. 5. Milo, Fred. 6. Trials (Murder)—
Ohio—Akron. I. Title.
HV6534.B343M64 1983   364.1'523'0977136   82–73032

ISBN 978-1-4767-7197-7

Published simultaneously in Canada by McClelland and Stewart Ltd.
Composed by Maryland Linotype Composition Company,
Baltimore, Maryland
Manufactured by Fairfield Graphics, Fairfield, Pennsylvania
Designed by Mary Cregan
First Edition

To my dad, mom and sister—
for all we've been through this year

"The Lord received Abel and his gift with favour;
but Cain and his gift he did not receive.
Cain was very angry and his face fell.
Then the Lord said to Cain, 'Why are you so angry and
    cast down?
If you do well, you are accepted;
If not, sin is a demon crouching at the door.
It shall be eager for you, and you will be mastered by it.'
Cain said to his brother, 'Let us go into the open country.'
While they were there, Cain attacked his brother Abel and
    murdered him.
Then the Lord said to Cain, 'Where is your brother Abel?'
Cain answered, 'I do not know. Am I my brother's keeper?' "

GENESIS 4:4–10
The New English Bible

Contents

Part Three: R E S O L U T I O N

This book could not have been written without the
cooperation and assistance of William C. Dear,
Private Investigator, Dallas, Texas

Acknowledgments

THIS work could not have been completed without the invaluable assistance of Lieutenants Larry Momchilov and William Lewis of the Summit County Sheriff's Department in Ohio; Richard Munsey of the Bath Township Police Department, also of Ohio; Richard Craven of the Scottsdale Police Department in Arizona; and Frederic L. Zuch of the Summit County Prosecutor's Office. These gentlemen were chiefly responsible for confirming or denying information I collected during my investigation of their investigation of the murder of Dean Milo. They were always accessible for questioning and ensured that I never went off the track with my work.

Special thanks are extended to those investigators and staffers who worked in an official capacity on the Milo murder investigation for various law enforcement agencies: David Bailey, Tom Bostick, Larry Coleman, Marv Dawkins, Ed Duvall, Peggy Koloniar, Ken Lockhard, Dorothy Madden, Mark Martin, Charles Pongracz, John Rege, Bob Scalise, Bill Stallworth, and Sheriff Dave Troutman, all of the Summit County Sheriff's Department: also to: LaVerne Ferguson, John Gardner, David Gravis, Chief William O. Gravis, Kirk Shively, and Mike Zorena, all of the Bath Township Police Department; also to: The Akron Police Department; the staff of the Bureau of

Criminal Investigations in Richfield, Ohio; Chief Ricardo Hawkins of the Stark County Sheriff's Department; Arlene D. Fisk, assistant district attorney in Philadelphia; polygraph operators William D. Evans and Forrest Marts; Special Agent William E. White of the Akron office of the Federal Bureau of Investigation; George Graham of the Arizona Drug Control Division; Maryann Eickelman of the Summit County Prosecutor's Office; Dave Cooper, Tim Smith, Dick McBane, and Dennis McEaneney of *The Akron Beacon Journal*; and to my good friend Tim Davis, the Summit County Auditor, who gave me confidence and compassion during a personal crisis, as well as many lectures on the political atmosphere in Akron and Summit County.

Sincere gratitude is also expressed to all of my brothers and sisters at The Institute for Policy Studies in Washington, D.C., especially Bob Borosage, Dick Barnet, and Marc Raskin;

And to those who have made my life—and, thus, my work—a little easier: Michael Allen, Annabelle's, Marylou Baker, Ann Beattie, Leonard Bertsch, Dick Billings, Mr. and Mrs. Bob Brady, Howard Bray, The Bucket Shop, Cristine Candela, Mark Carson, Isolde Chapin, C.P. Chima, Pat Clawson, the physicians and staff at the Cleveland Clinic, Diane Cole, Carole Collins, Kay Constantine, Donn Cory, Ana Craciun, Ann Marie Cunningham, Bob Davis, Nancy Davis, Mike deBlois, John Dinges, Janet Donovan and her children, Ariel Dorfman, Jack Dover, Celia Eckhardt, Mike Ewing, Lou Farris, Rachel Fershko, Bob Fink, Hamilton Fish, Sid Foster, Arthur Fox, Mike Gale, Marjorie Gaus, Fred Gloss, Jeff Goldberg, Barry Golson, Sue Goodwin, Don Greene, Jim Gross, Chester Hartman, Mary Heathcote, Mark Hertsgaard, Bill Hill, Jim Hougan, Perdita Huston, Doug Ireland, Pam Johnson, Kitty Kelley, Mary King, Ron Koltnow, Alex Kura, Saul Landau, Todd Lane, Bob Lawrence, Rev. Fr. Lawrence Lazar, Isabel Letelier, Nancy Lewis, Neil Livingstone, Bob Loomis, Dave Lubell, Ann Lynett, Joe Madigan, Scott Malone, John Marks, Steve Martindale, Rudy Maxa, Janet Michaud, Ethelbert Miller, John Naum, Gary Nesbitt, Carl Oglesby, Bob Pack, Ken Paff, Michael Parenti, David Parker, Tom Passavant, Mark Perry, Pat Pringle, Barbara Raskin, Barry Reighard, Judy Saks, Tom Sawyer, Harold

Shantz, Carl Schoffler, Curtis Seltzer, Frank Selzer, Walter Sheridan, John Sikorski, Tom Slocum, Georgiana Smith, John Solomon, Jeff Stein, Kitty Stone, Joel Swerdlow, Jim Switzer, Marge Tabankin, Dawn Trouard, Judith Turner, Bob Verdisco, Tom von Stein, Jimmy Warner, Susan Waters, Rozanne Weissman, Danny Wexler, Herb White, Wendy Wilson, and all my neighbors on New Hampshire Avenue in Washington and on Elmore Avenue in Akron.

Finally, I would like to thank my literary agent, Philip Spitzer; my attorneys, Nick Roetzel and George Farris; my writing coach, Nancy Nolte; and my patient editor, Neil Nyren at Atheneum, who believed in and fought for this project from the outset.

Preface

THE police investigation of the murder of millionaire business executive Dean Milo in Bath, Ohio, is a sensational but complicated story. It is, perhaps, the most talked about case in the state since the slaughter of Dr. Sam Sheppard's wife in 1954. That is understandable, considering that fratricide—the act of killing one's brother—is such a classic crime.

Because of the fascinating characters, the smoking guns, and true confessions contained in this plot, I was never tempted to sensationalize what was already sensational. In short, I have attempted to minimize my power as the author of this work. I try not to use my words to take any moral stands for or against any characters or their acts. I do not claim to know what any character was thinking—unless he or she explained it to a police officer or to me in an interview. In short, I have tried to avoid all hit-and-run tactics. This is a story of a brilliant, year-long police investigation; and I wanted the reader to learn about the case as it was developed by the police.

Everything contained in this work is based upon confidential police reports, court records and transcripts, and tape-recorded interviews with a variety of speakers, both suspects and cooperative witnesses. All of these interviews were conducted by either law enforcement officials or me.

The names of several characters—who are innocent of all crimes stemming from the murder of Dean Milo—have been changed, on the advice of law enforcement officials involved in the investigation.

In order to limit the number of minor characters who were interviewed, three composite characters—Peter Hartmann, Nick Terpolos, and John Hastings—have been introduced. These fictitious people have been created in this non-fiction book for the purposes of clarity, continuity, and confidentiality. No charges of criminal misconduct or illegal acts have been alleged by any of these composite characters. Of course, I am prepared to defend any statements attributed to them.

Other specific liberties—such as the use of re-created conversations, interviews, and scenes—taken by me in this work are listed in the Appendix.

Also, for the record, I have been personally acquainted, for nearly ten years, with Barry Boyd, a principal character in this book. Boyd was one of several people who encouraged me to write it.

Dan E. Moldea
Dupont Circle
November 19, 1982

Principal Characters

(*) NAME CHANGED

The Hunters

DAVID BAILEY: Detective-Sergeant, Summit County Sheriff's
Department

THOMAS BOSTICK: Commander of Detectives, Summit County
Sheriff's Department

RICHARD CRAVEN: Detective, Scottsdale Police Department

WILLIAM C. DEAR: Dallas private investigator

EDWARD DUVALL: Chief of Investigations and Intelligence,
Summit County Sheriff's Department

DR. A. H. KYRIAKIDES: Summit County Coroner

WILLIAM E. LEWIS: Detective-Lieutenant, Summit County
Sheriff's Department

MARK MARTIN: Detective, Summit County Sheriff's Department

LARRY MOMCHILOV: Detective-Lieutenant, Summit County
Sheriff's Department

RICHARD MUNSEY: Detective-Sergeant, Bath Township Police
Department

DAVID TROUTMAN: Summit County Sheriff

FREDERIC L. ZUCH: Chief of the Criminal Division, Summit
County Prosecutor's Office

Associates of William C. Dear

BOB DARE
TERRY HURLEY
CARL LILLY
DICK RIDDLE
JOE VILLANUEVA

Paid Informants

*WILLIAM DAILY
*RAY RADDOCK
*JACK TAYLOR

The Conspirators

FRED MILO: President, the Milo Corporation
BARRY BOYD: Counsel to Fred Milo
TERRY LEA KING: Akron go-go dancer
THOMAS MITCHELL: Vietnam combat veteran
RAY SESIC: Former employee, the Milo Corporation
TONY RIDLE: Former employee, the Milo Corporation
HARRY KNOTT: Vending machine operator
†FRANK PICCIRILLI: Vending machine operator
JOHN HARRIS: Loan shark and juice collector
BOBBY O'BRIAN: Drifter and occasional construction worker
THE KID: Speed freak
The Mystery Woman

Composite Characters

PETER HARTMANN
JOHN HASTINGS
NICK TERPOLOS

† awaiting trial

Dean Milo's Sphere of Influence

*ROBERT BENNETT: Comptroller, the Milo Corporation
*PATRICIA DOUGLAS: Dean Milo's friend and former lover
BUD EISENHART: Dean Milo's personal aide
LOUIS FISI: Dean Milo's financial advisor
*ANGELO GIERI: One of Dean Milo's business associates
NICK GONATOS: Maggie Milo's father
*ARTHUR KNOX: Regional manager, the Milo Corporation
ROD KYRIAKIDES: Chief buyer, the Milo Corporation and
   Dr. Kyriakides's son
*JAMES LICATA: Ohio businessman and associate of Dean Milo
MAGGIE MILO: Dean Milo's wife
*MR. AND MRS. WALTER TERESA: Dean Milo's neighbors
*WARREN TOBIN: Vice president, the Milo Corporation
GEORGE TSARNAS: Dean Milo's attorney and best friend
GEORGIA TSARNAS: George Tsarnas's wife

Fred Milo's Sphere of Influence

LONNIE CURTIS: Sophie Curtis's husband
SOPHIE CURTIS: Dean and Fred Milo's sister
RICHARD GUSTER: Attorney to the Milo-Curtis families in suits
   against Dean Milo
KATHLEEN MILO: Fred Milo's wife
KATINA MILO: Dean and Fred Milo's mother
SOTIR MILO: Dean and Fred Milo's father and founder of the
   Milo Corporation
GEORGE PAPPAS: Fred Milo's criminal attorney

Boyd-King Sphere of Influence

*LARRY BENSON: Terry Lea King's lover
DENNIS KING: Terry Lea King's husband
*MELISSA MACKEY: Akron go-go dancer

Knott-Piccirilli Sphere of Influence

*BOBBY "SILVERMAN" GREY: Massage parlor manager
*JIMMY JONES: Professional streetfighter and legbreaker
*MOLLY TRIOLA: Former employee, the Star System bar
*JOEY WASHINGTON: Phoenix low-life

Part One

QUESTIONS

1 | *"Dean's dead."*

IT WAS A HOT AND SUNNY MONDAY AFTERNOON, August 11, 1980, in Bath Township, a small suburb of Akron, Ohio. Georgia Tsarnas, a dark, attractive woman in her early thirties, parked in millionaire Dean Milo's driveway at the top of the hill, at the end of the large cul-de-sac, and left her three children in the station wagon. Sweltering from the heat, she walked up to the garage and peered through a window; both Milo's red and white Cadillac Eldorado and his blue Mercedes were inside. She paused momentarily, then started up the brick steps, bordered by paths of bright flowers, to the front door and rang the doorbell. When there was no answer, she began to tremble a bit. She nervously opened her purse and took out the house key Milo's wife had given her. Her hands were shaking as she opened the storm door and pushed the key in the lock. Before she could turn the key, the large wooden door snapped open.

There, on the foyer floor, was a man lying spread-eagled and face down in a pool of dried blood. A yellow, foam-filled cushion with white trim rested on his head and shoulders. It appeared to have been taken from a living-room chair about ten feet from the body. The center of the cushion showed the clear impression of a gun barrel and the burned outline of a single bullet hole.

The man was wearing only a gold bracelet on his right wrist

3

and a pair of urine-stained, blood-splotched jockey shorts—which were on backwards, the fly over the buttocks.

Startled, Mrs. Tsarnas recoiled, then carefully approached the body and lifted the cushion, praying that he wasn't who she already knew he was.

Milo's head, turned slightly to the right, was a chalky-white and purple color, like the rest of his body, except where he was splattered with his own blood. His bruised eyes were closed tightly.

And his mouth, which was partially open, was covered with cotton.

Trying to compose herself so she wouldn't upset her children waiting in the car, she walked slowly through the living and family rooms into the kitchen and called her husband, Dean Milo's attorney and best friend, George Tsarnas. When he came on the line, her voice was barely audible.

"Dean's dead," she mumbled. "There's blood everywhere. What should I do?" After a long choking pause, he told her to call the Bath Township Police and then go outside until they arrived.

She found the number for the police on a sticker attached to the phone and did as she'd been directed. Then she paused once again, wiped the tears from her eyes, and walked from the kitchen, this time directly into the foyer, stepping over Milo's body on her way out the front door.

Outside—away from the blood and again in the midst of bright flowers—as her composure began to crumble, she told her inquisitive children to remain in the car . . . because Uncle Dean was very sick.

2 | *"Just another suburban killing."*

AT 2:52 P.M., Bath police officer Kirk Shively—a twenty-six-year-old, three-year veteran of the department—patrolling at the northern end of the township, received a dispatch to investigate a possible homicide at 2694 Everest Circle. Within eight minutes he arrived at a large, brick, colonial home and parked in the driveway next to a burnt-orange Oldsmobile station wagon. As he climbed out of his patrol car, he shielded his eyes with his hand to block the bright sunshine and saw a woman who looked badly shaken sitting on the front steps.

"Our friend . . . inside . . . he's dead!" Her words mixed with sobs as she looked up at Shively.

"Who's dead?" the patrolman asked.

"Our friend! Dean Milo! He's dead! There's blood everywhere!"

Mrs. Tsarnas stood up and led Shively through the double wooden doors into the foyer. A rush of cold air from the central air-conditioning units met him as he walked toward the body, but in spite of it, beads of perspiration formed on his brow. This was a first for him. He'd never been the first cop at the scene of a murder.

As his heart pounded faster and his leg muscles began to quiver, he glanced around the room. It appeared to be clean

5

and in order, with the exception of a wadded-up piece of yellow paper on the brick-pattern, vinyl-tiled floor near the clear plastic runner by the entrance. Also, the light in the crystal chandelier was on.

There was no gun in Milo's hand or near the body—which seemed surrounded by cotton dust.

Shively told Mrs. Tsarnas to stand outside to prevent anyone else from entering, then called his dispatcher from the phone in the kitchen to ask for back-up units. There was no longer any question about this being a "possible" homicide. And, for all he knew, the killer might still be there in the house.

His adrenaline pumping, Shively walked from the kitchen back into the foyer, drew his gun and climbed the staircase next to the body. As he reached the top of the steps, he heard a voice coming from one of the bedrooms. Quickly, he pressed against the wall in a combat crouch and then silently, slowly moved toward the room at the end of the hallway. Outside the doorway, he paused for a moment before entering, gathering himself together—and then the voice turned into music. It was the radio. Shively let his breath out, placed his service revolver in his holster, and made a cursory search of the room upstairs.

Returning to the body, Shively heard the phone ring. He hesitated for a moment and then went to the kitchen and answered it. The caller identified himself as Bud Eisenhart, Milo's assistant and a close friend of both the Milo and Tsarnas families, and asked to speak with his boss. Shively replied that he was not available.

"Is everything all right over there?" Eisenhart demanded.

Shively said nothing.

Then, more quietly, Eisenhart murmured, "I just talked to George Tsarnas. . . . Is . . . is Dean still alive?"

"No, sir. He's not."

Pausing momentarily, obviously in grief, Eisenhart said he'd heard that Mrs. Tsarnas was at the house and asked to speak with her. When she came to the phone, Shively heard her ask Eisenhart to come over right away.

Standing outside the house while Mrs. Tsarnas was on the telephone, the patrolman saw Detective-Sergeant Richard Munsey drive up the cul-de-sac in his Bath detective car. Shively gave him a brief report as the two men walked into the house to begin their formal investigation.

"Just curious, Rich," Shively asked, "have you ever been involved in a homicide case before?"

"Just one," Munsey replied, as they walked up the steps. "Two years ago, a water softener delivery man killed a housewife with a pop bottle after she walked in on him burglarizing her house. He stuffed her body in a steel chamber and dumped her in a swamp. . . . Lotsa crazy people out there."

Munsey was a tough professional who'd started with the Bath police as a dispatcher at seventeen. Now twenty-six, he had established himself as a crack investigator, specializing in burglary, robbery, and general theft cases. Even for him, however, this crime scene was something new.

Munsey handed Shively a .35 mm camera and told him to take some photographs; then he called the Summit County Sheriff's Department in nearby Akron for assistance. Munsey specifically asked for the help of his mentor, Lieutenant Larry Momchilov, a homicide investigator who also taught a few courses in the law enforcement department at the University of Akron. Because of the relationship between Momchilov and Munsey, there existed a personal, as well as institutional, association between the Bath Police and the Summit County sheriff's office.

Returning to the body after his call, Munsey found a spent cartridge shell near the dead man's head, possibly from a .32 automatic pistol, then spotted a second casing a few feet from the body, as well as the crumpled yellow paper near the entrance.

Hoping to deter the anticipated horde of investigators from disturbing the area around the body near the front door, he walked back to the kitchen and opened the door into the garage and then the garage door. As he walked out onto the driveway, the sun began to disappear behind dark clouds, and the gentle breeze turned into a stiff wind.

Shively continued taking pictures of the dead man and various rooms in the house, while Munsey tried to talk to Mrs. Tsarnas. Her voice occasionally cracking with emotion, she explained, "Dean is a very good friend of ours; he's my husband's best friend. . . . Everyone has been trying to reach Dean since yesterday. He was supposed to have dinner with us. When he didn't show up, we figured he left town on business. Then, when he didn't come to work today—and still no one had heard from him—my husband called me at home about an hour ago and asked me to come over here to see if anything was wrong."

"Tell me about Mr. Milo," Munsey said. "I know his name, but who is he?"

"He's the president of Milo Barber and Beauty Supply Corporation. It's a national wholesale distribution firm owned by the Milo family. George, my husband, is his attorney. The company's located over there on Allen Road in Stow, just north of Akron."

"Where's his wife? Was she here?"

"No. Maggie—Magdaline—is down in Clearwater, Florida, with their three kids. . . . Listen, I can't talk about this right now. Later, for sure, but not now. . . ."

As Mrs. Tsarnas returned to her station wagon, a steady procession of cars began pulling into the cul-de-sac and up the hill to the house. First out were officers from the county's scientific investigative unit, carrying suitcases full of more cameras, fingerprint and ballistics equipment, and everything else necessary for a crime scene search. Munsey led them through the garage and into the kitchen, explaining that Mrs. Tsarnas, who had found the body, had touched only the cushion over the body and the telephone in the kitchen.

Following the investigators into the garage was George Tsarnas, who had tearfully embraced his wife, and then Bud Eisenhart. Munsey told the two men to take Mrs. Tsarnas and her three children home and to wait for the police to contact them.

Also entering the home were two investigators from the county coroner's office, James Crano and Richard Scott. The county coroner, Dr. A. H. Kyriakides, was out of town and not expected to return until the following day, but a few minutes later Rod Kyriakides, the coroner's son—and an employee of the Milo Corporation—called and asked to speak with Scott.

After the crime technicians completed their preliminary investigation—measurements and photographs of the scene both inside and outside the residence, a check of the flow and

direction of the blood, and diagrams of specific blood splotches—
the coroner's investigators took control of the crime scene and
began their work, joined by two detective-sergeants from the
Summit County sheriff's office.

Meanwhile, Lieutenant Momchilov and his new partner,
Lieutenant William Lewis, had been caught on the highway.
The dark clouds had exploded into a thundering summer rain
and they'd been forced to pull over and stop on the side of the
road until the storm subsided. Lewis, who was going on his first
murder investigation, asked Momchilov, "What do you make
of this murder in Bath?"

"Nothing really, except that it's just another suburban killing.
These are the toughest, too. You're going to see that the further
out of the city these things happen, the longer it takes to solve
them."

"Why's that, Larry?"

"Damn houses are too far apart. More isolation. Crimes are
committed, and, sometimes it takes days, sometimes weeks, before they're discovered. Trails go cold really fast. If this guy in
Bath has been lying dead out there for a few days, the guy who
did it is probably long gone."

Somehow, as he glanced over at Lewis, Momchilov sensed
that this Bath case was not going to be a quick fix.

At forty-two, Momchilov—a medium-built man with graying-
brown hair and boyish features—was the senior officer in the
detective bureau and had seen a little of everything since he'd
joined the department in 1967. Recently returned to homicide
after heading the prosecutor's office's white-collar and organized
crime division, Momchilov was widely regarded as an expert at
crime scene evaluation and review, and as a stickler for minute
details. An FBI-trained cop, he solved most of his cases.

His partner, Lewis, had just been promoted to the detective
bureau out of the traffic division, where he'd served since 1966.
A street-wise, wise-cracking cop, he knew, at the age of thirty-
seven, that this case would be his first big break.

"Sounds like you picked a helluva time to get married,
Momchilov," he cracked, knowing that Momchilov had just
returned from his honeymoon the previous week. His new wife,
Joan Rice, was a staff reporter at the *Akron Beacon Journal*.

"What the hell are you talkin' about, Lewis?" Momchilov snapped back. "You're married and got all them kids and shit."

"Hey, man! I've always been married. The only difference between you and me is that my wife misses me when I'm not home; your wife is so goddamn busy at the newspaper, she's not even gonna know when you're gone."

The rain finally let up and the two of them drove on; their fifteen-minute trip from Akron now stretched to forty-five minutes. At the house, they were greeted by Munsey and the other officers, who filled them in on the details of the investigation thus far. "Who's the dead guy?" Lewis asked.

"Just some multimillionaire executive type," one of the investigators replied. "This is the way we found the body. Weird, ain't it?"

"Let's get some light in here!" Momchilov shouted. "We can't see a damn thing!"

"Can't, Lieutenant. Power failure. The storm knocked out the lights."

"Well, open the front doors at least. Let's get some light in here."

Kneeling by the body, Momchilov saw that—despite the single bullet hole in the cushion over Milo's head—he appeared to have been shot at least twice, in the head and in the back of the neck. He was particularly intrigued with Milo's assbackward shorts and the cotton on his mouth.

"How the hell do you figure that?" Momchilov asked himself. "What was this guy doing before he was killed?" He also noted the position of the shell casings and the yellow paper on the floor.

"What's that wadded up thing over in the corner?" Lewis asked coroner investigator Scott—who nonchalantly picked up the paper with his bare hand and unfolded it. "It's just a blank telegram," he shrugged, throwing it back on the floor.

Lewis was stunned. "How can you be so casual with that piece of paper, Scotty? That's evidence! That might be how the killer got in the house!"

While Scott apologized to Lewis, Momchilov ordered one of his officers from the crime lab to place the telegram in an evidence bag and mark it for further analysis.

Now taking charge of the probe, Momchilov asked for more pictures to be taken of the area. "I want them in black-and-white and color, both inside and outside the house. I want this whole place on film."

As the lights went back on in the house, he called all of his investigators together in the family room and started making assignments. "I want to know where every member of this guy's family has been during the last seventy-two hours. I want to know every move he made before he was killed. I want to know everything about his business. I want this neighborhood canvassed. And I want all of this done before we leave tonight."

While Momchilov laid out his strategy for his men, Lewis asked Crano, the other coroner investigator, what he thought about the case.

"I think it's a suicide," Crano responded.

"Jesus Christ!" Lewis exclaimed. "Where are you on this? What the hell do you mean, 'suicide'? Where's the goddamn weapon?"

"Hey, the lady who found Milo's body is a good friend of his family. She might've taken the gun to protect the family and their insurance claims."

Lewis exploded. "How do you explain two shots in the back of the man's goddamn head? How the hell could he have done that to himself?"

"Okay, Lewis," Crano conceded, "it's probably a murder."

While Lewis and Crano argued, Momchilov and Captain Thomas Bostick, chief of the sheriff's detective bureau, who had also arrived on the scene, began to search the house. First, they went to the bedroom. The venetian blinds were raised and the curtains were spread. Although Momchilov had a clear view of the cul-de-sac from the window, he could not see the front door; a five-foot ledge between the first and second floors obstructed his view. Had the killer come to Milo's front door, Milo probably couldn't have seen him.

The radio and a night light were still on. On top of the dresser was Milo's wallet, which contained $33 and several credit cards. Nearby, on the television, was another $40 in cash, a gold watch, and gold wedding ring—as well as a check made out to Milo from the U.S. Internal Revenue Service for $24,000. On the other dresser sat a woman's jewelry box, filled with pearl necklaces, diamond rings, gold bracelets, and an emerald brooch, among other items. Nothing of value seemed to be disturbed.

They also noticed that someone had obviously been lying in the king-sized bed: the blue satin sheets were wrinkled and pushed to one side, two pillows were on the bed, and a third was leaning against the nightstand on the floor. Milo's clothing was scattered on the floor as well, and near the pillow on the floor, Momchilov found a piece of tissue paper, later found to be stained with dry semen. "This guy might not have been alone," Momchilov speculated, as he placed the tissue in a plastic evidence bag.

Matching nightstands stood on either side of the bed. Under one, by the telephone and a walking cane, lay a stack of *Playboy* and *Penthouse* magazines; under the other, by the radio, a collection of religious reading material.

In Milo's closet, Bostick came upon a plain, brown paper bag. Opening it, he found four pornography films—*Deep Throat, Wild Beauty, Super Cock,* and a fourth movie exploiting gay male sex, *The Crisco Kid*—all packaged in colorfully explicit boxes.

They also found several prophylactics by the nightstand with the girlie magazines, a gross of rubbers in a cabinet in the adjacent bathroom, and one in Milo's travel kit.

When the search of the bedroom was completed, Momchilov turned to Bostick, grimacing. "You know, Captain, I have a feeling we're not gonna figure this one out today."

Staring at the box containing *The Crisco Kid*, a movie about fist-fucking, the conservative, fifty-one-year-old Bostick looked up at his detective and said, shaking his head: "Or tomorrow either."

3 | "One-third, one-third, one-third . . ."

GEORGE TSARNAS was a mass of nervous energy when sheriff's detective David Bailey arrived at his home, which was just around the corner from Milo's residence. Normally a calm and even-tempered man, Tsarnas was also a fast, intelligent speaker and a brilliant corporate lawyer who specialized in tax shelters. He had a reputation for shrewdness and persuasiveness. And, at forty-one years of age, he had already become the man top business executives wanted on retainer when push came to shove.

"Tell me about the Milo Corporation, can you?" Bailey asked.

"God, where do I start," Tsarnas replied, pushing his dark hair straight back with his hand. "There's so much. . . ." The Milo Barber and Beauty Supply Company was the largest wholesaler of barber and beauty supplies in the country, he explained. It had grown from a single, full-service dealership in 1969 to a major American corporation, with ninety-two stores in seventeen states east of the Mississippi; and it had planned to expand into Colorado, Kansas, and Nebraska soon. Just that year alone, Milo B&B would be grossing over $45 million.

Milo was the big fish in the little pond of the beauty supply business; the whole industry yielded about $400 million a year—

and Milo had over 10% of that. Its nearest competitor was a quarter its size.

The industry itself was very conservative, a very closed, close-knit society. Everyone knew everyone. Everyone was very protective of their labels and reputations.

"Was Dean Milo pretty well liked in the business?" Bailey asked.

"Well liked?" Tsarnas said. "Detective Bailey, Dean Milo was like the bastard son at a family reunion." Milo had taken control of the business from his father, Sotir, who, with his wife, Katina, had immigrated to America from Albania decades before. During the late 1940s and early 1950s, Sotir had started the business out of the basement of his home. It had been a straight full-service operation. Sotir Milo had carried his supplies in a handbasket around to the barber and beauty shops in Akron. When Dean Milo took over in 1969, however, he scuttled the full-service operation and adopted a discount approach. He began opening discount stores which stocked cosmetics and beauty supplies, undercutting the cosmetic dealers who had exclusive distribution contracts with manufacturers, such as Fabergé, L'Oreal, and Clairol.

At first, Dean just made everybody mad, but, by 1980, Milo B&B had become bigger than most of the cosmetics manufacturers. Everyone criticized him, but he had revolutionized the beauty supply business.

This was how the beauty supply industry worked. Traditionally, the manufacturer's distributor—such as Milo had been before 1969—sent its salesmen to the thousands of barber and beauty shops in its region. They extended the shops credit for their purchases and permitted returns if the stores couldn't sell their inventory. Milo's discount operation was different. There were no salesmen hustling goods and so no sales commissions. Milo sold everything by mail or in his company-owned stores—strictly on a cash-and-carry basis. By cutting out the middlemen, Milo could offer a fifteen to twenty percent discount compared to full-service prices. The approach was so successful that by 1980 Milo B&B could open a new store every four weeks—and all those company-owned stores generally showed a profit within the first six to nine months. Some stores were in the black by the end of their second operating month.

Milo B&B got so big, so fast, because it extended no credit. Milo had maneuvered himself into the enviable position of getting all the credit he needed—because of his success rate—and yet never having to extend any.

"Well, didn't the competition complain or something?" Bailey asked.

"God, yeah. When Milo began expanding the business in 1969—opening stores in Columbus and Cincinnati, in addition to those that already existed in Akron, Canton, Cleveland, Mansfield, and Youngstown—all of his competitors screamed about it." For instance, the national sales manager of the Wella Corporation charged that Milo's discount operation gave him an unfair edge—while cheapening the business. Some of the manufacturers viewed Dean's discount operations as illegitimate. Many of them just flat out refused to sell to him. The marketing plans of these cosmetic firms—and their glamorous public images—couldn't tolerate something as distasteful as the sales of their cosmetics at discount prices.

"So, if companies refused to sell to him, how did he, you know, survive?"

Dean bought two full-service wholesale dealerships, Tsarnas explained: A. A. Lovelace Beauty Supply in Charleston, West Virginia, and Capital Beauty Supply in Columbus. Essentially, both companies became legal bootlegging operations. They simply purchased products in bulk from manufacturers at wholesale prices. Those suppliers—Lovelace and Capital—then diverted to the Milo Corporation. Even though some industry people knew what was going on, the charade was a face-saving device for the stubborn manufacturers—because they weren't selling their products to a discount firm.

Milo had other subsidiaries as well, two partnerships, which served as legitimate tax shelters: the Milo Company—which was different from Milo B&B—and the Heritage Investment Corporation. Both of them were operations that leased property, equipment, and vehicles to the parent company. Neither of them, however, had an office, telephone, or employees. In addition, the Milo Corporation controlled Mico, Inc. Mico was created in 1972 and purchased merchandise—such as shampoos, hair conditioners, and even hair dryers—from various manufacturers and placed the "Mico" label on them. Ninety-nine percent of Mico's products were sold to other Milo family enterprises.

"So, Mico was like a dummy corporation, too?"

"Well, it was a legally-operated company, used primarily for corporate tax purposes. Strictly legal, just like all the others."

"And Dean Milo owned all of this?"

"Well, no," Tsarnas said. "Up until 1975, Dean's father, Sotir, had the real control of the company and owned most of its stock. Then, with my help, Dean proposed a recapitalization plan to his parents, his brother, Fred, and his sister and brother-in-law, Sophie and Lonnie Curtis. According to this proposal, Dean would have the sole voting power in the corporation. See? In other words, Dean would have the full authority to act unilaterally on behalf of the family business. But Dean only had one-third of the total company, just like his brother and sister. Each of them had one-third. But the two-thirds owned by Fred and Sophie was 'non-voting common stock.' Do you see what I'm saying?"

"Okay, Dean ran the corporation, even though his brother and sister, combined, owned a majority of the stock. And they couldn't interfere?"

"Well, Dean had the final say in the decision-making process. However, Fred and Sophie and even her husband, Lonnie Curtis, were all vice presidents in the company and had daily jobs."

"Did Lonnie Curtis have any stock in the company?"

"He wasn't a part-owner, no. He had a job."

"So Fred and Sophie were also salaried employees?"

"Right. And, according to this recapitalization plan, their salaries were tied to a ratio. It was a hundred percent, seventy-five percent, and fifty percent. By that, I mean, if Dean's salary was a hundred dollars, then Fred's salary had to be seventy-five dollars, and Sophie's salary had to be fifty percent of what Dean made, or fifty dollars. There were a lot of protections put into this plan for the family which, in turn, allowed them to give voting control to Dean."

"Yeah, but we're not talking a hundred dollars, seventy-five dollars, and fifty dollars. How much did they make in salaries?"

"Off the top of my head, I can tell you that, in 1979, Dean made $260,000, just in salary and bonuses; he expected to make over $400,000 this year alone."

"So everyone's happy, right?"

"No," replied Tsarnas. "Not at all. In late August of last year, Dean fired Fred and Sophie, as well as Lonnie Curtis, from their jobs. And those firings touched off a barrage of lawsuits against Dean, all filed by his parents, his brother, and sister. They charged that Dean had fraudulently taken control of the company. It's kind of ironic, because Dean's father—who remained as the corporation's chairman of the board at his $50,000 annual salary—had taken control of the business from *his* family after there was a falling-out during the 1950s. But, now, thirty years later, there was much more at stake."

"What was the reason for the firings?"

"It's hard to say really, competition, internal family squabbling. You see, Dean's sole voting power applied only to matters directly affecting the Milo Corporation—which was the only real big money-maker in the Milo empire. In matters involving the subsidiaries, as well as their interlocking relationships, his vote was only one among three. . . ."

"One-third, one-third, one-third: Fred and Sophie against Dean?"

"Right. Consequently, in another move against Dean, Fred and Sophie, using their two-thirds interest, took over the corporation's subsidiaries, firing anyone who was loyal to Dean. Fred became the president of Lovelace Beauty Supply in January of this year; Lonnie Curtis, who had been working for Fred at Lovelace, was named head of Capital Beauty Supply in March. So, being forced to accept really steep paycuts, Fred and Lonnie, with Sophie's blessing, refused to allow Lovelace and Capital to continue as the Milo Corporation's bootlegging operations, forcing Dean to purchase cosmetics from other businesses at higher prices."

"So then, there were a lot of hard feelings within the family?"

"Hard feelings? Detective Bailey, Dean Milo has been murdered."

"So you're saying . . ."

"I'm not saying anything. But I would talk to Fred about this. You see, several weeks ago, Fred contacted a friend of Dean's, Louis Fisi, and asked him to arrange a meeting with his brother: Fred was willing to consider being bought out by Dean. That's why Dean came back into Bath on Saturday. He was supposed to meet Fred and talk about this."

"Let me ask you, Mr. Tsarnas, did you see Mr. Milo on Saturday?"

"Like I said, Dean came home from Florida on Saturday. About 6:00 P.M. that day he arrived at our house to have dinner with my wife and me. We were together about an hour and a half. We barbecued a lamb and talked business. At that time, Dean told me that Fred had phoned him. They were going to have a meeting the following day at the home of Barry Boyd, one of Fred's attorneys."

"That was yesterday, the 10th?"

"Yeah. I think Barry thought he would look good as an attorney if he could help get this thing settled. . . . Anyway, we'd asked Dean to come to a concert at Blossom Music Center with us, but he said he'd already made plans."

"What was he going to do?"

"A friend of his was getting married. Dean wanted to go to the wedding reception, so I told Dean to join us at a restaurant when he was done, which he did, at about 11:00 P.M. He didn't eat anything, and I don't believe he had had much of anything to drink—Dean was never much of a drinker—so he certainly was sober. But he was tired—he told us that—and left a little after midnight to go home."

"That was the last time you ever saw him?"

"The last time. We wanted him to come over for dinner on Sunday—with his wife still down in Florida and all. So, we called him and kept calling. No one answered."

"So, you're not sure whether Dean and Fred had this meeting on Sunday over at Barry Boyd's place?"

"On Sunday? I don't know. But I think that if they did have the meeting, Dean would've called me. That's why I believe Dean was killed early Sunday morning."

*   *   *

When Detective Bailey returned to Milo's home, Momchilov was still conducting a thorough search of the house. But after hearing the details of the Tsarnas interview, he paused and regrouped his investigators, instructing Lewis and Munsey to go to the homes of Sotir and Fred Milo to inform them of Dean's murder and to collect whatever information they could. Meanwhile, Momchilov would try to locate Barry Boyd.

As Lewis and Munsey left, Shively returned, saying that, during his canvass of the neighborhood, several people had expressed fear for their own safety because of Milo's murder. He added that the only person with any information had been the newspaper boy, who'd said he'd seen Milo's garage door open Saturday night and that, earlier in the day, he had seen a man he hadn't recognized standing on Milo's front porch. "The kid said the man was driving a gray car," Shively said, "and that it was parked in the driveway."

By the time Lewis and Munsey arrived at Fred Milo's residence, just four blocks from Dean and Maggie Milo's home, the rain had stopped and the early evening sun had reappeared. They knocked on the back door.

Fred's wife, Kathleen, a petite and pretty thirty-four-year-old brunette, answered. The officers identified themselves and asked where her husband was. "He's down in Charleston," she replied.

"Could you tell us when you last spoke with him, Mrs. Milo?" Lewis inquired.

Sensing that something was wrong, she asked, "Has something happened to Fred? Is Fred all right?"

"Your husband is fine," Munsey assured her, glancing at the kitchen table and seeing it was set for dinner. "There's nothing wrong with him."

"Well, Fred manages Lovelace Beauty Supply down in West Virginia, and I get worried sometimes. He works there Monday through Friday and returns home only for weekends and holidays. I talked to him this afternoon, at about three."

"What was he calling about?"

"He bought a birthday gift for his brother-in-law, Lonnie Curtis."

"Is that unusual for your husband to call you in the middle of the day like that to tell you he bought a birthday gift?"

"Yes, it was a little strange, but . . . hey, fellas, what's going on here?"

"Dean Milo was found dead at his home this afternoon. He had been shot twice in the head."

Stunned by the news, Kathy Milo sat down suddenly. "I don't know of anyone who would've wanted to hurt him," she said quietly. "I saw Dean at a party about two months ago. . . ."

"Well, we understand that there has been some trouble between your husband and his brother. Is that true?"

"Well, yes, but I know it couldn't have come to anything like this. There were some problems over control of their company, but . . ."

"When did your husband last speak to his brother?"

"They talked on the telephone around five Saturday afternoon; they were trying to arrange a meeting for Sunday afternoon at Barry Boyd's home. He's one of Fred's lawyers."

"Do you know what that meeting was all about?"

"God, I'm just shocked about this!"

"The meeting, Mrs. Milo, what was it supposed to be about?"

"Dean was going to make an offer to Fred—to buy him out of the family business. . . . I know Fred tried to reach him all day Sunday, but he never could."

"I'm sorry to put you through this," Munsey said, "but we have to know these things. Could you tell me what you and your husband did on Saturday night?"

"We had a . . . wait a minute . . . I'm wondering whether I should answer any more questions. Maybe I should call an attorney."

"These are routine questions, Mrs. Milo."

"Well, I certainly don't have anything to hide. . . . What was the question?"

"You and your husband? What did you do on Saturday night?"

"Oh, we had a cookout. Some friends came over at about seven-thirty, and we ate and talked. Then we watched some television, and we went to bed by midnight."

"What about on Sunday?"

"Fred was home all day. I went out only once; I went to the market. Then, at about three, my sister-in-law, Sophie, dropped off her four-year-old son, Alexander, to play with our kids. Fred left the house once, to take his nephew home. That was at about six."

"Where does your sister-in-law live?"

"About six blocks away, on Bath Hills Boulevard."

"So Dean's house is midway between yours and theirs?"

"I guess that's right, but Fred came right home!"

"Does your husband own any guns?" Lewis asked sternly.

"No!" she exclaimed. "We have never, ever had a gun in this house!"

"Okay. Lonnie and Sophie Curtis, do you know if they're home now?"

"No, sir, they run Capital Beauty Supply down in Columbus. They work away from home Monday through Friday, too."

While Lewis and Munsey were questioning Kathy Milo, Momchilov, still at the scene of the murder, ran a check on Barry Boyd. He discovered that Boyd, who had run in the Democratic primary for county prosecutor in 1973, had four cases pending against him—three for default on credit-card payments totalling over $10,000 and a fourth for driving while intoxicated. Summit County Sheriff David Troutman was acquainted with Boyd and, after speaking with Momchilov, called Boyd at home, informing him that Sergeant Bailey was en route to interview him. He also told him that Dean Milo had been murdered.

"I understand that you were supposed to set up a meeting between Dean and Fred Milo yesterday," Troutman said. "Did it ever take place?"

"I don't know anything about any meeting, Sheriff," Boyd replied.

A little after 7:00 P.M., Lewis and Munsey arrived at the home of Milo's parents and were admitted into the house by seventy-year-old Katina Milo. Her seventy-eight-year-old husband, Sotir, was standing in the kitchen, wearing his pajamas. Seeing no grief on their faces, Lewis asked them if they had heard the

news about their son. In their broken English, they replied that
they hadn't heard anything. Then Mrs. Milo cried out, "What's
happened to Fred? Tell me what's happened to Fred!"

"I'm very sorry to be the one to tell you this," Lewis said
slowly, "but your son, Dean, is dead."

Overwhelmed with shock and despair, the elderly couple
began wailing and holding each other for comfort. "No! No!
No! You're wrong! You're wrong!" screamed Mrs. Milo.

"Was he shot or what?" sobbed her husband.

Munsey looked at Lewis, who was also surprised by the old
man's response, and said feebly, "Yes, we believe he was
murdered."

Speaking in Albanian while he cried, Sotir Milo left the
kitchen. Suddenly, Mrs. Milo regained her composure and was
actually able to answer some questions. "I haven't seen either
of my sons in nearly a month," she explained. "My daughter,
Sophie, came by with her family last night."

"Was there any special reason for that visit?"

"No reason. Just stopped by."

Mrs. Milo was just beginning to explain the nature of the
family's lawsuits against Dean when the old Mr. Milo returned,
fully dressed and clutching a framed picture of Dean. Upon
seeing her husband, Mrs. Milo broke down again, repeating
over and over, "Our eldest son . . . the most educated. We
gave him the business."

Realizing that they could answer no more questions, Lewis
and Munsey left and returned to Dean Milo's house. It was
about 7:25 P.M.

Milo's body had been turned over. Small cotton balls were
on the floor where the body had been, and his hands had been
bagged for further investigation and fingerprinting. The
coroner's investigators would examine his fingernails for skin or
hair particles, and Momchilov had insisted that Milo's remains
be placed on a sheet so that anything falling from the body
could be analyzed.

At about 7:30, Milo's body was removed from the house,
placed in an ambulance, and taken to Akron City Hospital,
where he was officially pronounced dead on arrival. The autopsy

was scheduled for the following day when the coroner, Dr. Kyriakides, would return to Akron.

Barry Boyd walked out of his house to greet Bailey as soon as
he arrived. Boyd, usually a snappy dresser though now he wore
blue jeans and a T-shirt, was a well-known figure among young
activists and politicos in Akron. Among the first of the VISTA
volunteers to organize local communities in New York, the
thirty-six-year-old attorney had also served as the executive assistant to a member of the U.S. Consumer Product Safety Com-
mission in Washington, D.C., and was now the sole law partner
of Dennis Shaul, a Rhodes Scholar and one-time candidate for
mayor of Akron.

Boyd insisted to the officer that he hadn't been home on
Sunday, but had spent the day with his twelve-year-old son in
Cleveland. "Let me ask you this," said Bailey. "Why did you
give Sheriff Troutman false information concerning the meeting between Fred and Dean Milo—saying that you didn't know
about it? We know for a fact that you did."

Pausing for a moment, Boyd became defensive. "I didn't
know specifically that Fred had set it up. I realized it when
Dave Troutman called. Fred didn't tell me specifically that he
had a meeting set up for him. And I found out later that he
had."

"So you're saying that you were aware of the meeting, but
you didn't know the specifics of the meeting?"

"Right. I didn't know that Fred and Dean were coming over
to my place. I didn't know the meeting had been specifically
set up. I didn't know, as I do now, that Dean had agreed to
meet at my house on Sunday."

"Is there any information you can give us that would aid us
in our investigation of Milo's murder?"

"Not really," Boyd replied with some defiance in his voice.

Back at Dean Milo's house, Momchilov and the other officers
emptied all of the wastebaskets, looking for anything with a
name or telephone number on it. He also asked the investigators
from the crime lab to empty the vacuum cleaner and analyze
its contents for possible evidence. From Milo's cars in the

garage, he retrieved two attaché cases. In one was a list of top executives at the Milo Corporation and their salaries.

Their search completed, they stacked all of the materials they wanted to take away in a large pile in the family room. Momchilov wanted to take some of the information—especially the material found in the attaché cases—back to his office for further study.

"Sorry, Larry, we're not going to release that stuff to you yet," one of the coroner's investigators said.

"What do you mean?" Momchilov argued. "I'd like to look at some of these papers."

"We'll make you copies—just mark what you want."

"Why can't I just take what I want right now?"

"You might be running this investigation, Larry, but we have control of this crime scene and everything found here—until K. Y. [Dr. Kyriakides] releases it to you. You'll get copies of what you want, guaranteed."

As they were cleaning up, Bailey returned and reported on his interview not only with Boyd but also with Bill Crocker, the owner of the restaurant where Milo had last been seen. Crocker had confirmed the information provided by George Tsarnas—that Dean Milo had left his place alone between 11:30 p.m. and midnight. Another officer also returned to report that neither Sophie nor Lonnie Curtis had been home, but that some neighbors—who had asked not to be identified—had said that the Curtises had left for Columbus and asked them to collect their mail while they were gone. "They said they already had learned about the murder from their son, the newspaper boy."

"Why did they want to remain anonymous?" Momchilov asked.

"The kid's dad said he could 'mention a name,' but was afraid to."

"What kind of name? Whose name?"

"Well, he finally said that Dean had part-interest in an area restaurant chain with a man named 'Licata.'"

"Okay, I get it," Momchilov said, shaking his head.

"Who's Licata?" asked Munsey.

"Oh, there's some talk that he knows some underworld people up in Canton . . . That's all we need now!"

As coroner investigator Scott locked up Dean Milo's home, Munsey posted two uniformed Bath officers outside to ensure its security.

Later that evening, at 10:21 P.M., Sergeant J. J. Gardner at Bath police headquarters was given a message to "call Lonnie Curtis at the home of Mr. and Mrs. Sotir Milo," which Gardner did. Curtis immediately asked, "Can we assume that Dean Milo is dead?"

"Yes, you may," Gardner replied.

"How was he killed?" Curtis continued. "And do you know who was responsible?"

"I suggest, Mr. Curtis, that you call the coroner's office tomorrow for that information."

Back at his office, still working overtime and hoping that his bride would understand, Momchilov sketched diagrams and jotted down dates, names, and places on a scrap of paper. As he had originally suspected, this was definitely not going to be a case that could be quickly solved. There was too much to do, too many leads to pursue—meantime, the killer's trail was already cold.

He called Ed Duvall, the Chief of Investigations for the sheriff's department, to discuss the day's yield. Momchilov knew that anything that would be done in the probe would be done under Duvall's authority. A tough, steely-faced cop with thirty-five years' experience, Duvall would be depended upon to oversee the investigation over the long term, to free investigators from other duties, and to mediate whatever internal disputes arose. Duvall was a respected and feared man, and he had the political clout to make things happen. No one messed with Ed Duvall.

Momchilov told Duvall that the only theory he had developed was that Milo had not been murdered in the midst of a burglary. He added that he continued to be intrigued by the cotton on Milo's mouth. He knew full well that whoever had put it there was somehow involved in the murder.

4 | *"I have nothing to hide."*

BATH TOWNSHIP is synonymous with wealth and class. Tucked away in the midst of the Cuyahoga River, which twists and turns to the north until it reaches Lake Erie, Bath appears to be a portion of New England seemingly misplaced in the Midwest. It is a beautiful haven for those who, like Dean Milo, have made it: rubber barons, industrialists, doctors, lawyers, and an array of other professional men and women. Many of its residents have found it to be an escape from the expanding urbanization of nearby Akron. Others live there simply to be as close as possible to nature but with easy access to the city.

Early Tuesday morning, August 12th, Bath detective Rich Munsey donned a three-piece suit and continued the neighborhood canvass. Milo's neighbors were still frightened that the Milo killing had been a random slaying; that it could've happened to any one of them. Murder was alien to this small Ohio community.

Only one of the interviews seemed to hold any promise. The home of Mr. and Mrs. Walter Teresa was at the bottom of the cul-de-sac and faced that of Milo. "Early Sunday morning," Mrs. Teresa recalled, "I was awakened by the sound of a car outside. I looked over at our digital clock on the nightstand,

and it was around 2:00 A.M. Then I got out of bed and went
to the window. It was warm and clear outside. . . ."

"And what did you see?" Munsey asked.

"I saw a parked car—with the motor running and its head-
lights on."

"Where was this car, Mrs. Teresa? Where was it parked?"

"Right at the opening of the cul-de-sac, at the bottom of the
hill."

"Okay. Could you see anyone in the car? Maybe the driver?"

"No, I couldn't see who it was, but I did see a man get into
the car. . . ."

"Okay, now, where was this?"

"Well, the car started moving up Bath Hills Boulevard really
slow, and then it turned into the next street. Then it turned
around again and came back down to the cul-de-sac. Its head-
lights were still on."

"Did it drive up the cul-de-sac?"

"No, it didn't. But that's when I saw someone walk down
the cul-de-sac and then get into the car."

"Could you tell if it was a man or a woman?"

"I really couldn't; it was pretty dark."

"Can you describe the car?"

"It looked like it was green with a black top. I do remember
that. It also had a bad muffler."

"And you're sure that this was late Saturday night, early
Sunday morning?"

"I'm pretty sure it was early Sunday morning."

Mr. Teresa said that he had been awakened earlier that same
night by the sound of a car. "I went to the window," he explained, "and I saw Dean parking his Mercedes in his garage
up the hill. I remember seeing the electric garage door go up
and the light go on."

"Was Milo alone?" Munsey asked.

"Yes, he was alone. I'm sure of that."

At 2:00 P.M. on Tuesday, Lieutenants Momchilov and Lewis
arrived at the county morgue for the Milo autopsy. As they
entered the coroner's office, the two officers were pulled aside
by investigator Scott—whom Momchilov had tried to cold-

shoulder because of their argument the previous night over possession of Milo's attaché cases. "Look, K. Y. [Dr. Kyriakides] is really upset," Scott told them. "He was a close personal friend of Milo's, and he's not taking this very well."

For reasons unknown, Kyriakides was not present at the beginning of the autopsy, so another pathologist, Dr. William Cox, performed the coroner's investigation.

"It looks like he's been dead for about three days," the pathologist said as he probed Milo's body. "His body is cold to the touch. . . . Rigor mortis is not present. . . . There's dried blood around his nose . . . upper lip . . . chin . . . and just below the lower lip. . . . He's in good shape for a forty-one-year-old man. . . . Six feet tall . . . two hundred nine pounds, slight weight problem . . . medium-textured hair, black and cut short . . . hazel eyes, pupils equal, round, and regular. . . . Thorax and abdomen are normal. . . . Two old scars on both arms and in his right groin. . . ."

As the pathologist began to explore Milo's head, Kyriakides walked into the room. Nodding, but not saying anything to those present, the coroner snapped on a pair of surgical gloves and immediately began probing his close friend's brain with his hands.

Now understanding the relationship between Milo and Kyriakides—and the raw courage the coroner was exhibiting, doing what he was doing—Momchilov and Lewis, both of whom had seen hundreds of autopsies, had to look away. There was something tragic about the scene.

Kyriakides discovered one gunshot wound behind Milo's left ear, measuring four millimeters in diameter. It had traveled from left to right, back to front, at a twenty-five-degree angle. There were no powder burns near the wound. A copper-jacketed slug, fired from a .32 automatic pistol, was found mushroomed just under the skin by his right temple. Momchilov immediately concluded that the bullet had mushroomed because it had hit the floor—thus, Milo had been lying on the floor when he'd been shot.

A second entrance wound, five millimeters long and three millimeters wide, was found on the back of his neck. There was no exit wound; the slug had to be dug out from behind his

Adam's apple. Again, no powder burns surrounded the wound. During the crime scene investigation the previous day, the police had found a second casing, from the same .32 automatic, near Milo's head.

A respected man with an unblemished seventeen-year record as county coroner, Kyriakides concluded that Milo had died from "cardio-respiratory failure, due to a penetrating, perforating gunshot wound of the brain." Unfortunately, the precise time of Milo's death could not be estimated—although it was thought to have occurred early Sunday morning. The coroner also determined that Milo had been clinically alive, although probably unconscious, for as long as a half-hour after he had been shot.

By the time he had completed his examination, Kyriakides appeared to be verging on anger. He tore off his rubber gloves and threw them into a small laundry bin; then, pacing the floor quickly, his speech rambling, he began advancing a suicide theory. Not wishing to challenge the coroner, considering what he was going through, Momchilov and Lewis pulled out their notepads and started writing.

"Look!" Kyriakides shouted at them. "Everything said down here is confidential!" Momchilov and Lewis quickly placed their pads back in their pockets. Then, rubbing his deeply-lined forehead, the red-eyed, white-haired coroner officially ruled that Dean Milo had been murdered.

Meantime, back in Bath, Sergeants Munsey and Bailey drove to Fred Milo's residence. He had returned from Charleston late Monday night.

Appearing calm and relaxed, the thirty-six-year-old man introduced himself and invited the two policemen into his home. Although not jovial, he was hardly grief-stricken and seemed more concerned with missing a day's work than with his brother's murder. Clean-cut, with brown, closely-trimmed hair and green eyes behind black-rimmed glasses, Milo was short and slightly built. He appeared brimming with confidence and ready to answer any questions the police could throw at him.

"Basically," Munsey asked, "you got along with your brother pretty well?"

"Yes!" Milo responded curtly, lighting up a cigarette.

"Did you have any arguments?"

"You are saying 'basically'?"

"Yes."

"Yes."

"Did you look up to him?"

"Yes."

"Did you think that he was successful in this business?"

"No doubt."

"He always did a good job?"

"I felt he was his own worst enemy the way he did the job—but the end results speak for themselves. . . . I can be critical from the 'how you do it,' but . . . what you accomplish? You're right."

"So, you felt, more or less, that he did a good job in his type of work?"

"Yeah!"

"You never had any arguments about . . ."

"About how the operations would be run?" Milo asked.

"Right."

"Plenty of arguments!"

"You felt you were right?"

"The problem was I handled half the company. He handled the other half of the company, and whenever I'd get into his side or he got into my side, there was always friction about it. 'You do it your way, and I'll do it mine,' or whatever. Those were the kind of arguments we had."

"When he left on vacation, who would be put in charge?"

"It'd probably be me, but the thing was so structured, where Lonnie would have the half that Dean would take care of. . . ."

"Okay, why would Lonnie take half? Why wouldn't Sophie?"

"That's just the way it was. Lonnie was like Dean's protégé. I mean, the part Dean handled on a day-to-day basis was the side of the company that Lonnie was involved in. We structured that thing in two parts. It was Dean on top, and me and Lonnie."

"What about Sophie?" Munsey asked.

"What do you mean? What was her position?"

"Yes."

"Just about every little thing that had to be taken care of, plus payroll, things of that nature. As the company grew and as her child grew, her responsibilities changed. . . ."

"When did you start negotiating with Dean about selling?"

"There were several attempts at negotiating, maybe, around April or May."

"April or May of this year?"

"Yeah. There were attempts prior to that from the other side that just never came off. Either the price was wrong, or something. Finally, [Dean's attorney] came up with the guarantee situation . . . which kind of changed the whole complexion of the possibility of negotiating this thing. We knew there was no way anybody could buy the other person out for cash. That was a given. So it had to be on a time-payment basis. The problem was: how sincere would the other side be in completing the payment? Was it a five-year deal? Ten-year deal? Fifteen-year deal? . . . 'What do you want to get rid of all the headaches?' That was appealing to me. 'But if I buy it, what happens to Sophie?' . . ."

"Okay, did Dean call you up on the Saturday he came home?"

"No, I called Dean."

"How did you know he was back home?"

"He called me Thursday—I can't remember, Wednesday or Thursday—in Charleston."

"He was in Charleston?"

"No. I don't know where he was."

"You had a conversation with him at that time about . . ."

"He wanted to get together the weekend coming up to follow up the negotiations that had ended in early July. . . . I agreed to meet with him over the weekend. . . ."

"On Saturday, did you call Dean up?"

"Yes."

"What conversation did you have with him at that time?"

"It sounded like I woke him up. I said, 'When did you get home?' He said, 'Just a little while ago.' I said, 'What do you want to do?' He said, 'Well, how about we meet right now?' And I said, 'No, I can't, because we have our next-door neighbors over. . . . I can come over after dinner.' He said, 'No, I can't. After dinner, I have a wedding reception to go to.' And then we talked about where to have the meeting. . . . He said, 'Well, think of a place.' I said, 'Well, I'll try to get Barry Boyd's place . . . but you think of a place, too, just in case.' He said, 'Okay.' And then we left it where I was supposed to call him back in the morning. . . ."

"Do you recall talking to Lonnie about it?"

"No, I don't."

"Could you have called and talked to him?"

"No, I wouldn't have talked to Lonnie. I wouldn't have talked to Sophie. . . ."

"Did they know that you . . ."

"They did not know that I was talking to Dean. . . ."

"What happened on Sunday?"

"Around 11:00 A.M., I called Dean. No one answered. I tried calling Barry Boyd to see if we could use his house. No answer. I think I got ahold of Barry around 2:00 or 3:00 P.M. I said, 'Can I use your house?' He said, 'Well, do you need me there?' I said no. He said, 'The house will be open. You can use it.' I must of tried to call Dean four or five more times; I'm not sure. At about 8:00 P.M., I finally got upset about the fact that he wasn't home. . . . I called Barry and told him, 'The meeting's off, but call the office in the morning to see what the hell happened.' "

On Monday, Fred said, he'd left his home at 8:00 A.M. and arrived in Charleston just before noon. He'd checked into his hotel and then gone to his office where he'd remained for an hour and a half. At 1:30 P.M., he'd gone to a men's clothing store to buy Lonnie a sweater for his birthday. He'd been back in his office by 2:00 P.M. to attend a sales meeting. After calling his wife and telling her about Lonnie's present—so she wouldn't go out and buy one, too—he and two of his employees had driven to Princeton, West Virginia, for a 7:00 P.M. presentation.

"And I was there around nine," Fred said, "when I got the news about my brother. So I told everybody just to wrap the damn thing up and 'Let's get the hell out of here.' I called my mother to find out what the hell happened."

Fred also disclosed that his brother had been having numerous problems with his partners in the area restaurant chain, adding that Dean had purchased his stock in the enterprise through some "shady" maneuvers. He said that one of his brother's business partners was James Licata—to whom Fred admitted introducing Dean in 1977, just before Dean had become a shareholder in the chain.

"How well do you know James Licata?" Munsey asked.

"I know him; I know his son. His son owns or ran a car dealership. . . . I bought cars from him. Through that relationship I met Mr. Licata."

"Has he contacted you or have you had any discussions with him since the death of your brother?"

"I've had no contact with him. . . ."

"Have you ever had any business dealings with him other than with his son through the car dealership? Investments?"

"We bought some . . . I bought some stock . . . everybody in my family bought stock in Adams Restaurants, a chain owned by Licata. Okay? At one time or another I sold mine."

Finally, Fred accused his brother of being a philanderer who had been seeing several other women during the course of his ten-year marriage. According to Fred, Dean had asked his wife for a divorce in about 1974. Fred claimed that he had pleaded with Dean to reconsider and to think about his three children. Fred quoted his brother as saying, "Fuck it, the kids are mine; she'll get nothing! The kids will go with me!"

He also mentioned a 1979 incident—just before he, Sophie, and Lonnie had been fired—when, during a seminar sponsored by the Milo Corporation, Dean had been caught by two people while he'd been "with" a woman employee. The two later told Fred what they had seen. Fred did not elaborate for the police. Fred said that Dean's wife, Maggie, had found out about her husband's extracurricular activities and threatened to leave him.

Finally, just before leaving, Munsey asked, "Would you object to taking a polygraph examination?"

"A lie detector?"

"Yeah. Would you be willing to take a test?"

"I'd have no objections. I have nothing to hide."

5 | *"Mr. Licata, who did it?"*

NEXT ON MUNSEY AND BAILEY'S LIST to be questioned were Lonnie and Sophie Curtis, whose home was just down the street. Like Fred Milo, the Curtises seemed to show little emotion over Dean's murder. However, both expressed shock over the incident—although neither had any idea who could possibly be responsible. They added, upon being asked, that there were no guns in their house.

Tall, brown-haired and somewhat lanky, with an air of cockiness about him, Lonnie Curtis had been a five-year employee of the Milo Corporation when he'd married Sophie Milo in October 1974. In fact, Dean had been his best man. Lonnie had met Sophie in 1967, while at the University of Akron, and two years later had begun working part-time at the Milo Corporation as a common laborer, making $1.25 an hour.

After the wedding, Dean had placed Curtis in charge of the company's accounting and computer operations, where he had made considerably more money. Curtis proved to be smart and tough, and immediately gained Dean's respect and confidence. At the time of his firing, Curtis had been vice president, responsible for three departments: inventory, purchasing, and the warehouse. Since his termination, he had become president of

Capital Beauty Supply in Columbus—where he and his wife had a small apartment. He would be thirty-one years old on Saturday.

Munsey asked, "What I'm trying to find out is what caused this whole thing: the bitterness between you and Dean. Can you tell me about it?"

"I had no bitterness towards him," Curtis responded.

"How did you get along with him?"

"Up until that time that he told me to go home, I got along with him fine."

"Well, what caused him to tell you to go home?"

"I haven't the slightest idea. Today, I still don't know why he told me to go home. Other than, after the fact and in retrospect, he was planning to fire everybody."

"Who is everybody? Who are you talking about?"

"Fred, Sophie, and I . . ."

"Okay, will you gain anything by Dean's death?"

"Nothing."

"Will you gain control of the company?"

"No, I won't. You're asking me, I . . ."

"Yes?"

"I have absolutely no capability of ever having any stock in Milo Barber and Beauty Supply. So I will gain absolutely nothing. . . ."

"On Saturday, August 9, were you home that day?"

"Yes."

"Tell me your day, what did you do that day?"

Curtis explained that he had done nothing out of the ordinary, spending nearly the entire day with his wife and son. He'd left home for only a few minutes in midday—to help his father-in-law with some repair work. Later that evening, the Curtises had taken their son to Sea World, stopped at a McDonald's for dinner, and then returned home. According to Curtis, the entire family was in bed by midnight.

"Somewhere around 3:00 or 3:15 A.M., Alexander [the son] woke up screaming," Curtis continued. "So Sophie tried to get me to go get him back to sleep, and instead she went and slept with him the rest of the night off and on. He was rather restless that night . . . so that's basically the whole day."

"Did you sleep with your wife that evening? . . . I mean, were you in your bed?"

"Yeah."

"And she slept in another bed?"

"After she . . . after Alexander woke up, yeah."

"You're saying that was about 3:00 or 3:30 A.M.?"

"Three, three-fifteen, somewhere in there. I believe it was three-fifteen. I remember looking at the clock and seeing three-fifteen on it."

The family woke up between 8:30 and 9:00 A.M. on Sunday morning, watched television, and then cleaned their swimming pool. In the afternoon, Sophie went shopping at the nearby mall and dropped off her son at Fred and Kathy Milo's house. While she was gone, Lonnie had a business discussion with Barry Boyd on the telephone. At 5:00 P.M., he drove his cream-colored Mercedes station wagon through Sand Run Park to check some property he owned. There he saw some friends, whose names he gave to the police.

While Lonnie was out, Sophie returned home. Boyd called again to speak to her husband, and when Lonnie returned home he telephoned Boyd and had a private discussion. At 6:00 P.M. Fred dropped off Alexander, talked to the Curtises briefly, and left. Having forgotten to give Fred some papers, the Curtises stopped by Fred's to drop them off and then went to Sophie's parents' home, where they stayed until 9:00 P.M., and then went on to Columbus. They arrived at about midnight.

When Kathleen Milo heard about Dean's murder from the police the next day, she tried to reach the Curtises in Columbus, but they were at the movies, and she called Ray Sesic, one of Lonnie's employees, in Columbus. Sesic later reached the Curtises and told them to call Sophie's mother: there was an emergency at home.

"Lonnie made the phone call and talked with your parents. Is that correct?" Munsey asked Sophie Curtis. Sophie was a brunette, twenty-nine years old, five feet tall, with a slight complexion problem.

"Yes," she replied.

"And then you took the phone?"

"I got on the phone—and still feel the chills just as I

felt. . . . When I got on the phone with my mom, she was just hysterical. And she said the police were at her house and that they said that Dean's . . . well, first, the way I heard it was Lonnie was talking to my mom. . . . I'm standing next to Lonnie, and he, see, I thought when I heard 'emergency phone call' it was my parents [who] were sick. And, he said, 'Dean's dead.' Like that. And I said, 'What?' You know, I said, 'It's impossible.' And the first thing that started going through my mind, 'Oh, God . . . airplane crash.'

"I didn't know where he was, or I didn't understand how he, you know, he was dead. And I got on the phone, and my mom said that the police were at her house and he had been killed. And she was just hysterical, and I did call the doctor from there."

"You called the doctor?"

"I called the doctor, because my parents are on medication . . . high blood pressure and medication. . . ."

Sophie explained that she and her two brothers had always been extremely close—until the firings the previous year. Everything their family did seemed to revolve around the business as far back as she could remember. "This business, I've been in all my life since I was a child, and my father . . . my parents first started the business. . . . On Saturdays, we'd go delivering with my dad. [We] put up orders at night, and we just grew up doing that and whatever had to be done. We all did it: sweep the floors or answer the phones or taking orders . . . always. All three of us kids have always been in it."

She also stated that it was not uncommon for Dean to walk around the house in his underwear. "He wasn't a bashful person," she said.

Finally, agreeing with Fred—and contradicting Tsarnas's statement—Lonnie and Sophie said they had both been aware of Dean's marital problems—which had resulted from his womanizing. They said it was the reason Maggie Milo preferred to spend so much time in Florida with her family.

Sophie and Maggie had never been particularly close. Sophie even admitted that after church on Mother's Day 1980, she and Maggie had exchanged cross words regarding the family problems.

When the argument had begun getting personal, Sophie had shot back, "I have . . . a letter in Dean's handwriting, that [says] he isn't as happily married as you act like you are. . . . He isn't happy." When Maggie had asked to see the letter, Sophie had responded, "No, I don't have it here, and I'm not going to show it to you, because I'm not going to break up any marriages. . . ."

"Where did you get this letter?" Bailey asked.

"I got it out of Dean's office."

"I assume that you made a copy of it and put it back?"

"Yes."

As they had with Fred, the police officers asked if Lonnie and Sophie were willing to take a polygraph test. They both replied that they would.

Returning to the Summit County Sheriff's office in Akron, Munsey and Bailey picked up a copy of the *Akron Beacon Journal.* Buried on page C2 and entitled, "Bath Man Is Found Shot to Death," an article, without a by-line, reported simply: "Summit County sheriff's detectives today were investigating the shooting death of Constantine D. Milo, 41, co-owner of a beauty and barber supply firm who was found dead with two gunshot wounds in the head Monday afternoon at his Bath Township home. . . ."

On Wednesday, August 13th at 10:00 A.M., every investigator in the Milo murder probe met at Milo's residence for a final search of the premises. Also among those present were Dr. Kyriakides and George Tsarnas. The coroner told Momchilov that his son, Rod Kyriakides, who worked for Milo, had given him a list of names of those who had recently locked horns with Dean. Among them were a competitor from Chicago and two former employees who had been fired from their jobs. One of the latter, representing the Teamsters Union, had tried to force a union recognition election—and had been fired for his pro-union effort. The second man was Ray Sesic, who now worked for Lonnie Curtis in Columbus.

While coroner investigator Crano tried to rub the blood from the foyer floor—in an unsuccessful attempt to find a dent

in the tile caused by one of the bullets that had struck Milo—
Momchilov led Kyriakides upstairs to the bedroom closet and
showed him the four porno films Captain Bostick had found on
Monday. Despite Momchilov's protests, Kyriakides insisted that
the films remain in the custody of the coroner's office. During
their brief discussion, Momchilov also requested an explanation
for Kyriakides's visit to Dean's house on Tuesday night. According to the Bath police officer assigned to guard the house,
the coroner had discussed details of the murder investigation
with several friends whom he had taken through Milo's home.
Without any response, Kyriakides walked out of the room with
the four films under his arm.

Meantime, back downstairs, Munsey telephoned Lonnie
Curtis and asked if he would consent to take a polygraph examination on Friday, August 15th. Curtis agreed to do so, and
Munsey said he would pick him up at his home on Friday
morning.

After the final search of the residence was completed, Kyriakides released control of the crime scene to George Tsarnas,
representing Milo's estate.

At noon, Munsey and Bailey met Milo's forty-three-year-old
assistant, Bud Eisenhart, at the Bath Township Police Department. Eisenhart had been Dean Milo's devoted, lifelong friend.
Responsible for the control of the Milo Corporation's distribution center since 1975, he described himself as being "like a
brother to Dean and a son to his parents . . . until the family
problems began."

Still overwhelmed with grief, Eisenhart, somewhat subdued,
explained that he had left his home near Pilgrim Square in west
Akron early Saturday morning.

"What kind of a car were you driving?" Munsey asked.

"A gray 1977 Chevrolet sedan," he replied.

"And you parked it in Dean's driveway?"

"Yes, that's right. . . . I opened Dean's house with the key
he gave me, and I went inside to take the mail and to feed his
fish. I did those kinds of things for him. So, then, I got his
Mercedes and drove to Pittsburgh. Dean had flown in there the
previous night. I picked him up, and we started touring Milo's

stores in western Pennsylvania—about four of them. Then we went to a fifth in Youngstown. We drove back into Bath. That was about 4:15 P.M. I remember the sky was dark and overcast."

"What did the two of you talk about on the drive home?"

"I don't know. . . . He said something about flying to Milwaukee on Wednesday and then to Chicago the following weekend. You know, that kind of stuff—business."

"Anything else?"

"When we drove into Bath, we saw Lonnie Curtis outside, watering his lawn."

"Did you stop and say anything to him?"

"Oh, no. There're just too many hard feelings. . . . So, when we got to Dean's house, I helped him carry in his luggage into the house. Then I suggested that he call his wife down in Florida, so he did. His WATS-line wasn't working, so he called her direct. When I left, he was talking to her."

"And that was the last time you ever saw or heard from Dean?"

"The last time."

"What was your first reaction or your first thought about the murder?" Munsey asked.

"I've had thoughts about it," Eisenhart replied, red-eyed and now choking occasionally. "But I've told George [Tsarnas] and Maggie that I didn't know that Dean was in anything that would result in something like this . . . in his death. I just can't conceive of it. It's still unbelievable to me. I do understand . . . I am aware of the problems he had with his family within the last year and a half. . . ."

"Of the individuals that have left the company or are no longer with the firm, could you describe or let us know who left with bitterness? Who left with the most animosity?"

"Obviously, the family wasn't happy. Lonnie was . . . no, I won't say it. . . . Lonnie did not leave on good terms with Dean. Fred and Sophie did not leave on good terms with Dean. Ray Sesic . . . did not leave on good terms with Dean, because he left, I'll say, almost out of his mind."

"Ray Sesic? Why did he leave?"

"Well, Dean caught Ray leaking corporate secrets to Fred and Lonnie—after they'd been fired. You know, it was one of those things where Dean suspected him of being a 'spy,' as he called it. So Dean intentionally gave Sesic some false information—only Ray knew about it. When it returned to Dean on the grapevine, he fired Sesic."

"Okay. How would you describe Dean, in general? What kind of guy was he?"

"Dean . . . Dean was decent, honest, generous. He was a devoted husband and father. There's been some talk over the years about some problems between him and his wife, but don't believe it. Dean was a loyal man."

"What about drinking and gambling, stuff like that?"

"He only was a casual drinker and an occasional gambler. That's it."

Later, on Wednesday night, from 6:30 to 9:30, Momchilov, Lewis, Munsey, and Bailey staked out the funeral home where Dean's family was having calling hours. Another officer sat in his unmarked squad car across the street from the funeral home, taking pictures of the callers. Bailey and Munsey took down license plate numbers and later requested and received a copy of the register of guests. Momchilov and Lewis remained inside, mingling among those who mourned—and some who did not. Momchilov also spoke to the embalmer, who said that he'd noticed no unusual marks on Milo's body—other than the two gunshot wounds in his head. Because of the amount of time which had already passed, Milo's head and body had swelled, forcing the family to request a closed coffin.

The scene in the funeral home was bizarre. Up front, near the casket, were the grievers and wailers, mostly close friends of Dean and Maggie Milo's and members of Maggie's family, the Gonatos clan of Clearwater, Florida.

In the back of the room, friends of the Fred Milo family, the Curtises, and Mr. and Mrs. Sotir Milo sat and stood. There were few outward signs of grieving and even some laughing and joking among the crowd in the back.

Fred was the only member of the immediate family not present. He had come alone earlier in the day. The funeral director had seen Fred weep uncontrollably and even speak to his brother's coffin during his short visit.

In between the two large divisions of people in the room were several rows of empty chairs and space—which somehow illustrated the clear split within the Milo family. The pressure in the room was intense, almost unbearable for some. At one point, Milo's mother, Katina—who, unlike her husband, was rather composed—walked up to the front of the room to offer her condolences to her daughter-in-law. "This is a time for the family to be united," the elder Mrs. Milo said. Maggie, who was sobbing and very bitter, nudged her away with her shoulder and sternly told her to return to the other side of the room where she belonged.

While all of this high drama was going on, Kyriakides stood next to Momchilov, identifying people as they came and went. Then, just before the Greek Orthodox wake began and while the two men talked, Kyriakides stopped in mid-sentence and stared at a man—accompanied by two, towering, twitching thugs out of the thirties—who was walking through the door. Momchilov followed Kyriakides's eyes and saw the man, too.

"That's Licata," Kyriakides said quietly and with great awe.

The loud talk and laughter at the back of the room turned into silent whispers as tall, smiling, white-haired James Licata made his way to the front of the room and to the casket. He then turned to Maggie Milo, whose eyes slowly rose and met his as he gently placed her hand in his. "I'm very sorry for you and your family," Licata said in a deep, robust voice.

"Mr. Licata," Maggie replied, angrily gritting her teeth, "who did it?"

Now clutching her hand with both of his, Licata, seemingly quite saddened, responded, "Mrs. Milo . . . I don't know."

6 | *"Dean's going to get his brains blown out."*

EARLY THE NEXT MORNING, Lieutenants Momchilov and Lewis were in their office making telephone calls to sources Momchilov had acquired while in the prosecutor's organized crime division. The amazing growth of the Milo Corporation had put the hook in both cops. They, like Milo's competitors, had begun to wonder what role, if any, the mob had had in the rise and, perhaps, the fall of Dean Milo.

From his own experiences, Momchilov knew that the underworld actively searched for companies like Milo B&B to acquire and exploit, particularly ones that were vulnerable because of internal dissension. When the right company was found and its players identified, one or more of the principals were targeted as unscrupulous enough to want to win at any cost. After the Faustian pact was struck, the target would then be set up, caught in the mob's web of illicit activities. Once the situation within the company was cleared up, the target might be permitted to remain in the controlling position—but only ostensibly. Any resistance could result in ruination, or even death.

"There are three areas we have to look into," Momchilov explained to his partner. "First, Milo had an incredible cash flow situation. Where did his initial capital come from? How did he manage to borrow so much money when he first began with so little collateral? Why did the banks trust him? Who were his major financial backers? And what did he give in return?

"The second thing is this stuff going on in Chicago. . . ."

"Right," Lewis replied. "We're being told that Milo literally invaded their turf up there. I guess he opened something like five stores, almost overnight—and that was after buying out the Chicago beauty supply business that was once the biggest in the country. That pissed everyone off—and that's what got everyone in Chicago talking about Milo's underworld connections."

"I talked to a guy yesterday," Momchilov continued, "and he said that the Chicago thing was the only one Dean was afraid of. The guy said Dean once told him, 'That's a tough market. You take your life in your own hands when you work in this business in Chicago.' That's what Dean said."

"So what happened in Chicago?"

"The worst thing, I understand, was the biggest beauty supply firm—next to Milo—filed suit against him and charged him with unfair advertising practices. From what we know, that's as rough as it got. I mean, the case was dismissed. . . . Anyway, the third thing we have to look into is Licata. The problem is that Licata has never been proven to be a part of the underworld."

"Yeah, but you want to know what the interesting thing about this Licata business is?" said Lewis. "Milo's top advisors warned him against joining the board of directors of these restaurants—Adams Restaurants—because the company really wasn't making any money. But, hell, just about everyone in Milo's family and just about all of his friends bought a lot of stock in the company, Dr. K. Y., too. Anyway, just before Dean's murder, there was some big shake-up within the Adams company. Supposedly, one of the members of its board of directors took on Licata, and then Licata claimed to have some information on the guy, saying that he was stealing food and equipment from Adams's main warehouse. From what I've been told, Dean sided with Licata and supported the removal of this other board member. In fact, Dean made the motion to get rid of this guy. Sometime after that, there was a fire at the main warehouse. The FBI came in and was pretty sure it was arson—but they could never make a case against anyone."

"So that's what that's about!" Momchilov exclaimed. "Guess what? I got a call this morning from one of my snitches. The U.S. Marshal's office issued subpoenas to several members of the board at the Adams company. Dean was among them. Guess when his deposition was supposed to have been taken?"

"No idea."

"Tuesday, August 12th, the day after his body was found."

While Momchilov and Lewis continued to pursue the possibility of underworld involvement in the Milo murder, Munsey and Bailey arrived at the office of Angelo Gieri in Macedonia, another Akron suburb. Gieri had telephoned Momchilov the previous night, saying he had some information he wanted to share with the police.

Gieri had met Dean in 1974 while Gieri had been selling a weight-loss product. Since then, he had remained in touch with Milo, talking to him at least twice a month. They also occasionally played golf together.

On Wednesday morning, Gieri had received a telephone call from his business partner, Phil Donner, who had told him about Dean's murder. Donner had learned about it from one of Milo's competitors in Chicago. Shocked by the news, Gieri called the Milo Corporation and received confirmation from Rod Kyriakides.

"Phil called me again that afternoon and told me that he was getting calls from Milo's competitors all over the country, asking for more details," Gieri said. "I told Phil that I had nothing more than confirmation. He said that one of Dean's New York competitors called and was real fucking happy about the whole thing. The New York guy said to Phil, 'Milo's fucked enough people in this business.'"

"Did he say anything else?" Munsey asked.

"Yeah. Phil told me that the guy said he 'knew someone would get him sooner or later.'"

"Why did he say that?"

"Well, Phil told me that this guy in New York was talking to Fred Milo one day. You know, they were just bitching about the way Dean did things. Then, in the middle of all this, Fred advised him not to deal with Dean anymore."

"Why not?"

"Because Fred supposedly said, 'Someday Dean's going to get his brains blown out . . . and it may happen sooner than you think.' "

Back at sheriff's headquarters, Momchilov, going through his mail, came upon an envelope with no return address. Inside was a mimeographed piece of paper sent to "Store Employees" and signed "A Friend." Although it was undated, it had obviously been written before Milo had been killed. In part, the letter read:

> Never before has there been so much turmoil and distrust as now exists for Milo Beauty Supply. Brothers sue brothers, turnovers of employees . . . Where will it stop? Will the people who make this company run be cast from their positions as were the people who still carry the Milo name? Will the only protection one has with this company still be "honest words" received from a two-faced home office management? . . . It is a sore that will take a long time to heal, and store personnel must protect themselves from this sore. We must unite and never be in a position where we are defenseless. THINK ABOUT IT! . . . It's time to talk to *people* in your *own region* about this . . . LET US BE WISE! LET US UNITE AND ORGANIZE!

"What do you think?" Lewis asked Momchilov when he finished reading the letter.

"You know, Bill," Momchilov replied, "I think we better find out more about this company. There's a revolution going on over there."

While Munsey was at Angelo Gieri's, a call came in for him from Lonnie Curtis. Curtis said that he and his family were considering flying to Florida for Dean's burial, and so he needed a postponement of his polygraph examination, scheduled for the next day. Munsey agreed.

Munsey then called Fred Milo and asked him if he, too, was planning to attend his brother's funeral. Fred replied that he had made no definite plans.

* * *

On Friday, August 15th, at 10:30 A.M., Dean Milo was lowered into his grave in Tarpon Springs, Florida. Other than his wife and children and her family, not one member of the Milo or Curtis clans—not even his mother and father—attended the burial.

As Milo's coffin was placed in the grave, another furious thunderstorm erupted—just as it had in the wake of the discovery of his body.

Meantime, back in Akron, Munsey and Bailey arrived at the Milo Corporation's general headquarters and began questioning Milo's personal staff and employees.

Milo's special assistant, Peter Hartmann, told the officers that his boss "was a legend in his own time in the beauty supply business. The guy was incredible. Because he was so big, he got bad-rapped with this reputation as being really hard and really ruthless. No doubt he was tough. But all that other stuff? No way. The man was a winner."

"What did his employees think of him?" asked Munsey.

"Generally, I think everyone looked at him as a genius. Everyone looked up to him for guidance, even inspiration. I mean, sure, some people hated the guy, and he was resented by some—but those of us who worked closest to him were loyal and devoted to the man. He made all of us feel as though we were, like, an essential part of the whole operation, like we were really important. He gave his staff responsibilities; he paid them well; and he rewarded everyone with promotions and cash bonuses if they made the grade. Hell, the managers around here operated with all the autonomy they could ever want. No one's head was chopped off for making an honest mistake."

"Well, how did Dean Milo view his corporation? How did he structure it?"

"Dean believed that Milo B&B should be run by professionals, not family. After the family split, he began putting together a new management team. He appointed three new senior partners in the company to replace Fred, Sophie, and Lonnie. It was common knowledge that Dean was thinking about phasing himself out of the corporation—in order to spend more time wheeling and dealing in the real estate market. He also wanted to spend more time with his family, particularly his son, Sotir. He has sickle-cell anemia, you know. A few weeks ago, he had his spleen removed."

"Poor kid," Munsey said.

"Dean had all kinds of problems."

"How about corporate finances?"

"Dean was completely up front with everything. The record proves that, you'll see. He insisted on an annual inventory and certified audit. He wanted to make sure he could gauge the growth of the corporation, so he monitored the growth and hoped someday to let it go public. That's what he really wanted."

"What about Dean's background for this kind of work?"

"Dean had a degree in accounting, but never really worked at it. But he was an excellent financier. He could really leverage a money transaction. Most manufacturers—even those who didn't like him—were willing to support him, because they knew he'd pay. If he said he would pay on X-day, they got paid in full on that day. And the same thing was true at the bank. He would go in and buy property at a good price. He'd find a $100,000 piece of property that was worth $100,000. Well, he'd go in, and talk the owner down to $80,000. If he couldn't, he wouldn't buy it—but he *could* do it. And then he'd go to the bank and borrow the full amount, based on appraisal. See, the bank will give you eighty percent of appraisal. Well, in fact, if he talked the seller down to $80,000—and he usually did—he'd get one hundred percent financing. He'd borrow the whole damn $80,000. He wouldn't have a nickel in it. Then, he'd go out and rent it or something, and make his payments. That's why Dean grew so big and so fast and was able to obtain the credit he did—because he always found some way to pay his bills when he said he'd pay them. . . ."

"There have been some questions during the course of this investigation as to how Milo B&B grew so fast," Munsey said. "I'm sure you've heard this, too. But what do you say about the allegation that organized crime is involved in the Milo Corporation? You know, the Mafia?"

"It's bullshit!" Hartmann said. "This company is clean!"

*   *   *

Most of Milo's employees agreed with Kyriakides's assessment that—other than the members of the Milo family—the two former employees who'd held the biggest grudges against Dean had been the Milo warehouseman who'd been organizing for the Teamsters and the corporate "spy," Ray Sesic. After being fired, the organizer, Bruno "King Kong" Kertzmayer, had threatened, "Dean will get his!"

Munsey and Bailey's next stop, then, after leaving the Milo Corporation, was the home of "King Kong" Kertzmayer. Kong was generally viewed as the kind of guy who would slap around the newspaper boy for throwing the afternoon edition in the bushes. In fact, he was a basically timid man who sought justice for working people. Still not working and barely surviving on unemployment compensation, Kertzmayer, in response to Munsey's question, replied, "Okay, yeah, I said that! I said 'Dean will get his!' I admit that, but, goddamn it, I had nothing to do with his goddamn killing! I respected the man! I just didn't like the way he handled the whole union thing!"

"But you don't have any information about his murder?"

"Absolutely not!"

"Are you willing to take a polygraph test?"

"You bet—anytime!"

Kertzmayer was dropped as a suspect.

On Sunday, August 17th, the *Akron Beacon Journal* ran a sensational, front-page, banner-headline and rather melodramatic story: "Mystery Surrounds Murder of Millionaire."

> By all accounts, he was a millionaire—a man who had started off with almost nothing and ended up with almost everything.
>
> A man who, in scarcely more than a decade, had scratched and clawed his way to the top of a little-known industry that afforded him a nationwide reputation—a reputation that made him respected and despised. . . . As a result, when Constantine R. "Dean" Milo was found shot to death Monday afternoon in the hallway of his Bath Township home, the incident drew little public notice.
>
> But within his tightly-knit trade where everybody's business is everybody else's, the news moved as a bulletin.
>
> One who knew him well put it this way: "The big question

now is going to be more like 'Who shot C.R.?' than 'Who shot J.R.?' "

The reference, of course, was to the fictional J.R. Ewing, popular villain of the smash-hit CBS-TV series "Dallas," [which] kept viewers in suspense since the season ended with J.R. being shot by an unknown assailant.

Some insist the analogy, in many respects, is apt.

7 | *"The soul won't rest until the murder is avenged."*

IN FACT, more and more, the Milo investigation did seem to be mimicking the fictitious probe of the shooting of J. R. Ewing—at that time being featured on magazine covers across the country. As in *Dallas*, the police were concentrating their research in three areas: the family, Milo's business associates and adversaries, and his possible extramarital affairs. Nearly everyone they contacted seemed to have had a run-in with Milo at some point; others would benefit from his permanent removal. As a result, nearly everyone was under suspicion.

However, the most intensive investigation had begun to concentrate on one man: Fred Milo.

While Lieutenants Momchilov and Lewis followed up on other leads, Munsey and Bailey spent most of Monday and Tuesday, August 18th and 19th, at the Milo Corporation, continuing their interviews with the employees. However, at midday on Tuesday, the two officers left the company and drove to Novelty, Ohio, to meet Phil Donner, the man who had learned second-hand that Fred Milo had been predicting his brother's murder.

Donner had had a strictly business relationship with Dean and had once tried to help him take over another beauty supply company. He hadn't seen him since January 1980—when he and his wife had flown to Las Vegas on the same plane as Dean and Maggie Milo.

"There were a lot of rumors. . . ." Donner explained. "You hear a lot of talking going back and forth, you know, everything from 'the guy was runnin' around' to 'somebody put a contract out on him. . . .' I heard stories that he had borrowed money from the underworld sources or . . . that he had borrowed money from some kind of organization, this family Greek or Albanian organization. And they were mad at him. The other story was that, supposedly, he was running around with some guy's wife, and that guy was mad at him."

"Was there any substance to any of these rumors?" Munsey asked.

"I never saw any evidence of things like that."

"Okay, Mr. Donner, Angelo Gieri told us that one of Dean's competitors in New York had had a conversation with Fred Milo. During that conversation, Fred supposedly told him, 'Someday Dean is going to get his brains blown out . . . and it may happen sooner than you think.' We understand that this New York guy told you about that. Is this true?"

"Well, I . . . There was a conversation between Jim Chanier—who's from New York and in the beauty supply business—and Freddy Milo. . . ."

"Okay," Munsey said, sensing that Donner was beginning to lose his memory.

"Well, Chanier said it to me . . . yes . . . that he said something . . . he and Fred were talking about it . . . that it would be better for everybody if Dean wasn't around, or something to that effect."

"Who made that statement, whose idea was it, that it would be better for everybody if Dean wasn't around?"

"I don't really . . . I didn't pay much attention to it. I don't know if Freddy said it to him or if he said it to Freddy or . . . that's the way it came off to me, you know."

"Anything else about that particular conversation?"

"Not really. Just that . . . nothing I can remember, you know?"

Munsey knew. That was all they were going to get from Donner.

In the meantime, Momchilov and Lewis were meeting with Nick Terpolos, a leader of the Greek community, an active member of the Greek Orthodox Church, and, himself, a successful area businessman. A large jolly man with a thick handlebar mustache and a houseful of children, Terpolos had grown up with the Milo children—Dean, Fred, and Sophie—and was well acquainted with the internal problems of the Milo Corporation.

"Tell us about Fred," Momchilov asked as Terpolos' wife served him a piece of souvlaki.

"All through Fred's life, he's been completely dominated by his mother. She's a loud, tough, matronly woman. In that respect, he took after his old man, Sotir, who was a gentle, dotty man who generally would do anything for anyone. Sotir sought peace at any cost within the family—but only as long as his wife approved. She is one strong lady. But she had such control over Fred that it drove a lot of people crazy. I mean, there were a lot of people who wanted to like him, but just couldn't because he was so tied to his mother."

"Okay, tell me about Katina, the mother. Who is she?"

"Katina is something else. She's a smart woman, first of all. She speaks something like five or six languages, and she has a hell of a business sense. She comes from a wealthy family. Her father was in the import-export business in Tripoli. She viewed the world as being a cruel place, and she wanted her sons—particularly her sons—to be as tough as she was. So she played them off against each other. She'd have one piece of candy, and she'd throw it between the two of them and make them fight over it."

"What about Sotir?"

"He'd let it happen. God forbid if he ever challenged his wife."

"Okay, I'm sorry, we were talking about Fred."

"Yeah, right. Well, Fred is basically a good-natured kind of guy who was manipulated by his mother. Like I said, Fred took after his father. But Sotir's pride and joy was Dean. Dean was the one who was brought up to be the successful businessman, not Fred. Dean was the one child whom the parents had high hopes for. Anything Fred, or even Sophie, did always seemed to be overshadowed by something Dean had done better. But for years neither Fred nor Sophie seemed to be bothered by this. They loved their brother; that's all they knew! They just loved him!"

"So would you say that Katina pushed Fred against Dean?"

"Yeah, she pushed him into a war with Dean! I know she never meant it to come to this. But it was against Fred's nature to confront such things head-on. Again, we're talking about basically a nice guy. He's no boat-rocker. Anyway, because he was naive, he was totally incompetent fighting his brother. He just kind of stumbled and bumbled through it all. And this bumbling by Fred started to really complicate something that was already getting pretty damned complicated. While Dean was busy being a winner, Fred was busy being a whiner. Get it? Fred had walked into this battle with his brother completely unarmed!"

"So Fred really didn't want to fight?"

"These two guys really loved each other. They really did. And all of this fighting really took its toll on the two of them. Fred had always viewed Dean as his big brother and his protector. In fact, when Fred decided to marry Kathy, it was Dean who went to Sotir and Katina on their behalf and asked them to accept Kathy into the family. See, Kathy's not Greek or Albanian, and the folks had their ways, you know? But Dean went to bat for his brother. He later did the same thing for Lonnie when he wanted to marry Sophie. Hell, I don't even know what the hell Lonnie is. He sure as hell ain't Greek. . . ."

"Okay, what about Dean and Fred in the office? How did they get along?"

"You know, Dean made some mistakes, too. He used to always introduce Fred to his friends like this, 'Hello, I'd like you to meet my brother, Fred.' You know? 'My brother, Fred.' He'd even do that with business associates. And then people would come up to Fred and say, 'Oh, you're Dean Milo's brother.' No one ever knew Fred just as Fred Milo; he was always Dean's kid brother."

"What about Sophie?"

"Sophie? Hell, her situation was totally different. She was her parents' little girl, and she wasn't expected to do anything more than get married and have babies. You know?"

"What's Fred's educational background?"

"Fred got, I think, a degree in English from the University of Akron and spent a couple of years behind a desk in the Army. He had virtually no qualifications to be a businessman, let alone the president of something as big as the Milo Corporation. In fact, until Milo B&B started making big money, he took only a casual interest in its operations outside of his own job. At best, he was a nine-to-five man. Dean usually sent him to shows and conventions their industry had around the country. But even they were too fast-paced and packed with pressure and deadlines. Fred was too laid back, too methodical to make things happen. He liked to play tennis, drive his Mercedes, and play with his kids and their pets. That's what he liked to do."

"And Dean?"

"Dean liked to work; Fred liked to play. And, for years, both did as they liked—and both of them were happy. Meantime, Dean made everyone in the family, including Fred, pretty god-damn wealthy. Fred once told me, 'Hell, if it wasn't for Dean, I wouldn't have what I've got now.' Okay, business? Fred was executive vice president of the company, right? He had an office adjoining Dean's. I think they were separated only by a corridor. Because they worked so close together, they were always talking to each other, you know, consulting each other. To Dean, asking Fred his opinion about anything was just, kind of, a *pro forma* gesture, you know, a common courtesy. From what I understand, Dean did this with all of his employees. But, in the end, Dean made all the final decisions—all of them."

"Okay, when did the problems begin between these two guys?"

"About early '79; that's when they really started. There was some sort of disagreement over the need for creating a new department—the personnel department, I believe. See, Dean hated unions. He was kind of screwed up in that way, and there were some people raising hell, trying to create a union. So, Dean had already started to pull his management team together. And he thought that the company was to a point that it needed a personnel department, right? You know, he thought it would offset everyone's demands for a union. So, how does Fred take it? He looks at it and says it's cutting into his responsibilities. Understand? In this period of growth for the company—which Dean is trying to control—Fred starts getting territorial and conservative, as well as secretive. Fred started making charges that Dean was going against his parents' long-term plans for the company—which included keeping it owned and operated by members of his family."

"So what did Fred do?"

"Hell, he got desperate, and he tried to create a sector within the corporation that reported to him—and only to him. To spite Dean, he'd issue orders to his staff that were completely contrary to Dean's directives. You know? I mean, it's like, say, I'm working for you, and you tell me to go sweep the sidewalk. And then I say, 'No, I think I'll go do the dishes instead.' See, Fred felt that he had to prove to everyone, particularly his parents, that he could do the job as well as, if not better than, his brother. Everyone suffered because of this."

"So what happened to Dean's personnel department?"

"Sometime in early '79, with no decision made yet, Dean gave Fred a 'special assignment.' You know what that is. . . . Get the hell out of my way for a while. Fred understood that, too, and he didn't want to go. But finally he did. He must've thought he could help ingratiate himself with the field staff of the company. But, for three months, I guess, all Fred did was visit stores around the country, ask a few questions, measure the physical dimensions at each place, and fill out forms. Like I said, everywhere he went, he was still referred to as Dean's brother. This whole special project was nothing more than busy work. Hell, the employees in the field knew which brother had the power and who could get them ahead."

"So when did Fred get back? What happened after that?"

"Well, he was still coming home on weekends. But he found himself being isolated from everyone at the company's headquarters in Akron. And, because he had so few friends over there, he really didn't know what was going on. I mean, decisions were still being made by Dean during the three months he was gone. I understand that while Fred was out West he found out from some field representative that Dean had gone ahead and created that personnel department."

"So what did Fred do?"

"Well, Fred was pretty goddamn upset. When he got back, he saw a bunch of changes had been made and some new people were hired to do the additional work—all during Fred's absence. Fred was fighting mad, and he and Dean really had it out. You know, Fred accused Dean of trying to take over and betraying his parents, and Dean accused Fred of being incompetent. Sure, Fred kept his title as vice president, but so what? He was the big loser in all of this, and he lost most of his authority in the company, as well. The guy was completely demoralized. So, without any bargaining power, or leverage, or even solid support from the other executives in the company, Fred could do nothing more than yell and scream at his brother —who had taken firm control of the family business. Because of the constant harassment from Fred, Dean told him to take off, take an extended vacation until they could sit down and talk under better circumstances. 'Fred, go home,' Dean said. 'I'll send you your salary. But, for now, go home.' Meantime, Dean had some big conference, and then he flew to Vegas for a while. And, so, during all this time, Dean and Fred never talked. So Fred just sat home. He played tennis, drove his Mercedes, and played with his kids and their pets. And, all the while, he kept getting his $150,000 annual salary and kept his one-third interest in the corporation and all of its subsidiaries. Goddamn, under different circumstances, life could've been pretty good for Fred —but then everyone else got involved and stirred things up again."

"And who was that?"

"Well, when Dean reshuffled the company, it also took its toll on Sophie and Lonnie. Because their child was so young, Sophie began to spend more of her time at home and came into the office only sporadically. Also, before the shake-up, Lonnie was being criticized for the way he was handling one of his departments. There was some guy named Ray Sesic who worked for Lonnie. There was another guy, too, but I can't remember his name. . . . Anyway, Lonnie was protecting these two guys, trying to preserve some sort of a kingdom for himself. He started playing the same games Fred had been playing, you know? Lonnie wasn't as big a loser as Fred in the war against Dean, but he saw his territory getting chipped away by Dean, too. Dean was big on giving jobs to people with the education and experience necessary to do the job the way he wanted it done. So, as a result of this, both Lonnie and Sophie became more intense, more defensive, and more critical of Dean."

"So the resentment grew?"

"The resentment within the family grew in equal proportion with their frustrations. Lonnie and Fred, who had never been particularly close, began calling each other on a regular basis, sometimes four and five times a day. And all of this was simply based on their mutual discontent with Dean. And, along with Sophie, they began meeting several times each week at Sotir and Katina's home. Well, the old man just sat there at the kitchen table nodding his head. But the man was praying for peace. But, while he was doing that, Katina was demanding war! She charged that everyone had made their contributions to the company and that everyone should be entitled to equal authority in the company. . . ."

"I don't understand this," Momchilov interrupted. "If the business was going well, and Dean was making everyone money, why the problem? Why did Katina want war?"

"Because Katina saw her son moving further and further away from her and closer and closer to his wife, Maggie, and her family. See, Katina wanted to control people, especially her family. She was just reacting to her losing control of Dean. But once again, I'm sure she never thought Dean was going to lose his life over this."

"So where did Lonnie and Sophie fit into this?"

"Lonnie sided with Katina right away and so did Sophie. I guess Fred hesitated at first, but he eventually yielded to his mother; of course, he did. Sotir, who had been dominated by his wife so long ago, had no choice but to side with her. It's been said that Lonnie was the one who got the parents all upset in the first place. And when Dean found out, he sent Lonnie and Sophie on vacation. He told both of them not to come back until further notice."

"So that was when the firings occurred?"

"No, not then. Something happened in mid-August. Whatever it was, that was what caused the final, irreconcilable split within the family. All I know is that Dean would tell his employees, 'Look, I have a family problem. I'll handle the problem myself. I don't want you people involved. Just do your jobs. I think I'm capable of keeping my family problems and my business dealings separate.'"

"And you don't know what caused it . . . the final split?"

"No, I don't."

Just as the officers got up to leave, Terpolos asked, "Can you tell me something?"

"Sure," Momchilov replied.

"They say that it stormed when Dean's body was found, and that it stormed while he was being placed in his grave. True?"

"That's what I understand. . . . Why?"

"It's an old Albanian belief—when such things in nature happen, it means that the soul won't rest until the murder is avenged."

8 | *"There were two checks—each for $150,000."*

THE INTERVIEWS CONTINUED. Next on Munsey and Bailey's list was Warren Tobin, a new vice president of the Milo Corporation and a member of Dean Milo's professional management team. Tobin had been with the company since the age of twenty-one—he was now twenty-nine—and had been promoted to vice president from general merchandise manager. Dressed in a blue pin-striped suit, white shirt, and red silk tie, Tobin fit the role of the young junior executive. After a brief conversation about clothes with Munsey—himself a poor but well-dressed plainclothes cop—they got down to business.

"Did Mr. Milo ever discuss with you any threats against him or to the company by any competitors?" Munsey asked.

"No. We were always a very competitive company, and we've stepped on a lot of people's toes over the years," Tobin replied. "But, no, I'm not aware of any threats whatsoever or anything of this nature. People say, 'Well, we're going to get back at you' in the business world, or 'We're going to fight you,' competitively, which is what we expect. That's what we do, too. . . ."

"Were you aware of a problem with Adams Restaurants and the U.S. Marshal attempting to come to Dean Milo to serve a subpoena?"

"Yes. I wasn't here that day. . . . I was in Nashville, but I've heard there was a staff meeting. Dean said not to be alarmed, that there was a federal marshal coming, and it had nothing to do with the family problem. That they wanted to question him on another matter. And then I've also heard that he didn't talk to them. He wanted to go to Florida and wanted to talk to them when he got back. They were supposed to talk to him immediately on his return. And that's really all I know [except] he was on the board of directors of Adams. I know he sold me some stock in Adams. . . ."

"Have you ever seen James Licata?"

"Yes, I've seen Mr. Licata . . . a couple of times. I met him once [at the company]."

"Do you know what the circumstances were that he was there?"

"Mr. Licata came [there] to have lunch with Dean. . . . I happened to be in the front conference room once and Dean, jokingly, said, 'I want you to meet another stockholder,' and introduced me to Mr. Licata. I said, 'Nice to meet you,' you know, and walked away. . . ."

"Do you know anything about Mr. Licata?"

"Well, all I know is what our advertising man [said]. When Dean first got on the board of directors and this whole Adams thing came up, he just said, 'I hope Dean knows what he's doing.'"

"What was he talking about?"

"Well, he had implied that, in his past, Licata had some underworld connections, or whatever you want to call them. This is what I was told. . . ."

"To your knowledge, has Dean ever borrowed money from Jim Licata?"

"No, not to my knowledge."

"Where did the money come from that Dean invested in Adams Restaurants?"

"That Dean invested? I'm sure it was personal money. I'm assuming it was."

"Did you know Ray Sesic?"

"Yes, I know Ray."

"Could you tell us a little bit about him?"

"He was the person who was leaking information out of the company after Dean had asked that nothing be passed on. Ray is not a stable human being. . . . He was not the cleanest person in the world. He was kind of grubby and didn't really take care of himself real well. . . . The last I heard, he moved down to Columbus to run this Capital Beauty Supply, which Lonnie was in charge of. So, to my knowledge, he's still down there."

The next member of Milo's tight-knit inner circle to be interviewed was thirty-two-year-old Rod Kyriakides, the coroner's son. As chief buyer and a nine-year employee of the company, young Kyriakides had been a close and trusted advisor to Milo, played golf with him and occasionally accompanied him on business trips. In addition, his father and Milo had been close friends.

Early in the interview, Munsey hit paydirt. He was trying to determine what had caused the firings of Fred, Sophie, and Lonnie, when Kyriakides said casually, "Fred made a tour . . . and we saw very little of him. He'd come in, say 'hello.' He would acknowledge your 'hello,' and he'd stay anywhere from ten minutes to an hour. And then he'd just walk out and wave as he was leaving. He would literally say nothing. He'd just come in, do what he had to do, and go out again.

"And, then, of course, last August, when we were at our show in Boston, I believe a couple of checks were drawn against the company, very large amounts of money. And I think Dean found out about it when we were in Boston. I didn't know about it, I don't think, until we got back."

"How much money are you talking about?" Munsey asked.

"I think there were two checks—each for $150,000."

"Do you know what they were for?"

"Supposedly—I have no verification for this—supposedly the settling of the account for the private label products company. We had a company, Mico, M-I-C-O, that would buy contracted merchandise. . . ."

Although Kyriakides was not certain who had drawn the checks, he indicated that both of them had been old checks, the kind used before the company had been computerized.

PART ONE | *Questions*   63

"So, then, the money went where?" Munsey continued.

"To Mico Beauty Products."

"Who was, at that time . . ."

". . . The three children again . . . Dean was outvoted, two-to-one. . . . So they took this money into Mico. . . . We came back from the show, and Dean was very angry. I know he was; he was hurt. And he said, 'Yeah [the money had to be returned]. We'll figure out what it is, and we'll pay you, but that's no way—to take it.' I don't know if they were going to do it or not, but he [Dean] finally said, 'If you don't return the money by such and such a date, I'm going to fire you.' And, obviously, they never did, and he let them go."

"Now, you say, 'they.' Are you referring to . . ."

"Fred, Lonnie, and Sophie."

As Kyriakides left the sheriff's office, Munsey rushed over to Momchilov, who was sitting alone in his office. "Larry! I think we've just found out why Dean fired his family!"

"What's that?"

"Dean apparently caught Fred misappropriating $300,000 from Milo B&B, with the blessing of Lonnie and Sophie!"

"Okay, Rich, you and Bailey get over to the Milo Corporation, and talk to Bob Bennett, the company comptroller. Press him on it. Get him to give you whatever evidence is available, cancelled checks or whatever. Then, pressure him into giving you everything he knows about Dean and Fred's negotiations. Find out how much money was involved. I want to know if Fred was bargaining in good faith or just trying to buy some time."

Robert Bennett, who had been with the Milo Corporation for only thirty months, had last seen Dean at the wedding reception on Saturday night. "He sat and ate at our table with my wife and me," explained Bennett, another member of the Milo brain trust. "Dean was in a great mood, nothing appeared to be troubling him. He only had one drink all night. Someone brought him a second, but he never touched it."

With regard to the two $150,000 checks, Bennett recalled, "One day at work, I think it was August 13th, a guy from the

bank called me and said, 'We have these two checks; they are
out of sequence here. What do you want me to do? How do you
want me to handle them?' I said, 'What two checks?' And [I
learned] they had taken monies amounting to $300,000. . . .
They [were signed by] authorized signatures on our bank
account. Okay? And they [Fred, Lonnie, and Sophie] had gone
down and got counter checks and written two checks for
$150,000 each. One was dated August 3rd, and the other was
dated August 13th. They pulled $300,000 out of the checking
account. And that's what blew the cork."

"And that was in 1979?" Munsey asked.

"Yes. And, on August 31st, Dean wrote them a letter stating
that they were terminated. . . . He fired them on August 31st,
and they haven't been paid since that time. . . ."

"Who were they [the checks] cashed by? Do you know? Who
were they signed by?"

"They were made out to one of the [subsidiary] companies.
. . . I think they were deposited in some kind of Mico account."

"Do you know who signed the checks?"

"Yeah, Fred. . . ."

"When these people were fired from the company, they lost
their salaries, but they didn't lose their other benefits?"

"No."

"So they still continued to get money . . . ?"

"I still accrued their salaries. Just for the record, Dean, at
some point, if he ever settled, had planned to pay them. Hell,
last year they got their bonuses, as usual, which were large
amounts. They get a year in bonuses—a large portion of their
pay based on how well the company did—and that was paid to
them last September. We always try to pay them something."

"How much was that, approximately?"

"Fred got $103,500; and Sophie got $69,000. . . ."

"If the company ownership is in thirds—Dean Milo, Fred
Milo, and Sophie Milo—how could Mr. Milo . . . ?"

"Fire them?"

"Right."

"Well, it also involved their employment agreements. Here's
how he could fire them, and it was also one of the court cases,

okay? The problem was that they didn't want to take orders from Dean—especially Fred. He didn't want to take orders, and then Lonnie went to the parents [and got] the parents involved, so Dean got really upset. . . . The employment agreements really state that Dean couldn't fire them unless [they did something illegal] . . . but he felt that [signing the two checks] had been an illegal act and was justification for it."

Munsey then began questioning Bennett about the discussions Fred and Dean had been having prior to the murder.

"My understanding is that Dean and Fred were about to arrive at a settlement," Bennett explained. "What Dean really wanted was to reach an agreement—you know, out of court—a buy-out."

"Do you know what the figure was?"

"Yeah. I think they started out asking ten million, Fred did, and Dean offered four. The last time I heard, it was six or eight million or something like that. It wasn't a straight buy-out. It had to do with financial arrangements and getting Fred a job with another company. It involved a lot of things."

When the two officers had concluded their interview with Bennett and returned to their car, Bailey wondered out loud, "Why would Fred have Dean killed if he was near a settlement and could walk away with at least six million dollars and maybe as much as eight million dollars?"

"You know," Munsey responded, staring off in the distance. "Maybe Momchilov is right. Maybe Fred was just buying time. Maybe he wanted it all."

"And maybe all of this bargaining and negotiating was just a charade."

Later that night, Munsey called Lonnie Curtis at his home and asked if he would be willing to take a polygraph test the following day. Curtis replied, "Wait a minute," and then gave the phone to his attorney, Richard Guster, who said that he represented both Curtis and Fred Milo. He informed Munsey that neither would take a lie detector test, because there were serious questions regarding its reliability.

Munsey protested the decision, to no avail, and finally could only ask when it would be convenient for Lonnie and Sophie Curtis and Fred Milo to give their formal statements. All three interviews were set for August 25th at the Summit County Sheriff's Department.

9 | "*There was a fuse burning.*"

ON THURSDAY, August 21st, Lieutenants Momchilov and Lewis met with Dean Milo's long-time friend and business adviser, forty-five-year-old Louis Fisi, at his Akron office. A tall, thin man with brown, graying hair, Fisi had known Milo since 1957 when they had been fraternity brothers at the University of Akron. They had also been in the Army Reserves together.

During the early 1960s, Fisi had become involved in the Milo family's then-small business operation, which had been located in a basement shop at Five Points on Akron's near west side. Fisi had been primarily a business consultant and tax advisor. He'd helped to create the family business's first accounting system and functioned as its first bookkeeper and accountant. Until 1970, he'd accepted only $75 a month for his part-time work. After that, Fisi had worked for free, continuing as the family's financial advisor. He had also grown close to Lonnie and Sophie, as well. The three of them and others had once pooled their money and invested in a couple of oil wells.

During the final year of Dean's life, Dean had asked Fisi to consider taking over as president of the Milo Corporation in the event Milo decided to step down. Fisi had not seen Dean since June. At that time, they had discussed Dean's strategy for his settlement negotiations with Fred, as well as for the lawsuits that had been filed against Dean by the other members of the family. Fisi told the two detectives that he, too, had been named in the major lawsuit, over control of the voting stock. Milo's parents had openly accused Fisi of malpractice in his role as intermediary. Of course, Fisi denied this.

"When Dean told Fred, Lonnie, and Sophie that they no longer worked there, is that when they filed the last lawsuit against Dean?" asked Momchilov. "There's ten of them, from what I understand."

"Yeah, but there's only one real lawsuit," answered Fisi. "That's the one I'm named in—to set aside the voting share. The others are all tactical lawsuits. They're significant, but they're all spinoffs from the one big argument [over] Dean's share of the voting. . . ."

"The way it was originally set up was that each one of them had a one-third interest in the business?"

"No. How far do you want to go back? There have been a lot of changes. . . . At first, the majority of shares went to the father, some to the mother, some to Dean, only one to Fred, and only one to Sophie. At that point, in 1965, I challenged Dean. I said, 'Dean, man, why don't you take control right now? You're going to run the company. Why don't you take control? You are going to make problems for yourself later. If you are going to run the company, get control now.' [Dean said,] 'No, in due respect for my parents, I've got to do this.' I said, 'Okay, it's your life. . . .'

"But when this agreement that they are arguing about was drawn, Dean's rationale was as follows: 'My parents have always promised me the authority to run this company as the eldest son. I want that in concrete, actual fact, because I want to build a warehouse. I want to make it twice the size it is now. And I'm going to be jammed for space. I can't run a business by having to answer to them [Fred and Sophie]. I want control. I want it so I don't have to answer to anybody.'

"So," Fisi continued, "Dean somehow got me hooked into talking to the family. I was a confidant. Everyone trusted me. Dean said, 'I want control.' You know, when you talk control, you say, 'Okay, that's fifty-one percent.' It got to the point where the rest of the family wasn't willing to pay for giving that control. . . ."

Puzzled, Momchilov asked, "But after you came up with the concept, they all agreed to it?"

"They all signed it, but they're all suing me now, so . . . that's the contention, yeah. The thing is, I worked very diligently to explain it thoroughly to all the children first, so that they understood it. Sophie understood it at the time that she signed those documents. Lonnie understood it. Fred said, 'Where do I sign . . . ?' Fred's kind of an artist, 'Just don't bother. I don't want pressure.' Dean, I don't think, ever really signed the documents until long after they were in effect. . . ."

"The parents understood the whole thing?"

"Well, they did at the time. No question in my mind. I would say this—whether or not my attorney thinks I should say it or not—because of the tremendous pressure, and the way the family got so angered about the whole thing, and then the firings . . . there was a fuse burning. People convinced themselves that other things were going on. . . . But, yeah, they understood it. . . ."

"In their faith, is it the custom for the oldest son to take over the business?"

"Yeah, the parents reared Dean to be a successful businessman. The mother was a strong entity. She's the one who raised him to be a businessman. The father, Mr. Milo, is a very weak man. Mrs. Milo is the matriarch, and that's the whole reason there's a big fight—because, finally, Dean no longer followed her orders. That's the big blowout right there. All of a sudden, he stopped taking orders, and she got very upset. And she's tough . . . a tough lady."

"Is she?"

"Oh, you better believe it. I have a lot of respect for her. She's tougher than hell, a hard woman."

"And she's what? Sixty-nine years old?"

"Yeah, she's got to be pushing seventy. She's tough. She's tough! I remember the last time I went over there when Mr. Milo called me about being thrown out [of the business]. . . . The conversation went like this: Mr. Milo started it, and, in about two minutes—Mr. Milo wasn't really getting to the punch line—Mrs. Milo stepped in and took over. Then it was her from that point forward. The old man was just shaking, really angry, very upset. . . . I was there at the appointed hour. . . . The parents are talking to me. 'We gave it to Dean, and we can take it away from Dean!' And then in comes Lonnie and gives me the shuffle and starts interrogating me. I said, 'Hey! Time out! Time to stop all this bullshit! I came out of respect to you people, but I'm calling an end to the meeting right now! I don't have to put up with Lonnie! And I'm not going to put up with Lonnie, and that's it! End of conference!'

"I walked down the center hallway to go to the door. Mrs. Milo, man, came after me, and I thought she was going to attack me. I thought the woman would attack me! She was in a frenzy, hollering and screaming. I walked out of there, and damn, she slammed that door; I thought the whole sucker was just going to fall off the hinges. She had that kind of anger. . . . She's a tough lady."

"What did the parents want? Did the parents want the control of the company back?"

"They felt Dean had abused his power, that they had the power to give, and also the power to take back. They didn't understand the legalities. . . ."

"Last year, of course, was the big break, after which Sophie left, Lonnie left, and Fred left. Supposedly, Dean was left running the business?"

"Right."

"As of this year, there was a court hearing he was supposed to attend?" Momchilov asked.

"And it was postponed until July, and then, in July, it was postponed until this coming December."

"Okay. How much has the bitterness grown from the time it was cancelled?"

"Every day. And I would say that the July 29th postponement could very well be a key factor. . . ."

"July 29th?"

"Because even the attorney, Dick Guster, went bananas. He was pissed off about that court case being put off. I know they felt that Dean had some kind of leverage with the court to be able to postpone that thing. . . . Fred [came to me] and said, 'Look, I'm sick and tired of all of this, and if I had my way I don't want to go through all of this. I just want to end it all. I can't stand the family bickering. I can't stand all the pressure. I have a future to worry about. I've got no job. I don't know what the hell to do.'

"He was shook. In essence, he said, 'How can we get this thing settled? What I want to do is cut a fair deal with Dean that I can go sell to [my parents, Sophie, and Lonnie]. I don't know how the hell I'm going to sell it to them, but I'll take it to them, and try to get them to move. Things are so polarized that if they don't move, then I've got to make my own decision.'

"Two weeks before the court case, scheduled for July 29th, we sat down, and Dean made an offer [to buy Fred out for] eight million dollars, plus interest and so forth. Every day that went on, though, things got worse. I think the players on the other side—Sophie, Fred, Lonnie, Mrs. Milo, and Mr. Milo— all became more bitter. It was just building and building."

"Did Lonnie ever know that Fred was going to sell?"

"That's a good question. I don't know. I would like to know the answer, because it could be a key question."

"Have you ever said anything to Lonnie or . . . ?"

"Hell, no! Absolutely not! Other people might've, because, you know, there was a certain amount of discussion."

"Okay. So, in other words, Fred wanted to get out of it, as far as you know—he wanted to sell his part of the whole thing?"

"Yeah, he was interested in finishing it. . . . You've got to remember that Fred is a very weak-willed person. He just doesn't want any hassles. That's the kind of individual he is. He couldn't deal with it."

Fisi had given a great deal of thought to the circumstances of Dean's murder; he and Momchilov discussed that, too.

"A theory I have," Fisi speculated, "is that somebody got entry with a Western Union telegram."

"Why was that?" Momchilov asked.

"Okay. How would you get Dean's attention? You know,

Dean was a spooky character. He would not go out in the dark. He didn't like strange noises. He didn't like dogs. He never put himself into a compromising position. He was physically, to some degree, a chicken. Okay? You know, like football players are willing to take a certain amount of punishment— Dean was a tennis player. And there's a big difference; he's never been one who could handle physical pain very well. He was kind of a sissy in that sense.

"So, if someone was knocking on his door, he would not admit them. No question in my mind. He would ask them who the heck it was. I know about that—that Western Union thing. [Richard] Scott is a good friend of my daughter, who told me that he found a piece of paper. [The killer] called him [Milo] up and said, 'This is Western Union. I have a telegram about your son, Sotir.' At that point, the guy [Milo] is bananas. He would lose his conventional cool about being cautious. Someone knocked on the door, handed him a piece of paper. He looked at it. It's blank. Gun. Okay? Stepped inside. 'Turn around.' Pow! That quick. No horsing around. Someone knew exactly how to get at him, exactly what would make him drop his guard. . . ."

"Anything else? Do you know anything else you can add?"

"No, except I have to tell you that whoever laid him in, was able to get to him somehow. . . . They got in without any signs of forcible entry. Dean had a strong upper torso, so anyone who got close to him would've been in a hand-to-hand type thing. He [Milo] could've at least handled himself reasonably well. . . . K. Y. [Dr. Kyriakides] said at the funeral that he had his underwear on backwards, [or] did he say inside out?"

"They were turned around," Momchilov replied.

"You mean the fly was on his butt?"

"Right."

"That leads me to some irate husband or lover thing. That's a sign, like, 'This is what I've done.' I don't know if it means anything, but, to me, I can't imagine putting your underwear on backwards. I don't care when it is. I don't care what kind of rush I'm in. I always get the fly in the right spot, you know?

That's the only way to put them on. That one bothers me.
That means something; but I don't know what it means. I
just don't think, you know . . . inside out . . . I can't see it.
That's haste. Somewhere along the line, they're on backwards.
That doesn't make a lot of sense."

10 | *"It's Fred."*

THE FOLLOWING DAY, Friday, August 22nd, Sergeants Munsey and Bailey returned to the Milo Corporation to interview Arthur Knox. Knox, a tall, distinguished-looking man, had been with the company for the past four years and was currently serving as a regional manager for the company. "The last time I saw Dean," Knox told the police, "was at about 5:00 P.M. on the Friday before he was killed. I dropped him off at the Harrisburg International Airport in Pennsylvania."

"What were you doing with Dean?" Munsey asked.

"He had come into Norfolk, Virginia—that's where I work— and I'd accompanied him on a tour of his three stores in the Richmond area. We spent the night in Richmond, then we continued on a tour of other stores in Virginia, then up to Philadelphia and Allentown, Pennsylvania."

"Tell me, Mr. Knox, did Dean seem to be particularly troubled about anything? Did he say anything?"

"Yes, he did. He was talking to me about his problems with his brother, Fred, and his brother-in-law, Lonnie Curtis."

"What did he say, in particular?"

"Well, he said that his dispute with Lonnie had hurt him even more than the one with his brother, because he had

74

placed an enormous amount of trust and confidence in Curtis.
That was about it, though."

"Did you do anything else with him?"

"We had dinner with an old girl friend of his."

"An old girl friend? Who?"

"Her name was Patricia Douglas."

"Tell me about it, can you?"

"Oh, Dean telephoned Patricia and asked her to have dinner
with the two of us. We met at the bar in the restaurant at the
Regency in Richmond. She came by at about 8:30 P.M. We
had a few drinks and then had dinner at some restaurant a few
miles away."

"Was Dean drinking?"

"Yeah, he had a few. He wasn't loaded, if that's what you
mean."

"What did you do after you ate?"

"We went to a discotheque."

"Did Dean and Patricia dance?"

"Yes, mostly the slow dances."

"What time did you get back to the Regency?"

"It was about 1:00 A.M."

"Did Patricia Douglas come back with you?"

"Yes, she had left her car there in the parking lot."

"Did she return to Dean's room?"

"No. Dean walked her to her car; I went upstairs to my
room."

"Did you see Dean again that night?"

"Yeah. He stopped in my room about twenty minutes later."

"Was he alone?"

"Yes, he seemed to be."

Later that afternoon, Munsey received a telephone call from
attorney Dick Guster, who informed him that his clients—
specifically Fred, Sophie, and Lonnie—had taken "polygraph
examinations from a private operator." He added that all three
had passed. Munsey demanded to know the name of the
operator, his firm, and a list of the questions asked, but Guster
refused to provide him with the information. In addition, in

response to Munsey's request for taped statements, Guster said that his clients had answered enough questions and would not answer any more.

On Monday, August 25th, Lieutenant Bill Lewis received a telephone call from George Tsarnas, who had arranged interviews for the police with Maggie Milo and her family in Clearwater, Florida. During their conversation, Lewis asked Tsarnas if he had talked to Licata since the murder. Apparently, Licata had come to Tsarnas's office the previous week. Lewis later told Momchilov, "It was just a general conversation [between Tsarnas and Licata] about the status of the company: who was going to be in charge, and if Dean's widow was going to have the only vote in the company as Dean did. Tsarnas replied that the company would probably be in the hands of Fred and Sophie now since . . . the voting power went back to them."

Later that afternoon, the *Akron Beacon Journal* carried an article, "Slain Businessman's Sister Sues to Get Will." According to the story:

> Attorney Richard Guster, representing Sophie Ann Curtis, said the suit is an attempt to learn the identity of the person who will handle Milo's estate in order "to have an orderly continuation of the family business."
>
> The suit was filed against the law firm of Samuel Goldman, George P. Tsarnas, and Michael L. Robinson, which represented Milo and his company.
>
> Larry Vullemin, an attorney with the law firm, who was asked to comment about the suit, said, "We will be prepared to argue against that motion on Friday. . . . Our interest at this point is finding out who is responsible for this murder. . . . The financial considerations are secondary to us. . . ."

The next day, Tuesday, August 26th, Munsey and Bailey returned to Milo B&B to reinterview Bud Eisenhart, who was still mourning deeply the death of his friend. Eisenhart was shown a document, found by Momchilov among Milo's personal papers and records during the search of the crime scene. Described as a "contingency plan," the secret document was apparently a description of what Milo and his staff were prepared to do in the event that Dean lost the company to his brother and sister.

"The purpose of the plan was to make it as difficult as possible for them actually to take control of the corporation," Eisenhart explained. "It was supposed to provide for the destruction of key company records and computer tapes."

"Where was this material kept?" Munsey asked.

"In the company's vault. It was dated, May 9, 1980, and everyone just called it 'The Worst Case Alternative.'"

"Who was authorized to carry this out?"

"Me, Bob Bennett, and maybe one or two others. Frankly, Rich, I hadn't heard Dean make any reference to this plan in several months."

"So he probably didn't view his family's challenges against him that seriously?"

"Oh, he took it all very seriously, but I don't think he ever really thought they could actually take the company away from him."

On August 27th, Munsey and Bailey drove to Columbus to interview fired corporate "spy" Ray Sesic. The slender, thirty-year-old Sesic sported a thick crescent-shaped mustache, which made him look more like a Mexican freedom fighter than a buyer at a beauty supply store. An employee of the Milo family since 1972, he had dropped out of college during his senior year and never returned to finish his undergraduate work. He had also been a former Ohio National Guardsman.

"Were you terminated [from the Milo Corporation]?" Munsey asked.

"Yes."

"Do you recall what happened when you were terminated? Did you leave on bad terms?"

"I was a little angry when I was let go. Yeah, but . . . well, what can I say? After seven years, I suppose I was a little let down, disappointed."

"Did you make any threatening statements at that time?"

"No. I yelled a little bit; mostly, I talked. . . ."

"What were the circumstances of why you were let go?"

"Well, I believe it was, more or less, I was talking to the

[Milo] family, and we weren't supposed to have any contact with the family. But they were close friends, and, well, I just called Lonnie. . . ."

"Were you let go for just talking to the family or for giving them information regarding the business operations at Milo?"

"Well, I admitted a few things. I said a few things that, probably, I shouldn't have. I guess he [Dean Milo] had a right to slap my guts. . . . It was just one of those things. . . ."

Sesic explained that he had heard about Dean's death from his wife—who had heard about it from one of Milo's employees. At first, Sesic said he understood that Dean committed suicide. Sesic then called Fred Milo's wife, Kathy, in Akron. She asked him to have Lonnie—who was with Sesic but in another part of the building—call her.

"And Kathy then told you of the death, too?" Munsey continued.

"Yes."

"And then you contacted . . ."

"I went upstairs and told Lonnie to call Kathy. It was an emergency."

"How did Lonnie take the news?"

"I don't . . . well, it's kind of hard to explain. It was . . ."

"We realize there were a lot of family problems."

"Yeah, I know. I can understand. There was shock in his face, and Sophie . . . it was bad. Sophie was very, very upset. I tried my best to calm her down. I really didn't know what to do. I was very shook up when I heard about it. . . ."

"Have you been given any promises or made any promises as far as maybe running Capital or any other position once the family takes over again at Milo?"

"No, I haven't. There has been nothing discussed."

"Do you have any knowledge of who was involved in the death of Mr. Milo?"

"No, sir, I don't."

"Were you involved in that death?"

"No, sir. . . ."

"To verify any possible involvement in the death of Mr. Milo, would you be willing to take a polygraph examination?"

"I suppose so. I'd want consultation from an attorney first."

"Okay."

"Which would be natural, but I can't foresee any objection."

"Okay. Do you have anything you'd like to add?"

"No, I really don't . . . sad, sad time."

"Okay."

"It's been hard on everybody," Sesic concluded.

While Munsey and Bailey concluded their interview with Sesic, Momchilov and Lewis arrived in Clearwater, Florida, to interview Maggie Milo. When they arrived at the home of Nick Gonatos, Maggie's father, they found she had arranged to have nearly every member of her family present. "Who do you want to talk to first?" she asked the two officers. Although Momchilov and Lewis were only interested in speaking with her, she insisted that the others be interviewed as well.

Seventy-year-old Nick Gonatos—a wealthy, hard-working businessman—was almost as bitter about the murder as his daughter. Gonatos had accompanied Dean and several of Milo's colleagues to Nassau for a series of business meetings from July 23rd to the 27th. He respected and admired his son-in-law. Although neither Gonatos nor any other member of his family could provide any direct information to the police with regard to the murder, he pledged his full cooperation in their investigation and allowed his home to be used as a makeshift office for Momchilov and Lewis during their stay in Florida.

Tall and slim, with short, dark-brown hair, brown eyes and a dark Mediterranean complexion, thirty-eight-year-old Maggie Milo had become a tough and bitter woman since the murder of her husband. Throughout the interview, her fists clenched and her eyes welled, as if she could barely contain her rage against her husband's family, particularly Fred Milo and his mother, Katina.

She recalled an incident which had occurred during the Milo Corporation's annual Christmas party in December 1979. The event had been held at one of Ohio's most extravagant restaurants, Tangier, on Akron's near west side.

"The purpose was to go and have a good time," Maggie said. "[But] as soon as we walked in . . . I saw his mother's face, and I completely panicked. I told Dean, 'Look who's coming.' He immediately went to the door and asked [his mother and father] to leave, because he knew her purpose was not to come to the Christmas party. Her purpose was to come and badmouth him to all of the employees. She had done that at the seminar [a few months before the party]. All she did was go around and try to make Dean look bad to the employees. The Christmas party, he felt, was a time for the employees to have a good time, and he just didn't want his mother in there making a fool out of herself. The mother and father came in as far as the lobby, and I could see through the doors. I just went in the back room and kind of hid. I was scared. I didn't know what was going to happen.

"They were hollering and yelling. . . . I didn't listen to the conversation. I only know from the people [who] walked in and heard it. Judy and Bud Eisenhart were there helping him. I'm sure it embarrassed the parents, but the more he asked them to leave, the more obstinate they were getting with him. It was very strange.

"Fred drove them to the party, to Tangier. Dean had asked them to leave, and Dean was going to have Bud call Fred and ask him to come back and get them. He didn't have to do that. Fred, all of a sudden, drove up in the car ten or fifteen minutes later. He almost knew. Like my husband told me that night, 'Why that so-and-so knew I was going to do that, and he was just waiting to come, drive up and take them home. . . .' "

Despite their problems with Dean's family, Maggie insisted that their marriage was a success. "I do, because if I was any other kind of girl, I couldn't've tolerated that family. . . . I'm not pinning a medal on me; I just feel that I've gone through so much with them and their obnoxious remarks and the accusations. They have hurt me through the years. I have continued to be with my husband, and he and I had a wonderful marriage together. He felt that his success was me, because I was his rock; I was his backbone. I'm the one who stayed home and took care of the kids. I didn't know about his business matters; he wanted it that way. My role was to stay home and raise his children and benefit by all we were going to share together."

However, she did concede that their relationship had been strained by her confrontation with Sophie Curtis after church on Mother's Day—when Sophie had threatened to reveal the letter Dean had written which could allegedly break up Maggie's marriage.

"Sophie was just shaking, you know?" Maggie said. "She was just furious with me. . . . Then the kicker was, 'If we go to court, I've got a piece of paper that Dean knows about that's going to destroy you and Dean. . . .' That shook me. I got into the car, and I said to my husband, 'What the hell is this piece of paper she's got? You're not telling me something.' He asked, 'What piece of paper?' And I explained the story. He said, 'She doesn't have anything. I don't know of any piece of paper.' And then I started accusing him. 'Did you have a child? Were you married before? Did you get in some trouble before we got married that I don't know about? Did you sign something that you were going to divorce me after doing something in particular . . . or what the hell is it?' Well, I was really shook. I didn't know what to think. And for her to come with an outright lie like that, I couldn't imagine it. Dean said, 'Mag, it's a threat. She's so desperate now that she's threatening you.' I was so upset that afternoon that I went to George Tsarnas. I said, 'George, this is what she told me. What is it, George?' He said, 'Maggie, don't worry about it. They're desperate. They know they've got a losing battle. It's just another one of their lies.'"

Regarding Dean's personal habits, Maggie explained that he was generally a messy person. Although she had never known him to throw his clothes on the floor, he had often placed them over chairs and on doorknobs. Over the past few years, she'd noticed that he had become a "big spender" of sorts, usually carrying at least $100 cash in his pocket, although usually he had charged everything on a credit card. For years, Milo had been known as a tightwad who had never had more than a couple of bucks on him.

She said that her husband had always taken off his wedding ring before he'd gone to bed and placed it on the television. However, he'd never removed his gold bracelet—which had been one of his favorite things. He'd basically been a non-drinker, who rarely gambled and did not take drugs. She'd never known him to be a womanizer—since their marriage—but she understood that he'd occasionally met a variety of women to discuss business.

Maggie Milo also knew about the four pornography films found in her closet. She explained to the officers that a friend of his had given him the films for safekeeping, and that Dean had told her about them as soon as he'd brought them to the house. She insisted that Dean had never viewed them.

She added that Dean had never liked to be alone. He would even refuse to eat by himself and often called friends on the spur of the moment to have dinner with him in lieu of eating alone. "He's not the type to go to restaurants and eat breakfast by himself," she said. "He would go out and impose himself on someone to fix breakfast. . . ."

Although there were three pillows on the bed, he would only use one. When his wife wasn't using the extra pillow, he'd had a weird habit of throwing the third on the floor. He'd usually slept in his shorts and rarely in the nude. She could not imagine why his jockey shorts had been backwards. She also confirmed what the police had suspected—that she'd slept on the side of the bed near the radio and the Christian magazines; and he'd slept by the phone and the skin magazines.

"He put the radio on, because he didn't like a quiet house. It drove him crazy. My husband had a little fear in him at night. I'm sure you saw that cane by his bed. That was a big joke with us. When he heard a crack on the wall or something, he was going to take that cane. And I'd ask him, 'Where in the heck are you going with that? What's that going to do?' He'd say, 'Man, you just never know.' So he would check every room. He was a very, very cautious man. If that cane was untouched, it has to make me believe that he either expected somebody at the door, or it was somebody that he just didn't fear. It was not a burglar or someone he might've heard downstairs. If he'd heard [something], I don't think he would have gone down there without his cane to protect himself. . . .

"If he'd heard a car door, without anyone calling him, he would've probably gone to the bedroom window and looked out to see if there was a car in the driveway. . . . He'd have looked out there to see who in the world was out at this hour. If he'd felt completely at ease, he'd have turned on the foyer light from the upstairs, but, before he'd ever open the door, he'd have flipped on the outside light to see who it was—even if the person had precalled him. He was always cautious. . . ."

Then Momchilov asked, "If somebody came to the door, would he have gotten up and then put on a robe or something? How would he do it?"

"If he went to the door and let somebody in, it would have to be somebody he knew. I mean, unless they just said something. The only thing that I could understand him opening the door for would be, 'Something happened to Maggie and the kids.' . . . My oldest son has a blood disease. My husband is always nervous about that; he always made sure everything was okay with him. So, unless somebody said something like that, I don't think [he would've opened the door]."

"What pants would he put on if he was going downstairs?"

"Either jeans or some of those cut-off pants."

Because the police were still completely baffled by the cotton found on Milo's mouth and around his body, Lewis asked Maggie if the house had any.

"I have cotton balls, I believe, in the drawers . . . in a plastic container. . . . I don't remember Dean ever touching it for a long time. I've never seen him with cotton."

"Do you think the canister was full?"

"I haven't touched it. I don't know, unless he took some. I wouldn't say it was empty."

Maggie last saw her husband on Thursday, August 7th, after he had returned with her father from the Bahamas and before he had left for Virginia. She had been planning to return to Bath with her children on August 15th, a few weeks before they were scheduled to go back to school. She had also been considering accompanying him on a trip to Chicago, set for the following weekend.

She recounted her final conversation with her husband on Saturday, August 9th, after Eisenhart had brought him home from Pennsylvania.

"I said, 'Dean, what are you going to do now?' He said, 'Well,

I don't know.' I made him come out and tell me why Marge [Dean's private secretary] had phoned, looking for him [before Dean left Florida]. He said, 'Well, that was about my brother who called about our meeting'—they were supposed to meet over the weekend. I said, 'Have you heard anything?' I was anxious to see if they had set up anything. He said, 'Honey, I just got home.'

"This was awfully funny," she told the police officers. "All of a sudden, Fred wanted to talk to Dean. I thought that his mother was really making him scared. He's running scared, so he thinks he better get what he can, and get out. But I couldn't believe he would leave his mother and sister out in the cold.

"The first time Dean was supposed to speak with Barry Boyd, I said, 'Why is he trying to talk to you? Your mother and sister are never going to settle . . . until they get back in that company. If you paid them $50 million, that wouldn't be what they want. They want the company!' "

As Dean and Maggie concluded their half-hour conversation, he told her that he'd try to call again the following day. When Maggie didn't hear from him, she just assumed that he was working and couldn't get away. On Sunday evening, a friend of Maggie's, Connie Kanakaredes, called her in Florida. During their conversation, Maggie asked her to call Dean and invite him to dinner on Monday night. Connie tried to reach Dean until 2:00 A.M. Monday morning without success.

Early Monday afternoon, Eisenhart called Maggie. Ostensibly, he just called to say hello. "Bud knew they hadn't been able to get hold of Dean that day," Maggie explained. "But he kept it to himself. I think Bud was really scared. I could tell by his voice that something wasn't right. But I didn't question him."

When Maggie and her aunt returned from shopping at 4:00 P.M., her father, who had been called by Eisenhart, broke the news that her husband was dead. Completely numb, she immediately flew back to Akron and was met at the airport by the Tsarnases, the Eisenharts, and Father Nekrides, the Greek Orthodox priest from Canton. She immediately demanded answers from all of them about what had happened to her husband.

When Maggie was asked by Momchilov and Lewis to speculate on who she thought was responsible, she replied, "Fred had
nothing to lose. He came to a point where Dean actually de-
graded him and humiliated him. When Fred started promoting
these negotiations with Dean, I thought something wasn't right;
but I didn't know what it was. I just didn't understand why
Fred seemed so anxious to sell out. And, now, I'm thinking that
maybe it was just a big act to make Dean think he was.

"Dean kept saying to me near the end, 'I think I've got my
brother on the home stretch; I think I've *finally* got him on the
home stretch!'

"But something just wasn't right about all of this."

"So who do you think is responsible?" Momchilov asked
again.

"It's Fred," she replied calmly. "There's no doubt in my
mind."

Part Two

DIVERSIONS

11 | *"We'll cut you in."*

ON TUESDAY, September 2nd, at 5:30 P.M., Sergeant Munsey cruised Dean Milo's home and found Bud Eisenhart's car parked in the driveway and the front door of the residence open. Munsey stopped and went into the house, where he surprised Eisenhart and another man examining the markings on the foyer floor where Milo's body had been found. Eisenhart quickly introduced the tall, slim stranger as William C. Dear, a private investigator from Dallas, Texas.

"What are you doing here?" Munsey asked Dear.

"I'm on this case," Dear replied, with a "don't fuck with me" glare in his eyes. "The Milo case. I'm here to solve it."

"On whose authority?"

"Tsarnas hired me, his law firm—with the advice and consent of Milo's widow. Anything else?"

"Yeah. I doubt that we'll be able to help you," Munsey shot back.

"Fine," Dear said curtly. "I'll go ahead without you."

Munsey was astonished that an outsider had been brought into the investigation and was particularly taken back by his apparent arrogance. Realizing that Dear was there to stay, however, Munsey simply suggested that he contact Lieutenant Momchilov at the Summit County sheriff's office. Dear nodded his head as Munsey, still stunned by the encounter, excused himself and returned to his car, leaving the two men in the house.

After hearing the news from Munsey, Momchilov telephoned John Hastings, an old friend from the FBI Academy who had left the Bureau and gone into private investigative work. Hastings—who now primarily protected foreign diplomats, business executives, and rock musicians, told Momchilov that he was acquainted with Dear and his reputation. "The guy's a professional manhunter, Larry," Hastings said. "He's a self-contained loner. He lives on some huge estate down in Dallas County. He has the works down there—you know, heliport, Beachcraft Baron airplane, labs, electronic surveillance equipment, all the toys."

"Is he any good?"

"Yeah, outstanding. Good record, good rep. He's got about seven people working for him, too. Two of them could be in business for themselves: Dick Riddle and Bob Dare; they're both top-notch investigators. Then, there's three of them he calls 'The Mod Squad.' "

" 'The Mod Squad?' "

"Yeah, a black guy, Carl Lilly; a Chicano guy, Joe Villanueva; and a white woman, Terry Hurley—you know, 'The Mod Squad.' They mostly work undercover and on surveillance. They do the job."

"Okay, what about Dear? What kind of a guy is he?"

"Dear's kind of a hot dog, but he's a class act. He appears to be a perfectionist—you know the kind: cocky as shit, bad temper. But, what the hell, he and I are in a business in which we're constantly called upon to prove ourselves. He's a survivor. . . . Personally, he's on his second marriage. He's like you, Larry, a newlywed; and he has a young son. I understand his home is something else—indoor pool, mirrors on the walls and ceiling of his bedroom. He thinks he's James Bond, you know. His lifestyle's a cliché. Oh yeah, Larry, he has a man Friday. The guy's name is 'Boots' Hinton. His father was one of the deputy sheriffs in Dallas County who ambushed and then gunned down Bonnie and Clyde way back when. Dear ran for sheriff himself down there a couple of times but was beaten both times. So he's kind of political and very much the public relations type. He likes seeing his name in the paper. But if you work it right with him, that shouldn't be a problem."

"John, what about his cases? What's he done?"

"Dear can take care of himself. He's got connections. He was a bodyguard to some Texas millionaire, H. H. Coffield, one of Lyndon Johnson's big money people. When Coffield died, Dear opened up his own business. He makes his living handling cases other people have given up on. You know, he looks for missing people, business people. That kind of stuff gets sticky. I know he's had his throat cut from ear to ear. I know he's been stabbed in the back. I mean, the guy's got brass balls."

"Specifically, what about his cases?"

"His biggest one—the one that made him famous—was up in Michigan. There was some kid, boy-genius type, at Michigan State. The kid disappeared. Everyone thought he was playing some Dungeons and Dragons game; they thought he got lost in a maze of steam tunnels under the school. . . ."

"Yeah, I remember reading about it."

"Well, that's Dear. Dear supposedly found him—nobody knows where or how. I know it wasn't in the steam tunnels. From what I understand, Dear actually went into the tunnels and looked. I understand he was almost killed doing that. The temperature down there was something like 120 degrees. You know, he's unorthodox and his technique gets a little unpredictable. But he really throws himself into his work, and he gets results. . . . Why? What's going on up there in Akron?"

"Well, Dear's been invited to work on a murder case we're into. I'm just trying to figure out what to do with him. Should we cut him in or cut him out?"

"Knowing him, Larry, I'll tell you: you should cut him in. Like I said, he's got a good reputation, and he's worked with people like you before, police departments and the like. You know, just put it to him, 'We'll cut you in, and you cooperate with us. . . .'"

The following day, September 3rd, Dear arrived at the sheriff's office—where he received a cool reception from Sheriff Troutman, Ed Duvall, Lewis, Munsey, and nearly the entire homicide division. "What'll happen if we don't cooperate with you?" Duvall asked.

"Well," Dear replied, shrugging his shoulders and fingering his mustache, "with or without your help, I'm going to work on this case. And I'm here to solve it. . . . I've worked in Akron before. A couple of teenagers disappeared up in north Akron. I got called in. . . ."

"Right, okay!" Momchilov exclaimed. "That's where I've heard of you. You worked with the Akron Police Department."

"That's right. And I think if you'll talk to them, you'll see they gave me high marks on my work. . . . Listen, I know what all of you are thinking. I understand it. I'm the odd man out. But I think we can work together on this. I think we can solve this thing together, as a team."

"How'd you come to be here?" one of the other officers asked.

"A week or so ago, I got a call from Bob Bennett over at the Milo Corporation. He was calling on behalf of George Tsarnas. He asked me if I was interested. I said, 'Sure.' So he sent me a packet of information about the corporation and the murder itself, and I accepted the case. . . ."

After several minutes of discussion, Duvall suggested that Dear leave the room to allow for a decision to be made.

With Dear pacing up and down the hallway outside, the officers stared at each other, trying to get a feel for the consensus of the group. Momchilov was the first to speak. "Look, we're experiencing a real lack of operating capital in the department. This budget crunch is probably going to cause some cutbacks, even layoffs. We already know that David Bailey is going to be taken off the case. Chief Duvall has done everything he can for us. Now, we get Dear. He's coming in here paying his own way. I mean, my yearly salary wouldn't be enough to fill up his private plane. Plus, we better consider that he has the support of Tsarnas and Maggie Milo. I say, let's use him; let him prove his worth."

With some reservations, the others agreed and then called Dear back into the room. "We're going to go along with you on this," Duvall said. "But here are the rules: everything you hear or see regarding this investigation is strictly confidential.

You are forbidden to talk to the press. We also expect you to share any information you develop on your own with us. In return, we'll cut you in."

After Dear agreed to Duvall's terms, he explained that he wanted to start his investigation from scratch. Among other things, he planned to recreate the murder, to reevaluate existing evidence, and to reinterview witnesses.

While Dear retraced the ground already covered by the police, the sheriff's office continued with its investigation. On Wednesday and Thursday, September 10th and 11th, Munsey, Lewis, and Momchilov conducted a marathon of taped interviews, taking the statements of Barry Boyd, Lonnie and Sophie Curtis, Fred Milo, and Sotir and Katina Milo. All but Dean's father and mother had to be subpoenaed. Boyd, an attorney, was not represented by counsel. The rest were accompanied by attorneys George Pappas and Dick Guster. It was an exhausting two days.

Boyd was first at 9:40 A.M. on Wednesday. He said that he had represented Fred Milo in certain civil cases over the past eighteen months, and added that he had grown up with Fred and had gone to school with him through high school. Although they had both attended the University of Akron, they had rarely seen each other then or later, but had regained their close friendship after Fred had been discharged from the Army. He also said that he had been brought into the negotiations between Fred and Dean by Lou Fisi and George Tsarnas.

"Mr. Boyd, when was this meeting on Sunday supposed to have been set up between Fred and Dean?" Munsey asked.

"Fred didn't say. I didn't know he had actually set one up. Fred told me, 'I'm trying to find Dean. Can we use your house? . . .'"

"So you offered them the use of your home?"

"Right."

"Let me ask you this, Mr. Boyd: Why, when the police contacted you on August 11th, did you give them false information, concerning the meeting between Fred and Dean—in the sense that you didn't know about it?"

"It concerns me that I gave you false information," Boyd

responded, almost desperately. "When Sheriff Troutman called and said, 'Did you meet with Dean? You were supposed to.' I said, 'I didn't know I was supposed to meet him the way it was set up. I just knew they were trying to get together.' If I misled him, I'm sorry."

Munsey asked, "Barry, do you feel that Fred was really pushing for a settlement?"

"I think he was very sincere in his efforts to settle [the lawsuits], because it was bothering him a great deal."

"And you have no knowledge of what the dollar amounts were?"

"The dollars amounts were large."

"Are you talking thousands? Millions?"

"Several millions."

At 2:15 P.M., it was Lonnie Curtis's turn. Momchilov wasted no time. "Do you know who killed Dean Milo?" he asked. "No, I do not," Curtis answered forthrightly.

Momchilov shifted to a subject that had intrigued him ever since Sophie Curtis had first brought it up. "What kind of letter does Sophie have that's going to break up Dean and Maggie?"

"I don't know if it's classified as breaking up Dean and Maggie. What I would say [is] she has a letter in Dean's handwriting that shows the strains between Dean and his wife."

"What kind of strain is that?"

"It's like a pro-and-con sheet. On one side, he said, 'I bought you a new home. You didn't like it. I get you a babysitter. You don't take enough time with the kids. I entertain your family in Florida and when you come back to Akron you won't even call my mother or my family. What kind of person am I? The guy that just pays the bills?' Those are the kind of facts. . . ."

"Where did she get that letter from?"

"I believe, the office."

"When?"

"Year . . . year and a half ago, somewhere in there."

"How did she get it out of the office?"

"She worked there. She saw it on his desk. . . ."

"Made a copy?"

"Made a copy, I believe. . . ."

"Are you aware of a letter that was sent by the mother and father . . . ?"

"I believe so, yes."

"What were the contents?"

"I don't have total recollection of it. . . . [The sense was] that [Milo B&B] is a family corporation; that the family is supposed to be as one; and that Dean should not do to the rest of the family what the rest of the family would not do to him."

"Do you know of a letter that was sent from Dean to the family, mother and father, explaining that all you—or Fred and Sophie—had to do was to grab hold of his shoe strings, and go along with whatever he says, and he'll make you a millionaire?"

"That's unfounded. . . . From 1975 . . . through 1979, the company was not run by Dean Milo. . . . The people [who] busted their backs and did the work and were there every day was not Dean Milo. It was the rest of the family. When he wanted to take a vacation or took his family back to Florida, it was the family that ran the corporation. It wasn't Dean that ran the corporation. It was the total family that ran the corporation."

"This was including you?"

"Yeah, it's [including] me."

At 4:10 P.M., Momchilov, Lewis, and Munsey interviewed Fred Milo. After some preliminary questioning, Momchilov began asking about the $300,000 allegedly misappropriated by Fred. "Last year, 1979, there were two checks written for $150,000, for a total of $300,000. Can you explain about those checks?'"

"Yes, I can explain that."

"Go ahead."

"My brother and my sister and I had a meeting. . . . We were all at odds with each other, and, during that conversation, we were trying to find out if there was a way of resolving [our disputes]. My position was, 'Let me go; run one of the other companies or whatever.' So, somewhere along the line, it became apparent that Lonnie, who had been running Mico, would end up running Mico as a separate corporation, independently— because we didn't feel that we'd be working at Milo's much longer, [considering] the way the [corporation] was running. So, when we got the notice that we were going to be terminated, and since Lonnie was going to end up running it anyway, Lonnie came up with the idea of 'Let's pay the debts that Milo Beauty Supply owes Mico.' He totaled them up, and they came to approximately $300,000, as I recall. Those debts, we paid. I think it might've been two checks. I don't recall. . . ."

"Who operates, or owns, or is on the board of the Mico Company?"

"That was similarly owned, I think: one-third, one-third, one-third."

"Still in the family?"

"Oh, yeah."

"So, in other words, what you were doing was really paying right back into . . ."

"That's all any of them really were, you know? They all went hand-in-hand. One was created because of a need for the other."

"Okay, do you know who killed Dean?"

"No. . . ."

The following day, Lewis and Munsey took the sworn statements of Sophie Milo, who corroborated the stories of Lonnie and Fred about the checks to Mico. Then they moved on to Sotir and Katina Milo.

At 11:30 A.M., the two officers recorded Katina Milo's sworn statement to be followed by her husband's.

"Mrs. Milo, on Saturday, August 9 . . ." Lewis began.

"Yes?" Mrs. Milo replied in her Albanian accent.

"Do you recall what you did that day?"

"I did my work, housework. I do every Saturday, you know?"

"Did your housework. Did you leave the house that day?"

"No."

"Stayed at home all day? Was anyone over that day?"

"Nobody, because, like I say, I do the cleaning house on Saturday, and that's it."

"And Mr. Milo was here with you?"

"Yes."

"And did he leave that day?"

"No. He stays home Saturdays, you know? Doesn't go to work."

"So you stayed home and did your housework and your dinners and went to bed? And that's the extent of your day? That's about all you did that day?"

"Yes."

"Okay, Sunday, which would have been August 10th, did you do anything that day? Did you leave the house?"

"No. We stayed home. We stayed home and rested."

"You didn't go anywhere that day? You both stayed home?"

"Yes."

"Okay, Monday, August 11th—did you go anywhere that day?"

"Monday . . . no. You came. We didn't go no place."

"You didn't go anywhere, and the only people that were in your house were Sergeant Munsey and I when we came over to inform you . . ."

"I lost my son. . . . I couldn't believe it! I still can't believe it!" she cried.

When it became obvious that Mrs. Milo couldn't continue, Lewis ended the four-minute interview.

Sotir Milo, too, was visibly upset. But contrary to what his wife had said, he had left home on Saturday, to do some repair work on a building owned by his family. Both Fred and Lonnie had accompanied him. In addition, Lonnie, Sophie, and their son had visited Mr. and Mrs. Milo before driving to Columbus on Sunday night.

Mr. Milo became increasingly upset as Lewis applied some pressure. "Mr. Milo," Lewis asked, "do you have any idea who would have killed Dean?"

"Please don't ask me that!" The old man started to cry.

"We need to ask you that, Mr. Milo."

"I don't! I don't!"

"Okay."

"I have no idea at all!"

"Sergeant Munsey, do you have anything?" Lewis asked his partner, who simply shook his head.

Meantime, Mr. Milo continued to wail, "You know, I want to go take hold of, please, as soon as . . . I don't like anybody . . . please . . ."

Mr. Milo's interview lasted for only five minutes.

Meantime, back in his office, Momchilov received a telephone call from a Columbus police detective. The detective had received an anonymous tip. Fred Milo, he had been told, had contracted "organized crime people" to murder his brother.

12 | "Why should I get tied up in a family squabble?"

THE ORGANIZED CRIME SCENARIO had haunted the police from the outset of the Milo murder investigation, but, despite the allegations of mob involvement in the Milo Corporation from corporate rivals, the sheriff's investigators had been able to find no evidence of such activity. There was only Dean Milo's personal relationship with James Licata, alleged to be associated with organized crime figures in northeastern Ohio.

Weary of all the speculation and hearsay, Bill Lewis finally decided to call the fifty-two-year-old Licata and ask him to sit down for an interview. To the surprise of both Lewis and Munsey, Licata agreed and came to the detective bureau.

"We know you've known Dean for three years," Lewis said, still somewhat awed by Licata. "Where did you meet him?"

"I met Dean through his brother, Fred Milo," Licata explained in his thick Italian accent. "Well, it goes back further than that. I owned . . . a pizza manufacturing plant. . . . I had my own aircraft. Milo Barber and Beauty Supply would hire my pilot and airplane for occasional trips. Then Fred showed up at an automobile dealership I own—and he would buy his cars there. That is how I met Fred. The first contact I had with Dean was after I sold [my plant] in '77. I ended up buying a plant on Allen Road, that Dean's place is on. He drove down to see me, we became friends, and I put him on my board of directors."

"How long was he on the board of directors?"

"I'd say darn near three years. . . . Dean was an outspoken gentleman, and he had a lot of merit. And that's why I say, it's a great loss to me. . . ."

"How many shares of stock does Dean have in the company, approximately?"

Licata pulled out a small notebook, leafed through it, and replied, "Dean did buy stock in this company . . . 26,100 shares, 2.4 percent."

"Have you had any contact with any members of his family, prior to his death or after his death?

"No, I showed up at the funeral parlor with due respect for the man. Boy, that was a hell of a shock. In fact, I think it was on Tuesday that I got calls from his attorney, George Tsarnas, telling me what happened. I was out in the field. . . . Then, I called George. In fact, I went up and sat with George one day. [I was] just upset about it. Prior to this happening to Dean . . . I met his mother and dad, the old people; and his mother and dad are just beautiful people. In fact, his mother speaks Italian like it's out of this world. [Dean] says, 'Jim, why don't you see Mom and Dad because of this problem [the lawsuits] that they got into?' A year and a half ago, he threw them out, and I was dead against that. I told Dean, as a father, I says, 'You know, Dean, you can always work things out.' He said, 'Why don't you go and talk to them . . . ?' [But] I never did follow through, because I'll tell you, why should I get tied up in a family squabble?"

"Have you heard anything, Mr. Licata, in the circle of people that you deal with as to who may have done this? Have you heard any talk about that?"

"Ohhh . . . you know, a lot of guys came up, and the first guy asks me, 'Was he a playboy? You know, maybe he was horsing around with somebody's wife or something.' 'No!' I would say. 'Hell, no! I don't believe that!' I never believed that Dean drank. I kind of—when you say, 'hear,' now this is just the street talk—that his brother-in-law really had a hard-on for him. Lennie?"

"Lonnie."

"Lonnie. This guy, Lonnie, really had a hard-on for him. You know, after I visited the funeral home, and I went up to [Dean's] wife, and, my God, she just got hold of me and everything. And I'm looking around for the family, and, to my surprise, the mother and father were there, but they weren't sitting with her; they were sitting way in the back. And I heard that Fred snuck in there in the real early hours and made a visit and then got out. And I heard that Dean's wife didn't want the mother and father sitting with her, to sit in the back. And I even went back to give them my condolences back there. And . . . I don't know."

"Have you talked to his wife since the funeral at all?"

"No. No, in fact, I was going to call her down in Florida, because I wanted to send Dean's board of director's fee. Somebody said, 'Send it to some church.' And then I called Tsarnas, and Tsarnas said, 'Well, why don't you just send it to her.' And that's what I did. . . ."

"You'd know if it could have been a hit?"

"This is my feeling: knowing Dean Milo [and] the way he was, upset inside, he never showed on the outside. After all these suits he was having with the family—and he was a strong man—he knew his direction. I feel whoever was with Dean Milo, whomever was with the gentleman—let me get this—there had to be somebody on the other side of the door that Dean knew. And there had to be somebody with that party to do what they did. Because, you know, when you read in the paper, it says, 'He was shot with a .32,' Okay. Then they said they found a pillow with a shot through the pillow. Okay? So what happened? Dean must have turned his back; they must've shot him; then they figured to secure it, they muffled a shot through a pillow. And, damn it, it had to be somebody that he knew, or he wouldn't have opened that door. . . ."

"Did you ever know anyone who hated Dean enough to do this? Did he ever say he was having problems with someone, particularly other than family? We knew he was having family problems."

"Never, never in my life have I heard Dean make any accusations like that—where anybody hated him."

"Were you aware of any threats? Any threatening phone calls? Did he owe any money to anybody?"

"No, not that I know of."

"Gambling debts?"

"No, I don't think Dean gambled. I don't know. . . . Then, this other thing comes to mind: you know—I don't know whether it's my looks or what—people take me for the bad guy, or whatever. Maybe because I'm Italian. Dean . . . called me up one day, and he says, 'Jim, [have] the boys got the shopping centers all tied up in the country?' I said, 'Dean, what the hell do you mean by "boys"?' [He said], 'Oh, you know what I'm talking about. . . .' And I always wondered what the hell was he bringing that up for? Did he run into something . . . that gave him a feeling or what? . . ."

"Let me ask you this . . ."

"What he's talking about is: [Is] there a Mafia, mob gang, or something?"

"Do you know who shot Milo?"

"No. If I'd known who shot Milo, I'd be right up there. I'd be right up there. I'm going to tell you that right now."

"Let me ask you this . . ."

"In fact, I had a call. There's a guy in Cleveland, and I can't think of his name, an investigator, well known; I jotted it down one day. I was going to go on my own expense and have it looked at, and I called this Tsarnas, and they told me that they hired somebody from Texas."

"Right."

"Big name from Texas."

"Would you be willing to take a polygraph based only on the death of Milo?" Lewis asked.

"What is a polygraph?"

"A lie detector test?"

"Oh, yes. . . . You know they talk about these lie detector tests. A lot of attorneys say, 'Well, I'd advise you not to take one because of what questions they ask. . . . What is a lie detector test? You tell the truth, what you know, and that's it. . . . As far as taking a lie detector test, I'd be more than glad to, if it's any help to you people."

"Okay, what we're basically doing . . ."

"Do you want a cigar? Do you smoke?" Licata interrupted.

"No, thanks, I'm not old enough yet," Munsey replied.

"Let me tell you, I got one bad habit."

"One bad habit?"

"That's it: cigars. These come out of Florida, where they're called 'Little Havana.' They get the tobacco in, and they roll the cigar. On this, you don't spit up your guts every morning either."

"That's a healthy cigar?"

"That's a good one."

Later, Licata was taken into a small room. Before the polygraph operator hooked Licata up to the lie detector machine, he asked him to sit down and get comfortable. Then he began to ask him several background questions and told him what questions he would be asked once he was connected to the machine. "This is standard operating procedure, Mr. Licata," the operator explained. "There won't be any surprises. Just answer no to all of the questions. We'll know if you're telling the truth."

With the preliminary questioning completed, the polygraph's sensors were connected to Licata's fingers, chest, and stomach. Because the machines had to warm up for a few minutes, Licata began to squirm in his seat, growing increasingly uncomfortable.

"Do you know for sure who shot Dean Milo?" the operator asked Licata.

"No."

"On August 10th or 11th, did you shoot Dean Milo?"

"No, sir."

"Did you plan with anyone in any way to hurt Dean Milo?"

"No."

"In any way were you involved in the death of Dean Milo?"

"No."

"Have you lied to me today in any way in reference to the true facts of the incident?"

"No, sir."

Lewis and Munsey, in an adjacent room, anxiously observed the operator as he removed the sensors from Licata's body and then examined the results of the test.

After several minutes, the operator pulled off his glasses and proclaimed, staring directly at Licata, "He's telling the truth. He wasn't involved."

Lewis and Munsey looked at each other. After all the hints and rumors they'd received concerning Milo's "underworld connections," it had finally all come to this: just another blind alley. Licata would have to be dropped as a suspect. They'd have to look elsewhere for a break in the case.

Unknown to them, that break was just a few days off.

13 | *"She offered me the contract twice."*

MEANWHILE, in Bath, Bill Dear was conducting his own investigation, beginning with Lonnie and Sophie Curtis. He arrived at their home, but had to knock several times before Lonnie came to the door and partially opened it.

"My name's Bill Dear, and I'm a private investigator working on the investigation of your brother-in-law's murder. I'd like to . . ."

"I really can't talk to you," Curtis said.

"Well, I'm really here working for you. You're part of the Milo Corporation, and I'm trying to solve the case. I'm trying to find out who did it, and I need your help."

"I can't talk," Curtis repeated. "Anyway, we've already given our statements to the police."

"Either help me or don't," Dear insisted. "But I'd be surprised if you didn't. If you weren't involved, you should cooperate."

Just then, Sophie came to the door and opened it wider. "I'd like to talk to you," she said, but her husband barked, "No! We have company!"

"My parents are here," Sophie added, conceding to Lonnie, who told Dear, "There's nothing we can talk to you about.

There's litigation pending, and we've been advised by our attorneys not to talk to anybody."

Dear left Curtis's home and went up the street to Fred Milo's residence. After identifying himself, Dear began to ask a question, but Fred abruptly interrupted him and, like Lonnie, claimed, "I can't help you."

"If you were involved," Dear replied sharply, pointing his finger at Fred who was standing in the doorway, "then I'm going to prove it. If you weren't involved, I can help you prove that, too; and you can help me prove who did it."

Shaking his head, Milo again interrupted, saying, "I can't talk to you. I hope you find out who did it, but I can't talk to you. I've been told not to."

Dear left Milo's home and immediately drove to his hotel, where he telephoned his staff in Dallas and instructed them to come to Akron and begin physical surveillance on Fred Milo, Lonnie and Sophie Curtis and, later on, Barry Boyd.

On Wednesday, September 17th—two days after George Tsarnas and his law firm offered a $25,000 reward for information leading to the arrest and conviction of Milo's killer—Bill Dear arranged for a re-creation of the murder. Returning to the house, accompanied by nearly every investigator involved in the case, Dear began to test his theory, using evidence developed by the Summit County Sheriff's Department as well as by members of his own staff in the intervening days. Starting upstairs and walking through the house, Dear began:

"Okay, Dean drives home alone at 12:30, 1:00 A.M. . . . . He takes off his clothes and throws them all over the floor. . . . He goes to sleep. . . . At about 2 A.M., someone knocks on the door or rings the doorbell. . . . He gets up . . . walks to the bedroom window and looks out. . . . He can't see anybody. . . . So, he puts on his underwear in the dark. By mistake, he puts [his shorts] on backwards. . . . He walks down the hall and down the stairs. . . . He turns on the foyer light. . . . He looks through the window in the door, and he sees either someone he knows or someone posing as a Western Union messenger. . . . He opens the door. And then the person shoots him twice. . . . The guy leaves, and the neighbor, Mrs. Teresa, who's at her window, sees the gunman get into a green car with a black top waiting at the bottom of the cul-de-sac. They then make their getaway. Somewhere along the line, they get rid of the gun."

Downstairs in the foyer, Dear produced a mannequin the size and shape of Dean Milo. He dressed the dummy as Milo had been found, wearing underwear backwards and a gold bracelet. Laying the body face down, Dear even placed cotton balls underneath the mannequin's head and body. In addition, he marked the spots where the bullets had entered and exited.

Dear pulled a .32 automatic from his jacket and fired into the dummy's head from several different angles. Judging by where the casings fell, Dear determined that the gunman had forced Milo to the floor and had been standing over him when he had opened fire. Also, Dear's associates, posted in neighbors' homes, reported that they did not hear any of the shots.

After taking a magnifying glass and examining blown-up photographs of Milo's head, Dear further speculated that the cotton balls had, in fact, been applied to Milo's wounds either by the gunman—who may have had second thoughts—or by another person in the house at the time Milo was killed. Bill Lewis was the only cop to taunt Dear on this theory, saying, "If I hear about that cotton one more time, I'm going to take it and jam it right up somebody's ass."

Dear had also arranged for a metal detector specialist to sweep the area in and around the house, in the hope that the murder weapon would be found—it was not—and he had asked Charles Pongrancz, the sheriff department's photographer, to take aerial pictures of Milo's neighborhood. While that was being done, Dear clocked the time it took to walk to Dean's home from his brother's residence. At a steady pace, Dear did it in three minutes and fifty-four seconds. Through his own independent investigation, Dear, like the police, considered Fred Milo to be his top suspect.

Meanwhile, Munsey and Lewis had been able to solve at least one small mystery. On Thursday, September 22nd, they flew to Richmond, Virginia, to interview Milo's former girl friend, Patricia Douglas. Douglas—a pretty, thirty-nine-year-old woman, with long dark hair—had met Milo in 1969 while she'd been the owner of a beauty salon in Massillon, Ohio. They had been introduced by one of Milo's salespeople and soon began seeing each other.

"Do you know who shot Dean Milo?" Lewis asked.

"Do I know?" Douglas responded, showing no emotion. "No, but I've kind of drawn my own conclusions. . . ."

"Okay, what conclusions have you drawn?"

"I feel like it had to be somebody in his family—from what he said when I was with him."

"When was the last time you saw Dean Milo?"

"I was trying to think of the date. . . . It was the Wednesday before he was murdered . . . at the Beehive Lounge at the Regency Hotel."

"Was he by himself?"

"No, he was with this regional manager. I think his first name was Arthur . . . Arthur Knox."

"How many drinks did Dean have that evening?"

"I hadn't seen him in eleven years. Before, he didn't used to drink more than two drinks. He had quite a lot that evening. Maybe, probably, about eight."

"So you got back to the hotel around 1:00 A.M.?"

"Uh-huh."

"Then what happened?"

"His regional manager went to his room, and Dean took me to my car and we talked for about twenty minutes to a half-hour. He said he would call me . . . when he got back home to Ohio. . . ."

"I realize that you probably only spent a few hours with Dean, but did he discuss with you having any girl friends in the Akron area or anything like that?"

"He said that he had never messed around—that he had been straight. That's what he told me. But, see, we almost got married."

"You and Dean?"

"I dated him about a year, and I was dating the man I'm married to now. Dean said I was more in love with Peter than him. So then he married. . . . I don't even know what his wife's

name is. He got married right before I did. . . . Now Peter
and I are separated."

"Had he been calling you from Ohio?"

"Yeah."

"When did he call you?"

"It wasn't every day—but it was sometimes three times a
day. . . ."

"Where would he be when he called you?"

"At home a lot. He called me late at night. We'd talk until
three."

"Would you consider Dean to be oversexed?" Lewis asked,
changing the subject.

"Uh . . ."

"Some guys like to do it, maybe, once a night, and that's
it. . . ."

"Yeah. No, I would say he's oversexed."

"Dean enjoyed his sexual life?"

"Right."

"Is that from your relationship?"

Douglas did not respond, and it became obvious to the police
that she was growing extremely uncomfortable answering questions about her sexual relationship with Milo—particularly
while being tape-recorded. As a result, they offered to turn off
the recorder and continue their questioning.

With the tape recorder off, Douglas explained that Milo had
been loyal to his wife. She made it clear that she had not had
sexual intercourse with Milo since he'd married. However, she
was under the impression that when sexually aroused, Milo
simply masturbated. Hearing this, the detectives felt they had
an explanation for the semen-stained tissue found on Milo's
bedroom floor.

On September 25th, with the approval of the sheriff's department, Dear held a press conference to announce that the
reward for information leading to the arrest and conviction of
Milo's killers had been raised from $25,000 to $50,000 by Milo's
wife and attorneys.

While Dear was with the press, Munsey and Lewis's big

break finally came. Ed Duvall received a telephone call from a man who refused to identify himself, but claimed to know who killed Dean Milo. Arrangements were made for Duvall to meet the informant at the Greyhound bus terminal across the street from the sheriff's office in downtown Akron. For protection, Duvall wired himself for sound and asked another officer to monitor the conversation from a car outside the bus station.

When Duvall arrived, the source introduced himself as Jack Taylor. He was a freaky-looking guy with long, blond hair pushed back in a ponytail. His blue eyes were sunk deep in his head, and he appeared to be badly strung out.

"Okay, what do you have for us?" the crew-cut Duvall asked impatiently, unimpressed by Taylor's appearance.

"I used to live at a group house on the west side," Taylor explained while wiping his runny nose with his sleeve, "and one of the women who lives there is a go-go dancer named Terry Lea King. . . ."

"Go on," Duvall said.

"Terry had been hired to find someone to kill this guy, Dean Milo. . . ."

"Right."

"Really! She offered the contract to me twice—the first time for $5,000 and the second for $10,000."

"And who hired her? Where was she getting that kind of money?"

"She was hired by an Akron attorney named Barry Boyd."

14 | *"This whole thing had come off."*

JACK TAYLOR was one very weird person, and the police had a hard time taking him seriously, despite his willingness to take a polygraph examination. A cursory background check indicated that he had never been arrested, however, and had never even received a speeding ticket. He had been born and raised in Akron and had worked in the local rubber factories on and off since graduating from high school in 1965. He was now unemployed and making feeble attempts to find work—and insisting that he was not interested in the $50,000 reward. However, he did permit himself to say that he would accept it.

Despite the officers' skepticism, Taylor's information about Terry Lea King and Barry Boyd rang true, and Momchilov met with Taylor again four days after his initial meeting with Duvall at the bus terminal.

"Jack, as you know, we are doing an investigation of the homicide of Dean Milo. Do you understand?" Momchilov asked.

"Yes, sir," replied Taylor nervously.

"And you're here to give us a statement, pertaining to information that you obtained from some [person] that you knew by the name of Terry Lea King. Is this correct?"

"Yes."

"Okay. And this information is in regards to her knowledge of the killing of Dean Milo. Is this correct?"

"That is correct. . . ."

"Prior to your current address, where did you live?"

"Two eighty-eight Gordon Drive, Akron."

"And who was living with you there?"

"Dennis King, Terry King, [their daughter], and [another friend]."

"Okay. Could you describe this house?"

"It's an A-frame house with an attic and three bedrooms and a bath on the second floor. [On the] first floor is a living room, dining room, kitchen, and basement—and a garage."

"Could you tell me who sleeps in what rooms?"

"Terry sleeps in the attic. Denny, [the daughter] and [the friend] sleep in separate bedrooms on the second floor. And, being that I was living there on a temporary basis, I was just sleeping in the living room, primarily on the sofa."

"And are the Kings married?"

"Yes, sir."

"What kind of a relationship is this that she sleeps up in the attic while he sleeps on the second floor?"

"Well, they're married in the legal sense that there's never been a divorce. But, over the years since they were first married, their relationship has changed. They really don't relate to one another as man and wife in the conventional sense."

"Okay so, in other words, each of them goes their separate ways?"

"Yes. . . ."

"Does Terry Lea have any work?"

"No."

"Do you know her previous employment?"

"She was a go-go dancer for five or six years. . . ."

"When did she become a go-go girl?"

"About 1972."

"So she's been a go-go girl since 1972 until when? Or is she still doing that?"

"Well, she's kind of retired in the last year."

"So she hasn't, to the best of your knowledge, been in a go-go girl employment this year?"

"Right."

"Where was her last employment?"

"She used to work so many different [places], several bars and a number of private doings and fraternity parties, that you couldn't really say she was employed at any one particular place. . . ."

"Do you know what private affairs she worked at?"

"Other than that she worked one time for a private party for the Cleveland Browns and several fraternity parties at the University of Akron, I really don't know anything other than that."

"Does she live on Gordon Street at the present time?"

"She stays there a good part of the time."

"And where does she stay besides that?"

"In Medina. . . ."

"Who lives there?"

"Larry Benson."

"Who is Larry Benson?"

"I guess you'd say he's Terry's boyfriend. . . ."

"Does she normally stay there most of the time—out in Medina with him?"

"I would say that it is about seventy percent of the time and the other thirty percent in Akron. . . ."

"Do you know of Terry Lea—some of her friends she socializes with or meets or talks to?"

"She doesn't have that many friends. I would say one of the few that I know about would be Barry Boyd."

"And who is Barry Boyd?"

"Barry Boyd is an Akron attorney and a friend of Terry's."

"How long has Terry known this Barry Boyd?"

"About ten years. . . ."

"Is this an attorney that she uses a lot?"

"They are friends. As far as how much she uses him as a legal counsel, I couldn't say."

"Has she ever gone and met him on any occasion?"

"Yes."

"Have you ever heard her talk about Barry Boyd in your presence?"

"Yes."

"Could you tell me when this was?"

"Lots of times."

"When was the last time she brought up Barry Boyd to you?"

"Oh, several weeks ago. Terry was talking about the wisdom of committing suicide, and we should all think about having a party; and Barry Boyd would even be into that, because he's really too nice for this world. And, you know, I listened."

"What did she mean by that?"

"I would assume—I'm interpreting what she was saying—that people that are too nice for this world would, you know—the assumption would be since the world is made up of so many evil people and since someone like Barry Boyd is an exception to this rule and such a benevolent-type person, maybe the way he copes with this problem . . . would be to commit suicide. That's all I could . . ."

"Has she ever been arrested?"

"I think she was arrested on a drug thing at one time, but the case was dismissed."

"Do you know who her attorney was at that time?"

"No, I don't know all the particulars."

"Is she on drugs now?"

"Yeah."

"What kind of drugs is she on?"

"Primarily cocaine and pharmaceutical."

"And is this an everyday occurrence with her?"

"As far as I can tell . . ."

"Did she ever tell you how much her habit is a year?"

"She talked in terms of $25,000 to $30,000 so far in 1980."

"Do you know where she would get the money for it?"

"Well, there are any number of possible explanations."

"Does her husband say anything to her about the drugs?"

"He doesn't approve."

"How about her boyfriend?"

"He doesn't like it, either."

"Has either one of them said anything to her about the drugs or tried to help her out?"

"Numerous times. . . ."

"Going back in the earlier part of this year, you were living there on Gordon Street in February?"

"Right."

"Okay. In February, did she ever approach you about being a paid 'hit' person?"

"Right."

"How did this all transpire?"

"Well, it was late February, early March, and she came downstairs, and I was sitting there. We were the only two people in the house. And she says, 'How would you like . . . I know you could use some extra money. How would you like to make $5,000 real easy?' And I think I thought, 'This is really my lucky day.' And I said, 'Sure. How am I so fortunate?' And then when she told me what was involved, of course, that changed my attitude about the whole situation."

"What did she say?"

"She said that there was a man that was involved in business with some other people, and he was very greedy and wanted it all for him when there was plenty to go around for everybody— and that he just wouldn't stop being greedy and give everybody their share. And he really was a very kind of low-life-type person, and he really needed to be eliminated. And that it could be very simply done and would really be doing a service to the other people and to the community at large."

"At that time, did she say who it was?"

"No."

"Did she say anything about how it was going to be done at that time?"

"The impression that I got was that someone would just walk up to him at some point, where he would be coming out of work or whatever, and shoot him."

"Did you ever see a gun?"

"Not on that occasion."

"But, on another occasion, you did?"

"Right."

"On this particular occasion, the first one in February or March, did she tell you how much money there was going to be?" Momchilov asked.

"You mean payment to the hit man?"

"Right."

"Five thousand," Taylor replied.

"Did she say how much she was going to get?"

"No."

"Did she say who hired her to do this?"

"No."

"Why did she ask you?"

"Well, I don't know. I think she figured I could use the money, but I suppose that anybody could use $5,000. So I think my only explanation—and it isn't probably a very good one—is that somebody as flamboyant as Terry either tends to have people around her who follow her lifestyle, or people like her husband and this gentleman in Medina who tend to be very judgmental or critical of her. My stance in relating to her was always a moderate round between the two. I would just tend to listen to her and not tend to comment too much and not be judgmental about the kinds of things she would say. So she probably was not exactly sure where I was coming from on a lot of things and wasn't sure what my reaction would be."

"Did she talk to you a lot about her problems?"

"Right."

"On an everyday occurrence?"

"No, not everyday, but over the years, many, many times."

"Has she ever talked to you before about being a hit man and killing somebody?"

"No."

"This is the first time?"

"Right."

"Did she mention any other names at that particular time, about if you didn't want the job somebody else could do it?"

"She said that there were a lot of people who would jump at the chance, but she didn't mention any names."

"Did she say when she wanted this man killed?"

"No. Well, you know, the impression I got was, at that time it would be done . . ."

"Okay, did she say anything else on that first occasion, pertaining to who the person was?"

"No, she just said that it was a very prominent person, and I would be very surprised if she knew who it was."

"Did she talk any more about it then?"

"No."

"When was the next time she ever brought up the conversation to you, pertaining to who the person was to be shot?"

"Well, now, she brought up the offer again. But, even at that point, she never really mentioned any names."

"What did she say when she brought it up, and when was this?"

"About two or three weeks after the initial time. She said that maybe she was now going to give $10,000 rather than $5,000. And she had a manila envelope in her hand that she flipped across the room. She was maybe five feet away, and it landed on the sofa next to me. [She] said this was my tool [a gun]. I inspected the envelope to some degree and, other than that, the conversation was very similar to the first—with me expressing no interest."

"What did she say about the gun?"

"Just that this would be what one would use."

"Do you recall what kind of gun it was?"

"Yeah, but not being familiar with guns, I couldn't say it was like a magnum or something. I mean, I remember . . . it was a black gun. It wasn't the standard-type police revolver that a patrolman carries on duty. And it was much too small to be a magnum or something, but it was just . . . almost shaped in a rectangle. It had a barrel [that] came to the back of the gun. . . ."

"I'm going to show you my service revolver, which is a .38. Did the gun look like anything with a cylinder. . . ? Did the gun have a cylinder to it?"

"No."

"Do you know how the bullets were loaded into the gun?"

"I didn't see any bullets."

"So, I presume, if it's not a gun similar to mine that we are talking about, possibly, an automatic-type of weapon?"

"I think so. Must have . . ."

"Okay, when she gave you this package, was there anything else inside the package beside the gun?"

"There were a couple of pieces or whatever that apparently

went in conjunction with the base part of the gun, because she said she would show me how to assemble it. . . ."

"This manila envelope that she showed you, were there any markings on it?"

"Not that I recall."

"And was it a big type of envelope?"

"Right."

"Did she say where she got that gun from?"

"No."

"So, when she threw you this package, was it sealed or was it already opened?"

"It was already opened. . . ."

"Okay, did you reach in and pull the gun out?"

"Yeah. . . ."

"Now, after you picked the gun up and looked at it, you put it back in the envelope?"

"Right. . . ."

"What was the next conversation, [in] this five minutes? That's what I'm interested in."

"Well, I just, you know, pointed out to her that regardless of how much money was involved, I wasn't interested in shooting somebody. And that, you know, I wasn't disputing the fact that whoever this person was might not be a real scoundrel. I wasn't arguing that point, but I just didn't feel it was appropriate for me to go out and shoot somebody, because they were a scoundrel. And she said, 'Well, there're a lot of people who would love to have this job.' And I said, 'Why don't you get one of them then?' "

"Did you mention any names to her, or did she mention any names to you at that particular time—who would do it besides you?"

"No."

"Did she mention anything about the name of the person at that time?"

"No."

"Going into a little later on, did you have another conversation after that about the same situation?"

"Not shortly after that. It was in August or [the] last part of August of 1980."

"Okay, in August, the last part of August 1980, could you tell me exactly what kind of a conversation, and where you were at this time?"

"We were leaving Gordon Street. I was going to drive Terry down to the carwash in Akron. And she was going to stop by and see her friend Barry Boyd. We were driving down West Exchange Street when the conversation started. I had seen a brief story on Barry Boyd on the news the night before, but there had been some interruptions because of conversations in the house, and I hadn't caught the whole thrust of the story. I said, 'Terry, that's sure strange that Barry made the evening news. He isn't a candidate for office or anything.' I didn't really think of him, personally, as being so prominent an attorney to be in the news for that reason. And, at that point, she informed me—this was the first time we'd talked about it in relation to this conversation—this whole thing had come off, and that he was involved in it."

"Well, excuse me, when you say 'this whole thing had come off,' what? When you had this conversation with her in a car, and you mentioned to her him being on television and everything, what were her comments to you at that time?"

"She was kind of uptight about it."

"And did she ask anything about what the program was about?"

"Right. And I just said I didn't see enough of it to really know for sure."

"And you were driving her to Barry Boyd's office?"

"No, I was driving her to a carwash at Main and Exchange in Akron."

"Whose car were you in?"

"Terry's. . . ."

"Did she ask you to take her car down and get it washed?"

"She said she just didn't feel up to driving, and that she had to run in and see Barry Boyd. This was prior to the conversation. . . ."

"Did she say why she was going down at that time to see Barry Boyd?"

"No, but I wouldn't have asked, because they were friends, and it seemed like being friends, they might be getting together for a chat. . . ."

"All right. Now, going back to this conversation in the latter part of August, was it before the holiday or after the holiday?"

"I'm not totally certain. I would just say it was the day after the story on WAKR [Akron's local television station], and I'm sure the date could be determined by determining when the story was on WAKR."

"What story are you talking about?"

"The story in relation to Barry Boyd on the six o'clock news."

"Was that radio?"

"Television. . . ."

"Fine. Now you are in a car, and you're down on Exchange Street, going to the carwash. She, Terry King, wanted to go to Barry Boyd's office."

"After we went to the carwash. . . ."

"When you said to her about him being on television, did she make a comment to you about it at that time?"

"She was concerned about it."

"What did she say?"

"This occurred just as we were driving into the carwash."

"Okay."

"And, you know, we were getting out the car. We were talking, and we were sitting on these little stools in the carwash, and she just, you know, reiterated that she was very concerned about Barry being on the news. And I was kind of laughing about it. I said, 'So what?' or something. She said, 'Well, do you remember what we talked about last spring?' And I said, 'Yes.' She said, 'Well, that all came off, and the guy's name was Dean Milo. Barry and I were involved. So can you see now why I'd be nervous?' And I said, 'Yeah, that makes sense.' "

"When she said that she and Barry were involved, what did she mean?"

"Well, in subsequent conversations, she made it clear that Barry had acted as a liaison between the Milo family and her;

and her part of the arrangement was to line up somebody to shoot Dean Milo. So that kind of makes it clear how they would be involved."

"She told you this?"

"Yes. . . ."

"Let me ask you this, did she ever mention to you while you were at the carwash who the person was who did the killing?"

"Not at the carwash, no."

"Was there any other conversation, while you were at the carwash, about Dean Milo's homicide?"

"No, it continued as we drove down the street, because we were only at the carwash about five or ten minutes."

"What transpired then?"

"Well, we were going up South Main Street through downtown to Barry's office, as she had planned even before this conversation started. She was concerned about this, and would feel better after she talked to him, but it was very serious. She said, 'Jack, don't you realize I could go to prison? And then she said, 'I think we're all right in this one respect: the person who did it.' She gave me the name, but I couldn't recall it later. [The alleged killer] was out of the area and left town immediately after the shooting. But she said that Barry was certainly involved, because she called him after the shooting and told him that it had been done, and now it bothered her that there were these questions on the news. . . ."

"When did she say she called Barry Boyd about the homicide of Dean Milo . . . ?"

"She said she called him around two, two-thirty, sometime in the wee hours of the morning, and [he] said he'd been taken care of. She never did actually say that it was right after the event, but I assumed that."

"But she did mention to you [who] the killer was?"

"Right."

"Did she say she hired this man to do it?"

"Right."

"Did she say how much money she gave this man to do the killing?"

"No. I had been offered $10,000, but whether that price stayed intact over that period of time, I don't know."

"Did she mention how much money she got for setting this up?"

"No."

"But she did state that she and Barry Boyd were involved, and that Barry Boyd was the mediator between the Milo family and also her?"

"Right. But when she used the phrase, 'Milo family,' she didn't say all of them, some of them. She didn't necessarily imply that every member of the family was involved—just that some portion of the family was involved."

"Okay, have you ever been there when she has called Barry Boyd?"

"Yeah."

"Pertaining to talking to him about this particular homicide?"

"No."

"All right. What happened after you got to Barry Boyd's office?"

"I dropped her off and circled the block a number of times, for thirty minutes or so, until she was standing back out in front of the building. I picked her up, and we headed back to west Akron. She said, 'Well, everything is cool, and nobody's going to make them talk. . . .'"

"When she got back in the car, what was her reaction at that time?"

"She seemed kind of relieved."

"And did she say she discussed everything with Barry Boyd about the homicide?"

"She didn't say she discussed everything with him. She just said that there was nothing to worry about."

"Did she mention anything else about the homicide or about the man who did the killing?"

"No."

"Did she say where he was at?"

"It seems to me that, at one point, she said he was down in Arizona or California, but I'm not always certain about that. Those things happened so fast. You just . . ."

"In other words, did she say he was out of town?"

"Yes, right."

"He wasn't around here? Did she say the man lived in the Akron area?"

"She didn't say; she didn't say one way or the other."

"She never said how she got ahold of this guy?"

"Well, what you've got to remember is that I really didn't want to have all this information. I didn't want to be aware of these things, so I didn't ask any questions. I mean, had I asked questions, I probably would've gotten the answers, but I didn't ask anything. I only heard what was told me. . . ."

"Was there any conversation about her having some of these items written down on paper, stating who was involved, or how it was suppose to go down, or what was suppose to happen next?"

"Right."

"What was that?"

"She said, 'I got to get it together and clean up the attic, because,' she says, 'I've got all these documents or plans or whatever in relation to this.' But she really didn't make it clear just what she meant by the term 'plans' or 'papers' or 'documents,' and that's a very vague term in itself. . . . 'Just get it together one day, and throw those out in the Tuesday morning trash pick-up.' "

"Is that when the trash company comes out there?"

"I think the city does. . . ."

"Did she ever mention to you about this job, as far as the homicide or the shooting, where it should happen? In other words, he was shot in his house. Did she ever mention to you about where it should have happened, or was this the place that it was all planned—that it take place in the house?"

"She kind of implied something. She said something about he had been shot in the house or around the house, and something to the effect that, 'It really shouldn't have been done that way, but I guess it's all right; it worked. . . .' "

"Now, on that particular day when you came back, you left, and she went about her business. Since that time, have you had any more conversations with her about Dean Milo's death?"

"Yeah, there was one. I remember now in regard to this one other conversation. . . . We were driving to Medina . . . and

Terry was saying, she was [wondering] if she could get the Milo family to agree to set up some secret trust fund for her daughter of $50,000 or $100,000, some figure like that, that her daughter could use for her future. She would be willing, perfectly willing, to come forth and say that she had killed Dean Milo herself because of a lovers' quarrel or some type of a romantic triangle, something of that nature. That would let everybody else off the hook, and it would give her daughter a certain financial security. And then, of course, before there could be any kind of a trial or anything, she would just commit suicide. And this would—well, it would in her eyes—settle the problem all the way around. It would leave them off the hook, and she wasn't too keen on living anyhow, and it certainly would provide her daughter with some money. She was, somehow, going to leave her daughter a note that would give a different twist to it altogether, so her daughter wouldn't feel that she had, in fact, killed this person. But she never made it clear how she would do that. About the only other conversation we had about this was out in Medina later that day. She said she just hoped Larry never found out about this, because [he] knew nothing about it. He would be very angry about it. . . ."

"Was there any other conversation?"

"No."

"About the Milo family and the homicide?"

"No. . . ."

At the conclusion of his interview, Taylor was asked if he was still willing to take a polygraph test, to verify his story. Taylor replied that he would. Within an hour, Taylor took the test—and passed.

15 | "You people already killed one person."

ON SEPTEMBER 26TH, the Milo case took another bizarre twist. Barry Boyd was arrested by the Akron Police Department—but not because of Jack Taylor's information. He was arrested for attempting to tamper with court records, stemming from a traffic ticket he had received for driving while intoxicated. According to the charges, Boyd, while working on another case, had pulled material relating to his own trial out of the city clerk of court's files, hoping to stop prosecution. After being released on bond, Boyd called Bill Lewis to inform him that he would have to postpone further questioning on the Milo case—until his own trial was resolved. He had no idea yet that he was now a prime suspect in the case.

Because of the press attention that Boyd, as an attorney, received from his arrest, Dear and Momchilov thought the time was right for their prized informant, Jack Taylor, to have a talk with Terry Lea King. At Dear's insistence, the telephone call was tape recorded.

"Hi, Terry," Taylor said, opening the phone conversation.

"Yeah!" she replied.

"I told you I'd give you a call today. Are you out of your spot, or are you still kind of stuck?"

"I'm still stuck."

"Well, I got, you know, a couple of those late checks . . . and you helped me sometimes . . ."

"Paychecks?"

"Yeah. How much do you need?" he asked.

"I'm trying to think."

"I owe you twenty bucks anyhow, so I'll pay you regardless."

"All right."

"You sound as frazzled as I am."

"We're short about $200."

"And I'd have it back, when? Two or three days or something? Week at the most?"

"Yeah."

"As long as it's in a week's time, you know."

"Oh, yeah. That's no problem."

"Are you you going to be in Akron later on?"

"I don't know. I'm supposed to pick up Larry [Benson] at the airport at seven."

"How can we get together tomorrow?"

"Barry Boyd just left."

"Barry left?"

At the mention of Boyd's name, Taylor tried to move in on King. "Barry better . . . you know, I worry about Barry," Taylor said. "I mean, I don't . . ."

"Barry worries about Barry," King replied.

"Because, you know, like I was telling you, there's all those stories about the Milo thing in the paper all the time and, you know . . ."

"Oh, yeah. He's cool."

"Well, just, you know, in a case like that, maybe he should go on the wagon or something . . ."

"Oh, he has . . . he did . . . when he had that DWI."

"Yeah. I heard something on the radio or something—some kind of case where he tried to fix a ticket or something. I don't know . . . you know how the stories are on radio."

"Right. Try to plant the stuff . . ."

"I guess . . . he was some kind of suspect in that, so, probably, everything he does, they take a report or something. And he's an attorney. You know how they get into it. . . ."

King immediately changed the subject away from Boyd and the Milo murder. Despite this and later attempts, Taylor was unable to ever get King to speak about the Milo murder.

On October 1st, Lewis and Munsey were driving north on South Main Street in downtown Akron, when they saw Fred Milo standing on a corner. He appeared to be waiting for someone. The two officers parked their unmarked car a half block away and watched. Soon, Boyd crossed the street and approached Milo. They shook hands and exchanged a few words before disappearing into the building on the corner.

Bill Dear had shifted into high gear with his investigation. Posing as a man interested in hiring King to dance for him and some of his friends, he approached Melissa Mackey, one of King's dancing friends. They met at a waterside restaurant near Akron's Portage Lakes on October 3rd. Dear was wired and being monitored by a member of his staff.

"Is Terry a nicely built girl?" Dear asked, hiding behind a pair of dark glasses and looking as sleazy as possible.

"Yes," Mackey replied. "Like me. But there's no way I'm dancing again."

"Why?"

"I've had enough, and so has Terry."

"You didn't appreciate all those guys googling at you? Just . . ."

"First six months, it was fun, because there was a lot of attention. But three and a half years later, it was just, more or less, you get up there and smile . . . and 'You stupid son of a bitch.' You get up there, and you make your money."

"Yeah, 'I know what you're looking at,'" Dear added.

"You know, I just got up there and made my money and got mostly what I want. And, now, I just want to forget it. I'll lead a normal life and be a good little girl."

"Oh, no slipping around on the old man, huh?"

"No, no way."

"Did you and Terry have an agent?"

"We'd go into a bar, and I'd want to see the owner. He'd

make you go on stage and check you out while you dance. If
he likes you, he'll book you; they'll put you on a schedule."

"What do they pay an hour for that?"

"Anywhere between $8 to $20 an hour."

"So, it's better to work a private party then?"

"Oh, yeah, yeah."

"You mean, like bachelor parties?"

"Yeah. You can get anywhere between $75 to $100 and up—
like, if you're going to do an hour and a half, $150."

"That beats $8 an hour, doesn't it?"

"Sure does. Terry was one of the highest-paid dancers; there
were six of us who were the top-paid dancers in Akron."

"So Terry won't dance anymore?"

"No, she won't."

"Why not?"

"Oh, she's in love with some guy out in Medina, Larry something; and she has problems of her own. Drugs and stuff, you
know. . . . I really shouldn't talk about that."

"I don't care to know about it. . . . I was just referred by Barry
Boyd."

"Barry? Do you know Barry?"

"Sure, I know Barry," Dear replied.

"He's a good friend of Terry's, and that's one of her
problems."

"What do you mean?"

"Oh, she's just all tied up in knots about some deal she had
with him. She wouldn't tell me anything more than that."

On October 16th, the detectives sent Taylor into King's
Medina house, hoping that Taylor could lure her into the car—
which was wired for sound—and begin a discussion about the
murder. Meantime, Dear was in the trunk of Taylor's car—an
old, beat-up Chevy, with exhaust fumes pouring out and into
the trunk where Dear lay curled up. Outside, the temperature
was well over 80 degrees; inside the trunk, it had to be nearly
120. Dear had brought only a small flashlight in order to see the
buttons on his taping device. He had no walkie-talkie and could
not communicate with Momchilov—who was parked down the

street and monitoring whatever conversation took place with his own equipment.

Taylor was inside the house with King, trying to persuade her to go out to eat with him, for nearly an hour. Because she was busy and couldn't go, Taylor left, returned to the car, and drove a few blocks, before he was quickly pulled over by Momchilov, who grabbed his keys out of the ignition and rushed to open the trunk.

Dear didn't move. His clothes were completely saturated with perspiration and grime from the hot and dirty fumes. His face was chalky-white. Momchilov shook him. "Bill! Bill! Get up, damn it!" Dear then winced and opened his eyes. He was weak and had a horrible headache, but he was alive. Momchilov concluded that Dear was incredibly brave and dedicated—or awfully crazy.

Because physical surveillance by Dear's staff on Fred, Lonnie, and Sophie had failed to yield anything, Dear instructed them to concentrate their activities on Barry Boyd and Terry Lea King. Although King's actual role was still unknown, both Dear and the police were convinced that Boyd was involved and probably the weak link in the murder conspiracy.

Telling his Chicano associate, Joe Villanueva, a member of "The Mod Squad," to follow Boyd, Dear also advised him to let Boyd know he was being followed, hoping that Boyd would be so unnerved that he would make a mistake. At one point, after several days of obvious but apparently unnoticed surveillance, Villanueva—a Freddy Prinze look-alike who usually wore sunglasses—walked up to Boyd, gave him his card, and *told* him that he was following him. As a result, Boyd buried himself in his home and stopped going to work.

At King's homes in Akron and Medina, those who visited her were photographed and their license plates listed. Dear hired a pilot to take aerial photographs of her neighborhoods. His collection of data began to border on overkill.

In short, Dear had become obsessed with the Milo case. Although a couple of inches taller and about ten pounds lighter than the dead man, Dear had begun to take the entire investigation personally, seeming to become a kind of self-appointed crusader to avenge Dean Milo's death. More and more, as the investigation rolled on, others began to compare Bill Dear to Dean Milo.

One of Dear's associates told Momchilov, "Have you noticed Bill lately? I mean these past couple of days? I've never seen him like this. He gets so mad about this case, he shakes. This has never happened before. He talks about the case all the goddamn time—and he has other work to do, too."

"It's ironic," Momchilov replied. "Both Milo and Dear are obsessives."

"Yeah, look at these two guys, Dear and Dean. They both have these dynamic personalities and the strong wills of their mothers. They're both wildly successful, and they kick ass in their own worlds. I mean, Larry, both Bill and Dean could put their arms around somebody who is standing still and make him move at the same time. . . ."

"And nobody's neutral about them."

"Oh, yeah, these are the kind of guys you either love or hate. They both have that weird aura around them. . . ."

Dear's obsession was so intense he insisted that the coroner's failure to perform a rectal smear and mouth swab on Milo during the autopsy was justification enough to exhume Milo's body from his Florida grave and conduct an independent autopsy with his own pathologist. Because no one else thought it was necessary, this was never done.

The following day, Dear and Lewis were sitting in their car continuing their surveillance on King, who was now at her Gordon Street address in Akron. Seeing the city garbage collector making his rounds, Dear got out of the car, walked up to him, and offered him $20 to pick up her trash—wrapped in a green plastic bag and lying on her front porch—and give it to them. The trash man, an elderly gentleman, marched right up on the porch of the Kings' three-story wood-frame house and grabbed the bag of garbage. Seeing this from inside the house, King and her husband walked out onto the porch and called the man, who then began running down the street toward Dear and Lewis's car. In plain view of the Kings, Dear, with no options, grabbed the trash bag, and they sped away. Later, while going through its contents, the police found drug paraphernalia and several telephone numbers, including three for Barry Boyd.

Because the King probe had also turned into a narcotics investigation, the sheriff's narcotics division had been invited into the case. One undercover agent, Mark Martin, was a personal friend of both Momchilov and Lewis's—and Dear had a proposal for him. Dear wanted Martin to telephone King, claim to have information that could implicate her in the Milo murder, and then try to blackmail her. Of course, the call would be recorded.

When Martin agreed to participate in the charade, the sheriff's legal advisor, Michael Wolff, warned of possible charges of entrapment. "We could have a bad time with this," Wolff said. But after consultation with other attorneys in the prosecutor's office, Wolff concluded that Dear's proposal was legitimate and based upon probable cause.

On October 20th, Martin called King at her home in Medina.

"Terry?" Martin asked.

"Yeah."

"Hi."

"Hi."

"How are you doing?"

"Who is this?"

"Well, that isn't really important who this is, just that I get to talk to you."

"Sure, it's important who it is. If you don't identify yourself, I'm going to cease the conversation."

"You are?"

"Yes, sir," she insisted.

"That would be very bad for you, because it concerns Dean Milo."

After a long pause, Martin continued, "So, I don't think you should hang up on me, do you?"

"Who is Dean Milo?"

"Dean Milo is the guy that was killed."

"Oh, that's right. A couple of months ago."

"Yeah. You remember Dean Milo, don't you? You and Barry did a little number on him?"

"No, I don't know what you're talking about."

"Oh, you don't?"

"No, I do not!"

"Oh, you wouldn't want to sit down, and talk to me about it, maybe?"

"I . . . Are you with the law enforcement agency or something?"

"Not hardly. I'm not with anybody. I'm with myself."

"Well, then, why would you want to talk about this?" she asked.

"Well, because I'm kind of hurting for money."

"I don't understand."

"You don't?"

"You know, I would love to talk with you about it—down at the Federal Building."

"The Federal Building?"

"Sure."

"Why the Federal Building?" Martin asked.

"Well, first of all, I have nothing to hide. Secondly, I would be most interested in what you have to say," King replied.

"You say you wouldn't be interested?"

"I would be."

"Oh, you would."

"Yeah. I don't understand what it is you're talking about."

"Well, what I'm talking about is the fact that you and your little buddy, Barry Boyd—how you arranged to have Dean Milo killed."

"This is absurd."

"Yeah, well for a small fee, I'll keep my mouth shut, and I won't tell that Texas dude—that wants to know all about it that's here in the Akron area. Now, that's strictly up to you, because I really don't care. Now, they are offering a lot more than what I want, but it means I have to work with the police. And I've been in trouble before, and I really don't want to work with them. So, it's strictly to your advantage. If you want to talk to me, I'll talk to you. If you don't, I really don't care. I'll just go talk to the police."

"Oh, my gosh! I just woke up!"

"Yeah."

"And . . ."

"Wait a minute, listen to me. You had better get your act together real fast, because I don't have a whole lot of time to screw around. Now, if you want to talk to me, you know where that Western Omelet is on Route 18 by I–71?"

"Western Omelet . . ."

"You know, just down from your house about four miles."

"Yeah."

"You know where it's at. Well, I'll tell you what, if you want to talk to me, you come all by yourself, and I mean I don't want anybody with you, okay? Because you people already killed one person, and I'm not going to take any chances. You come by yourself, and meet me at that Western Omelet at two."

"What time is it now? I just woke up."

"It's twelve-thirty. You throw some water on your face, honey. And you get your butt down there if you want to talk to me. Because, if you're not there at two, I'm going to go talk to that Texan. I'm trying to give you and Barry a chance."

"To a Texan. Why would you do that?"

"Because I don't want to have to help the police. I need some money bad. I got to get out of town, so it's up to you."

"This is crazy!"

"Yeah, well, you killed a person. That's crazy, too."

"No, I most certainly did not," she responded.

"So, if you want to meet me at two, I'm going to be at that Western Omelet right on 18 by 71."

"Yeah, that's close to the intersection, right down here."

"Yeah. And I'm going to be wearing a yellow-knit stocking cap and green Army jacket. And I don't want to see anybody other than you."

"Are you . . . you sound like an adult."

"I am an adult, honey; kids don't extort money."

"No, I, you know, you said Army jacket. . . . I was thinking someone young, but you sound like an adult to me."

"So, I'll expect to see you there at two, and I want you to . . ."

"I'll have to go put in my contact lenses. This is . . ."

"I don't care what you do or how you get yourself dressed up. If you're going to be there, you be there at 2:00. Don't be there at 2:05, because I'm not going to wait. This is the one chance you've got. That's it."

"Okay, fine."

"Okay, bye."

"Bye, bye."

Martin was then wired for sound by the detectives. He drove to the restaurant and arrived at about 1:45 P.M. With Dear again in the trunk of the car, preparing to monitor the conversation, Martin—dressed in a yellow stocking cap and green Army jacket—went in and sat down at a table; but 2:00 P.M. came and went—with no sign of Terry Lea King. By 2:25, it was obvious that he had been stood up. She had probably never had any intention of showing.

However, just to make sure that there wasn't another reason why she hadn't appeared, Martin—again on tape—telephoned King the following day.

"Hello?" she said, answering the phone.

"Terry?"

"Yes."

"It's me again."

"Are you the man that called yesterday?"

"Yep."

"Well . . ."

"I thought maybe I was a little bit too hard with you or something like that, and give you a little time to think about it."

"If I had time to think about it, I'd still feel the same way I did yesterday when we hung up. . . ."

"Well, you know, I'm not asking for a whole lot to keep my mouth shut about what you and Barry Boyd did. I can't . . ."

"I have done nothing. Barry has been a friend of mine for at least ten years."

"Well, I know how long Barry has been your friend."

"Barry is a very wonderful person. You're not . . . I don't know what we're supposed to have done."

"Well, you know, I know that you and Barry helped make

the arrangements to have Dean Milo killed. Okay? And the thing . . ."

"This is upsetting. You know, I don't know much about this man."

"Well, the thing is . . . is that, like I said, I don't want to have to go help the police. Okay? I can't really, because I've got my own problems. All I want is $5,000, and I'll keep my mouth shut. That's going to get me out of the Akron area, and that's really my main concern. I wouldn't really be doing this to you, but you are involved, and you are my only way out of town. That's it. I've got to have some money or some dope or something that I can use to get my way out of town."

"This is utterly crazy! Now, I don't know why you're talking to me like this!"

"The reason I am is because you are involved! That's why!"

"But I'm not involved! I don't know this man that you are talking about! I don't even know that much about Barry—other than he's been a friend, and that he's a nice person! The type of things that you are doing . . ."

"I'm not doing . . . listen, I don't like doing what I'm doing, but you guys were involved in the killing of a guy, okay?"

"That is an absolute lie! I will go to the police department with you, and you can tell them whatever you want! And I can tell them what I know to be true!"

"I don't want to argue with you, okay? Because I've got my own problems. I've got to get out of town."

"I'm not arguing about this! There is nothing to argue about!" she shouted.

"You know . . . I get . . ."

"There is nothing to talk about! I was very serious yesterday! Now, I do not need you calling me on the phone! If you're talking about a prank or something . . ."

"This is no prank, you know? You and Barry were involved in it, and I know that, okay? And, like I say, I don't want to have to go to the police."

King stood tough and then threw a scare into the police by naming their key informant. "You tell, you know, Mr. Taylor— who also talks about this—if he thinks this is a joke, it has gone too far!"

"I don't know who you're talking about," Martin replied quickly, "but all I know is what I know. Hey, all I'm asking for is $5,000! That's it! That's all I want!"

"I have to go now. I have no more to say to you. I'm very sorry."

"Okay, if that's the way it's going to be."

If King was lying, then her performance was again outstanding. Not only had she refused to concede any role in the murder, she had also accused Jack Taylor, the prosecution's top witness, of spreading fictitious stories. The investigators were facing a dilemma: should they continue to believe Taylor's story or not? If they did, they would have to base their belief on his polygraph results alone, and on the one piece of information that rang true: the involvement of Fred Milo's attorney, Barry Boyd.

16 | "Life must go on in spite of the grievous loss of a son and brother."

ON MONDAY, October 20th, Dean Milo's will was read in the county's probate court. As expected, his wife, Maggie, was named as the executrix, responsible for dividing his multimillion-dollar estate, half of which went to her and the other half to their three children. Milo had written his will on December 27, 1975, but there was a codicil as well, filed on January 23, 1980. It excluded his brother, Fred, from becoming the executor if Maggie was unable to handle the job, instead naming his banker and George Tsarnas. The amended will also removed Fred as the guardian of Milo's children and trustee of their trust fund.

When asked by reporters to comment on the sheriff's handling of the murder probe, Maggie Milo remained silent except to express support for the ongoing investigation.

That same day, in Momchilov's office, a loud argument was going on among Dear and the sheriff's deputies over whether or not to arrest Terry Lea King.

"Jesus Christ!" Dear shouted. "We've got probable cause on this bitch! We've got plenty to arrest her!"

"It's not there, man!" Lewis retorted. "We can't get a god-damn conviction with what we have!"

"If we bust her—I'm telling you—all the other actors will get

137

flushed out!" Dear insisted. "I'm telling you, I know what I'm saying!"

"Listen, Dear," Munsey interrupted, "it's our tails, not yours, if you're wrong. You've got nothing to lose in this."

"Lose? I've got my damn reputation! I've got this case!"

"Listen, all of you settle down!" Momchilov said, trying to be the peacemaker. "Just take it easy. . . . I think we ought to pop her."

"Larry, I think we'd be making a big mistake," Lewis protested. "And the prosecutor's office agrees."

"Not if we handle this right," Momchilov explained. "Now, I'm going to get both an arrest warrant and a search warrant for Terry's places in Akron and Medina. We'll arrest her, search both places, bring her down here and try to get her to flip against Barry. . . . Here we are, right here. We have Taylor's statement, saying he was offered the contract. That's probable cause. And Chief Duvall backs me on that."

"So that's it?" Lewis asked. "Okay, then I'm with you."

"That's it," Dear said. "Tomorrow, we nail her."

With this unity among the investigators, they worked to convince cautious prosecutors concerning the merits of the case against King. While the evidence against her was weak, the officers were certain she'd confess.

The following day, just after noon, nearly the entire Summit County Sheriff's detective bureau, and officers from the Medina County sheriff's office and the Bath Township Police, as well as Bill Dear, drove to Terry Lea King's residence in Medina. Without drawing their guns, Momchilov and Lewis walked up to the front door and knocked. There was no answer. They continued knocking for several minutes until King's boyfriend, Larry Benson, answered, wearing only a pair of jeans.

After identifying themselves and asking a woman deputy to accompany them, the officers walked into the bedroom. King was standing in the middle of the room, completely naked. Momchilov immediately asked the woman deputy to take King into the bathroom, and get her dressed. When she returned, the tall, willowy King, dressed in blue jeans and a purple blouse, was placed under arrest. King didn't even react as Lewis read her rights. Her head simply nodded downward, forcing her long brown hair to fall and cover her pretty face and half-closed eyes. She did little to conceal the track marks on both arms.

While the police served Benson with a search warrant, King, without any resistance, was placed in Momchilov's squad car and taken to her Gordon Street address. Momchilov told her they had a search warrant for that address as well, but to his surprise, she consented to sign a "permission to search" form, allowing them to conduct their search without producing the actual warrant.

Specifically, the police were looking for a .32 automatic pistol and any notes or papers making reference to either Dean Milo or the murder of Dean Milo. The search lasted for two hours. It yielded little more than a few scraps of paper, peripheral to the actual murder but indicating a friendship between King and Boyd. In addition, Lewis found no fewer than thirty bags of garbage stacked up in the basement.

No weapon was found. King and her husband, Dennis—who had been home during the search—were given an inventory form detailing the materials taken; then she was taken to the county jail and charged with complicity to commit aggravated murder.

While Momchilov and Dear escorted King downtown, Lewis and Munsey conducted an interview with her husband. After establishing that she stayed at the Gordon Street address about one night a week and spent the rest of her time in Medina with Benson—whom she said she planned to marry one day—Lewis got right to the heart of the matter.

"Did Terry ever discuss with you anything relating to the possibility of being involved in a homicide, possibly killing another person, possibly being hired to kill another person?"

"She has never indicated it to me that she would be involved," Dennis King replied. "She had, at one time during the summer, mentioned—and it is probably even related to this, I don't know —but she came in from the bar [where] she hangs out, the Night People, and she said, 'Boy, did I hear something tonight. Anybody want to make a quick $10,000? Somebody needs to be killed.' [I] just dismissed it."

"What did you think about this?"

"Just a bunch of shit, you know. She comes in with these stories all the time."

"Where is the Night People located?"

"Corner of Rhodes and Market."

"When Terry made the statement, do you recall what month that would've been in?"

"I believe it was in August. . . ."

"What specifically did she say, or what did she allude to?"

"Insofar as I can remember, it was just bar gossip—well, that's the way I treated it. She didn't indicate to me that she really knew how to get $10,000 for killing somebody. She just kind of mentioned it in passing: 'Boy, did I hear something at the bar.' "

"Did she say who she heard it from?"

"No. . . ."

"Do you know how Terry met Barry Boyd?"

"Well, I can tell you we all met Barry Boyd about the same time. It was 1972, somewhere around there. Some very close friends of ours . . . had a run-in [with the law]. I think it was drugs; I can't remember for sure. Barry Boyd was full of fire, one democratic lawyer, you know? He was [their] defender. It was kind of a charity-type thing. And we got to know him after that. And as the years came on, Terry got close to Barry. . . . They saw a lot of each other. I never really got into their . . . let's put it this way, Barry never got into me. . . ."

"How close would you describe their relationship?"

"Platonic friends, mostly conversation."

"Did Terry ever mention the killing of Dean Milo?"

"Not specifically, no."

"In your estimation, did somebody approach her and ask her if she knew of anybody who wanted $10,000?"

"From what I got from her . . . she was sitting at the bar. She overheard somebody talking. But then again I couldn't say that for sure. All I know is that she felt somebody could net $10,000 for doing something. I remember, back in 1973, she brought this guy around the house, and he said he could have anybody killed for $100. . . ."

"Do you know who killed Dean Milo?"

"No, I have no idea. . . . I'll tell you what else I believe—for the record: Terry had nothing to do with it."

While running Terry Lea King through the booking process, Momchilov noticed her right hand, which was swollen from a lack of blood circulation. It was also obvious that she had hepatitis, as a result of years of shooting up perocodine. Although she insisted that she wasn't an addict, she admitted to having taken quaaludes every night for the past three years and nearly every other kind of drug at one time or another.

Still, there was something indescribably alluring about the thirty-one-year-old former go-go dancer. Knowing she was in big trouble, she remained scared; but she was calm and police officers described her as "polite and cooperative" on her rap sheet.

She smoked Marlboros, but said she didn't drink, except for an occasional beer. She owned a nickel-plated .38 Colt revolver and a .22 caliber long rifle. She had been arrested once, in October 1972, for possession of marijuana, but the case had been dismissed. She had been unemployed for the past three months.

Because the police disputed her claim that she was not a drug addict, and because she was viewed by the court as being undependable, her bond was set at $500,000 cash.

Meantime, Akron attorney Larry Vuillemin, George Tsarnas's law partner, had asked a judge, on behalf of Maggie Milo, to prevent Fred and Sophie from conducting a meeting scheduled for the end of the week with the Milo Corporation's stockholders. Vuillemin also charged that the meeting was Fred and Sophie's latest attempt to take over the company—which, since Milo's murder, had been operated by Dean's hand-picked professional team, with Tsarnas serving as the overall fiduciary manager.

In court, Fred and Sophie's attorney, Dick Guster, responded, "My clients, including their parents, have an interest in knowing who caused this act to be committed on their son . . . and I resent and protest any suggestion on the part of Mr. Vuillemin and his client that there is any callous[ness] or disinterest on the part of my clients . . . in ascertaining and learning the identit[ies] of the persons responsible for the crime.

"Having said that . . . it is equally clear that the interests of this family business and the persons who have a right and ownership in that business must be attended to. If you will, life must go on in spite of the grievous loss of a son and brother. . . ."

Called to testify by the court, Momchilov said that Fred Milo was a suspect in the murder of his brother and was currently under investigation. Consequently, the court agreed with Vuillemin and blocked Fred and Sophie's attempted takeover of the corporation—temporarily.

With King behind bars, police pressure concentrated totally on Barry Boyd—who seemed to have fallen off the face of the earth. No one could find him. Dear's "Mod Squad" associate, Joe Villanueva, placed a cigarette in the crack of Boyd's front door—after nearly a week, the cigarette hadn't dropped. Either Boyd was still buried inside his home or had slipped out and not returned. In frustration, Dear drove to Cleveland and interviewed Boyd's girl friend. She hadn't seen or heard from Boyd in several days and was worried, adding that he had been "really upset" during the past few weeks and had started drinking heavily.

Meantime, back in Akron, Bill Lewis had dismaying news. He had discovered that the prosecution's key witness against Terry Lea King, Jack Taylor, had been in Fallsview Mental Hospital and the psychiatric ward of Akron General Hospital no fewer than seven times since 1963, including two separate year-long stays. Furthermore, according to Lewis, Taylor had been found to be "suicidal, has girl friend problems, [is] very emotional and schizophrenic, and always talked a lot of being President of the U.S. one day."

Lewis's information nearly gave Momchilov and Dear heart failure. Taylor would be ripped apart in court when King's defense attorney learned of his mental history. There was only one thing to do: find Barry Boyd.

Lewis could have gloated but didn't. Instead, he and Munsey joined the massive search for Boyd.

Finally, on October 26th, Boyd surfaced, insisting that he had been in his home for the past week and just not answering the door or the telephone. He was immediately taken to the sheriff's office, where he was interviewed again by Lewis and Munsey—and peppered with questions about Fred Milo and Terry Lea King.

"At this point," Lewis began, "I would like, for the purposes of the record, to remind you of the Miranda Warning. You understand that you have the right to remain silent? Would you answer audibly for the tape, please?"

"I understand the Miranda Warning. . . ." Boyd replied.

"Okay, what is your current relationship with Mr. Milo? Fred Milo?"

"It's a business relationship. . . . It's social, in that he listens to my advice, and we talk—but it's mostly about business. . . ."

"Are you on retainer now? Is he paying you for your services?"

"Yes, we do have cases pending . . . but nothing related to the larger lawsuits [against Dean Milo]. . . ."

"When was the last time that you talked to Fred Milo?"

"A few days ago; we talk often."

"Was that on the phone or in person?"

"He comes down. He doesn't come down that often. We meet in Guster's office, and he sometimes comes over. . . ."

"Have you had any conversations at all with either Fred Milo or Lonnie Curtis, since the death of Dean Milo, concerning his death and their feelings on it?"

"I don't press them on that; we've talked about it."

"What do they feel?"

"About who did it? They have no idea. They're just, just very upset. You know? They're upset that the finger is even pointed at them by anyone."

"Are you representing Fred and Lonnie, together, on a lawsuit?"

"We have one lawsuit. They purchased a beauty supply house—and Sophie's more in on this. Dean, Fred, and Sophie personally signed a guaranteed letter of credit, and Dean hadn't been paying, so we sued. It's a minor thing. . . ."

"You mentioned that Fred and Lonnie had different theories on how to handle the problem of Dean . . ."

"Well, yeah. Lonnie and Sophie are much, much more hard-nosed than Fred. Fred wants to get it over with. Fred is more practical—as you and I would be. You know, you file a good suit, and no one wins if you go to court. Fred realizes that. He's got a great deal of insight and is willing to compromise. And he wanted to get this thing over, because he saw what it was doing to him and to his parents and to Lonnie and Sophie."

"Do you know Terry Lea King?"

"Terry Lea King and I are friends."

"How close are you to you to her?"

"Terry Lea King and I are friends."

"What did you think about her arrest this week?"

"She's my friend. . . . I can't believe that she'd be involved in something like that."

"Did you ever discuss the murder of Dean Milo with her?"

"No, never."

"Are you sure?"

"Never."

"Do you know who killed Dean Milo?"

"No, I don't have any idea."

"Do you have any information at all that could lead or help lead us to . . . ?"

"No. And, if I did, you'd be the first to know. Believe me."

Skeptical of Boyd's story, Lewis challenged him to take a polygraph test. Boyd agreed. However, when the test was analyzed, Boyd was told that he had failed. Asked whether he would be willing to try it again, Boyd replied that he would have to consult with his attorney.

On October 27th, as Terry Lea King was officially being indicted by a grand jury for her alleged role in the Milo murder, Boyd's attorney, Ed Pierce, called Ed Duvall to inform him that his client was suffering from "acute anxiety and depression" and would be unable to take a second lie detector test.

Dean Milo

Dean and Maggie Milo

Fred Milo

Sophie Curtis

Lonnie Curtis

Sotir Milo

Katina Milo

Barry Boyd

Thomas Mitchell

Terry Lea King

Tony Ridle

Harry Knott

Ray Sesic

Frank Piccirilli

John Harris

Bobby O'Brian

David Harden, "The Kid"

William C. Dear

Larry Momchilov

Richard Munsey

William E. Lewis

Rich Craven

17 | *"The purge of Dean Milo . . .*
was now complete."

THE SUMMIT COUNTY PROSECUTOR, Stephan Gabalac, had fully cooperated with the sheriff department's probe of the Milo murder and expressed a willingness to grant immunity to witnesses, if and when necessary. On the top of Gabalac's list for immunity was Barry Boyd. However, this and the Milo investigation in general was further complicated when Gabalac was defeated in his reelection bid on Tuesday, November 4th. His successor, Lynn Slaby, knowing he had inherited the Milo case, promptly contacted Ed Duvall—who advised him to follow Gabalac's lead with regard to immunity.

But even though the murder probe was "popular" among official investigators, as well as with the public and in the press, the prosecutor's assistants were less enthusiastic. To them, the evidence against Terry Lea King was so weak that they were embarrassed to try her in court; none of them were interested in what they began to call "this dirtball case." Finally, Slaby approached assistant Summit County prosecutor Fred Zuch—with whom he had attended law school—and asked him to handle all prosecutions stemming from the Milo investigation, beginning with King. Zuch agreed to consider it—with the proviso that *no one* be granted immunity.

* * *

On November 6th, King lost one battle and won a second. Summit County Common Pleas Judge Frank J. Bayer denied her plea to drop the charge of complicity to commit aggravated murder, but the Ohio Ninth District Court of Appeals reduced her bail from $500,000 to $100,000. However, she was still unable to raise the cash, so she remained in jail.

The following day, the stockholders of the Milo Corporation, after months of litigation, elected a new board of directors, the majority of whom supported Fred Milo. The directors included Sotir Milo, Lonnie and Sophie Curtis, and, in the minority, Tsarnas's law partners, Larry Vuillemin and Michael Robinson. The meeting and election were approved by the court. Thus, effective November 10th, Fred Milo would become president of the Milo Corporation and all of its subsidiaries. Lonnie and Sophie would become its two vice presidents. The Fred Milo–controlled board immediately announced that—although the estate of Dean Milo would maintain its one-third ownership in the company—all benefits due it, including death benefits due Milo's widow, would be terminated. In addition, the board of directors fired all the members of Dean's professional management team.

The purge of Dean Milo from the Milo Corporation was now complete.

On November 13th, Fred Zuch was officially named as the prosecutor's point man in the cases against Terry Lea King and any others indicted in the Milo murder—with full power to grant or deny immunity. An ex-cop who had received his law degree by attending the University of Akron's evening law school, Zuch had achieved a reputation for toughness by maintaining strict standards with regard to plea-bargaining and immunity. Immediately upon his appointment, Zuch accelerated the pending case against Barry Boyd, in connection with his alleged tampering with court records. Zuch also said he was going to offer Terry Lea King a seven- to twenty-five-year sentence—instead of the life sentence Ohio state law required—in return for her cooperation, adding that he wanted it understood from the outset that he would not give immunity to anyone involved in the Milo murder.

Later that day, King asked to make a telephone call and was taken from her cell. The duty officer handcuffed her to the cage near the booking area. Because King claimed that she had hurt her wrist, the handcuffs were loosened.

King telephoned Larry Benson in Medina, but his line was busy and the officer told her that she could call again in five minutes. During the interim, the officer answered another phone call and turned her back on King. When she turned around, King was gone. Frantically, the officer began searching the area, along with another uniformed policewoman—and finally found King hiding between a door and the gun lockers.

When the duty officer asked her what she was doing, King replied that she was "playing a game." She was promptly returned to her cell and not permitted to make her call.

On November 22nd, King's attorney, Jerry Montgomery, charged that the prosecution's entire case against her was based on hearsay. He told *Akron Beacon Journal* staff reporter Dennis McEaneney, "We want them [the prosecution] to give us every name, every date, every time, and every incident involving her and any other alleged co-conspirators. So far, we don't have that kind of information.

"So far, all the prosecutors have indicated to us is that they have a statement from a man we believe to be a highly unreliable source, a man whose track record isn't the greatest."

Montgomery seemed to know about Jack Taylor—whom he stated was part of King's social circle—but he refused to publicly name him, adding, "We feel he is motivated solely by the $50,000 reward."

On November 26th, as the state prepared for King's trial, Judge Frank Bayer issued a gag order, prohibiting all law enforcement officials, witnesses, lawyers, and anyone else connected with either the Milo investigation or King's trial from making any statements to the press.

Meanwhile, that afternoon, all of the disputes between the sheriff and the coroner's office, with regard to the Milo murder

investigation came to a head. The confrontation occurred after
Dr. Kyriakides returned only three reels of pornography film to
the sheriff's investigators instead of the four that had been
found in Milo's closet. *The Crisco Kid*, Momchilov charged,
had been removed from the package.

"Wait a minute!" Kyriakides protested. "You did not give me
four rolls. You gave me three rolls!"

"They were in a bag!" Momchilov replied angrily. "There
were four rolls of film."

"You pulled them out of the bag and showed me?"

"Tom Bostick found them. I even came back, because I
thought I was mistaken. I asked Tom Bostick whether or not
there were four rolls of film. . . . He says, 'There were four
rolls of film. . . .' "

"That's a damn lie, because . . ."

"We verified it by talking to somebody who furnished the
film. We asked the man, and the man said he did give four
rolls of film. . . ."

"Bostick may have seen four, but you only turned three over
to me. And if you want to search my house, if you want to
search the coroner's office, if you want to search any damn house
of any of my people, if you want to search anything, go ahead
and do it!"

"I don't want to search anything!" Momchilov shot back.
"I'm saying what I saw. . . ."

Lewis then charged that Kyriakides had been leaking evidence to members of the Milo family, specifically Fred, Lonnie,
and Sophie, each of whom had told the police they had learned
details of the murder from Kyriakides.

"You know, you guys think the leaks are in our office,"
Kyriakides said. "You know, the leak could be in your office,
too. . . . I don't remember [telling members of the Milo family
about the evidence found at the scene of the murder]."

"Larry and I went out and talked to Fred [Milo] a few days
after the homicide," Lewis said. "I said, 'Jesus Christ . . . we're
trying to work together on this, and K. Y. is going back to the
family and telling them stuff. I'll be goddamned if we'll tell
him anything."

"Lewis," Kyriakides said, "you should have known better;

and you should have called me up and braced me with it, because I don't play that way."

"I went to my chief."

"Your chief should've called me! I wish he had . . . !"

"Because I didn't have balls enough to . . ." Chief Duvall began to say.

"Oh, no, you've got balls," Kyriakides said sarcastically. "There's no question about that."

"Because, let me tell you," Duvall yelled, "I'll have your ass any time I see fit to . . . !"

"And," Kyriakides fired back, "just remember, I'll jump on your ass, too."

"Hey!" someone shouted.

"Well, let's go at it! Right! Any fucking time you want to . . . !" yelled Duvall.

"Cool off!" Sheriff Troutman insisted.

"I don't know," Duvall continued, pointing at the coroner, "you're too mixed in with this, with the family."

"I'm not mixed in with this family . . . !"

"Like hell you're not! You were in business with Dean . . . !"

"What the hell do you mean I was in business with Dean!"

"You don't have any shares in Adams Restaurants?"

"That's not business with Dean!"

"Well, Dean was on the board!"

"Sure, Dean is on the board, but I'm not in business with him! When I buy Coca-Cola stock, and you have Coca-Cola stock, we're in business together?"

"Why did you buy that stock?"

"Because Dean comes to me, and he says, 'Doc, this is treasury stock. . . . It can become yours in November. Do you want to buy some?' I said, 'Dean, why are you messing around with those guys on that damn board?' He says, 'Well, I'm trying to find out how to run the company [the Milo Corporation] when I get directors and my company goes public.' Horseshit! Dean would never let his company go public. So he said, 'Will you buy some?' He sold some to Rod [Kyriakides], too. And he sold some to Tsarnas, and he sold some to a couple other guys. So I'm not in business with him."

"Well, I didn't mean it that way, but . . ."

"Well, all right, goddamn it, say what you mean! . . . The point is that you guys take it any way you want. You start out by telling me what a great friend of Dean's I was. And that's right. You don't think I'm interested in finding out who killed him? Hell, yes! I'm interested in finding out who killed him. Supposing I knew that his . . . brother [killed him], do you think I wouldn't tell you?"*

On November 29th, at 7:30 A.M., Bob Dare, another one of Dear's associates, received a telephone call from a man who refused to identify himself but claimed to have information about the Milo murder. Because the informant feared that he was being tape recorded—which he was—he hung up. But, ten minutes later he called again, informing Dare that he wanted the reward money and asked for a meeting as soon as possible.

The informant and Dare agreed to meet at a restaurant in nearby Norton Township, southwest of Akron, at 10:00 A.M. Dare was accompanied by two other Dear associates—one of

* Author's note: The Summit County Sheriff's Department charges against Kyriakides were not without merit. On September 17, 1982, county and city law enforcement officials raided the coroner's county offices. After presenting Kyriakides with a search warrant, sheriff's deputies found a secret file on the Milo murder, which had been maintained by the coroner from the outset of the investigation. Momchilov and others contended that, although the sheriff's department eventually became aware of all Kyriakides' private information, it would have been collected sooner had the coroner cooperated. In addition, the police found taped conversations, recorded covertly by Kyriakides, in which he discouraged several persons from cooperating with the sheriff's investigation.

The raid was precipitated after Kyriakides—just one week earlier—suddenly returned a load of Dean Milo's personal property to his widow. Mrs. Milo, who was unaware that these items had been in the coroner's possession, immediately informed the sheriff's department of what Kyriakides had done. Included among those items totalling over $110,000 were Milo's wallet and $3,000 gold bracelet, his $24,000 IRS tax refund check, as well as other things found at the scene of the murder in August 1980. To date, however, the missing fourth film, *The Crisco Kid*, has not been located.

On December 23, 1982, Kyriakides was indicted for tampering with evidence in connection with the Milo murder investigation. Subsequently, however, he was convicted of "theft in office" in an unrelated case, resigned as county coroner and was placed on probation. At the time of his sentencing, the charge against him stemming from the Milo case was dropped.

whom, Dick Riddle, checked out the informant's license number when he arrived. The informant—whom Riddle identified as William Daily, an ex-convict with a long criminal record for theft and bank robbery—told Dare that he knew who Milo's killer was. He added that he, too, had been approached by Terry Lea King to do the killing.

That afternoon, Daily met with Dear. When Daily arrived at the Cascade Holiday Inn and went to Dear's room, he had no idea that it, too, was wired for sound—and was being monitored by Larry Momchilov in the next room.

"If the information that you have is factual, I'll see that you get the money," said Dear. "That's not a problem. . . . Now, did Terry approach you?"

"She asked me to do a hit, yes. But she didn't say Milo. She stated, 'Bill, I've been trying to get ahold of you.' Ten grand was named, and they wanted this guy hit. . . . During the conversation, Tom Mitchell's name was brought up. And Mitchell was going over there. I can't tell you for sure that Tom Mitchell did the killing, but I would just assume that he did, because I don't know anywhere she could have got . . ."

"All right. Where was this? And where did she contact you, Bill?"

"I went to her place over there on Gordon Street."

"How did you happen to go there?"

"Me and Terry have been friends for years."

"Did she call you to come over and talk to her about it?"

"Yes. I don't go there that often, because of all the drug traffic and everything. I just dropped in. . . ."

"What date? Do you recall when this was?"

"It was early June or late May. . . ."

"And who was present in the house?"

"Me and Terry."

"All right, did you talk to her on the first floor, second floor . . . ?"

"See, now, you're gonna use this! I'm not going to go on! I'll screw . . ." Daily began to freak out.

"I know you will, Bill, but I've also got to know. For $50,000, I've got to know if you're being straight."

"I'm not lying to you! I'm losing my home and things like this!

I'm not into snitching on somebody innocent. I wouldn't do it for $50,000. How do I know? I told you guys . . . I'll bet my life on Mitchell doing the killing, because I know he was over there, and . . ."

"When you were? Or later that night?"

"No! No! No! Listen to this! During the conversation, I said, 'Okay, Terry, find out as much as you can and let me know.' You know, I thought she was just bullshitting me, you know? Not that I'd do that. Me and Terry had high games, and I thought she was crazy. She'd like to have got me under her thumb. I've been convicted of bank robbery. I'll go out and rob a bank before I'll kill somebody for $10,000. I'm not into hurt; I've never hurt anybody in any way. . . ."

"Well, let me ask you, are you involved in the Milo murder at all?"

"No, sir! I knew I was going to get into this! No, sir! I would take a lie detector test! I'm here because I would like that fifty grand; fifty grand and that's all."

"You can do a hell of a lot on fifty grand; so could I. But I'm going to ask you if you were involved in the murder?"

"No way I was. Terry was drugged, you know? And I took it that Terry was trying to act the cool role, because she likes to impress people. I don't know. Terry was just on an ego trip. I didn't realize [that she was serious] until I read it in the paper—when Terry was arrested—that she wasn't bullshitting about that killing. She was straight up. . . ."

"Were you up in her attic? That's where she stays most of the time."

"Yeah."

"Is that where the discussion was?"

"Yes, sir."

"Well, did you ever see the $10,000?"

"No, sir. She told me she gave it back. She thought I could get it again. . . . I could take a lie detector test or whatever, if you want me to. I won't tell you guys if I was involved in anything."

"But you're not asking for immunity. I could understand that."

"I could use immunity, because there'd be charges [over]

drugs. . . . Maybe [Terry] would try to hurt me that way. I'm not even worried about that. I got out of the drugs. It's been quite a while. . . . I saw her again in July, and it was on July 5th. And, then, that was it."

"What did she say on July 5th?"

"Wasn't even brought up. But Tom Mitchell left town at the same time. I know, you guys probably think you're going on a wild goose chase. Tom's going to be up there and digging the morphine. Tom's the only other one that I know that could do that killing. . . ."

"Did she mention his name?"

"She said she talked to Tom Mitchell."

"When was the last time you saw Mitchell?"

"It's been a year."

"Do you know if Tom was here during the month of August?"

"He left. He was selling his furniture. He left the week of the killing."

"The week of the killing?"

"He left town. . . . He's a pretty bitter individual. I've been with him a few nights, and he'd cut my throat for some money. So I really don't have that much to do with him anymore."

"Did he ever carry a gun?" Dear asked.

"Thirty-eight."

"Thirty-eight?"

"Terry has it. . . ." Daily replied.

"All right, where were you when Terry said she knew about . . ."

"I was sitting in [a] bar, and she said, 'You know who did the killing?' And I says, 'Yeah, Tom Mitchell.' And she said, 'Yeah.' And she also said that [she] could do that killing. She was really strung out at the time. And then she came back with that. I thought of Mitchell before, because Terry brought Mitchell's name up that day. And he was up her ass about this and that, you know. You'd have to know the guy. He probably got involved in that just to show Terry he could do it. You know, just for an ego trip. The guy is kind of a strange guy, with a couple of chicks."

"What about Terry? She has an appeal over men. I've never seen anything like it."

"Me and Terry . . . like, I never screwed the girl. Me and Terry were really close friends, you know?"

"How come you never used Mitchell? Can't [he] be trusted?"

"Well, we weren't close. I didn't know Tom. I met him in prison. We celled together for a while, and then I escaped. Then I came back like nine months later, and they transferred me to another prison, and I didn't see much of Mitchell at all. I seen him when he got out. And he screwed my old lady. You know, I thought [he was just trying] to get back at me. . . . I was going to college here and in prison, and I was sending her money. . . ."

"How did Terry meet Mitchell?"

"Through me. . . ."

"Was she screwing Mitchell?"

"I couldn't tell you, you know? He probably tried, but, hey, Terry . . . I can't tell you that. . . ."

"Why would she approach you and Mitchell instead of [someone else]?"

"Well . . ."

"You know the answer."

"I can't kill anybody. I can't even . . ."

"I don't care if you killed ten. It makes no difference to me," Dear exclaimed. "This is the only case I'm interested in."

"I know, but I haven't killed anybody! I have never killed anybody! I never let anybody fuck over me. I have that reputation. I don't let anybody fuck over me. . . ."

"Do you know Barry Boyd?"

"Barry Boyd? Yeah."

"What do you know about Barry Boyd?"

"Oh, Terry's friend. Terry and me went over to his house. I went to get some coke over there one time. . . ."

"If Barry Boyd had contacted Terry to find somebody to do the killing, then, if she contacted you and Mitchell . . ."

"She said I was the only one she knew. I mean, Mitchell's name was brought up once again. I walked out of there, and I didn't get back with her. . . . I'd drop in there just to, hey, do a little coke or . . ."

"Did Mitchell ever tell you that she had . . . made contact with him?"

"He used to go over there, selling Terry drugs. . . . Mitchell took some morphine over there. I'd stop in there . . ."

"All right, because I want to wrap it up this month, when I leave here on the 31st of December, I want to have it wrapped— your money to you and me gone."

"I understand that you already have a witness."

"No! No! Wrong! That's not true! If I promise you are going to get the money, you will get the money."

"I can put a lot of time in this and never get [it]. I sat here and helped you a lot. I think I ain't getting nothing from it."

"Except for one thing: I have been in business eighteen years. If I make deals, I always keep them," Dear boasted.

"I'm not mistrusting you. I'm just saying that what I've done for you so far, I'm no further ahead. And, if you decide you don't need me . . ."

"Not really. What?"

"What I did for you was a waste of my time. So I go back on Plan B, you know."

"Well, keep that Plan B to the side, all right?"

"I don't know if I can. . . ."

"Well, here's what [Terry] will do: As the trial gets close at hand—It's the fifteenth of the month—her mind's starting to work, because we've had a good case against her. All right, when it gets down to nut-cuttin' time, do you think she's going to ride to prison, or do you think she'll turn on those who are involved to keep from going to prison? If I offer her . . ."

"I'll tell you what. I think if you offer Terry [something, she'll think], 'Man, that's the rest of your life in prison,' " Daily said.

"That's right. She'll be old and gray. She won't be worth nothing. The legs and arms will be gone."

"She's such a cutthroat deadshot. I really believe she would . . . I'd be a dead goner. I'd be scared to death, I think. Because, you know, I wouldn't mind prison, but she's going to ride to prison no matter what, because . . ."

"[We] might work a deal with her. I want the rest of them. I want the Milo family. That's who I'm interested in: the Milo family. If they are the ones who caused this to happen, that's who I want."

"Well, I can't see why she would run that to me about how

the guy fucked over his family. I wish I could remember the whole conversation that day, but, you know, I just [didn't] pay attention."

"Did she say how she wanted it done?"

"Oh, we discussed it. She said, 'Get the guy's routine down and everything.' She [said] get it all pretty well set up. No problem."

"In other words, she knew the business and everything?"

"Yeah. . . ."

"Well, at least you know where both of us are. I want to solve this case, and you want fifty grand. . . . I'll come up with the money; I always have. . . ."

"All right. I'm counting on that, because there isn't anything . . ."

"I'm counting on it; I'm counting on you. I'm going to make you earn your $50,000, but I'll see you get every nickel of it. So I've got to figure out an air-tight plan so that when we go in that courtroom, I get a conviction. You get your money, and I get my conviction. That's the name of the ballgame."

18 | *"I know you killed him!"*

ON DECEMBER 8TH, Dear, Momchilov, Lieutenant Bob Scalise, an expert at undercover surveillance, and Daily flew to Dallas, hoping to locate Mitchell. The night before Daily had managed to learn from Mitchell's former Akron landlord that their quarry was living with two women in Farmer's Branch, Texas.

The following day, after contacting the local police and informing them of their investigation, Momchilov and Dear found Mitchell's home. It was a white, one-story house at the base of a hill in a low-income rental area. Because Dear did not want to monitor Daily and Mitchell from the top of the hill, he once again climbed into the trunk of a car—the rented one Daily was driving. Momchilov stayed in a van—supplied by the local police—parked across the street from Mitchell's home. Scalise was parked in a car up the street. Both Momchilov and Scalise, like Dear, had their own electronic equipment.

Daily walked onto Mitchell's front porch and knocked on the door. There was no answer. Hearing loud Beatles music coming out of the house—a radio tribute to John Lennon, who had been killed the previous night—Daily peered into the house through a window. Mitchell's home was decorated for Christmas. Daily knocked again, but still there was no answer.

Momchilov instructed Daily to return to the car, and drive away; they would return later in the afternoon.

At 4:15 P.M. they returned to Mitchell's home. Again, Daily went to the front door. "Happiness Is a Warm Gun" played loudly from inside the house. However, again when Daily knocked there was no answer.

Less than a minute later, a car pulled into the driveway. Tom Mitchell climbed out of the driver's seat alone. He immediately recognized Daily.

"Hi, ya!" Mitchell shouted from the driveway.

"Tom!" Daily responded.

"What the hell are you doin' down here?"

"Didn't Andy [Mitchell's Akron landlord] call you?"

"Yeah. He called me last night, but he didn't say you were coming."

"He didn't know I was coming. Nobody knew I was coming."

"Is that your car?"

"No, rented."

Mitchell opened the front door and invited Daily in.

"How long have you been down here?" asked Daily.

"Little while."

"Are you working?"

"Oh, yeah. . . . So how's everything going with you?"

"Well, Tom, it depends. Are you hip to what's going on in Ohio?"

"I heard about Terry. . . ."

"I think you know that I wouldn't come all this way for nothing, Tom."

"Yeah, I know that."

"They got me scared to death up there, Tom," Daily said, his voice filled with hesitation and fear. "Me and Terry talked, Tom. It was my understanding that you did that, and they all think I did it, Tom. It leaves me in a fucking bind."

"Well, I'm not going to go back and tell them that I did it."

"I know, but . . ."

"I had the opportunity the night I left. She gave it to me the day before. . . . How'd she get busted, though?"

"Hey, I don't know. She asked me to do that murder. Apparently, she asked you to do that murder."

"I . . ."

"Hey, everybody thinks I did that murder, Tom—which leaves me up . . . Terry told me that you did it."

"I . . ."

"She was apologetic and everything. Hey, I'm glad you did it, but that leaves me out in the cold. Terry's trial comes up fuckin' next week."

"Yeah, is she going on trial by herself?"

"Yeah, she's the only person . . . they got a witness."

"Oh, God, she wasn't right there, was she?" Mitchell asked.

"Hey . . ."

"Is she in jail or out on bond?"

"She's in jail. . . . I think you should give me some money."

"Give you some money? I ain't got none. Where you gonna go with the dough?"

"I don't know, just away from here. Hey, it protects you, Tom."

"What? I'm not worried about nothin'. I'll help you out if you gotta go someplace. I can buy you a plane ticket, but that's about it. I don't have any cash."

"Also, I can't see how they can pin a murder on me that I didn't do."

"True."

"True. . . . I've lasted out this long, but I'm scared to death now," Daily continued. "Hey, we haven't been that close. . . . You don't think Terry would try to set me up. Make it look like I did that murder, do ya? What'd she say to you about it, Tom?"

"Nothing. We talked about it a little bit, and that's about it. And then she sent over some information, and that was it. And then I flew here. I don't think she'll set you up."

"Hey, if they offer her a deal—to get off for murder—all she's got to do is say, 'Oh, Bill did it.' And then fucking Bill goes to jail. . . . Hey, she told me you did it."

"Is she talking?"

"Hey, she isn't talking, but, apparently, we're not the only ones she offered it to. They have a guy to testify against her."

"All right, I've got nothing to say."

"Well, you've left me in an awful fix."

"Did I?"

"Oh, yeah, I would think so."

"Well, if she hasn't talked by now, she's not going to talk. How long ago did she get busted?"

"A week from this Monday, she goes to trial, so . . ."

"She doesn't have to talk if she's strong in her case. . . ."

"Oh, I know, Tom. I know. But, hey, that damn fucking . . ."

"She offered it to me, but I left . . ." Mitchell insisted.

"She gave you the information, and then you didn't do it?"

"No, because I had to fly out that night."

"You had to fly out the same night as the murder, and you didn't do it?"

"The night I got the information. No, I was thinking about going back to do it . . . and contact her. . . ."

"I'm A Loser" began to play on the stereo in the background.

"Hey, I backed away from it. You couldn't see that Terry was so loose, Tom? That fucking this could happen? I said to Cathy [Daily's wife], I couldn't even believe she offered it. I said to Cathy months before that she was going to get busted. Hey, there's not a mind-game going on there. But, if, fucking, she thought she could make a deal, Tom, and hang me, fucking she would."

"Well, I don't . . ."

"Hey, I'm afraid of that . . ."

"How's everything else back at home . . . ?"

Mitchell and Daily talked briefly about Daily's family, and then Daily interrupted, saying, "See why I'm scared to death?"

"Well, I can imagine why. . . . I don't want to ask you questions. I don't want to speculate. . . . Well . . ."

"Tom," Daily said, deadly serious, "she only knew me and you."

Mitchell changed the subject and began talking about the two women he was living with, Texas, and mutual friends who lived nearby. Anxious for the conversation about the murder to get underway again, Daily asked, "Tom, you don't think you put me in a hell of a fix?"

"Me?"

"Yeah."

"How?" Mitchell laughed. "Because I'm down here? How, Bill, did I put you in a fix on that murder?"

"According to Terry, Tom, you did it!" Daily shouted. "There ain't nobody else. . . ."

"I should be in the fix if Terry says I did it. Now, I'm telling you, I didn't do it. Does that put you in a fix? If I tell you I did it, I did it."

"Would you tell me you did it?"

"Not any more than I'd expect you to tell me. . . . And, if I did do it, I'm not going to go back up there, and say I did it. . . . So much for Bill Daily."

"Yeah, I can understand that. I'm not saying, 'Hey, Tom, go up there and confess to the murder.' It isn't that. You just should've stayed away from it, Tom."

"What?"

"You should of just stayed away from it."

"Well, we'll have to wait it out in court, and see what happens. . . . Did you drive or fly?"

"I flew down here and rented a car. I invested all my money into this, figuring that you had money."

"I got American Express," Mitchell said laughing. "I would've offered that. I owe about $600 this month."

"Did Terry approach you for that murder before me or after?"

"When did she ask you?"

"She hit me up in May for it."

"I don't remember."

"Did she give you all the information on it?"

"Yeah. I had two sheets [of paper], pictures, and all of that stuff. It was like a scrapbook. . . ."

"You don't think you owe me any money? I mean, why disappear here, Tom! All of the blood of the murder has gone on me!"

"I don't have any goddamn money . . . !" Mitchell shouted.

"Well, what'd you do with all the money from the murder, Tom?"

"What?"

"What'd you do with all the money from the murder?"

"I don't know nothing about that. We just talked about pay."

"Well, you must've been pretty serious about doing that murder."

"I didn't do it!"

"Gimme a pencil, Tom."

"What for? Last will and testament?"

"Nope, general information to you. Something for you to think about, because—and remember, this is business, Tom, just straight out business. . . . Terry told me you ought to be able to come clean with two or three grand."

"If you're trying to blackmail me, call the police."

"Yeah, well, you don't care if I go to them and tell them that you and Terry did it? It don't matter to you?" Daily asked.

Mitchell paused for a moment and replied quietly, "It matters."

"Well, I'll tell you what, I'll be at the Holiday Inn until tomorrow morning when I fly back. You decide whether you want me to go back with the information she gave me. What the fuck! It's two or three grand of what you made, Tom! Fucking, and they think I did it back there! Hey, I'm in a real rut, you know? You did me wrong. And you know, it's not the first time you've done me wrong. I didn't invest this little bit of money to come down here because I didn't know nothing. Because when Terry gets high, she does some talking, Tom. . . . So, hey, think about it."

"Hey, thanks a lot! You've got my answer!" Mitchell shouted.

"No? Think about it, Tom."

"Have a good flight."

Daily then stormed out of Mitchell's home, talking angrily to himself and the police. "Well, Dear, they got the fucking recording," he lamented. "You got one helluva lot, but you didn't get a confession! Hey, he owned up. . . . He got all the information on the guy; he left the night of the fucking killing, but he said he didn't do it! Fucking, I don't believe the guy! I know, but look at what he told me! I know he did that! I pray to God that they were able to get that over that fucking tape! The music was really loud!"

"Why don't you ask him to go someplace, maybe to dinner,

with you?" Dear said softly to Daily from inside the trunk. "Is there anybody in the house with him?"

"No, Bill!"

"Are you sure you can't get him to go eat with you?"

"Bill, I don't know! I just fucking blackmailed him! He wouldn't come across with a confession!"

As Daily drove off, with Dear still in the trunk, Mitchell's neighbor climbed over his back fence and entered Mitchell's home. Moments later, Mitchell charged out of his front door to Momchilov's van, still parked across the street. Momchilov tried to cover the window with a small rag, but it was too late. He'd been caught.

"Are you some fucking cop!" Mitchell screamed to him through the window.

"What the hell is it to you?" Momchilov yelled back, trying to tuck his electronic surveillance gear under a box.

"Come on out of there, or I'm calling the cops!"

When Momchilov didn't reply, Mitchell returned to his house—and actually called the Farmer's Branch police, which was also involved in the surveillance effort.

A few hours later, Daily telephoned Mitchell, and the police again recorded the conversation.

"If I don't get that money, Tom, I'm going to turn you in to Bill Dear—because Dear is offering a $50,000 reward. If you don't give me some money, I'll get it from him—because I know you killed him."

Mitchell slammed down the receiver.

Despite Mitchell's claim that he had not committed the murder, both Momchilov and Dear were convinced he had, in fact, been the triggerman. They relayed the information back to Duvall and Zuch in Akron, and though the evidence was very thin, reluctantly authorized an aggravated murder warrant on Mitchell.

Finally, that night, at 1:30 A.M., Momchilov, Scalise, Dear, and members of the Farmer's Branch police department's SWAT team—a bunch of locals armed with shotguns—returned to Mitchell's home to arrest him. Because Daily had told them that Mitchell would not be taken alive—and probably had a .357 magnum in his house—Momchilov decided on a ruse. Knowing that Mitchell had twice called the Farmer's Branch police about him in his van, Momchilov changed into some shaggy clothing, clutched his .38 service revolver, and placed his hands behind his back as if he were handcuffed. He was then escorted by two uniformed Farmer's Branch officers to Mitchell's front door.

Mitchell came to the door wearing blue jeans, a pink shirt, and cowboy boots, and holding a can of Budweiser. "What's going on?" he asked.

"Mr. Mitchell, you filed a complaint earlier today about a van parked in front of your house," the officer said. "Is this the man who was inside?"

As Mitchell began to focus on "the suspect," Momchilov swung into a combat crouch stance and pointed his .38 at Mitchell's nose. A lighter shade of pale, Mitchell froze and quickly surrendered. While being taken to a squad car Mitchell noticed Daily sitting in a police car parked down the street. At that point, he knew he'd been double-crossed.

At police headquarters, Momchilov tried to convince Mitchell to sign a document waiving extradition. Mitchell balked. Then Dear said wryly, "Hey, partner, I live in this state, and I will harass your ass from the time you breathe. You're going back." Finally, Mitchell signed the document.

At one point, as Dear and Momchilov questioned Mitchell, they showed him a picture of Terry Lea King. "Do you know who this is?" asked Momchilov.

"It's Terry," Mitchell responded.

Momchilov then showed him a picture of Barry Boyd. "Do you know who this is?"

"Dean Milo?"

Convinced that Mitchell would continue to plead his innocence, Dear responded sarcastically, "Yeah, right. Dean Milo."

Mitchell was held in the Dallas County Jail overnight; his bond was set at $300,000 by a local judge. That afternoon, Mitchell, accompanied by Momchilov and Dear, returned to Akron.

* * *

Meantime, back in Akron, Terry Lea King had been given a polygraph test.

"Do you know for sure who shot Dean Milo?" Lewis asked.

"No," she replied.

"Did you offer anyone money to shoot Dean Milo?"

"No."

"Did you offer money to Thomas Mitchell to kill Dean Milo?"

"No."

"Did Barry Boyd tell you that someone in the Milo family wanted Dean Milo killed?"

"No."

As expected, Terry Lea King failed the lie detector test.

The police felt confident. With the capture of Tom Mitchell, the Milo murder case had been solved.

How wrong they were.

19 | *"No, I did not kill the man."*

THIRTY-TWO-YEAR-OLD Thomas D. Mitchell had joined the U.S. Army in February 1969 and served thirteen months in Vietnam. Honorably discharged in September 1970, he had returned to Akron and begun hanging aluminum siding on other people's homes. Within his first year at home, he'd married his high-school sweetheart, fathered a son, and—unhappy with his life and circumstances—gotten divorced. Mitchell had become a speed freak during the war and had continued cranking up when he'd come home. When his wife had had enough of his friends and their drug habits, she left him, taking their son with her.

Soon after their separation, Mitchell—a handsome man of medium build and height, with shoulder-length, reddish-blond hair and blue eyes—had met Bill Daily. Prior to meeting Daily, Mitchell had only been in trouble once with the law. While in high school, he'd been arrested for grand larceny, but hadn't done any time in prison. However, after meeting and befriending Daily, Mitchell's crime activities had intensified. Between 1971 and 1973, he'd compiled a long arrest record, including charges of armed robbery, grand larceny, breaking and entering, malicious injury to property, and carrying a concealed weapon.

166

In 1973, he'd been sentenced to five to twenty-five years in the Ohio State Reformatory, and been released in 1977.

Walking away from his five-year jail term, Mitchell had become a pipe fitter, working occasionally while attending the University of Akron and later completing his junior year at Ashland College. He'd become comfortable with college life, but, when his money had run out, he'd been forced to quit school and return to hanging aluminum siding. Again, he'd begun doing drugs and flaunted a new tattoo on his upper left arm, an eagle over a swastika. Mitchell and Daily had become reacquainted and begun sharing an apartment together in Akron, but Daily had been forced to move out after he'd been caught going through Mitchell's dresser drawers.

Tom Mitchell was in a jam now, and everyone knew it. The *Akron Beacon Journal* printed a banner headline story, "Break in the Milo Murder Case?" on the front page. Because the police were not talking, not even confirming or denying the rumors circulating throughout the city—other than the fact that Mitchell had indeed been arrested—reporter Dennis McEaneney speculated: "The aggravated murder charge could mean that he [Mitchell] was suspected of being the gunman who killed Milo or that he was an accomplice who aided the triggerman."

However, Dear and the police were sure that they had caught Milo's killer. Soon after he'd been returned to Akron—and fully understanding the charges against him—Mitchell decided to talk.

"Did you kill Dean Milo?" Momchilov asked.

"No, I did not kill the man," he firmly responded.

"Now, come on, Tom. Did you kill Dean Milo?"

"I'm telling you, I didn't do it! Okay, yeah, I was made the offer by Terry Lea King—and she might think I did it! But I didn't do it!"

"So you're saying that you're not guilty?"

"I'm not guilty of murder. I might be guilty of something, but I did not commit this murder."

"So how did you find out so much about it?"

"Anything I know about this thing I learned from friends here in Akron—after Terry was busted."

"Okay, Tom, how'd you meet Terry?"

"I met her and Dennis [King] sometime around Thanksgiving last year through Bill Daily. Dennis was making a turkey downstairs in the kitchen while me and Terry and Bill were up in the attic, Terry's room, getting high."

"When's the last time you saw her?"

"Terry? Hell, I haven't seen or heard from her since May; it might've been longer."

"And she asked you then to kill Milo?"

"I didn't know who it was! I never even thought about it! I sure as hell never got any money! When Daily showed up at my place in Texas, hell, I thought he did it. I thought he did it and was on the run. I thought he was setting me up, making me the fall guy."

"What was Terry Lea King's relationship with Daily?"

"Drugs. It was strictly drug-related. She was a real user. She always had money. No one ever worried about selling her drugs. She never resold them; she used them all herself."

"So that's how you got to know her . . . through drugs?"

"Pretty much, yeah."

"And you knew her well enough that she could ask you to do things?"

"I guess so, yeah."

"And did she ever ask you to kill Dean Milo?"

"Actually, I went to her, asking if she knew some way I could make some money. That's when she told me that she knew of a murder contract. She said the person who took it could make $10,000."

"Did she say who was supposed to be killed?"

"No, never."

"Never?"

"No, I really didn't take her that seriously. But rather than say no right then, I told her I'd think about it."

"And did you think about it?"

"Not really. She was so strung out, I just didn't take her seriously."

"When did you see her next?"

"She came over to my place, once, in the middle of June, to change from her dancing costume into her street clothes. Then she came over again at the end of the month just to get high. . . . I remember that, because I had just gotten back from Texas. I was down there looking for a job . . . planning to move there all along."

"All along?"

"Yeah. And then on the day I was supposed to leave, July 12th, someone came by to see me and to give me a package."

"And who was that?"

"I don't know. I never got his name."

"What were you doing when he came over?"

"I was having a shaving cream fight with one of the girls I lived with. We were cleaning up in the shower, you know. . . ."

"What? Then somebody came to the door?"

"Yeah. I came downstairs, and this guy asked me, 'Are you Tom Mitchell?' I said, 'Yes.' And he said, 'Terry King told me to give this to you.' "

"What was it?"

"A large, brown envelope."

"Was there anything written on it?"

"Not that I can remember, no."

"What did the guy do then?"

"He just left. I just had a towel wrapped around me, but I followed him out."

"Did you see his car?"

"Yes. It was a white Ford. I remember I got part of the license number and put it on the envelope."

"Do you remember the license plate number?"

"No."

"Do you still have the envelope?"

"I might. I threw the other stuff away, but I might've kept the envelope. It would be down at my place in Texas."

"Okay, what'd this guy look like? How would you describe him?"

"White guy, twenty-five to thirty, clean-cut, light-brown hair."

"Had you ever seen him before?"

"Never."

"Since? Have you seen him since?"

"No."

"Okay, what'd you do after he left?"

"I went back in the house and opened the envelope. There . . ."

"What was in it?"

"There were two pieces of long paper, legal-sized paper. There was some handwriting on them. There were also two photographs; they looked like they had been cut out from a book or something, maybe a magazine. And then there was an index card; it described two cars. . . ."

"Anything else?"

"No, that was about it."

"The two pieces of legal paper with the handwriting on them, what did they say?"

"Well, I remember that the one paper had writing on it about halfway down; the other started in the middle and went down to the bottom. . . ."

"And this was handwritten?"

"Yes."

"Do you remember what it said?"

"I remember one thing it said was, 'Please burn this after you have read this. . . . His name is Dean Milo. . . . He will be at a banquet tonight, July 12th, at Tangier . . . should be leaving late and alone . . . his wife is out of town.' . . . And that this would be the best time to make the hit. . . . And he would be driving a blue or silver-grey car. . . ."

"On which paper was that?"

"That was on the first paper, the top one. The second one said, 'I'll meet you at the airport or any place of your choice. I will be alone and have a newspaper folded next to me.' I think it was a *Wall Street Journal*. 'Sit down. Don't talk to me. . . . I'll get up and leave, leaving the newspaper there. . . . Wait a few minutes, then pick up the newspaper and leave.' The money was supposed to be in the newspaper—$10,000. Then, like on the first sheet, I was told to destroy the paper when I was finished with it."

"The photos . . . could you describe the photos?"

"Yeah. There was a person standing . . . a front shot of the person. Then there was a side shot of the same man; he looked like he was reaching out to shake hands with someone."

"Had you ever heard of Dean Milo before?"

"Never."

"Not from Terry?"

"No, never. This was the first time."

"Okay, what did you do with the envelope and its contents?"

"Well, I was packing, getting ready to fly to Texas. I looked at the stuff and then packed it in my suitcase."

"And you didn't see it again until you arrived in Texas and unpacked?"

"Right. . . . I didn't do that killing. I thought that Terry was involved. I thought she must really want this guy out of the way. She was also the one I was supposed to contact if I did the job. . . . She'd arrange for the delivery of the money."

"Okay, so you went to Texas . . ."

"Right."

"And then what?"

"Well, I was met at the Dallas Airport by two girl friends. . . . Like I said, this had all been arranged in May—when I was down there looking for a job. They had a place down there, and I moved in with them. I got a job on a construction site, and I was making about $7.15 an hour."

"When did you hear that Terry Lea King had been arrested?"

"Well, my landlord in Akron called me sometime in October —about the middle of the month—and he told me, 'Your friend, Terry King, has been busted for murder. . . .'"

"And what did you do?"

"I asked him who she was supposed to have killed; he couldn't remember the guy's name. I told [him] to hold on, and I went and got the envelope. . . ."

"The one you received on July 12th, the day you left Akron?"

"Right, that one. . . . I went and got the envelope. I came back to the phone, and I asked if the guy's name was Dean Milo. He said, 'Yeah, that's the name.' That's when I went outside and destroyed it."

"The envelope?"

"Yeah. I went out on the back porch and burned the envelope. . . . Well, I burned the contents; I might've kept the envelope itself."

"Were you alone when you did this?"

"Yeah."

"Did you have any further conversations about the Milo murder after that?"

"No, none. . . . Well, not until Bill Daily came down. . . ."

At the conclusion of the interview, Mitchell was asked to take a polygraph test. He agreed to do so—and passed. It was obvious that Tom Mitchell had not killed Dean Milo after all.

In return for his cooperation in their investigation, the charge of aggravated murder later would be reduced to obstruction of justice, stemming from his destruction of the documents. Mitchell pleaded guilty and was sentenced to a year in prison.

Bill Daily received a $10,000 reward.

With Terry Lea King's trial scheduled to begin on Monday, December 15th, all the pressure came down on her. After interviewing Mitchell and waiting for the afternoon edition of the *Akron Beacon Journal*—with the report of Mitchell's arrest—to circulate, particularly to King, Fred Zuch called King and her attorneys into his office, where they were met by Momchilov and Munsey.

"This is the story, Terry," Zuch told her. "We now have two witnesses who can implicate you in the Milo murder. You can get life for what you're being charged with—or you can make a deal with us now. At most, you'll do four years. Talk to your attorneys; it's your choice."

King conferred with her lawyers for a few minutes and then returned to Zuch's office. "What do you want?" she asked.

"Just tell us the story," Momchilov responded.

She hesitated momentarily, then said, "One day, I was at Barry Boyd's house, and he started telling me about this guy who was really greedy. He said that there was someone who wanted him out of the way, and that there would be cheers all over town when he was dead."

"Did he tell you who wanted him dead?"

"All I knew was that this guy, some businessman, had come down on his mother and dad. They had some sort of a family business, along with their children, and this guy was trying to move all of them out of the business."

"How well did you know Barry Boyd at this time?"

"Well, I had a key to his house. I'd go over there once in a while."

"How did you meet him, Terry?"

"Oh, one of my girl friends took me to his office, maybe ten years ago. We've kept in touch since. He got me a part in a movie called *Nightmask*. I never even saw a cut of it, but I was filmed and everything."

"What did Barry Boyd think about this man he wanted killed?"

"I didn't get the impression that he, personally, had anything against him. He just kept talking about him pushing the family out."

"When did he want this job done?"

"As soon as possible . . . that was very clear. He said he could pay $10,000 for the contract—but could get more if he had to."

"Did he ever give you any information about the man he wanted killed?"

"Yeah, he did. I got a small aluminum packet, like aluminum foil. Inside, there was a slip of paper with Dean Milo's name, address, and telephone number on it. His business address and phone number were on it, too. Let's see . . . there was some information on his two cars—a Cadillac and a Mercedes, I think —and stuff like the license plate numbers for the cars. Then there were three pictures of Milo. They looked like they were cut out of some brochure or a magazine. . . ."

"Did Barry say anything about where he wanted him hit?"

"Barry wanted it to happen either at his home or at his office. He also knew that he had gone to Florida. Once he said, 'It'd be nice to hit him out of the state.' He knew he was going to Florida even before he left."

"Okay, what did you do with all of this information."

"Well, Barry gave me one of those 'zip-lock Baggies' with rubber bands around it. Inside this plastic thing were twenties, fifties, and one-hundred-dollar bills—$5,000 in all. I know that I gave him back the money a couple of days later. I think I gave him back the information on Milo at the same time, but I'm not sure. That was a while ago."

"Did he ever give you any guns?"

"Guns?"

"Yes. . . . Did he ever give you a gun?"

"I . . . yeah, I don't remember when. . . . I was over at his place. He started talking about a gun he had, and then he went downstairs in his basement and got it. I remember it was in pieces. He put the gun in an envelope and handed it to me. He asked me to see if I could get it fixed. My boyfriend and some of his friends collect guns. I thought maybe they would know something about it. They thought the gun would work—and was worth the cost of repair—but then Barry asked for it back; so I gave it back to him. It was still in pieces when he got it back."

"Did you ever see the gun again?"

"No."

"Was this the gun used to kill Dean Milo?"

"I really don't know."

"Did you show this gun to anyone else—besides your boyfriend and his friends?"

"I don't think so, but maybe I did. . . . I don't know."

"What about Tom Mitchell? How did he get involved in all of this?"

"Tom called and asked me if I was interested in buying some airline coupons. I kind of knew him from before. He had been to my place—maybe, six times. And I had been to his house once or twice, too. Anyway, I told him that I didn't need any of those airline tickets, but if I heard of someone who did, I'd have them call him. So he said that he was moving out West or something and needed some money. Right after Tom hung up, Barry called me, and I told him Mitchell needed money and was selling airline tickets. Later on, Barry called me and asked me to give all that information on Dean Milo to Mitchell. That's when I thought that maybe Barry was going to ask Tom to kill Milo. So I gave Barry directions to Tom's house; I told him that I wouldn't deliver the package."

"So Barry delivered the package to Tom Mitchell?"

"I guess so. He never told me for sure. But, later on, I remember Barry was upset, because he thought Tom had not thrown all that stuff [the information packet] away."

"Why was Barry upset about that?"

"Because it was in his handwriting."

The police knew that King was still not telling the complete truth—that she had offered the contract to Jack Taylor, Daily, and, finally, to Mitchell—but it was a moot point now. Momchilov's new target was Barry Boyd. They had the evidence—and the witnesses —to arrest him.

20 | *"I want to give you the whole thing."*

IMMEDIATELY AFTER Terry Lea King's interrogation, Lewis and Munsey drove to Cleveland Heights, a suburb of Cleveland, where Barry Boyd was spending the weekend with his girl friend. They were backed up by officers from the local police department.

While the cops waited in their cars outside the two-story town house, Momchilov received a warrant for Boyd's arrest that charged him with aggravated murder. He then drove to the Cascade Holiday Inn and picked up Bill Dear. The two men drove to Cleveland Heights and met the other officers.

As the local policemen watched the back door of the town house, Momchilov, Lewis, Munsey, and Dear went to the door and knocked. Boyd—dressed in blue jeans, tennis shoes, and a navy blue shirt—answered the door. He had obviously been drinking and offered no resistance when arrested, looking almost relieved as he was handcuffed and taken to Lewis and Munsey's squad car. Dear and Momchilov remained behind momentarily to help calm down Boyd's girl friend.

En route back to Akron, Boyd began rambling, telling Lewis and Munsey that he and his attorney had tried to make a deal with former Summit County prosecutor Stephan Gabalac. According to Boyd, he had been offered immunity and had

176

accepted. But when Gabalac had been defeated, the deal fell through.

To the surprise of both Lewis and Munsey, Boyd offered to tell them the whole story of Milo's murder—but first he wanted his attorney to talk to Fred Zuch, in the hope that immunity could be renegotiated.

A short time later, while Boyd was in a holding cell at the police station being processed for booking, Dear walked by. Boyd extended his hand, and Dear took it. As the two men shook hands, Boyd said he wanted to talk. "I want to tell you all about it."

"Tell me all about what?" Dear asked.

"The Milo murder. . . . I want you to know that I was involved. But I want you to know that it would've happened without me."

"What are you saying?"

"I'm saying that I can tell you everything; I can give you all the details. I can name all of the people involved."

Puzzled, Dear fell silent.

"Fred Milo met with the killer in Cleveland. Fred gave him the money. The parents had nothing to do with it; it was all Fred."

"Listen," Dear interrupted, "I'm advising you to remain silent. Everything you're saying can and will be held against you. . . . Really, Barry, you'd better wait for your attorney to get here."

"I'm a goddamn attorney! I understand my rights! Listen! I've been wanting to tell you all of this since November. If you can get me out of here, I can get you all the records: the phone numbers, places, and addresses that will lead you to the killer. . . ."

At that point, Captain Kenneth Lockhart, the booking officer who had overheard the conversation between Boyd and Dear, came to Boyd's cell. In front of Lockhart, Dear repeated, "You don't have to talk to me."

"I want to give you the whole thing," Boyd repeated.

"Barry, who was the shooter?"

"That's what I'm saying: Fred took the money to Cleveland and met with the killer. . . ."

"The killer . . . What's his name? Give me his name!" Dear insisted.

"I'm giving the whole thing away! If you set a reasonable bond, I'll tell you everything!"

"But you're saying that the family was involved?"

"Fred handled the whole thing."

"Where's the shooter? Where's the gun, the murder weapon?"

"I wanted to tell you all of this last November, but my attorney advised me against it!"

"Listen, Barry, again, I'm advising you of your rights. You have the right to remain silent. . . ."

"Listen! Give me a sheet of paper and a pen. I'll write the whole thing out."

As Momchilov joined the three men, Dear handed Boyd a piece of paper and Lockhart gave him his pen. Boyd sat down on his bunk and started writing. Then he suddenly stopped and shouted, "I'm giving it all away!"

Momchilov insisted that Boyd wait until his attorney arrived. Lockhart returned to the booking area, and Momchilov and Dear went to Momchilov's desk in the detective bureau. A half-hour later, Boyd, accompanied by another officer, walked up to Momchilov and Dear.

"I gave a package of information about Dean Milo to this Mitchell guy," Boyd said. "I was promised the Milo Corporation's legal work after the murder. . . . I've been taken advantage of enough. Now, I want to talk."

"Have you talked to Fred Milo since Terry Lea King was arrested?" Momchilov asked.

"No, I haven't. He still owes me $6,000."

"For the killing?"

"No, for some legal work I did for him. . . . I was going to use the money to go to Denver. But, yeah, I was involved in the murder. I'm not putting a halo around my head. I was involved. Like I said, I wanted to tell Dear about it in November. The deal was made with the prosecutor, but he reneged.

"I remember the first time we talked," Boyd said to Dear. "You said you weren't going to leave Akron until you solved this case, and I knew that sooner or later, you guys were going to get me. . . . And now that you have, I want a deal. I want you to offer me something."

As Boyd attempted to negotiate, the sheriff's legal advisor, Michael Wolff, was quietly obtaining a search warrant for Boyd's residence. There, the investigators discovered, among other things: a map of Dean Milo's neighborhood, with his home marked in red; a zip-lock bag containing several pictures of Dean; several money wrappers, dated in August and September, with $1,000 denominations; and copies of two court cases— one on the Miranda decision and the other on a passion murder.

When the officers returned to the sheriff's department and confronted Boyd with what they had found, Boyd's head dropped. Rubbing his forehead with his hands, he looked up in despair at everyone standing around him and asked, "What kind of a deal can I get?"

"No immunity," Momchilov said. "Zuch won't give it to you."

"Get me the best deal you can, and I'll talk."

"You got it, Barry."

"Okay, what do you want to know?"

Part Three

RESOLUTION

21 | "He must've had a dozen plots to kill him."

"STATE YOUR FULL NAME," said Ed Duvall, glaring into the eyes of his prisoner, who kept looking away.

"Barry M. Boyd," he replied, while organizing several pages of notes.

"Now, I want the entire story about your involvement in the murder of Dean Milo. Would you please start at the beginning?"

"In January 1980, Fred Milo came to my home and asked me if I knew of anyone who would take care of his brother. . . ."

"Who would kill his brother?"

"Right. He wanted me to find someone to kill him."

"Go ahead, continue."

"Anyway, I didn't take him seriously at first—but Fred kept bringing it up. So I contacted a friend of mine who told me that the job would cost $5,000. The following month—February, I think—Fred came over with $2,500 and a couple of pictures of Dean. . . ."

"I thought you said it was going to cost $5,000?"

"Yeah, right, $5,000. Fred brought over $2,500, and I owed him $2,500. He'd overpaid me for some legal work I'd done for him. . . ."

"So you had $5,000?"

"Yeah, right."

"Then what?"

"I contacted Terry Lea King sometime in March. I remember she had just gotten back from Florida. I called her and asked if she knew of anyone who could take care of Dean. She came over to my place that night, and we talked about it."

"Did she have someone in mind?"

"Not until about a week later. She called me and told me someone was interested; she said she was going to see the person at a wedding."

"Did you know who it was?"

"No. I just gave her the $5,000, a wad of money with a rubber band around it."

"Go on."

"She called me again a few days later and said she wanted the license plate numbers of Dean's cars. I called Fred down in West Virginia, and he gave them to me. I wrote them down and then put the note in Terry's car. I think I put in a second note—again in the car—sometime later on, telling her the make and color of Dean's cars. . . . Anyway, the first person Terry contacted, the guy at the wedding, said no."

"You never found out who the guy was?"

"No, I never knew. . . . I picked up the $5,000, and that was the end of it for a while. Then, about April, Fred started getting obsessed with having Dean taken care of. I was having my own problems then: the DWI charge and some traffic ticket problems. Fred was calling me all the time, always asking about 'the other thing.' That's what he called it: 'the other thing.' He'd even stop by my house. 'What're you doing about it? Are you gonna get someone? When will this be taken care of'"

"He was harassing you about it?"

"Right. It was constant, constant harassment. He really wanted Dean taken care of, and, I mean, right now. He wanted it over with. . . . So on June 4th or 5th, Fred came over with a big stack of money, about $6,000. That, plus the $5,000 I already had, made it $11,000. Fred said that he had set it up with some of his former employees, and that someone was going to be flying into Cleveland."

"Did he identify these people?"

"Not on that day. But the next day, June 6th, he met a guy

named Tony Ridle; he had flown into Cleveland from Phoenix. Fred had wrapped the money in a grocery bag, and he gave it to Ridle."

"Did you accompany Fred on this trip to Cleveland to meet Ridle?"

"No. I was doing a weekend sentence at the county workhouse for my DWI matter. I couldn't go; I was in jail."

"Did Fred mention any other names?"

"Yeah. He said that Ray Sesic—who used to work for him in the warehouse—had set it up. . . ."

"The murder?"

"Yeah."

"Okay, who was Tony Ridle?"

"Fred said that he owned a bar down in Phoenix. He got it after he left the Milo Corporation."

"Okay, who had Ridle gotten to handle the murder?"

"Supposedly Ridle's friends got some guys out of the Philadelphia mob."

"The Mafia?"

"Yeah. Dean was going to be out west at a conference. They were supposed to take care of him there; it was supposed to look like an accident."

"When was that?"

"Sometime in late June."

"So why wasn't he killed then?"

"I don't know, really. I do know that Fred thought he'd been ripped off."

"Because the murder had not been committed?"

"Yes, that's right. Then, on June 29th, sometime in the afternoon, Fred came over to my place. He told me that he'd been contacted by some guy in Cleveland, who said they needed more expense money."

"Did Fred pay it?"

"The money? Yeah, he gave me a personal check. . . ."

"A personal check?"

"Yeah. I cashed it here in Akron—at the BancOhio Wallhaven branch office over in west Akron."

"Was the check made out to you?"

"Yes."

"Okay, what'd they need the money for?"

"Fred told me that they wanted to buy a used car to drive to Florida. That's where Dean was—in Florida."

"How much was the check?"

"No more than $2,000."

"Go ahead."

"The next day, June 30th, I drove to the Holiday Inn near the Cleveland-Hopkins Airport and went to room number 136, like Fred told me. I knocked on the door, and some guy with fuzzy hair answered. I gave him the cash, and he took it and slammed the door."

"Do you know who the guy was?"

"No. I just did what I was told to do: deliver the package and drive back to Akron."

"Who put the package of stuff together?"

"Fred did. . . . He said that he was willing to pay an extra $5,000 bonus if the job was taken care of before July 5th."

"Why wasn't it?"

"I don't know, but word got back to Fred—either through Tony or Ray—that Dean had been killed in Florida."

"Killed? In Florida?"

"Yeah; then it turned out that Dean was still alive, so Fred really started to think that he was being ripped off. So I went out to see Terry again, out in Medina. We were doing some coke, and, while I was high, I wrote down Dean's name, home and work addresses, and all that."

"Were you still in touch with Fred, I mean, regularly?"

"All the time. He was calling me, always telling me about where Dean was and what he was doing. And he told me that Dean was going to be at some party on July 12th at either the Fairlawn Country Club or the Tangier restaurant. And me and Terry talked about this for maybe ten, fifteen minutes. The next day, I went over to this guy's house and gave him another package of information. This one I put together, based on what Fred was telling me. The guy was a friend of Terry's. He needed money and was trying to sell some airline tickets. . . ."

"And that was . . ."

"Tom Mitchell, I guess . . . but I didn't know it at the time."

"While all of this was going on, were you still attempting to

negotiate a settlement between Dean and Fred—with regard to
their lawsuits?"

"Yes."

"So what you're saying is that these negotiations were nothing
more than a smokescreen? Fred had no intention of selling out?
He was simply buying time until his brother was eliminated?"

"Essentially, yes, that's what was happening. But I didn't
know it. I thought the negotiations were an alternative to the
murder plot."

"So, after Tom Mitchell failed to kill Dean, what happened?"

"Fred really got weird. He even asked me to do it myself. He
wanted me to jog by Dean's house and shoot him as he was
coming out. Another time, after the court had agreed to another
continuance in July, Fred showed me a loaded revolver and told
me to ask Dean over. He wanted me to kill him in my home
and then plead 'temporary insanity.' He once told me that he
thought about doing it himself and pleading the same defense—
temporary insanity. . . . He must've had a dozen plots to kill
him."

"What about other members of the family? Did they know?
Were they involved?"

"I don't think any of them knew about this. I'm pretty sure
that none of them were involved. But Fred did tell me once,
after I was questioned by the police, to steer them toward
Lonnie Curtis."

"Fred wanted Lonnie to be the fall guy? And he didn't know
anything?"

"Right. Fred told me never to talk to anyone about this."

"What else?"

"Well, before Dean was taken care of, that's all I knew."

"What do you mean? What about the week before the
murder?"

"I don't know. Fred called me on August 7th or 8th and told
me that Dean was going to be in town and wanted me to set up
a meeting. He said he wanted to use my house; I told him,
'Sure.' "

"Did you know that Dean was going to be killed on August
10th?"

"No, I didn't; I had no idea. That was Sunday, right?"

"Right, Sunday."

"I had no idea. That was the day Fred and Dean were supposed to meet at my place. I wasn't in town that weekend; I was up in Cleveland with my son and girl friend; we went scuba diving up there. I got home sometime around three-thirty, four that afternoon, and Fred called me, saying that he had been trying to reach Dean all day, and couldn't. He asked me to call him, but I never even tried. . . . Then, Fred called me later on that night, maybe eight, and told me he still couldn't find Dean. He asked me if I had, and I just told him no. Then Fred asked me to come over to his house. I drove over there, and he was outside, standing on the sidewalk. He told me to turn my lights off, and then he gave me a piece of paper. He told me to call the numbers on the paper to see if anything had happened. . . ."

"Like whether Dean had been killed?"

"Yeah. I was supposed to call, and ask for Tony Ridle, I guess, but Fred wasn't making a lot of sense that night."

"So did you call Ridle or anyone else on the paper?"

"No, never did. I called Dean's office the next day and left a message with his secretary, telling her to have Dean call Fred in Charleston when he had a chance."

"So you still didn't know that Dean was dead?"

"No, I had no idea about it."

"And you never called the numbers on the paper?"

"Well . . . yeah, I guess I did. That night, Monday night— somewhere around five, five-thirty—I called one of the numbers from a pay phone. A guy with a deep voice named Tony answered. Tony said he didn't know anything either."

"So when did you find out about it—that Dean was dead?"

"I found out a couple of hours later when Sheriff Troutman called me, and then a couple of your men came out to see me."

"So what did you do after that?"

"I tried to call Fred in West Virginia, but couldn't get through. Then Lonnie called me around midnight and asked what was going on. I just told him that Dean had been shot. . . . Then Lonnie called back about an hour later and said that he had talked to Dean's priest, Father Bartz, who knew someone in the coroner's office. The priest told Lonnie that Dean had probably been killed by the mob. And so Lonnie was worried about protection."

"Lonnie was afraid he was going to be killed, too?"

"That's what he said."

"So when did you finally talk to Fred again?"

"He called me somewhere around one, two in the morning, Tuesday morning. Fred had already found out about it and was calling to tell me. I told him that I already knew about it, and that the police had been out here to see me about the Sunday meeting."

"What'd he say about that?"

"He really didn't say anything, except that he was coming back to Akron . . . and to divert attention to Lonnie."

"When was the next time you saw Fred?"

"Let's see . . . I saw Fred and Lonnie and Sophie on August 21st, or maybe it was the 22nd, in Dick Guster's office. Guster was calling you guys to tell you that they had taken polygraph tests and had passed. . . ."

"Did they really take the tests?"

"Yeah, I guess so. Lonnie and Sophie passed, supposedly, with no problem. But I understand that Fred passed by the skin of his teeth. . . ."

"Do you know what questions they were asked?"

"No, no idea."

"Did you and Fred talk about the murder at all?"

"No, but while we were in Guster's office, Fred took me in another room and we called Tony Ridle."

"What was the purpose of this call?"

"To find out how much more money he wanted."

"How much more?"

"A lot more. When I heard it over the phone, I couldn't believe it, so I asked him to repeat it. He said he wanted $39,900. I couldn't believe it, so I gave the phone to Fred. He couldn't believe it either."

"So what'd you think about that?"

"We both thought we were going to be blackmailed; they were trying to shake us down. That's what we thought."

"Did you pay it?"

"Well, they wanted $5,000 immediately. I took $2,000 from

my own bank account and borrowed $1,000 from my girl. Then Fred Milo wrote me a check for $1,500. He listed it as a loan to me."

"What did you do with the check?"

"Endorsed it and cashed it. A day or two later, I went to the Western Union office at 9th and Euclid Avenue in Cleveland and wired $4,500 to Ridle in Tempe, Arizona."

"Ninth and Euclid . . ."

"I know that I sent money from there at least twice."

"There was more?"

"Yeah, there was more."

"Can you tell us how much? Use your notes if you have to."

"Let's see . . . well, there was the initial $11,000 from Fred in June. I passed $2,000 at the Holiday Inn and another $6,000 was sent by Western Union. That's $19,000."

"Any more?"

"We sent another $12,000 total in two other trips to Western Union, and we sent another $20,000 from the Cleveland-Hopkins Airport. That's $32,000, plus $19,000; that's $51,000. . . . There might've been more."

"Where was Fred getting the money?"

"Well, I know on one occasion, he sold a diamond ring he gave to his wife. I remember that, because he was really mad. He thought he should've gotten more for it, you know."

"And it was all because Ridle was blackmailing you guys?"

"We were pretty sure that it wasn't just Ridle. Ray Sesic told Fred that Ridle was getting pressure from the guys who did the job. Ray said that Tony had to get a second mortgage on his bar to pay these guys off himself."

"The killers?"

"Yeah, I guess."

"Was all this money by check?"

"Most of it was."

"And how would the checks be made out? To Tony Ridle?"

"No, mostly to his band. He owns a band called 'Troutfishing in America.' The checks were made out to them to cover Tony, from what I understand. . . . Essentially, Fred had invested in Tony's band."

"Do you know the names of Milo's killers?"

"No, I don't. I just dealt with Fred and once or twice with Ridle. I never really talked to Sesic. But Ridle knows everyone. You're gonna have to get him."

"One thing puzzles me, Barry: what did you get out of all of this?"

"Nothing."

"No money?"

"No. In fact, Fred still owes me money for some other legal work."

"So why did you do it? Why did you get involved?"

"I guess I was just too loyal to Fred. He manipulated me, and I allowed him to do it. . . . And now I'm going to have to live with this for the rest of my life."

"One final question, Barry. At the scene of the murder, there was a whole bunch of cotton found all around Milo's face and mouth. Do you know how it got there?"

"No, I don't know."

"Do you know if anyone else was in the house, perhaps to administer first-aid or something?"

"No. I never heard anything like that."

At the conclusion of the interrogation, Boyd was asked to take a polygraph test to verify his story. Boyd agreed to do so—and passed. Later, in return for his cooperation, the charge of aggravated murder against him was reduced to conspiracy to commit aggravated murder. The charges of tampering with court records were also dropped. Like King, he would probably serve no more than four years.

22 | *"I'm glad it's over."*

"AKRON LAWYER BARRY BOYD who represented the brother and sister of slain millionaire, Constantine 'Dean' Milo, was charged Friday . . . in the death of the Bath Township businessman," the *Akron Beacon Journal* reported in its front page, banner headline story: MILO LAWYER IS CHARGED IN MURDER. "His arrest for the first time links members of the Milo family with Terry Lea King, a former Akron go-go dancer who is to go on trial Monday on a charge of complicity in the shooting."

Accompanying the story was a picture of Boyd—dressed in prison fatigues, handcuffed, and a "I-can't-believe-this-is-happen-ing-to-me" look on his face—being led down a jail corridor by two police officers.

Earlier that morning, Boyd had appeared defiant in court during his arraignment and had been ordered held under a $200,000 cash bond. The fact that Boyd was now cooperating with the police became a closely-guarded secret, but the charade was important to the investigation. The initial Boyd-King-Mitchell plot—which had clearly been unsuccessful—had been eclipsed by a second murder conspiracy. And, according to Boyd, this latter plot—consisting of Boyd, Fred Milo, Ray Sesic, Tony Ridle, and persons unknown—eventually led to the murder of Dean Milo. For tactical reasons, it was decided by Momchilov and his superiors that once Boyd's story had been completely confirmed, then Milo, Sesic, and Ridle would be arrested—simultaneously.

On Monday, December 15th, at 9:00 A.M., Terry Lea King—wearing a lace shirt, black cloth skirt and sweater, and twenty-five pounds heavier since her October arrest—pleaded guilty to conspiracy to commit aggravated murder before Judge Bayer. Soon after, informant Jack Taylor received a $15,000 check from the Milo reward fund, administered by George Tsarnas and Bill Dear.

In the meantime, Bill Lewis and Rich Munsey had had Boyd quietly released from the county jail and driven to the Holiday Inn near the Cleveland-Hopkins Airport. There, Boyd showed the officers the room where he had taken the $2,000 payment in July. From the motel's records, they learned that the room had been registered to a "Ray Rodriguez" of Tempe, Arizona. "Rodriguez," which the officers presumed was an assumed name, had paid cash for his one-day stay.

While at the airport, they also went to the American Airlines office and slapped down another subpoena, which gained them access to the records of two deliveries made to Ridle on August 28th and October 7th. The sender was not identified. They made copies of the orders and requested copies of the receipts in Arizona.

Returning Boyd to his cell, they obtained a subpoena for the Western Union office on South Main Street in downtown Akron, and found a $1,000 money order to Anthony Ridle in Tempe from Boyd. Boyd, according to office records, had refused to leave his address or telephone number.

The following day, Lewis and Munsey returned to Cleveland and presented a subpoena to the manager of the Western Union office at 9th and Euclid streets. There, as Boyd had indicated, they found two more money orders sent from Boyd to Ridle. The first, on August 22nd, was for $4,500; the second, for $900, had been sent on September 5th. The two officers then drove to Columbus and subpoenaed the telephone records of Capital Beauty Supply and Ray Sesic—which showed numerous calls between Columbus and Tempe.

A paper trail in the Milo murder investigation was finally taking shape.

On Thursday, December 18th, Dear and Momchilov brought Boyd to the detective bureau and had him telephone Fred Milo at his office in Stow. The call was recorded by Dear.

"Is Fred there?" Boyd asked the receptionist.

"Yes, he is. May I ask who's calling?"

"Barry."

"Just a moment."

After a short pause, another voice came on the line, "Good afternoon, this is Mr. Milo's secretary. He's not answering his phone. Could I take a message?"

Then another voice came on the line. "Hello?"

"There he is," said the secretary.

"Fred?" asked Barry.

"No, it's Lonnie," Curtis replied.

"Hi, Lonnie. Barry."

"Oh, hi, Barry."

"I called Fred . . . about helping out on bond."

"Well, I . . ."

"Where is he?"

"You'll have to call [inaudible]. We've been told not to talk."

"Who told you not to talk . . . because Fred knows I helped him a month or so ago when he really needed it. These guys haven't talked to me at all."

"Barry, you will please have to talk with him."

"Thank you."

Meanwhile, down in Columbus, Lewis and Munsey were conducting physical surveillance on Capital Beauty Supply—a small, old brown building near the downtown area. When nothing happened there after several hours, they drove to the home of Ray Sesic, who lived in nearby London, Ohio. His home was a small, gray Cape Cod, freshly painted, with a vegetable garden in back and a tulip patch in front. Through a window, the two officers saw Sesic talking on the telephone. Assured they could easily locate Sesic, Lewis and Munsey returned to Akron.

* * *

On Friday morning, December 19th, a meeting was called by Duvall to coordinate the simultaneous arrests of Fred Milo, Tony Ridle, and Ray Sesic. While Milo and Sesic could easily be found and taken, the Arizona officers were having trouble finding Ridle. The decision was made at the meeting that if Ridle could not be located by Monday, December 22nd, the officers would proceed with the arrests of Milo and Sesic. If Ridle was located, Milo and Sesic would be taken into custody immediately—before they were alerted of Ridle's arrest.

That night, at about 10:00 P.M., the word came from Detective Richard Craven in Scottsdale, Arizona. Ridle had been arrested at his mother-in-law's home and had been booked. Momchilov sent word to Lewis and Munsey, who returned to Sesic's home. Upon arrival, the two officers charged up to his door, backed up by other Summit and Madison counties law enforcement officers. Hearing the pounding on his front door, Sesic, who had been drinking, answered; he was promptly arrested. Offering no resistance and showing no emotion, Sesic simply picked up his jacket and kissed his wife goodbye.

On December 20th, at 1:00 A.M., Momchilov, Dear, and a delegation of officers from the Summit County Sheriff's Department and the Bath Police arrived at Fred Milo's home with a warrant for his arrest. The Milos had just returned to their house after a party, and their babysitter was pulling out of the driveway as the car caravan parked in front of his residence. The mood among the officers was solemn as Momchilov knocked on the door.

Kathy Milo answered.

"Is your husband home, Mrs. Milo?" Momchilov asked.

"He's upstairs. Can I help you?"

Without answering, Momchilov and the others entered the house. Momchilov went to the staircase and asked Milo to come down. As he walked down the staircase, Milo asked Momchilov, "Who are all these people in my house?" Momchilov reintroduced himself and the small dragnet. "We have a warrant for your arrest, Mr. Milo." As Milo was read his rights, his face quickly turned pale. Milo interrupted, "I have to go to the bathroom."

Momchilov nodded his head and accompanied Fred back upstairs. "I don't want to say anything," Milo told him.

"Don't," Momchilov replied sharply. "We'll be happy to call your attorney, or you can do it."

Now a little confused and spaced-out, Fred mumbled, "No, I guess I'll have my wife call him."

"Were you at a party tonight?" Momchilov asked, making general conversation.

"I can't answer that. I have nothing to say."

Milo was handcuffed, driven to the county jail, and imprisoned, charged with arranging the murder of his brother.

Meantime, en route from London back to Akron, Ray Sesic asked if he could stop and go to the bathroom at a nearby service station. Munsey, who accompanied him, asked how he felt. With his eyes starting to well up, Sesic replied, "You know, I'm glad it's over."

23 | "He asked me if I'd do him 'a big favor.'"

WEARING A PAIR of brown suede shoes, blue jeans, a red pullover shirt, and a dark blue jacket, Sesic was clearly nervous as he sat in the back seat of the car. With Munsey driving, Lewis asked, "On a scale from one to ten, what was your involvement in this case? But, remember if you answer, it can be held against you."

"If I answer that," Sesic replied with a half-smile, "I might as well tell you everything."

Lewis again read Sesic his rights, but Sesic said he understood them completely. "I'm ready to talk," he said quietly.

A few minutes later, Sesic began. "Sometime in mid-May, Fred Milo came over to Capital Beauty Supply and asked me if I knew anyone who could do him 'a big favor.' A real big favor. I asked him what he meant. Then Fred said, you know, 'to have someone permanently removed.'"

"Did he say it was Dean?" Lewis asked.

"Not then, but I had a pretty good idea of who he meant."

"Okay, go on."

"I told him I'd check around and see if I could find someone. Then, later on that month, Fred and me were together, and he says, 'Did you find anyone to do that big favor for me?' I told him I hadn't. That's when he told me that it was Dean he wanted killed. So I called a buddy of mine, Tony Ridle, over

197

in Arizona, and I told him that Fred was looking to have somebody offed. I asked if he knew of anybody who could do it, if
he knew of anyone who might be interested. Tony said he'd
check around and get back to me. A couple of days later, Tony
calls me and says he's got two guys. For $22,000 cash, they'd do
it. I then called Fred and told him what Tony said. After that,
Fred pretty much dealt directly with Tony. I was only called
when one of them was trying to reach the other. I was a go-
between."

"Like how?"

"Oh, like on the day before Dean was killed, Fred told me
to call Tony and tell him that Dean was in Akron."

"Okay. Tony Ridle—what do you know about the guy?"

"We're good friends. I met him around '72, while he was
working at some trucking company. Later on, he came to work
at Milo B&B over on Allen Road as their traffic manager; I
helped him get the job, introduced him around. I guess he quit
at Milo around '76, '77, to move out west. We lived together
for, maybe, six months before he went to Arizona and opened
his bar."

"He owns a bar?"

"Yeah, some place called the Star System. I know that he
hasn't been doing too well with it."

"Does he do any drugs or anything?"

"I know he's an epileptic, and he's been on Dilantin. I guess
that's supposed to control it."

"Why did you leave Milo?"

"I'm still there."

"I mean, why did you leave Milo here in Akron."

"Dean, you know, Dean thought I was being a spy for Fred
and Lonnie."

"Were you?"

"I don't know. I'd hear things, and tell them what I heard.
Does that make me a spy or a gossip? I never cared too much
for Dean anyway. I never thought he was real fair with me."

"Is that why you got involved in this?"

"It's hard to say what I was thinking back then. I guess,
partly, it'd have to be. But, mainly, I was really loyal to Fred. I
considered him to be a good friend."

"When did you find out that Dean was dead?"

"Tony called me Sunday night, August 10th, and told me that the job was done. Even though I wasn't sure, I immediately called Fred Milo and let him know what Tony had said. I knew Dean was really dead when my wife called me on Monday night, August 11th. She said that Dean had been found that afternoon."

"Did you talk to Fred about it after that?"

"Not until, maybe, September. Fred was down at Capital, and he told me that some guy named Dear, a private eye, had been brought into the investigation."

"Anything else?"

"Not really . . . except he asked me if there was any problem with Tony Ridle. I told him that I didn't know of any."

"One final question, Ray," Lewis asked. "Tell me, was anyone else in the family involved in this?"

"No," Sesic replied. "I don't think so. I work for Lonnie and Sophie Curtis, and if they were involved in any way I'd be really surprised."

"So you never talked to Lonnie about this?"

"Never."

Later, like Boyd, Sesic was asked to take a polygraph test. He, too, agreed to do so—and passed. Also, like Boyd, in return for his cooperation with the prosecutor, Sesic was later permitted to plead guilty to the lesser conspiracy charge.

On Saturday morning, Lewis and Munsey subpoenaed the telephone records of Fred Milo's home and office, both in Bath and Charleston. They then drove to BancOhio and subpoenaed his bank records. They also contacted his attorney, Dick Guster, and asked him for his cooperation regarding the remaining civil suits filed by Milo in his attempt to take control of the family corporation. Guster indicated that he would cooperate whenever possible.

Meanwhile, after spending the night behind bars, Fred Milo was arraigned—and, not unexpectedly, pleaded not guilty to aggravated murder. Despite the protests of his attorney, George Pappas, Milo's bond was set at a record two million dollars. A hearing on the possibility of reducing the bond was set for

December 22nd. Throughout the forty-five-minute court hearing, Milo, looking worn and angry, remained silent.

A few hours later, one week after it had reported the arrest of Barry Boyd, *The Akron Beacon Journal* ran a headline story—which stretched across the entire top of the front page—BROTHER IS ARRESTED IN MILO SLAYING. Included was a photograph of Fred, up against a jailhouse fence, being frisked by a uniformed officer. He, too, had that "This-must-be-a-bad-dream" look on his face.

The story also reported the arrests of Sesic and Ridle.

Although the police were still mum on Boyd's role in the investigation, both the press and the public—as well as his alleged co-conspirators—generally assumed that Boyd had flipped and turned state's evidence. Because of the public fervor over the case, there was concern for Boyd's safety, as a result of rumors that he, too, might be the target for a contract killing. To protect his chief witness, Momchilov, with judicial permission, quietly authorized Boyd's release from the county jail. He was placed in a small apartment on Akron's west side. During his stay there, he was under twenty-four-hour guard by sheriff's deputies and members of Dear's personal staff.

Upon hearing that Tony Ridle—in jail in Phoenix, Arizona—was planning to hire an attorney to fight extradition, Dear, Munsey, and Zuch flew to Arizona, hoping to apply pressure on him to reconsider.

Ridle looked smug as Detective Craven introduced him to his three visitors from Akron. "I'm not talking," Ridle insisted. "I'm not saying anything. My attorney will do all of my talking."

Once alone with Ridle, Dear jammed his finger into his chest and threatened, "Ridle, you may fight extradition! You may think you're a big ass! But let me tell you something: I'll stay on your frame from day's dawn to day's end! I'll stay here as long as I have to! I will eat you alive—mentally, physically, financially! I can outwait you, because you're going home. . . !"

As the others moved back into the room after Dear's tirade, Ridle appeared to be stunned by his remarks and to be having second thoughts. Then, eavesdropping on a conversation between Munsey and Craven, Ridle heard Munsey say, "I think we better go talk to Harry."

Suddenly and mysteriously, Ridle changed his mind. "Okay, I'm willing to talk!" Ridle exclaimed. "But you gotta offer me something."

Puzzled by Ridle's dramatic turnabout, Zuch told him he would offer him the same deal he'd given Boyd and Sesic: permission for a reduced plea of conspiracy, in return for his cooperation. Ridle agreed, waived extradition, and started talking.

Thirty-two-year-old Tony Ridle—who, like Sesic, had no previous criminal record—had worked for Dean and Fred Milo for two years before moving to Tempe and starting the Star System, a disco bar, in 1978. A short man, with green eyes and long brown hair, Ridle—one of six children from a deeply religious Roman Catholic family—began his confession.

"Why did you get involved?" asked Munsey.

"Because Dean was a despicable person, a terrible man. He was trying to take a business, built by his entire family, and use it for his own purposes—while pushing everyone else in the family out."

"So you did it because you hated Dean?"

"That, and because I was loyal to Fred."

"Why's everyone feel so loyal to this guy anyway?"

"I don't know. I was one of the few friends Fred had. He's basically a loner. Plus, he's always been loyal to me. He's been a good friend."

"Okay, Tony, who was the first person to approach you . . . to become involved in the Milo murder?"

"Ray."

"Sesic?"

"Yeah, Ray Sesic. He called me up last May and asked me if I'd do him a big favor. He said he needed a hit man—that Fred wanted somebody to kill Dean."

"And you knew Ray Sesic pretty well?"

"Oh, sure, I met him back around '72 when he was an assistant buyer for Milo B&B. Sesic helped me get my job there; I was Milo's traffic manager, and I handled Milo's trucks and drivers, about eight of them."

"And who was your supervisor?"

"Well, I answered to both Fred and Dean—but mostly to Fred since Dean wasn't around that much."

"Did you ever live with Sesic?"

"Well, yeah, I guess. He moved in with me and my wife when he was having some marital problems . . . that was around 1977, just before we moved to Arizona."

"When did you leave Milo?"

"In the fall of '77, October."

"Why?"

"I resigned on my own; there was no pressure. I just couldn't take the cold weather in Akron anymore; and the pressure around the Milo Company was incredible. I just wanted an easier life. . . . They threw a dinner for me when I left."

"So you left on pretty good terms with people?"

"Yes, I did."

"Okay, go ahead . . . Sesic called you and said he needed a hit . . ."

"A hit man . . . yeah. Well, I knew I could trust Ray. And he was telling me that Fred was getting desperate. He was running out of money, and Dean was going to take everything away from him. Then I talked to Fred. He told me that Dean was coming to Arizona in three days, and he wanted to talk about 'the big favor.' He said he wanted Dean's murder to look like an accident; he wanted it done while Dean was in Arizona for a convention."

"Did you agree to help out?"

"Well, I still felt a lot of loyalty to both Ray and Fred. . . . So a couple of days after I talked to them, I contacted a guy named Harry Knott, who said he could handle it."

"Harry . . ."

"Knott, K-N-O-T-T, Knott."

"And who is Harry Knott?"

"He was handling the vending machine business in my bar. You know, pinball machines, cigarettes, stuff like that. He worked with his brother-in-law, a guy named Frank Piccirilli.

Their company was called Action Amusement, and we worked together."

"Describe Harry Knott."

"Oh, I don't know . . . He's, maybe twenty-eight, five-ten, 200 pounds. He drives a green Ford LTD with Arizona plates. He has been living with some woman for a long time. . . . He used to be a drill sergeant in the Marines, but left the service when he got a bleeding ulcer. I remember that he went to Williams Air Force base for treatments."

"Was he from Arizona?"

"No, he and Frank were both from Philadelphia."

"Okay, go ahead."

"Well, I was having some financial difficulties with my bar; I was starting to lose money. So Harry and Frank came in, and we became partners."

"In your bar?"

"Yeah, we split the profits. . . . They did a good job. I started making money after they came in. Then a new place was set up, a disco. It was built nearby and took away a lot of my business. A new, pretty seedy crowd started coming to our place, and it started to fall apart. We did everything to try and keep going. We remodeled, changed the music format to rock 'n' roll, everything. Then Harry said he wanted to take over and see what he could do on his own. The Star System wasn't going anywhere. I was even looking for a buyer. So I let him do it. Harry talked about getting a second mortgage on the place to get us even—that was worth $39,000."

"When did Harry Knott start running the business?"

"May, last May."

"Okay, so Harry said he could handle the contract?"

"Yeah. So he flew to Philadelphia that same day. He was gone, maybe, ten or eleven hours. He left in the morning and got back that night. I remember that he flew American Airlines and bought his ticket—with cash—at the airport. I also think he was using the name 'Paul Johnson.' That was one of his aliases. . . . When Harry got back, he told me that the job could be done for $12,000—half up front for expenses, and the other half within forty-eight hours after the job was done."

"Twelve thousand?"

"Right, half now, the other half later. So I called Ray in Columbus and told him that it would cost $22,000. I added $10,000, just in case there was any trouble."

"Did you tell Harry you were doing that?"

"Oh, yeah. He said, 'Fine. . . .' So Ray said he'd talk to Fred. Then Fred called me back, I think, the next day, sometime in the evening. He told me to grab a plane and get to Cleveland and to tell Ray the time and flight number and all of that. Fred said he'd meet me there, and he'd have the money then—you know, the first half, $11,000. I went back and told Harry what Fred had said. Harry told me to pay for the ticket in cash and to use an assumed name. I got the reservation and then called Ray, telling him the flight number and stuff."

"What day did you fly into Cleveland?"

"I don't remember the exact date, but it was like on a Tuesday or Wednesday in June. I flew from Phoenix Sky Harbor Airport to Cleveland-Hopkins. As I went through the gate in Cleveland, I saw Fred. He was holding a black briefcase. We started walking down that long hallway, and, while we were walking, Fred handed me the briefcase; he said the money was inside. I remember that he asked me if everything was going to go okay. I told him, 'Sure.' "

"How long did you stay with Fred? Did you leave the airport with him?"

"No, he had to get back to work and left right away. I just took another flight back to Phoenix. I was only in Cleveland for about ten, fifteen minutes. I flew right back to Arizona. I went home, cleaned up, and went to the bar. Harry was there, and I gave him the money."

"How much?"

"I gave him the $11,000 Fred gave me. Harry gave me back $1,000."

"What were the denominations of the cash?"

"Hell! Just about everything. Fifties wrapped in amounts of $1,000 packages. There were hundreds, twenties, even fives. The money was in a white envelope in the briefcase, along with a picture of Dean Milo. Harry took the rubber bands off when he counted it."

"Did Harry tell you about the mechanics of the hit?"

"Yeah, that night. He said that there were three guys coming to Phoenix—two hit men and one middleman. They were going to buy a used car in Phoenix, using an assumed name, which I never knew."

"Were these guys coming in from Philadelphia?"

"Yeah, Harry was supposed to watch over them while they were here."

"Do you know their names? That's important."

"No."

"Okay, then what? What did you do after you heard about these guys?"

"Then I called Ray. He was the one who gave me the details of Dean's trip to Arizona."

"And when was that supposed to be?"

"Sometime in late June, I think. He was going to be staying at some hotel—I think the Regency—in Scottsdale. . . . So I got right back to Harry and told him, and he said he would take care of it. Then the day before Dean was supposed to arrive, Harry told me that his friends from Philadelphia were in Phoenix and were buying a car. On the day Dean got there, Fred called me and told me. I told Harry at the club. He left and went to meet the guys from Philadelphia. . . . So they started following Dean, but they couldn't get him; he was never alone. He was always with somebody; they just couldn't do it. The guys from Philadelphia stayed around Phoenix for a couple of days after Dean left, and then they flew back home. I called Ray and told him what happened, and he said he'd pass the information along to Fred. Fred then called me and said that Dean was going to be in Ohio. He wanted the guys to come to Ohio and do it. He kept saying that he wanted it to look like an accident. I got ahold of Dean's home and work addresses and gave them to Harry. I remember that I also drew a diagram of the Milo warehouse for him."

"So what did Harry say?"

"He said that the three guys were going to fly to Ohio, and he'd meet them there. Harry used the name 'Paul Johnson' again and flew to Akron. While he was there, I got a call from Fred. He said that Dean was in Clearwater, Florida, and he gave me the address. Right after that, Harry called me from Ohio and said he needed more money. He said he'd be at the Holiday Inn, near the Cleveland-Hopkins Airport. He gave me his room and telephone numbers. I remember that he said the three guys were with him, and that they had bought another car in Ohio."

"What happened to the first one?"

"Oh, they abondoned it in Phoenix after Dean left town. . . . So I called Ray and told him what Harry said. Ray said he'd call Fred and took down the information Harry had given to me. About a half-hour later, Ray called me back and said that everything was taken care of—that the $2,000 would get to them that day. I then called Harry and confirmed."

"Did they get the money?"

"Yeah, because Harry and the three guys flew to Clearwater and stayed there for a few days. They still couldn't get close to Dean—close enough to make it look like an accident—so Harry flew back to Phoenix and left the others behind in Florida. Then the next day—this is sometime in early July—Harry got a telephone call, and while he was on the phone I heard him say, 'Thank God!' He hung up and told me it was over; Dean had been killed."

"Wait a minute! This is . . . They said Dean had been killed in Florida in early July?"

"That's what they said. Dean was dead. . . . So I called Ray Sesic and told him. The next day, I got a call from Fred, and he yelled, 'What are you trying to pull?' I asked him what he was talking about. He said, 'Dean's back in Akron!' I couldn't believe it! I told Fred that I would get back to him after I found out what was going on."

"So you went to Harry?"

"Yeah, and Harry told me that they killed the wrong guy."

"Killed the wrong guy?"

"Yeah, they killed some guy who looked like Dean Milo. Supposedly, it was a hit-and-run in Clearwater."

Munsey trembled momentarily when he heard that a second murder had been committed, resulting from nothing more than a simple case of mistaken identity. "You mean there's some family living down in Florida that's wondering right now why their daddy was murdered!" he shouted. Ridle said nothing and simply shook his head. "That's what Harry told me," he murmured. "They didn't know who he was."

"What did Fred say when he heard this?" Munsey asked, with anger in his voice.

"Fred said that he'd pay a $10,000 bonus if they would get Dean within a week—before their lawsuit went to court. After what happened in Florida—the wrong guy and all—Harry wanted to get out, but the $10,000 bonus kept him in. We all needed the money badly. . . . So Fred started calling me a lot, calling me at the bar. He mostly called with information about Dean's whereabouts. Then the court case was postponed, and Fred was really upset. He kept the pressure on me. I told him that Harry wanted to know when Dean was going to be staying in one place for a couple of weeks. But Fred kept the pressure on; he was pushing real hard. He wanted Dean dead—and, I mean, right now. He kept on asking, 'Why hasn't this been done?' I didn't know what to say; I wasn't in control. I just kept telling him to hold on. Finally, Fred called me in early August, and he said that Dean was going to be in Akron for a while. I called Harry, and he called Philadelphia. Then he called me back and said it would all be over in a week. Harry came back to me in a few days and said it was finished. This time, Dean was really dead."

"When was this?"

"I don't remember exactly when, but I called Ray and told him. Ray asked how he could be sure, and I told him that some-one was going to have to find the body."

"Did you talk to Harry about it? I mean, what did he say? How did it happen?"

"Harry told me on Sunday night, 'Dean Milo has been shot twice in the head. It happened at his house. The job is com-pleted.' A couple of days later, he called and said that the two guys who did it were in Phoenix and wanted their money. Harry wanted the other $11,000, since the first $11,000 was used up for expenses."

"So Harry wanted another $11,000, in addition to the second half of the payment?"

"Right. So I called Ray and told him. He called Fred, and

Fred told him that he was under a lot of pressure and couldn't get any money for a couple of weeks. I told Harry, and he was mad—but he said he thought he could stall if there was more money involved."

"Did Harry ever tell you anything about the murder itself?"

"He told me that Dean had been shot in the head at his home; that Dean was really scared . . . and that Harry was really pissed off because they threw the gun in the woods somewhere near the house."

"Okay. Now the money, what about the money?"

"I called Ray back and told him that I took that second mortgage out on my bar. That wasn't true, but I was desperate. That's when I got a call from someone saying he represented Fred—Barry Boyd, I guess—and I told him that it was going to cost another $39,900. Fred got on the phone and asked what this $39,900 was all about. I told him, and he said that someone would get back to me. Okay? So the guys in Philadelphia started pressuring Harry for some more money. I already had everything I had soaked into this; there was nothing more I could do. So I called Ray again. And then Fred wired me $4,500 by Western Union. I picked up the money at the Western Union office in Tempe."

"So you gave this money to Harry?"

"Yeah, but it wasn't enough. He wanted more. So I called Fred at home, and he was really pissed at me for calling him there. He just wouldn't talk to me. But later that night, he called me back; he went someplace to make the call. I told him that I needed more money, and he said he'd get back to me. A couple of days later, I got a call from someone, but it wasn't Fred; it was someone else. The guy said that he was sending me $10,000 by American Airlines, and that it would be in my hands the next day. I said okay and got all the information. I drove to the airport with Frank Piccirilli, and he knew what I was going to pick up. We got into the terminal, and I signed for the package—which I then gave to Frank. He put it in the trunk of his Cadillac and then dropped me off."

"What did the package look like?"

"It was a small, brown package, with my name on it. I signed my own name when I received it."

"And what happened to the money?"

"I don't know after Frank took it. All I know is that Harry didn't pressure for more money for at least a week. The guys from Philadelphia went back home. Then I got a call from Fred. He told me that he was going to take over the company on October 20th, and that all unpaid bills could be dealt with at that time. I told this to Harry, and he relayed it to the people in Philadelphia."

"What happened on the 20th?"

"I don't know. I called Ray, and then Fred called me. He said that there was some trouble, and he hadn't been able to take over the company. I then told him that, regardless, I needed more money. A couple of days later, Fred called me and said he was sending me a ring, worth $40,000, again by American Airlines. So I went to the terminal and picked it up, again signing for it in my own name."

"Who was it from?"

"Fred Milo."

"Did Frank go with you again?"

"No, Harry came himself. I gave the ring to him."

"What did he get for the ring?"

"Well, he took it to five or six places, trying to get the best price."

"What did the ring look like?"

"Three-carat emerald-cut diamonds, with VS-2 quality. There were nineteen smaller stones around one big diamond."

"Where did he finally sell it?"

"He sold it to Sandoval-Marshall in Scottsdale. They gave him $10,600 for it."

"Do you remember the date?"

"No, it was on a Friday or Saturday morning in late September, early October."

"How did the jeweler pay Harry Knott?"

"Partially by check, partially in cash."

"Who was the check made out to?"

"Harry J. Knott."

"Okay, what about your own financial situation?"

"Well, Harry had given me around $1,500, and I had been talking to some people about investing in my band. . . ."

"Like who?"

"Well, Ray Sesic, but he didn't have any money. And then I talked to Fred Milo, and he said he'd send me a contract for $25,000—as a payoff for the Dean debt."

"What was the name of your band?"

" 'Troutfishing in America.' The contract was in the name of Heatwave Management."

"When did you talk to Fred and Ray about this investment?"

"It was around October 1st. I kept pushing Fred for more money. He just told me to send him the $25,000 contract with Heatwave Management. So I did. Fred kept two copies, and I gave Harry one."

"What about the guys in Philadelphia? Were they still impatient?"

"Oh, yeah, Harry said he got a call from them, and they were tacking on another $500 for each day that the payment was late. At that time, the outstanding debt to them was only about $3,000 to $4,000. So I called Ray Sesic and told him that I needed $7,500 right away. I was in L.A. on business for the band, so when Ray called about sending the money, I had my wife pick it up from American Airlines. That was on October 8th."

"Did your wife know what was going on?"

"No, she didn't know anything, absolutely nothing."

"So what did she do with the money?"

"I told her to go to the bar and give $4,500 to Harry Knott."

"I thought there was $7,500?"

"I kept the other $3,000. Harry didn't know about that at first, and he got real pissed off when he found out about it. He called me in L.A. and started climbing all over me. I just told him that I had to worry about the bar and the band; I needed the money, too. Then Harry told me that he was afraid that the guys in Philadelphia were going to kill him, and that he had been keeping records about the money. Then I got mad and told Harry that I was fed up with him. We started shouting at each other, and then Harry told me to get more money. Well, at that point, I was starting to get scared. So I called Ray and told him I was getting caught right in the middle of all of this. I told him to tell Fred to send me more money—the balance of the $25,000 for the band."

"Did Fred send the money?"

"Yeah, he sent it to our post office box in Tempe. . . ."

"Our?"

"Yeah, me and Harry Knott. . . . Harry told me that he got two checks, totaling $12,000. He signed them and deposited them in our account for the bar. Then Harry gave the guys in Philadelphia $7,000, paid off some bills at the bar, and then called me again and said it still wasn't enough. I told Harry to fuck off. Then, in November, Harry called me and said that the guys in Philadelphia had called him and threatened to kill him. He told me that if I didn't get more money, he was going to give me to them."

"Harry was going to have you killed?"

"Yeah, well . . . he was going to turn them on me. He said he wanted another $20,000. By that time, my bar was completely shut down; the phones were turned off. So what could I do? I called Fred from a pay phone and told him that—if I didn't get another $20,000—I'd be killed. Fred seemed to want to help, and he started talking about the band. He said he'd call me back. Then I called Harry. Harry said he didn't want to wait anymore and wanted to call Fred himself. So I said fine and gave him Fred's number. He came back a few minutes later and told me that Fred said the money would be in Arizona within three days. A $20,000 cashier's check, made out to me, would be arriving by the end of the week."

"How did the check come?"

"Federal Express; it came to my home. . . . I signed the check over to Harry. He got $4,500 in cash and then had a bunch of cashier's checks made out. He cashed them at other banks."

"How much did he send to Philadelphia?"

"Well, he said we owed them $18,000, so he and I split the remaining $2,000. I then told Harry that the bills with the band were $1,800, so he gave me the entire $2,000."

"As a loan?"

"Of course."

"Okay, when was the next time you talked to Fred?"

"A few days after the money arrived. Fred called me and said that the $20,000 payment had put him in a helluva bind. He said I should expect some heat over this—that someone might start asking questions about it. Fred also mentioned that he was really in a financial jam and needed to come up with $280,000 in a short period of time for business and didn't know where he was going to get it."

"Okay, all in all, how much money was received for the death of Dean Milo: $77,600?"

"Yeah, that's right. That's the figure I came up with."

"Can you tell me if anyone else in the family was involved?"

"I asked that to Ray once. He told me that it was just Fred; no one else was involved within the family."

"One final question," Lewis continued. "Why did you decide, all of a sudden, to talk to us? What caused that?"

"Well, you got Harry Knott, didn't you?"

"Harry Knott? No, we don't have him."

Ridle was astonished. "I thought you guys were putting me on in here; that stuff about knowing nothing about Knott."

"No, we don't have him. Why did you think we did?"

"Munsey. Just after me and Dear talked, I heard Munsey out in the hallway tell Detective Craven that he was going to 'go talk to Harry.' That wasn't Harry Knott?"

Starting to laugh, Munsey and Craven looked at each other. Then Munsey said, "No, Tony. We were gonna go talk to Harry Balion, the extradition officer for the Maricopa County Sheriff's Department."

Shaking his head, even Ridle had to produce a reluctant smile, as everyone in the room erupted with laughter.

Like Boyd and Sesic, Ridle took and passed a lie detector test.

When Ridle was placed back in his cell, Munsey telephoned Momchilov and summarized Ridle's statement, including the information about the alleged "mistaken identity" murder in Florida. Momchilov immediately called a friend he'd made on the Clearwater police force during his trip to Florida to interview Maggie Milo. "Do you have anything about a hit-skip in the Clearwater vicinity, sometime in early July?"

"Hold on, Larry," the officer replied. "Let me check the computer."

Several minutes passed. When the officer returned to the

phone, he asked Momchilov to give him a few hours to do some further checking.

At 5:15 P.M., the Clearwater officer called. "Hello, Larry? Nothing. I have absolutely nothing on this hit-and-run. Are you sure it really happened?"

When Momchilov hung up the receiver, he began wondering the same thing.

24 | *"This might be your man."*

ON MONDAY, December 22nd—after the court of appeals had reduced Fred Milo's bond from two million dollars to $200,000 —his attorney, George Pappas, came to the sheriff's booking desk and presented a receipt from the Akron Municipal Court for $200,000. Somehow, Fred had managed to raise $200,000 cash. After receiving confirmation from the clerk of courts, the booking officer released Fred Milo from jail.

The following day, at 11:30 P.M., Rich Craven of the Scottsdale Police called Munsey at his home. Munsey was half asleep when the call came, but quickly regained his senses when Craven told him that he had recovered a receipt for $7,000 cash and a copy of a cancelled check for $3,600 from Sandoval Marshall Jewelers in Scottsdale—for the purchase of a diamond ring. According to Craven, the check had been made out to, and endorsed by, Harry J. Knott. A second endorsement appeared on the back of the check underneath Knott's name, "Molly Triola," who had signed on behalf of Ridle's bar, the Star System.

"The owner of the store took the ring apart and sold it to a jeweler in New York for $11,600," Craven explained.

214

"What about the setting?" Munsey asked. "If we can get the setting, it's evidence against Fred Milo. Go back, and try to get the setting!"

"There won't be any problem with that."

"Why's that? How do you know?"

"Because it's over at the jeweler's right now; they still have it. When you guys come up from Akron, we'll go pick it up."

Now wide awake, Munsey nearly jumped out of his bed. "What about Knott?" he asked.

"I went out to his place today," Craven continued. "He wasn't around, so I went next door and talked to his neighbor. She said that he and the woman he lives with—a Margaret Thompson—went to Disneyland with their two kids."

"When will they be back?"

"She says they'd return some time around the first of the year."

"Is she being square with you?"

"I think so. I went back and checked his mailbox. There was stuff in there, dated December 19th, so I think she's telling the truth. I'll keep in touch with you on anything I hear on Knott. Rich, I've been checking out Knott's associates—and I came up with the name John Harris."

"John Harris?"

"Yeah, John Harris. And we can't find him."

While Craven couldn't locate Harris, he had no trouble finding information on him. Harris was described as five-ten and two hundred and seventy-five pounds. Using his sources, Craven learned that Harris had compiled a lengthy arrest record, consisting of twenty-three separate arrests since 1967, when he'd been sixteen years old. He had been picked up for everything from hit-and-run to grand theft auto, to possession of narcotics, to aggravated assault. There was every reason to believe that Harris was a ruthless, violent man.

In addition, Harris had worked as a loan shark, juice collector, numbers runner, and pimp for the Farentino mob in Philadelphia, a low-level underworld family operating in the Kensington and south Philadelphia areas. Harris had returned to

Arizona in early 1977 and begun his own vending machine business, initially concentrating on pinball machines, but later getting into half-dollar slot machines. On the side, Harris was also dealing cocaine and speed. He was generally known as a fast-talking, high-pressure salesman, who could get anyone anything from a new television to M-16 rifles. For a while, Harris had become a business partner of Harry Knott in his vending machine company—but Knott later bought out Harris for $12,000.

During this Arizona phase of the investigation as the Milo case began to open up, Dear's obsession with, and personalization of, the probe intensified, and his almost fanatical zealousness began to take its toll on his home life. His wife of less than a year had grown impatient with his work and activities, and demanded he return home. Dear refused, whereupon his wife flew to Arizona and confronted her husband with an ultimatum. He had to choose: it was either her or his work. She demanded that he give up his business and return to Texas, adding that she wanted him to come to work for her father, who owned a steel products company near Dallas.

Dear balked and asked for time. She agreed, but made it clear that the clock was ticking and his time was running out. For the time being, she remained in Phoenix, occasionally living with Dear in the family's local condominium.

On Saturday, January 3rd, 1981, just after noon, Momchilov, Lewis, and Munsey, along with Fred Milo's attorneys, went to Fred's home with a search warrant. Fred was present when the entourage arrived and, after speaking with Pappas, agreed to give the detectives several cancelled checks he made out to Barry Boyd and Tony Ridle.

Two hours into the search, while in Milo's basement, Munsey discovered a receipt from a local jeweler—for the purchase of an emerald-cut diamond ring, with the same setting recovered by Craven in Scottsdale. According to the receipt, Fred had purchased the ring in 1977 for $19,500.

*   *   *

Two days later, Craven telephoned Munsey: Harry Knott had called him. "What did he say?" Munsey asked.

"He said he'd 'think' about turning himself in."

"Why not now?"

"I don't know. He said he wanted to contact an attorney and get his affairs in order."

"Do you know where he is now?"

"No, I don't. He wouldn't tell me. But he's not at home; I called there. . . . You should also know that he said he wouldn't come back to Ohio."

"We've heard that before. . . . What do you think?"

Craven paused for a moment and replied, "If Knott doesn't show up soon, get your prosecutor to request a federal interstate flight warrant on your murder charge."

"We should also concentrate on finding John Harris," Munsey added.

"Since I can't locate either one of them, they might be together."

On January 7th, while speaking with a state narcotics officer in Arizona, Munsey was told that Knott's brother-in-law, Frank Piccirilli, had been in close contact with members of the Farentino family for several years. He added that Piccirilli, a former resident of Philadelphia, had often boasted of his contacts in the underworld.

Further, Munsey was told that Harris had been arrested for receiving stolen property from a jewelry store robbery in August, but that he never returned for his hearing. As a result, there was a bench warrant for his arrest.

"Do you know anything else about Harris?" asked Munsey.

"Yeah, there's one thing you might find interesting," the officer replied. "When Harris was picked up with the stolen property they found a telephone number on him. Hold on, let me check this. . . . Yeah, the number is to a motel near Cleveland, the Valley View Motel."

"When was he staying there? What does the receipt say?"

"August 3rd through the 10th. When did you say that murder was?"

"August 10th."

"This might be your man. Anything else I can do?"

"Yeah, tell me does the receipt say anything else about another man being with Harris?"

"Well, apparently two people were staying there."

"Does Harris have a partner or anything that you're aware of?"

"There was another guy involved in the hold-up, but he was never captured."

"Did you get a name or anything?"

"Yeah, his name was something like Dave or David. But that's all I know."

On January 15th, Momchilov arrived in Phoenix and joined Dear and Craven in their investigation of Harris and Knott. During a meeting in Craven's office, and using information Lewis had obtained from the U.S. Marine Corps, Momchilov explained, with some frustration, "Well, we know [Knott's] a white guy, twenty-nine years old, and that he's been a Marine sergeant. He did about six months in Vietnam, and I understand that he's a combat veteran. We've also got a set of his fingerprints. In about 1977, he asked for and received a medical discharge from the corps—because of ulcers. The Marines said that his last known address was in Atlantic City, New Jersey."

Dear then added, "He's about five-ten, two hundred and fifteen pounds, blue eyes, brown hair. He's of Scotch-Irish descent, and I understand he's got a real mean temper. He's never been arrested for anything, not even a traffic violation. The guy's clean as a whistle on the surface, but he and his brother-in-law, Piccirilli, are both supposed to be close to the Farentino family in Philadelphia—and that's where Knott was born."

"I laid out some subpoenas at the Arizona National Bank," Craven told them. "I received cancelled cashier's checks made out to Knott, totalling $17,500—all cashed in November 1980, just like Ridle said. Two of them were made out for $5,000 each, three of them were for $2,500 each. All of them had been endorsed by Knott—with the exception of one, which had been signed by Piccirilli's wife, who is also Knott's sister."

The three men then drove to the Western Union office in Tempe and found three money orders, sent to Ridle by Boyd and Fred Milo. Receipts showed that two of the money orders had been made out for $2,000 each and the third for $500. All three had been picked up, signed for, and cashed by Ridle.

Finally, Dear, Momchilov, and Craven drove to Sandoval Marshall Jewelers in Scottsdale. There, they were shown the gold setting for Kathy Milo's emerald-cut diamond ring. Dear slapped $400 on the table and bought it for evidence.

The next day, Momchilov and Craven went to the home of an employee at the Star System, Molly Triola, to ask her what she knew of her bosses' activities. In addition, they wanted to know why she had been the second signator on the $3,600 check first endorsed by Knott—after the sale of Milo's wife's emerald-cut diamond ring.

"What do you know about Harry Knott?" Momchilov asked Triola, a petite, dark-haired beauty, with a clear, olive complexion.

"I don't know . . . What do you mean? I mean, he helped Tony with the Star System. He ran the place."

"That's it?"

"Well, what do you want to know?"

"What's the relationship between Harry Knott and Frank Piccirilli?"

"They're in business together, pinball machines and all of that. Frank is Harry's brother-in-law. Frank and his wife's trailer is right next to Harry and Margaret's."

"What else about Frank?"

"Well, I don't know if Harry knows it or not, but he's been seeing some other woman, stepping out on his wife."

"Who's that?"

"Her name is Joyce Servadio. She drives a white El Dorado that Frank bought for her. Nice guy."

"He just bought her a Cadillac?"

"Yeah, just like that. Must be love."

"Okay, going back to Harry, have you ever had any financial dealings with him."

"He borrowed $500 from the Star System a few months ago,

May or June. He told me that he was going out of town for a few days."

"Did he say where he was going?"

"Yeah. . . . Harry said he was going to Atlanta for a board meeting with the mob."

"The mob? The Mafia?"

"I guess. He called me from Atlanta, at the end of June, to tell me that he was sick. He said he wouldn't be back for a few days, but I saw him with his woman at the bar a couple of days later."

"Well, what was he doing with the mob?"

"I don't know; don't have the slightest idea."

"Do you know, from memory, whether Harry was in town, say, from August 6th through the 11th?"

"I know that he was."

"How do you know that?" Momchilov asked.

"Because we had a party at the bar on August 9th; that was a Saturday night. Harry was there," she replied.

"On August 30th, Harry sold a diamond ring and received part of the payment, like $3,600, by check. Harry signed the check, and you signed the check. What was that all about?"

"I remember Harry showing me a diamond ring; it was beautiful. He said it was an emerald-cut diamond ring. I asked where he got it. And he said he got it from some friend who owed him money. . . . I remember signing a check that Harry gave me; it was probably that one. It was for a lot of money; $3,600 sounds right. The money was put back into the bar."

"Have you ever seen Harry carrying a gun?"

"Yeah, I have. I saw him with a revolver. It had masking tape around the handle . . . looked pretty cheap."

"What'd he do with the gun?"

"He gave it to Big John. I think he used it for a robbery of a jewelry store."

"And who's Big John?"

"John Harris."

"Right, John Harris! And have you ever seen Harris at the bar, the Star System?"

"Oh, sure. I've seen him there a lot."

"Do you know who he was with?"

"I remember one guy; but I don't know his name. He was about five-eleven, about a hundred and eighty pounds, maybe twenty-five to thirty. He had blond hair and a mustache."

"What else about him? Did you notice anything else?"

"Yeah, he was a real loudmouth, acted like a slob. Big drinker. Always tried to pick up the girls. If they didn't respond to him, he called them a buncha names. He was a tough guy, built solid. Cocky . . . smoked Winstons . . . that's about it."

"When did you see them together?"

"Sometime in late August, I guess. They were talking about something real serious. I remember Big John called Harry and wanted to know when they were going to get paid. I remember they threatened to burn down the bar if they didn't get paid."

25 | "Everyone just called him 'The Kid.'"

THIRTY-THREE-YEAR-OLD Richard Craven had the reputation of being a good and honest cop. He had no enemies, even among those he had helped put away. It was hard not to like the guy; his red hair and freckled face seemed to enhance his boyish innocence. However, his appearance of innocence disappeared when he grew a beard for his undercover narcotics assignments. Married with two children, Craven neither drank nor smoked. He sang in his church choir and taught classes in Bible school. And all of his clean living was paying off in the Milo murder probe.

Acting on a pure hunch, Craven thought that Momchilov and Dear might find it interesting to talk to Bobby "Silverman" Grey, the manager of several local massage parlors—since one of the men they were pursuing, John Harris, had managed a string of parlors in Arizona. Strictly on an educational trip, the three men went to Grey's home on January 19th. There, they were told that Grey was in the hospital. Just the night before, one of his girl friends had fired five shots at him, hitting him once in the upper arm.

Craven, Momchilov, and Dear went to Scottsdale Memorial Hospital, where Grey was recovering from his wound. The fifty-year-old Grey had spent over half of his life in prison. The deep

lines in his weatherbeaten face seemed to account for each day
spent behind bars. Although his arm was in a large plaster cast,
raised and extended, and he was obviously experiencing some
discomfort, Grey welcomed the three investigators, and seemed
prepared to do anything he could to help.

After some preliminary questioning, Craven asked, "By some
chance, would you know someone by the name of John Harris?"

"Yes, sir," Grey replied. "As a matter of fact, I do."

"You do? How well do you know him?"

"Not that well. I've known him for about two, three years."

"Where did you meet him?"

"Just through the course of the parlors. You know, he had
one of his girls working in Houston; I used to hang out down
there. I met him through Joey Washington. I knew Joey from
Houston, and I met Harris through him."

"Did Harris work with you at all?"

"No, sir. He never has."

"Okay, do you know Harry Knott?"

"I know Harry very little. I knew him when he was on what
they call 'the vending machine route.' They had a bar out there
by the parlor, and he had the pinball machines. He had the
jukebox and the pool table. And he'd come by about twice a
week to collect the money."

"So you've had no financial relationship with either Harris
or Knott, other than Knott's vending machines?"

"Well, Harris owed me some money. He had charged some
telephone calls to my phone. . . ."

"About when in time was this?"

"Oh, late July, early August. He just asked me if he could
charge some calls to my phone. I told him he could as long as
he paid me."

"And how much did he owe you?"

"Oh, 'bout $300, probably more."

"Did you ever get it back?"

"Yeah—and that's where Harry comes in—but it was a helluva
time. That Harris character is one crazy fucking individual. . . ."

"What do you mean?"

"Well, I heard from Fats . . .'"

"Fats?"

"Yeah, fucking Harris. That's his nickname. Anyway, Fats or Harris was headin' for Ohio with this guy named Jimmy Jones. And they were traveling around and making calls, charging them to my phone."

"And they were going to Ohio?"

"Yep."

"And this was about July, August?"

"That's right."

"Where were these calls made from?"

"Oh, Philadelphia, Florida, and Oklahoma. That's it."

"Ohio?"

"No, just those places I mentioned."

"Okay. And who's Jimmy Jones?"

"Jimmy Jones is real crazy, crazier than Harris even—and that's pretty goddamn fuckin' crazy. He's one mean guy."

"What do you mean? Is he a killer?"

"Well, I don't know if he kills, but I wouldn't be surprised if he did. The guy's probably one of the meanest streetfighters I've ever seen. Does it for pleasure."

"Could you describe this guy?"

"Five-ten, hundred and sixty-five, kinda gray now. Maybe forty-two, forty-three years old. Tough motherfucker, real tough."

"Okay, so Jones was going to Ohio with Harris?"

"Yeah, they drove Jimmy's car. . . ."

"And what kind of car was that?"

"This old, beat-up 1971 Oldsmobile 98."

"What color?"

"Olive green body, black vinyl top."

"Okay, so what were they doing in Ohio?"

"Like I say, I don't know. But I do know that Jimmy came back."

"What do you mean he came back?"

"He came back to Arizona. I asked Harris later on what happened to Jimmy, and he said that Jimmy had left him stranded. He said something like, 'He chickened out on me and just left me.' "

"And Jones came back to Arizona?"

"Yeah. That's all I know."

"So when did you see Harris after that?"

"Fats? Well, when he got back to Arizona, he called me up and asked me to pick him up at the airport. He said he was coming in from Cleveland. I said okay, and he gave me the flight number and everything. Just before I went to pick him up, I ran into a friend—well, hell, it was Joey Washington. I told him that I was going to the airport to pick up Fats. He asked me if he could go with me, and I told him to come on. So we went to the airport and picked up Fats and some other guy. The two of them got off the plane together."

"What was the other guy's name?"

"The only thing I ever heard was Don or Dave or something. Everyone just called him 'The Kid.' "

"Don or Dave?"

"Something like that. I never got a last name."

"Okay, can you describe this guy? The Kid?"

"To me, he looked 'bout twenty-three, twenty-four years old. He had blond hair, dirty blond, you know? His two front teeth were missing; I kept lookin' at that. And this fucker was loud, extra loud. He was boisterous. . . . Is that the word you use? Extra boisterous. Just, you know, extra vulgar."

"How was he built?"

"He was pretty solid. I'd say five-ten, hundred and seventy-five. No fat, just solid. I figured he was a weight-lifter or something."

"Clothes?"

"At the time he got off the plane, he had on khaki pants and some kind of colored shirt. He was carrying an overnight bag—black, long, the kind that zips up. . . ."

"Okay, how about Fats? Can you describe him?"

"Oh, sure. He's about five-eight or nine. Oh God, he must weigh three-ten, three-twenty. I mean, he's just fat. Curly brown hair. Tattoos all over."

"Okay, so you picked them up at the airport. Where'd you take them?"

"Well, we went over to the bar in the airport and had a drink. And Fats tried to hit me up for some money. Hell, I told him he already owed me money, but he said, 'Don't worry, I've got plenty of money coming. I promise you I'll pay you back in five or ten days.' So I asked him how much he needed, and he said he wanted $200. So—what the hell—I gave it to him."

"So he now owed you $500?"

"Right. After that, me and Joey dropped off Fats and this kid, Dave or whatever, over at the Caravan Inn. Then I dropped off Joey and went home."

"Did you ever see Fats and this kid, Dave, again?"

"Yeah, the next afternoon. Fats called me and wanted to rent one of my cars, my white Eldorado—the one I picked him up in. I told him he already owed me $500, but then he said he wanted to buy my car."

"So you let him have it?"

"Yeah, I did. I said I wanted $1,700 for it, and he said okay. So, now, he owed me $2,200."

"So when did you see him again?"

"The very next day."

"Okay, what date are we talking about?"

"Oh, maybe August 13th or 14th."

"Okay! Fine! All right! That's good! Okay, what happened?" Momchilov exclaimed.

"Well, I knew Harry knew Fats, so I went to Harry, and I told him that Fats owed me $2,200. I told him I wanted the money before Fats wrecked my car. So Harry said, 'What if I give you a post-dated check for $2,200?' I said okay but asked when the check would be good. He said he needed about ten days. Then I asked him whether it was his personal check or what. He told me he'd write a check from this bar he ran, the Star System. So I said okay, and he wrote me the post-dated check."

"Harry Knott did?"

"Yeah. So, later on that night, we all got together for a drink. . . ."

"Who?"

"Me, Fats, and The Kid. We were waiting for Harry. So we started talking; I bought a round of drinks. So we talked. When the next round came, The Kid said, 'You paid for the last one, let Fats pay for this one.' And Fats said, 'No, let him go ahead and pay.' And The Kid said something like, 'Well, it's a goddamn shame. I kill a motherfucker and ain't got enough money for a fucking drink."

"That he killed somebody?"

"Yeah, something like that."

"Did he say who or where it happened?"

"No, and I wasn't about to ask neither. . . . So we were there in this restaurant, and there were a bunch of bikers in there—you know, motorcycle riders? And then The Kid starts getting picked on by this biker. The Kid doesn't say a goddamn thing. The guy keeps riding him. The Kid doesn't say a fucking word. Then the guy put his hand on his shoulder, and The Kid kicked the livin' fuck outta this guy. I mean, he kicked the shit out of him. And all of the guy's biker friends are watching. Didn't do a goddamn thing. They had to call an ambulance for the guy. So, of course, the cops come. . . . That was over at Sambo's restaurant in Tempe."

"Were they arrested?"

"Nope, no one got arrested. They started asking for names. Harris was the only one who gave his real name," Grey added.

"What about The Kid?" Momchilov asked.

"He gave some fake name. . . . In fact, Harris took his I.D. and put it behind the visor in my car."

"Your car?"

"Well, my white Eldorado. The one Harris bought off me."

"Where's that car now?"

"Harris sold it to a friend of Harry Knott."

"Who?"

"Frank Piccirilli."

"Piccirilli? Piccirilli! And then Frank gave it . . ."

"To some woman he's been fuckin' . . ."

"Joyce Servadio?"

"That's it! She's friends with Fats, too, you know, through Harry."

"Did you ever notice whether the Kid ever took his I.D.

"No. For all I know, it's still there."

back? Did you see him get it from the visor?"

"Okay! Okay! I don't know where to go with this. . . . Piccirilli. Do you know him?"

"Only to say hello; that's about it. And that he's Harry's friend."

"So Harry paid you the money? I mean, the check finally cleared?"

"Well, a few days after the fight, Fats came over to my house. He showed me three trays of rings; pulled them right out of a pillowcase. He wanted me to take 'em off his hands. I told him, 'No way.' He said he needed $800 to get The Kid out of town. From what I understand, he said The Kid had held up a jewelry store."

"The Kid was involved in the robbery?"

"Yeah, the one Harris jumped bail on, concerning the stolen property."

"Do you know any of the details about this?"

"No, sir. I didn't want to hear it. I got enough problems of my own. I don't wanna get involved in nothing else."

"So when did you get paid?"

"I called Harry on the date the check was dated. He told me he had just gotten some money from a friend in Ohio. He told me to come down to the bar, and he'd pay me in cash. So I went down there, and he gave me twenty-two $100 bills; then he tore up the check, right in front of me."

"Were you not curious," Dear interrupted, "what Fats and this Dave were doing in Cleveland?"

"No, sir, I was not. You see, Mr. Dear, I've been in the penitentiary half of my life. And you don't ask questions—you know what I mean. I know you live on one side of the fence, and I live on the other. . . . I learned a long time ago: the least you know, the better off you are. No, sir, I was never curious about anything—except when I was going to get my money. That's all."

26 | *"The Kid . . . shot the guy twice."*

ON TUESDAY, January 20th, at 1:30 P.M., Lewis and Munsey arrived at the Valley View Motel in Fairview Park, Ohio, just outside Cleveland. Speaking with the manager of the small motel, they asked whether he remembered John D. Harris, who had been registered from August 3rd through August 10th. The manager replied that he did remember him and his friend.

"Could you describe the other man, who was with Harris?" Lewis asked.

"I'll never forget him," the manager shrugged. "He had no front teeth. We joked about it around here later on. We called him 'Fang.'"

"'Fang?'"

"Yeah, no front teeth, a real mean-looking guy. Young, early twenties. A kid. Five-ten. Hundred and seventy-five pounds. Blond, messy hair, shoulder-length . . . Yeah, he was the one with the big, fat guy."

A few hours later, after returning to the Scottsdale Police Department, Momchilov received a telephone call from Lewis and Munsey, telling him that they had obtained the booking records of the Lookout Motel in Fort Wright, Kentucky—

where Harris and "Fang" had stayed. According to the motel's records, they were driving a 1971, four-door Oldsmobile 98, olive-green with a black vinyl top. During their stay, Harris had received a $700 money order via Western Union in nearby Cincinnati, Ohio.

Momchilov had also learned that, on August 1st, there had been a collect call made to the Star System from the Trave-Lodge, a motel in Cleveland. Munsey told Momchilov that he and Lewis would check that motel to see if Harris had stayed there as well.

The following day, with the help of Craven, Momchilov and Dear obtained a search warrant for Harry Knott's trailer. When they arrived in mid-afternoon, his common-law wife, Margaret Thompson, told them that she hadn't seen or heard from her husband since the holidays. She added that she had no idea where he could be found.

During the search, Momchilov found a receipt for a Western Union money order, dated August 10th, for $600. It had been sent to John D. Harris in Cleveland from "Paul Henderson," one of Knott's aliases. When shown the receipt, Knott's wife said she had written it out—upon the instructions of her husband. In addition, three other money order receipts were found. One was for $750 and dated July 24th; another, sent on July 29th, was for $400; and the third, dated August 5th, amounted to $200. The first was sent to Cincinnati; the latter two were wired to Cleveland. All three were received by Harris.

Further, the officers located several of Knott's phone bills and address books, containing Harris's various phone numbers, as well as a crude chronology of Knott's previous whereabouts. Included in the information collected was evidence that a telephone call was made to a second motel in Cleveland on August 4th—just six days before the murder.

After completing their search, the three investigators then proceeded to the home of Harris's mother in Tempe, who also stated that she hadn't seen or heard from her son since Christmas. Although she admitted wiring him $700 while he was in Cincinnati, she denied knowing, until recently, that he was running from the law.

* * *

Two days later, on January 23rd, Momchilov, still in Phoenix with Dear, received a telephone call from Bobby "Silverman" Grey's attorney. Grey had received a telephone call earlier in the day from Harris, who'd said he was in Trenton, New Jersey, and needed money.

After calling the New Jersey state police and providing information on Harris, Momchilov received another phone call from a man who identified himself as Mark Tate, an acquaintance of Harris's. Knowing about the investigation of the Ohio murder, Tate told Momchilov that he had talked to Harris a few weeks earlier. During their conversation, Harris had told him that he had recently been involved in a contract killing in Ohio. When questioned by Momchilov, Tate, probably a fictitious name, hung up.

In Akron, Dean Milo's widow, Maggie, filed a civil suit in the Summit County Common Pleas Court, alleging that since Fred Milo and his sister, Sophie Curtis, had assumed control of the Milo Corporation on November 7th, the company had been mismanaged. Specifically, she charged that they had paid themselves excessive salaries, diverted corporate funds for personal use, and funneled corporate products to their other subsidiary companies. In addition, she was able to document that—during the first three weeks after the November takeover—Fred and his sister had paid themselves $790,000 in salaries and loans. Two hundred thousand dollars of this money was used by Fred to post bond after his arrest for his brother's murder.

On Wednesday, January 28th, Detective Craven received a telephone call from Joey Washington—whom "Silverman" Grey claimed had been with him when he'd picked up Harris and The Kid at the Phoenix Airport. Craven arranged to have Washington meet with him, Momchilov, and Dear at a nearby hotel.

To all intents and purposes, Washington corroborated Grey's story—adding that Harris had admitted to him that he and The Kid had been involved in the Ohio murder.

"The Kid went into the house and shot the guy twice, putting a pillow over his head," Washington said. "Harris was out in the car, waiting."

"Did he say anything else?" asked Momchilov.

"Yeah. He said the guy [Milo] was scared as hell. Before he was shot, he said, 'I'll just lie here on the floor and won't move.' Then The Kid plugged him. . . . Harris said The Kid had balls."

"How did the whole thing come down?"

"Harry Knott gave them the money they needed to get around."

"Anything else?"

"Yeah, Harris was telling The Kid that he had fucked up. There was supposed to be something like $20,000 and a bunch of jewelry up in the guy's bedroom, and he didn't go get it."

"What about the gun? What'd they do with the gun?"

"Harris said something about throwing it over a bridge."

"Anything else about the murder?"

"No, but they did talk about the jewelry store heist."

"What about that?" Craven interrupted. "What do you know about that?"

"The Kid did that, too. Harris and Knott pumped him up, telling him how great he was. Then he got a wig and went in and did the job. They got a whole bunch of rings. Some of them were worth between $450 to $1,000—about $42,000 worth. They just divided it up: Knott, Harris, and The Kid. If they're runnin' now, that's how they're payin' for it."

After the Washington interview, Dear peeled off and went on his own. Used to working alone, Dear needed the space, especially now. Just the previous night, after nearly a year of battling over his line of work, Dear and his wife had finally split up. It had become apparent that he wasn't going to give up his work for her, and she'd left him after one of those "I-can't-take-it-anymore" scenes. Announcing that she was filing for a divorce, she'd left Dear in Phoenix and returned to Dallas.

Dear now buried himself in his work. He drove to Joyce Servadio's trailer and was able to get into her Eldorado—the one previously owned by Grey, Harris, and Piccirilli. There was a chance that the Kid's I.D. was still there inside, on the visor—but it wasn't. Dear retreated, but only momentarily. He needed to find a way to pressure either Servadio or Piccirilli to talk.

*   *   *

In the meantime, Momchilov and Craven were interviewing Jimmy Jones, whose 1971 Oldsmobile 98 had been driven into Ohio by Harris and The Kid.

"I don't want no trouble with anyone," Jones insisted. "I wasn't involved in nothing."

"We're not saying that you were," Momchilov said. "We just want to know what happened to your car—and what you and Harris did."

"I got nothin' to hide."

"Then this should be no problem for you. Tell us what you know, okay?"

"Well, back in July, Fats wanted me to drive him to Cleveland. He said he wanted to kick the fuck out of some guy who stole his girl."

"So you drove him to Cleveland?"

"No! We never got there—at least, I didn't. . . . We were in New Mexico, Tulsa, Oklahoma, Louisville, and, then . . . let's see, oh, yeah, Covington, Kentucky. That's it."

"When did you go to Cleveland?"

"I'm telling you, I never went to Cleveland! The closest I got was Cincinnati, across the river. I called my old lady, and she told me she was sick or something, so I took a Greyhound bus back to Phoenix."

"Well, what did you do with your Oldsmobile?"

"I left it at the bus station. I left the keys and the registration papers in the car."

"So you gave the car to Harris?"

"Right. He called me up and was pissed off, 'cause I left. I told him where to find everything. I told him to take the car, and keep it, sell it, whatever he wanted to do."

"Have you talked to him lately?"

"Nope. Haven't talked to him since. No idea where he is."

"Okay, when you were traveling with Harris, who was paying the expenses?"

"He did. He paid for everything. When we went to Cincinnati, he picked up $700 at the Western Union office. . . . he just said it was money to help him get to Cleveland to whip this guy's ass."

"Did he say who the guy was?"

"No, he didn't."

"Did he use any credit cards during your trip?"

"Yeah, as a matter of fact, he did. . . . His Union 76 credit card; he used it to buy gas for the car."

Knowing the Piccirilli was having an affair with Joyce Servadio, and that she was a friend of Harris's, Dear decided, unilaterally, to place some additional pressure on both Piccirilli and Servadio, hoping that one or both of them would flip. To provoke this situation, Dear simply told Harry Knott's common-law wife, Margaret Thompson, that Piccirilli was seeing Servadio. "I don't believe you," she told Dear. "He promised he'd never do that again."

"Well," Dear replied, "he's lying."

At that moment, Dear and Thompson saw Piccirilli's wife walking up to Knott's home. "Don't you say a word to her!" Thompson ordered Dear. But, as soon as Mrs. Piccirilli walked in the door, Dear told her, "Your husband's running around with Joyce Servadio. You're being made a fool of."

Mrs. Piccirilli's face contorted while Thompson grew pale and walked into another room. "You should at least cooperate with me," Dear insisted. "Try to help me, because he's not telling you the truth."

Angrier than ever, Thompson returned to the room and ordered Dear out of her house, calling him a liar.

Later, Dear staked out Servadio's trailer, waiting for Frank Piccirilli to show up. When he finally came, Dear called Piccirilli's wife on the telephone and said, "If you want to know where your husband is, go over to Servadio's trailer. I know he's not at home, because he's over there in bed with Joyce Servadio."

Dear resumed his surveillance on Servadio—until he saw Piccirilli's wife park her car and run full speed toward the trailer looking like she was going to blow a hole through her husband. Dear quickly left the area, hoping that Piccirilli and Servadio were prepared to do or say anything to get him off their backs.

Within hours, everyone from Joyce Servadio to Piccirilli's wife was complaining to Craven about Dear's tactics. In an effort to relieve the growing bitterness, Craven arranged a meeting with Servadio and also invited Momchilov and Dear to attend. However, soon after the "sitdown" began, Dear, in a heated exchange with Servadio, called her "a whore." Then Dear stormed out of the room, leaving Craven and Momchilov behind to deal with a very angry Servadio.

Dear's tactics must have worked, though. On Friday, January 30th, Piccirilli broke down, saying that both he and Servadio had had enough. He telephoned Craven and told him he wanted "to clear the air." Piccirilli said that he didn't mind if Momchilov came along—but he did not want to see or hear from Bill Dear ever again.

A short, chunky man in his late thirties, with greasy, black hair pushed straight back, Piccirilli was a throwback to the 1950s, or at least to some second-rate Paul Muni gangster film.

"Okay, Frank you're married to Harry Knott's sister, correct?" asked Momchilov.

"Yeah, that's correct."

"And we understand that you're in business with him, correct?"

"Harry?" Piccirilli asked.

"Yes, Harry."

"Yeah, the vending machine business."

"And you've been friends with Harry for how long?"

"A long time."

"Do you know how long?"

"We go way back to Philadelphia. We both grew up there."

"Do you know Tony Ridle?"

"I've met the guy."

"At the Star System?"

"Yeah, I guess. He and Harry were partners in the club."

"We understand that you went with Tony Ridle to the Phoenix Airport to pick up a package at the American Airlines counter. Is that correct?"

"I seem to remember something about that, yeah. . . . He called me and asked me for a ride to the airport. I picked him up over by the bar."

"And you were driving the white Eldorado?"

"Yeah, that's right."

"Okay, so you went with Ridle to pick up the package and . . ."

"Yeah, we went in and got the package."

"Did you know what was in the package?"

"No, sir. I never even asked."

"You never did?"

"No, I wasn't even interested."

"But you took the package, didn't you? Didn't you place it in your trunk?"

"No! Why would I take it?"

"I understand that you did, Frank. That's not true?"

"Completely untrue."

"So what are you saying—Ridle kept it?"

"All I know is that he picked up the package, and I drove him back to the bar. Then, I went about my own business."

"Okay, what about Harry Knott?"

"I haven't seen or heard from him since before Christmas."

"What about John Harris?"

"I haven't seen or heard from him either."

"Do you know that he's in trouble with the law?"

"All I know is that he got involved in some kind of scam back east."

"A scam?"

"Yeah, I heard that he was milking some guy out of a lot of money."

"And where did you hear this from?"

"Just around. I don't even remember who told me."

"Was it Harry?"

"I just don't remember."

"Have you been sending Harry any money?"

"I told you, I haven't seen or heard from him in over a month."

"How about the Farentino family out of Philadelphia?"

"What about it? They just distribute amusement machines or something. They're just businessmen."

"Have you seen or talked with them?"

"No, I hardly know them."

"Okay, well, we have a warrant out for Harry's arrest. So, if you do see or hear from him, tell him to call us."

"Yes, sir. I certainly will do that."

"Is there anything you'd like to tell us?"

"You just tell that goddamn Dear to stay the hell away from me."

"Anything else about Harry or John Harris or anything else?"

"No, sir. I don't have anything more to say."

As Piccirilli quickly left the room after the interview, Momchilov turned to Craven. Without saying a word to each other, each knew, instinctively, what the other was thinking: Piccirilli was not telling the truth. Because of his tone, his friendship with Knott, and his statements—which were contrary to those that had been made by Ridle, who had passed the polygraph test—the two officers firmly believed that Piccirilli was somehow involved.

27 | *"They were hoping to shake down both guys."*

IN THE LATE AFTERNOON of Tuesday, February 3rd, Momchilov received a telephone call from Rich Craven. The Oklahoma State Police had told Craven that a man fitting Harris's description and using the name "David Ross" had boarded an Eastern Airlines flight three days earlier. According to the Oklahoma trooper, Harris had been bound for Nassau and had probably made a stop in Miami. Also, Harris's ticket had been booked by "Paul Johnson"—one of Harry Knott's aliases—who had accompanied Harris.

Momchilov quickly called Dear, who immediately grabbed the first plane to Miami, in hot pursuit. Once in Nassau, Dear called his law enforcement contacts on the islands, including the FBI, to ask for an all-points alert on either Harris or David Ross, as well as Harry Knott. Later that day, one of his sources came through: Harris, still using the Ross alias, had been spotted by customs agents.

On February 6th, in Akron, Judge Frank Bayer heard two motions pertaining to the Milo case. The first, prepared by George Pappas, asked that Fred Milo's trial be moved out of Akron due to pretrial publicity. Bayer agreed and rescheduled

238

the trial for April 27th in Columbus, Ohio. The second motion, pleaded by Fred Zuch, asked that Milo's $200,000 bond be revoked, since it was "tainted money," obtained as a result of his brother's murder. Bayer rejected Zuch's motion, and Fred Milo remained a free man.

In the meantime, Lewis and Munsey, still responsible for the collection and organization of evidence for the paper trail, received confirmation from the Lookout Motel in Fort Wright, Kentucky, of Harris's registration—with another, unknown person—from July 19th through July 30th, as well as similar confirmations from the TraveLodge motel in Cleveland, for July 31st through August 2nd, and the Valley View Motel in Fairview Heights, Ohio, for August 3rd through August 10th. In addition, the Cincinnati office of Western Union had taken a routine photograph of a man picking up money. He was identified as John D. Harris of Tempe, Arizona. The picture showed a three-hundred-pound man wearing a pair of glasses with two different colors of lenses—one dark and the other clear. The desk clerks at each hotel positively identified Harris as one of the two men who had checked into their motels.

Inspecting the motels' records, the detectives were able to get a description of the car the two men had been driving throughout their odyssey: a green 1971 Oldsmobile 98 with a black vinyl top, with Arizona plates, VDP348.

On Wednesday, February 11th, Sergeant Munsey received information that a 1971 Oldsmobile 98—a four-door sedan with an olive-green body and black vinyl top—had been reported stolen by a Cleveland man. The serial number of the stolen car was the same as Jimmy Jones's car—which Harris and The Kid had used to drive into Ohio. Calling the man who'd filed the report, Munsey was told that he had purchased the car for $100 on September 5th from another Cleveland man—whom he identified.

Two days later, Bill Lewis received an accounting of all gas charges made by Harris on his Union 76 credit card, prior to and following the murder. The information also confirmed the story Jones had told the police—that the two men had been in

Covington, Kentucky, before Harris had driven into Cleveland.
The records also showed he had been in Akron and Columbus.

Later that same day, Fred Milo appeared in court with his
battery of lawyers and amended his plea of "not guilty" to
include "not guilty by reason of insanity."

On Tuesday, February 24th, after tracing the ownership of
the 1971 Oldsmobile 98 through its five previous owners,
Munsey and Lewis talked to Juan Chavez, who had purchased
the car from "a big, fat guy" on Sunday afternoon, August 10th.

"How did you meet this guy?" Lewis asked.

"I was called to the Pizza Pan restaurant that day. My wife
works there. There was this guy—the fat guy and a friend of
his . . ."

"Then there were two guys?"

"Yeah, two of them. . . . So the guy wants to sell his car, the
Olds. He said he needed some money to leave town."

"Did they say where they were going?"

"Arizona. They were going back to Arizona."

"Yeah?"

"So the guy asked me for $50 for the car."

"Didn't you find that kind of weird?"

"Yeah, I did. I asked the guy for some identification. He
showed me his driver's license . . . from Arizona."

"Did you write down the name on his driver's license?"

"No, but I got a receipt."

Chavez went into another room and returned a few minutes
later with a sheet of paper in his hand.

Munsey took the receipt and read it to Lewis: " 'On this date,
I, Jimmy Jones, do sell to Juan Chavez, for $50 one 1971
Oldsmobile 98. August 10, 1980.' . . . And it's signed by Jimmy
Jones."

"Mr. Chavez," Lewis continued, "are you telling us you
bought this car from Jimmy Jones? That this Jones was the fat
guy?"

Chavez hesitated momentarily, then admitted, "Okay, listen,
it wasn't Jones that sold me the car. The fat guy said he was a
friend of Jones, and that Jones had given him the car. That's

how he got the title. He told me the car wasn't stolen. And I believed him."

"So he just signed Jones's name and turned the title over to you?"

"Yeah. . . . Was the car stolen?" Chavez asked.

"No, but what you did was illegal, understand?"

"Yeah, but I got a legal title from Ohio. . . ."

Chavez then produced a second receipt; this one was signed by "John D. Harris."

"I told him I wouldn't buy the car unless he gave me something with his own name on it. I knew he wasn't this Jimmy Jones guy."

"Describe this fat guy, okay?"

"Like I said, he was really fat, almost three hundred pounds, maybe more. Six-foot. Real sloppy. He was wearing some flannel shirt and a T-shirt underneath; I could see holes in it."

"Okay, what about his friend? What'd he look like?"

"Five-nine, five-ten, hundred and seventy-five pounds, blond hair. Real well-built. . . . And, oh, yeah, he had his front teeth missing. He looked real mean."

"How old was he?"

"Young guy, early twenties."

Munsey then showed Chavez six photographs of different people. "That's the guy!" Chavez said, pointing to the picture of Harris taken at the Western Union office. "I know him by those glasses—one's darker than the other."

"Okay, fine, anything else you can tell us?"

Chavez excused himself and returned to the back room. When he returned, he was carrying a small box filled with clothes and papers. "These guys were really messy," he said. "When I took the car, this is the shit they left in it: beer cans, food, bottles, and this stuff."

Munsey rummaged through the box and then pulled out a shirt big enough to wrap around a car. Holding it up, Munsey quipped, "I think this belongs to our man."

While Dear tracked Harris and Knott all over the Bahamas, another member of Dear's "Mod Squad," Carl Lilly, began staking out the Miami home of Harris's estranged wife, Linda.

Dear instructed Lilly to begin the surveillance after hearing rumors that Harris had bought passage on a boat and shipped off to Florida. After having sat in his car watching her apartment building for a total of forty-five hours over a period of four days, Lilly finally spotted Linda Harris's parents, whom he identified through photographs. He got out of his car, walked up to them, identified himself, and asked for their help in apprehending John Harris. Without hesitation, they said that they would do anything to get Harris out of their daughter's life, adding that her divorce from Harris had been finalized on February 20th.

With the parents' help, Harris's ex-wife agreed to speak with Lilly. During their conversation, she said that Harris had been calling her collect, and that the calls had been originating from three different locations: Cleveland, Cincinnati, and Atlantic City. He had been trying to hit her up for money, but she'd refused to help him.

On March 5th at 2:00 A.M., during a routine patrol, Craven located a stolen car parked by a fleabag motel. Craven went to the front office and received the room number of the man driving the car. Backed up by another officer, Craven went to the man's room and, acting like he was drunk, knocked on the door. When the man answered, wearing only his underwear, Craven told him that he wanted him to know he had hit his car in the parking lot. When the man identified the stolen car as his own, Craven and the other officer arrested him.

En route to the Scottsdale Police Department, Craven and the man, who identified himself as Paul McCarthy, discovered that they both knew "Silverman" Grey. While they were talking, McCarthy mentioned that he also knew John Harris—who had approached him to kill someone.

"Who did he want you to kill?" Craven asked.

Seeing Craven's eyes light up, McCarthy replied, "Wait a minute. I want you to know up-front that I had nothing to do with that."

"Right. . . . Now, who'd he want killed?"

"Harris was looking for someone to kill some big executive type in Akron."

"Did he say who hired him?"

"No. I got no idea about that. That's all he said, except that he was offering $10,000 for someone to do it. I got the impression that Harris was gonna end up doing it himself."

"That's it? That's all he said?"

"He said something about they'd tried to find the guy they were supposed to get down in Florida. When they couldn't find him, they just called the guy that hired them and said the guy was dead."

"That he'd been killed?"

"Right, that they knocked him off—when really they hadn't."

"Why would they say that?"

"Because they were going to extort the guy who hired them. Apparently, he had a lot of money. They were going to threaten to tell the guy he wanted killed who was trying to kill him, hoping they could get some money from him, too. They were hoping to shake down both guys. It was a fucking scam."

"So they never killed the guy in Florida?"

"Naw, it was just talk, leverage."

"Well, why, then, was Harris looking for someone to kill the guy when he came to you?"

"I guess there was more money in it for him. Anyway, I thought it was Harris just talkin'. More bullshit. The guy's a real bullshitter."

"But you were offered the contract?"

"Listen, okay? I was offered, and I told him, 'No way.' I didn't want to have a goddamn thing to do with it! Nothing!"

"Have you heard from Harris since?"

"Yeah, kind of, he called me a few weeks ago in Fort Worth. He wanted a place to stay. I told him he couldn't stay with me."

"And do you know where he called you from?"

"No idea."

At 5:30 A.M., Akron time, Craven woke up Momchilov to tell him McCarthy's story. "There was no murder in Florida!" Craven exclaimed over the phone. "It was just a scam!" Sharing Craven's excitement—and waking up his wife in the process—Momchilov, unable to go back to sleep, cleaned up and drove to his office, arriving just after 6:00 A.M.

28 | *"I think the guy's name was 'Milo.'"*

ON THURSDAY, April 23rd—one week before jury selection was to begin in Columbus for Fred Milo's murder trial—Rich Craven was sitting behind his desk at the Scottsdale Police Department when he was struck by a remark "Silverman" Grey had made during their interview with him. Specifically, Craven recalled Grey's mentioning something about The Kid giving the police a fictitious name after his fight with the biker in the Phoenix restaurant. Shuffling through a stack of papers, he pulled out the transcript of Grey's taped interview, noting one specific section:

> Grey: . . . I mean, he [The Kid] kicked the shit out of him. And all of the guy's biker friends are watching. Didn't do a goddamn thing. They had to call an ambulance for the guy. So, of course, the cops come.
>
> Momchilov: Were they arrested?
>
> Grey: Nope, no one got arrested. They started asking for names. Harris was the only one who gave his real name.
>
> Momchilov: What about The Kid?
>
> Grey: *He gave some fake name.* . . .

Craven called a friend on the Tempe police force and asked him to check his dispatch records for the name of the officer or officers who had been called in to break up a fight at Sambo's

244

restaurant between August 13th and August 16th. Within an hour, the officer called back and gave Craven the name of the cop who had written the report on the fight. The policeman was in the office, so Craven was switched to his extension.

The officer remembered the fight and went to his file, while Craven waited on hold.

"Okay, I got it here, Rich," the officer said. "What can I do for you?"

"There were a couple of names you took down of people involved in the fight."

"Well, there were two of them."

"I know, but I need the name of the fellow with no front teeth."

"Yeah, I remember him. He was with some real fat guy and a couple of other people."

"Right! That's him!"

"Here it is . . . John Harris?"

"No, that's the fat guy. . . ."

"Wait, I got it! 'David Bass.' That's B-A-S-S, just like it sounds. He's the one with no front teeth."

Craven then ran Bass's name through a central police records index used by five Arizona police agencies to cross-reference aliases with real names.

Finally, after about two hours of work, Craven discovered that a "David Bass" was wanted for burglarizing a mortuary in November 1979—and that a warrant for his arrest had been issued.

Cross-checking Bass's real name, Craven came up with "David Harden," a five-foot-ten-inch, hundred-and-seventy-five-pound twenty-one year old, with blond hair and green eyes, who had been born near Covington, Kentucky. Playing his hunch, Craven called Momchilov in Akron and told him what he had found.

"This might be a shot in the dark, Larry," Craven said, "but I think we might have something here. I think we have the name of Milo's killer."

"Who is he?"

"David Harden. H-A-R-D-E-N. He was the guy who was in the fight 'Silverman' Grey told us about over at Sambo's in

Tempe. He was using the name 'David Bass' that night. We've got a warrant for him here in Arizona. He's been arrested, one, two, three . . . six times since he was fifteen, mostly for grand theft and burglary. He fits all the descriptions we've received on The Kid."

"What can you send me, Rich?"

"Everything I have: prints and arrest record—I even have a photo."

"Missing front teeth?"

"His mouth is closed in this picture."

Momchilov told Dear, who was sitting in his office, what Craven had found—both men had been preparing for Fred Milo's trial—then Momchilov notified Lewis and Munsey, who were returning to Akron after some follow-up work in West Virginia. On their way home, the two officers stopped in Covington and received a copy of a traffic ticket Harden had received in September. Unfortunately, he had been driving someone else's truck and given the police a fictitious address.

However, with the help of the local police, Lewis and Munsey managed to locate Harden's father in nearby Bellview, Kentucky. The two officers called the elder Harden, and they identified themselves as Covington police officers.

"We have a bench warrant for your son, Mr. Harden," Lewis said, putting on a Southern accent. "He's wanted for a traffic violation."

"I haven't seen or heard from him in months," old man Harden replied. "I have no idea where the hell he is."

After this and other futile attempts to locate David Harden, the two officers returned to Akron.

A few days later, Dear called his associate Dick Riddle, who was also in Akron, and had him dispatch "Mod Squad" members Carl Lilly and Terry Hurley to Covington.

On Friday, May 1st—while the jury was being selected for Fred Milo's trial—Dear's associates arrived in Kentucky and began their search for David Harden. Having no luck, however, Hurley called Momchilov in Akron and asked him what they should do. Remembering the traffic ticket Lewis and Munsey had brought in, Momchilov gave them the name of the owner of the truck Harden had been driving. "Go check this guy out," Momchilov suggested. "Maybe he'll know where Harden is."

Because they were going to the backwoods area, Lilly, dressed in a $400 silk suit, and Hurley, wearing a high-fashion designer dress, decided to change into more modest clothing. They parked Dear's Lincoln Continental at their hotel and unloaded the motorcycles they were hauling, deciding that in this area of small, square-block towns, they'd be better received as bikers than city folks. They had to consider other problems as well: Lilly was a black man and Hurley a white woman.

Dear's two associates went to the owner of the truck's home in Bellview, Kentucky. They were told that Harden was staying with his girl friend in Mentor, just a few miles away. While asking for directions, the man volunteered, "You know, you better watch out for him. He's been goin' around sayin' he's a hit man. . . ."

"What do you mean?" Hurley asked.

"I don't mean nothin'. I'm just tellin' ya'll what's bein' said."

When they arrived at Harden's girl friend's home—one of five trailers in a small clearing, surrounded by a large forest—she insisted that she hadn't seen or heard from him in several days, and suggested that they contact a close friend of his, Ray Raddock, who lived just outside nearby Canton, Kentucky.

Raddock wasn't an easy person to find, but they finally located him in an area bar. And, once they found him, Lilly and Hurley were direct.

"Do you know David Harden?" Lilly asked.

"Why, yes, I do," Raddock replied, with some surprise in his tone. "Why would you want to know about him?"

"We're looking for him. If you can help us find him, there could be something in it for you. Can you help?"

"What're you looking for him for? He do something wrong?"

"He's wanted by the law."

"Well, you two sure don't look like the law."

"We're private investigators."

"Yeah, I know Harden's wanted."

"You already knew?"

"About that thing in Ohio?" Raddock asked.

"What thing?" Lilly replied.

"The murder."

"Can you tell us about that . . . the murder?"

"Are you asking me to talk against my friend?"

"I'm asking you to tell me the truth. He might be in more danger if we don't get to him first. . . . For what it's worth, there's a reward available."

"I don't know if I can be bought to turn in my friend. . . . That would cost a lot."

"Okay, how much would it cost?"

"Five to ten thousand dollars."

"We could get you that, and I could have it here pretty quick. . . . Will you cooperate with us?"

Raddock asked the two investigators to drive him into Covington, where both he and Harden lived. After some trepidation—fearing a possible ambush—Lilly and Hurley decided to go with him.

Within minutes after arriving at his home, he received a telephone call from Harden, who asked whether anyone had been looking for him. Glancing at the two investigators, he replied that no one had.

"You're willing to help us?" Hurley asked, as Raddock completed his conversation.

"I'll help—but not because of the money, mind you. Harden's in a lot of trouble. He's in the hospital right now with hepatitis. Too much drugs. Fucked himself up."

"Which hospital is he in?"

"Nope, I'm not going to tell you that—not until I get the money. Besides, he's there with another name, not his own."

"We can get the money. That's no problem," Lilly interrupted. "But we gotta make sure you know what you're talking about; that you really know something we don't. How're you going to prove that if you don't tell us where he is?"

Instructing Hurley to remain behind, Raddock took Lilly outside, and they walked through the woods until they reached a small stream. They both sat on a fallen, decaying tree and started throwing small stones into the water. Lilly was afraid to turn his back on Raddock; Raddock was deciding whether or not he should trust Lilly. For several minutes, neither man said anything.

Then, while he was looking up toward the sun, through the leaves and branches of the tall trees surrounding them, Raddock said quietly, "When Dave got back from Arizona, he told me all about it. Some guy came to him and asked him to kill someone up in Akron. I think the guy's name was 'Milo,' some corporate owner or something.

"Dave was really smashed that night, really loaded. Dope and booze, I guess. Dave's a speed freak, a mainliner. He shoots up, loves the stuff. Crystal, you know? This guy who hired him took him around, paid for everything. He met him in Covington; they were drinking at some bar. He drove him to the guy's house and gave him the gun, a .32 automatic.

"The guy parked at the bottom of some hill, and Dave walked up this hill to the guy's house. When he got there, he pulled out a blank telegram they'd got at the Western Union office. He rang the doorbell or something, the guy came downstairs in his underwear and opened the door, and Dave shot him twice in the head.

"Right now, Harden just wants to get out the hospital and get out of town. He knows people are looking for him. He thinks those guys who hired him are gonna kill him. And he's scared.

"I know what you must be thinkin' about me—turnin' my friend in for money and all. . . ."

"No, I don't . . ." Lilly said.

"Don't worry about it, Carl. I gotta do what I gotta do, too. I need the bread. But I do care a lot about the guy, and I don't want to see him get his ass shot off. And I don't want to see him die because of the dirty needles he's stickin' in his arms. He's killing himself, and if he don't, someone else is going to. I think, deep down, he wants to get caught, and get it over with. And, like I say, I don't want to see him get hurt. . . . So you get me my money, then I'll tell you where he is."

Raddock and Lilly returned to the house. Lilly asked Hurley to call Dick Riddle in Akron and then took the phone, explaining what he had just heard. "You stay put!" Riddle barked. "Wait there until I get ahold of Bill!" Riddle then called Dear at the sheriff's office and told him he thought Lilly and Hurley might have a lead on Milo's killer. "It sounds like Harden," Riddle declared, and explained Raddock's terms for delivering Harden.

Dear reported to Momchilov, who was sitting with Fred Zuch at Milo's trial. "This could be a real problem," Zuch said. "We'll discuss this after court today."

When Zuch returned to his Columbus hotel room, Dear and Momchilov were waiting with their arms folded, like a boy's parents waiting to hear why the lamp in the living room was broken. "Okay, Fred, what's the problem?" Momchilov demanded.

"The jury's been selected and we're going to start the trial on Monday," Zuch explained. "Our whole case has been laid out. We're ready to go. If you guys arrest this Harden guy today or tomorrow, there'll be an automatic postponement in Milo's trial. And something else could happen later on that could cause a mistrial. And I just don't want to chance it."

"I'll be damned!" Dear exclaimed. "We may never have another chance to arrest this killer! There's no way I'm going to allow this killer to go free! To hell with the trial!"

"Listen, Bill," Zuch retorted, "this is what we have: We have a paper trail, showing eleven separate financial transactions, involving Fred Milo, Tony Ridle, Barry Boyd, Harry Knott! And that totals almost $80,000 paid for this murder! We even have Milo's wife's diamond ring sale covered!

"We have telephone records to and from Milo, Ray Sesic, Ridle, Knott, and John Harris! And these calls came from the homes of Milo, Sesic, Ridle, Knott, Joyce Servadio, and the Star System bar, among other places!

"We can trace Harris's movements, almost daily, since July 14th! We have his credit card records, his Western Union receipts, and his motel registrations!

"We've traced the car he drove into Akron, the '71 Olds 98! We know where he got it, how he got it, where he drove it, and who he sold it to!

"We know the structure of the Milo Corporation inside out! We know all of their internal and external problems! We know about the power struggle for control of the corporation! We know Fred misappropriated $300,000 and was fired because of it! And we can trace just about all of the corporate money and what he did with it after he took control!"

"We can show that Fred had the means, opportunity, and motive to have his brother killed—plus we have the testimonies of Boyd, Sesic, and Ridle to back all of this up!

"Face it, you guys did a helluva job breaking this case! It's up to the prosecution now! We have the case! All we have to do now is go into court and deliver it!

"Now, if capturing this Harden guy right now and getting his story is going to force a delay or even a mistrial, I don't want him! Get him on something else; take him into custody! Hold him! Do whatever you have to do! Make sure he doesn't get away! But we don't need him for this trial!"

"You know, Harden's wanted on a Phoenix warrant for burglarizing a mortuary. What do you think?" asked Momchilov.

"I say, arrest him on that," Zuch replied. "Go down there and arrest him on the Phoenix warrant! Hell, take him back to Arizona! Put him in jail there! I don't even want him questioned about the Milo case now! It's just not in our best interests to do that right now! Wait until this trial is over! If he fights extradition, fine; we'll get him later! But not now! I don't want him now!"

Agreeing with Zuch and planning to arrest Harden on the Phoenix charge and not question him on the Milo murder until after Fred Milo's trial, Dear telephoned Michael Wolff, the sheriff's legal advisor, and had him arrange the pick-up of $5,000 from George Tsarnas for Raddock. Then Wolff called Craven in Phoenix and had him arrange for a copy of the arrest warrant to be sent to the Cincinnati Police Department.

While the warrant was being teletyped to Cincinnati, Dear leased a private plane and, along with Bill Lewis, flew to southern Ohio. They were met at the airstrip by Lilly, Hurley, and Raddock.

"I have $5,000 cash here in my hand, Ray," Dear told Raddock. "Now, it's your turn. I want the name of the hospital Harden's in. I want the room number. And I want the name he's using."

"First, I have to tell you that Dave's been sayin' all along that he ain't gonna be taken alive. You oughta know that, because I don't wanna see him get hurt, you know?" Raddock warned.

"We'll do all we can. Now, give me the information! Now!"

"He's in Cincinnati General Hospital, room 7004. He's using the name 'David Bass.' "

"That's the name he used in Arizona."

"That's the name he always uses."

Just after noon on Saturday, April 25th, Dear, Lewis, and officers of the Cincinnati police force crowded into the emergency room of Cincinnati General Hospital. According to a member of the hospital staff, Harden was indeed in room 7004.

Dear and Lewis then donned long, white doctors' coats, placed stethoscopes around their necks, and went to the seventh floor—with no less than fifteen uniformed and plainclothes officers behind them. After two nurses cleared the hallway, the investigators moved in.

Dear, holding a clipboard, and Lewis entered Harden's room. He was lying on his side, with several pillows propped behind his head. As the two men walked in, Dear said cheerfully, "Well, Mr. Bass, how are you feeling today?"

"All right," Harden grunted, flashing a quick, toothless smile. Harden looked just as he had been described. He was solidly built, with green eyes and blond hair parted down the middle. Although the rap sheet discovered by Craven mentioned that he had six tattoos, Dear and Lewis could only see two: a skull with hair and fire around it on his right forearm and a fire-engulfed demon on his left arm. They also noticed track marks on both arms.

Lewis clutched his wrist, appearing to read his pulse.

"Let me make you a bit more comfortable," Dear said, reaching under Harden's pillows to check for weapons. When he found none, he nodded at Lewis.

"FREEZE!" Lewis shouted, pulling his service revolver from his pants and pointing it between Harden's eyes—which immediately grew to the size of silver dollars from his surprise. "Just lay there, Harden! Don't even think about moving!"

"Don't shoot!" Harden pleaded, throwing his hands up in the air.

Dear stripped his bedsheet away to uncover any concealed weapons, and the Cincinnati police force rushed into the room. Harden was quickly handcuffed, and his legs were shackled to the bed. Dear introduced himself, and Lewis read him his rights, emphasizing that he was from Akron, Ohio. Although Harden knew he was being charged on the Phoenix warrant, he clearly understood what was really happening.

29 | *"Tonight's the night!"*

ON MAY 25TH, Judge Frank J. Bayer in Columbus announced that the jury hearing the murder case of Fred Milo had been unable to reach a verdict on his "not guilty by reason of insanity" plea. Bayer immediately declared a mistrial and ordered a new trial, scheduled for July and again in Columbus.

Immediately upon hearing the news, Lieutenant Momchilov telephoned Bill Dear, who had returned to Dallas. "What the hell happened?" Dear angrily shouted into the receiver.

"George Pappas was brilliant," Momchilov explained. "He conceded that Fred had plotted to kill Dean, but told the court that he had been insane while he was doing it. . . ."

"And that the murder was committed by someone else."

"Right. Were you here for the Detroit psychiatrist's testimony?"

"Yeah, I just got back yesterday. Tanay's his name. Dr. Emmanuel Tanay."

"Yeah. He said that Milo did, in fact, plot to kill his brother —but that he thought his brother had been replaced by 'an impostor.' He even called it 'The Impostor Syndrome'—a delusion caused by turmoil within the family. Can you believe it?"

"That kills me! Did Fred ever tell anybody that?" Dear asked.
"Not that I know of. Our psychiatrist who examined him
said he told him that he mentioned it to several people, but
when he was asked to come up with a name, he said he couldn't.
Didn't want to get anyone in trouble."

"Well, I was there when Tanay said that Fred had thought
that George Tsarnas had replaced Dean with a double. . . ."
"A robot!" Momchilov added.
"Right! A robot! Isn't that amazing? I still say he never told
anybody. Barry says he never told him. Sesic never said any-
thing about it. Neither did Ridle."
"The psychiatrist said that was consistent with his mental
illness. He said Fred couldn't resist killing his brother . . ."
"Because he didn't think that Dean Milo was really Dean
Milo!" Dear exclaimed.
"He's supposed to think that Dean's still alive—that's what
his psychiatrist said. . . . Did you hear Fred's comments to the
shrink on the plots?"
"Which ones?"
"He said he thought about tying him to the mouth of a
cannon or tying him to railroad tracks! Can you believe it? He
admits this, and he almost got off."
"Well, Zuch agreed that he was mentally ill. . . ."
"Yeah, but Zuch said that he could determine right from
wrong and that he was criminally responsible for his actions."
"Yeah," Dear added, "but some of the jurors didn't think so."
"Hell, some of the jurors?" Momchilov exclaimed. "Ten out
of the twelve thought he *was* nuts! He was almost acquitted!"
"That's incredible. . . . When's the next trial?"
"In July. Then, with a little luck, we'll have Harden
testifying."

On June 19th, Detective Craven—along with Ed Duvall,
Bill Lewis, and Harden's attorney—interviewed Harden, with
the understanding that if he cooperated with the prosecution
and pled guilty to aggravated murder, he would do fifteen years
at a federal prison. In addition, all other potential charges
against him in Arizona would be dropped.

Further investigation showed that Harden—despite his crime —*was* still a kid, constantly looking for cheap thrills and fast highs. His mother and father, both of German-Scottish descent, had split up when he was five. Leaving her old man as far behind as possible, Harden's mother, a battered wife, had taken her four children and moved to California. There had been little discipline around the house; Harden and his brothers and sisters had done pretty much as they pleased. Because of domestic problems, Harden had dropped out of high school at fifteen and left home. Once on his own, he'd begun hustling drugs, primarily crank, and become a speed freak himself, mainlining crystal and anything else he could get his hands on or make. While dealing drugs, he always sensed that someday, sooner or later, he'd end up shooting and killing someone. He'd fantasized about the notoriety of such crimes, imagining his name in the paper and seeing himself on television.

He'd settled down for a few years in Phoenix—after meeting and falling in love with a young nurse. Wanting to get married, he'd found steady work as a cement worker and finisher with a local construction firm. However, his girl's parents—who wanted her to marry a doctor or lawyer—had insisted that she rid herself of Harden. After three years of intense pressure from her folks, she reluctantly jilted him.

The break-up had had a devastating effect on Harden. He'd quit his job, gone back to drugs, and started getting in trouble again. For kicks, he would cruise gay bars, pick up someone, take him home, and then beat and rob him. He was a bully and a thief, a cocky young man with little self-esteem, who, nevertheless, viewed himself as Clint Eastwood, walking into a western town: feared by all men, loved by all women.

Two years before his arrest for the Milo murder, Harden, after twice attempting to commit suicide, had been admitted to the psychiatric ward at Phoenix City Hospital. Considering his criminal record, his violent behavior, and his bizarre fantasies, a murder rap against Harden was as inevitable as the sun rising in the east. As Craven conducted his interview, however, the officer also couldn't help noticing Harden's sincere remorse for his role in the murder. As the interrogation progressed, he concluded that Harden's actions had derived from his own desperation, and that whatever fantasy he had once had about killing another human being had quickly turned into a nightmare—even before his capture.

"I met John Harris in a bar in Covington," Harden explained to Duvall. "It turned out that we'd seen each other before. Back in Phoenix, some people I was with got into a hassle with some people he was with, and he took a shot at one of my friends."

"When was that meeting with Harris in Covington, Dave?"

"Sometime in July."

"What did you do then?"

"We got drunk. Then we went to the motel where he was staying. I stayed there that night. Before we fell asleep, he told me I could make some money. When I asked him how, he told me he'd tell me in the morning."

"Do you remember the name of the motel?"

"Yeah. The Lookout Motel in Covington."

"Okay, so the next morning . . ."

"So the next morning, he told me I could make $2,000, plus expenses. He showed me a picture of this guy, and he told me that someone wanted him bumped off. . . ."

"Killed? He wanted someone killed?"

"Right. He wanted me to kill this guy for $2,000."

Craven then showed Harden a photograph of Dean Milo. "Is this the man you killed?"

After only a quick glance, Harden replied, "That's him. That's Dean Milo. Harris said we were going to drive up to Akron and kill him."

"Did he tell you how you were going to do it? Did he already know?"

"Yeah, he showed me a gun. He said, 'We're gonna shoot 'im.'"

"What kind of a gun was it?"

"A .32 automatic. Rusty-black. That and a silencer."

"You used a silencer?"

"Yeah, he gave me that, too."

"Okay, how long did you stay at the Lookout Motel?"

"Four or five days."

"And what kind of car were you driving?"

"He was driving a '71 Olds 98, green body, black top. Arizona plates."

"How was he paying for gas?"

"He had a credit card, Union 76, I think."

"Okay, where'd you go after you left Kentucky?"

"We went to Cleveland. . . . Well, we stopped first in Akron to pick up some stuff."

"What kind of stuff did you get?"

"Plastic gloves and trash bags. He didn't give no reason for wanting that stuff."

"Did you do anything else in Akron?"

"Ate and drank, that's about it. Then, we went up to Cleveland. We needed some money."

"And where did you get the money?"

"It was waiting for us at Western Union."

"And who sent the money?"

"I don't know."

"Okay, what'd you do then?"

"We checked in at the TraveLodge; we were there for about three or four days."

"What happened while you were there?"

"We went to this town outside Akron—the place where Milo worked, his corporation. John showed me where this guy parked his car. He told me that I was supposed to walk right up to him, say, 'Mr. Milo?' And then I was supposed to pull my gun and shoot him. . . . He said he usually drove a red Eldorado with a white top."

"Okay, what was your reaction to that idea?"

"Well, I didn't like it. No way I was gonna walk right up to somebody in broad daylight—and in a parking lot—and shoot him. It was crazy! I told him I wouldn't do it that way."

"How did Harris get all that information on Milo—the color of his car, where he parked?"

"He made a lot of calls to someone. He'd get the information, and pass it on to me. Once, we got word that Milo was in town, and we were getting ready to go kill him. Then, John got a call. When he came back, he told me to relax, because the guy wouldn't be back for a few more days."

"How many trips to Western Union did you make?"

"Four or five."

"And how much of this money did you guys pick up?"

"About $3,000."

"How much of this did you see at this point?"

"For myself, nothing. He was scared that I'd take the money and go home. He kept saying that if we didn't do the job, we'd both be killed. So I guess he just didn't trust me with the money."

"Did he ever say who'd kill you?"

"No, never did."

"Okay, when you left the TraveLodge, where'd you go?"

"To the Valley View Motel, outside Cleveland; we were there for about four or five days."

"Did you go back into Akron?"

"We went to Bath—where Milo lived—and we checked out his house. We had all the information in a white envelope somebody gave him. That's where he got the picture of Milo and everything. We went back to the motel and just waited, you know, eating and drinking all the time. Then, John got a call from someone—I don't know who—telling him Milo was in town."

"When was that?"

"The night before, Friday, I guess. So, we drove back to Bath to his house. He still wasn't home. John called, and there was no answer. Then we went to Riviera bowling alley over in Fairlawn and drank some more. We kept calling, but there was still no answer. We must've called until two, two-thirty in the morning. We stayed until they closed the bar. We called one last time and then drove back to Cleveland."

"And what happened?"

"Then we went to sleep and got up the next day. He got another call, and he says, 'Tonight's the night!' And he took some bullets and loaded the gun. He had to show me how to use it. He showed me where the safety was and how to put the silencer on. . . ."

"Harris did all of this? John Harris?"

"Yeah. He used the plastic gloves to handle the gun and the clip. He filled the clip with bullets. Handled the silencer, too."

"What color was the silencer?"

"Gray-metal color. He showed me how to assemble it."

"So what time did you go back to Akron . . . or Bath?"

"I guess it was around seven, eight that night. We drove past the house again. Still, there were no lights on. So we just started drinking again. I kind of needed to do that. My nerves were shot."

"You were scared?"

"Real scared. He had to keep trying to calm me down."

"Okay, then what?"

"Kept calling, still no answer. John called the guy again in Arizona, and he said something about him coming in late. So we drank until about one in the morning. Then John left to make another telephone call. When he got back, all he said was, 'It's time.' So I took another shot of whiskey, and we walked out to the car."

"Did John call Milo?"

"Yeah, he pretended he got the wrong number when he answered or something. But we knew he was at home."

"Okay, go ahead."

"So he went to the car. He handed me the gun and the silencer."

"Were you wearing gloves?"

"He was; I wasn't."

"Okay."

"Then we drove about two miles to his house. On the way over, he handed me a blank telegram. We'd picked it up over at the Western Union office."

"What was that for?"

"To get into the house."

"Okay, go ahead."

"So he parks the car at the bottom of this hill, leaves it idling. Milo's house is up at the top of the hill. There's a few houses, no other exit or entrance—what do they call that?"

"A cul-de-sac?"

"Yeah, a cul-de-sac. He parked at the bottom of the cul-de-sac. We talked for a minute, and then I got out."

"What did he say to you?"

"Just pep talk stuff. 'You can do it!' All that. He told me to turn the porch light on when it was okay for him to come in."

"Why was he going to come in?"

"We were going to rob the place. He'd been told that there was $20,000 upstairs and a bunch of jewelry."

"Okay, you got out of the car and started up the hill?"

"Yeah."

"Were there any lights on in his house?"

Suddenly, Harden started to choke a bit. "Is there anything wrong?" Duvall asked. "No," he replied, his voice beginning to crack. "This is tougher than you think, particularly this part."

30 | *"I got the feeling the man knew he was going to die."*

WHEN DAVID HARDEN regained his composure and his voice, Rich Craven continued his questioning about the specific mechanics of the murder. "When you were walking up that hill towards his house, what was going through your mind?"

"It's hard to remember everything, because I was really loaded that night. But I was scared, really scared. My legs were shaking; I was shaking all over the place. I was afraid if I didn't do it, John would kill me."

"When you got to the front door, what did you do?"

"I rang the buzzer. I didn't get any answer, so I rang it again. Then I saw someone coming down the stairs. He looked at me through the window, and I said, 'Western Union. Telegram for Mr. Milo.' So he turned on the light inside."

"Did he say anything to you at that point?"

"No, nothing. I heard him playing with the lock, so I opened the storm door and drew my gun."

"Where was the gun?"

"In my right back pocket. I drew it with my right hand. . . . So, he kind of cracked the door open, and I pushed my way in."

"You forced your way into the house?"

"Yeah. He just jumped back and looked really surprised."

"What was he wearing?"

"He just had on his underwear."

"Okay, then what?"

"I stuck the gun right in his face, and I said, 'This is a robbery! Get on the floor!' "

"What was his reaction to that?"

"He was really scared. He kept saying, 'Anything you say! Anything you say!' Then he got down on the floor, face-down."

"What was going through your mind at this point?"

"I got the feeling that the man knew he was gonna die. And I was just freaking out. I just wanted to get it over with."

"Was the silencer already on the gun?"

"No, I took the silencer out of my left back pocket."

"Where did you stand?"

"I stood right over him. I had the gun in my right hand and then put the silencer against the barrel with my left."

"Was Milo saying anything?"

"He was just mumbling something; I really couldn't hear him."

"Then what?"

"I put the gun to the back of his head and fired. I shot him!"

Again, Harden was having more difficulty, but Craven bore in. "Did you shoot him once or twice?"

Harden was silent.

"Dave, did you shoot him once or twice?"

"Once, right then. . . . Then, for some reason, I thought the bullet didn't work."

"Why did you think that?"

"I don't know. Didn't see any blood, and he was still mumbling."

"What'd you do?"

"I was so scared. I just kept saying, 'Hey! Hey! Hey! Don't move! Just stay there!' Then, I went into the living room, and I got a pillow off a chair, and I put it over his head. Then, I pressed the gun against the pillow over his head, and I shot him again."

"Was the silencer still on the gun?"

"No. I stuck it in my pocket."

"Then what?"

"He didn't move—just made some funny sounds. Death rattle, I guess."

"Did you think about shooting him again?"

"No. I was really panicky, and I just wanted to get the hell out of there."

"Did you search the house?"

"No."

"Did you turn on the porch light for Harris?"

"No. I just ran out."

"Did you hear anybody else in the house?"

"No, I didn't. I was pretty sure he was alone."

"Did Harris come back to the house?"

"No. He wanted to, but I panicked so much, I just wanted to leave. I just left, and I ran down the street to the car."

"When you left the house, did you do anything in particular? Turn off the lights?"

"Yeah, I hit the lights on my way out, but I think there was still one on."

"Did you close the door behind you?"

"Yeah, I did."

"Did you lock it or anything like that?"

"No. . . ."

"Okay, Dave, do you know who it was that wanted Mr. Milo killed?"

"I found out it was his brother that wanted him killed."

"Why?"

"For the purposes of ownership of the Milo Corporation."

"When did you find that out?"

"A few days before the job was done. Harris told me."

"What did you do with the gun? We never could find it."

"Got rid of it; threw it over some bridge or something."

"Did you eventually receive any money for this killing?"

"Yeah, I got $400."

"Were you promised $2,000 originally?"

"Yeah."

"Did you ask about the rest of the money?"

"I asked John if I was going to get it. I thought he would give me more, but I only got $200 more."

"So, in all, you received $600 for killing Dean Milo?"
"Right."
"I have a final question, Dave," Bill Lewis interrupted. "Throughout this entire investigation, a lot of us have been puzzled by the appearance of cotton at the scene of the murder, around the wounds and in the victim's mouth. Do you know how the cotton got there?"
"From my silencer."
"Your what?"
"The silencer. . . . It was homemade, a steel pipe stuffed with cotton. When I fired the first shot, all the cotton blew out. That's why I used the cushion for the second shot. The silencer could be used only once."

On July 29th, with Harden testifying for the prosecution, a Columbus jury, composed of seven men and five women, found Fred Milo guilty of aggravated murder in the shooting death of his brother. He was sentenced to life imprisonment.

During the final hours of the jury's deliberations, just before it reached the verdict, yet another thunderstorm raged over the city. As its members returned to the courtroom and passed judgment on Cain, eyewitnesses claim that the storm passed and the sun shone.

Abel had been avenged.

| *"This murder was never supposed to happen."*

WITH DEAN MILO'S DEATH and Fred Milo's conviction and imprisonment for his brother's murder, the Milo Corporation was officially turned over to Sophie Curtis, their sister. Because of her responsibilities at home and to her child, her husband, Lonnie Curtis, became the president of the company.

Maggie Milo, Dean's widow, immediately challenged Sophie and Lonnie's claim to the company, filing a wrongful death suit against Fred. Mrs. Milo claimed that she should have control of the corporation, because, according to Ohio law, "No person who is convicted of [murder] shall in any way benefit by the death." The basis for her argument was that she should receive Fred's one-third interest in the corporation, which—along with her husband's one-third interest—would give her control of the company.

To enforce her claim, Mrs. Milo appointed a new board of directors that met on August 18, 1981. Then, accompanied by Bill Dear, her father, and six private security guards, she literally seized control of the corporation early in the morning on August 24. She ordered the locks on the doors changed, issued new employee identification cards, and had the armed guards escort the Fred Milo–appointed comptroller off the premises.

266

According to a report in the *Akron Beacon Journal* on the day
of the takeover, Mrs. Milo told the company's workers: "The
company is now going to be operated by a management team
brought together and trained by my husband, and with your
help we will continue to expand the business and continue to
provide jobs and security for all of us.

"Your job is the same. We want our employees to continue in
the same way before the brutal assassination of my husband."

She added that she had taken control of the corporation
"because my husband would have wanted me to."

Sophie and Lonnie Curtis, who were attending a beauty
supply convention in New Orleans, were promptly contacted
by allies inside the corporation and informed of the takeover.
By midday, their attorneys were standing before a Summit
County common pleas court judge, who ruled that Mrs. Milo's
action had probably been illegal and was subject to review by
the court. He then issued a temporary restraining order against
Mrs. Milo and her new board of directors. The Curtises also
filed a six-million-dollar suit against her. Lonnie stated that the
suit had been ordered "to protect the integrity of the company
and its property, the rights of the employees to feel physically
safe from invasion by armed guards and other individuals without authority, and in the interest of protecting the public from
such violent and unlawful acts."

Legal experts agree that the battle for control of the Milo
Corporation will be in court for years. Prosecuting attorney
Fred Zuch reflected: "Fred Milo thought his problems would
be over if Dean was removed from the scene. Instead, his problems had just begun. But even in the wake of this heinous crime
and all this poor family has been through, there is no apparent
remorse, no moves for conciliation. There was no middle ground
at all, only more bitterness, more hatred, and more battle-
grounds. It was this same attitude that cost this family the lives
of two brothers—the one who is dead and the one who is now
in prison."

Meantime, on August 11—the first anniversary of Dean Milo's
murder—John Harris's mother in Tempe, Arizona, made a telephone call to Rich Craven in Scottsdale. She informed him

and, later, Momchilov, that her son had contacted her brother, who was supposed to wire Harris $50 in Denver, Colorado. Because she was afraid that her son could be shot by the police, she decided to turn him in and gave Momchilov the location of the Western Union office where the money was being sent. Momchilov immediately contacted the FBI, who arrested him later that day.

Still pushing three hundred pounds, with tattoos up and down both arms, the polite but defiant Harris refused to talk, deciding instead to take his chances in court. His trial, which began on January 11, 1982, lasted ten days. He was found guilty of aggravated murder and, like Fred Milo, sentenced to life imprisonment.

The day after his conviction, Harris—whom I had interviewed on three previous occasions—called me at my home in Washington, D.C. This conversation was arranged by Larry Momchilov, with whom Harris had had several off-the-record discussions prior to his conviction.

During my interview with Harris, he admitted to me, on the record, that he indeed had been involved in the Milo murder. Specifically, he cited that he had hired Harden to kill Milo and had driven him to Milo's home on the night of the murder, among other acts already known by the police.

I asked him for the details of the crime, especially with regard to the role of the conspiracy's alleged mastermind, Harry Knott. Surprisingly, Harris stated that Knott had not directed the murder plot. Instead, he alleged, the driving force behind the murder conspiracy had been Knott's brother-in-law, Frank Piccirilli.

"One day, Frank Piccirilli called me up and said he wanted to get together," Harris explained. "He owed me $100 or something, I forget. So we met at this restaurant. While we were talkin', he said that he had tried to get some guy to do this thing. The guy said he murdered somebody for Frank when he really didn't."

"Give me that again, John?" I asked. "I don't understand."

"That was the first plot. A guy named Bobby O'Brian was involved in that one. He was supposed to kill Milo in Florida but never did. Everyone just thought he killed the wrong guy, because that's what he told everyone."

"Everyone?"

"Well, Frank and Harry. . . . So Frank told me he had this guy in Ohio he wanted killed. And he was offering $5,000. So I said, 'Why don't you let me make the money?' He says, 'Can you handle it?' I told him I could get it handled. So I knew this guy named Jimmy Jones. He's a dangerous-type guy. So we talked about it, and we made the deal. I told him that he'd get a couple of thousand for it. I wanted to fly to Ohio, but he wanted to drive. So we took his car."

"What kind of car?"

"A dark green, 1971 Oldsmobile."

After allegedly receiving $2,200 cash for expenses from Piccirilli, Harris and Jones began their cross-country drive to Ohio. However—as Jones had explained to the police when they interviewed him in late January 1981—Jones left Harris in Cincinnati, leaving his car behind, along with its keys and title. For one reason or another, Jones had decided not to go through with the murder.

"So I took Jones's car, and I drove to Covington, Kentucky," Harris continued. "At some bar, I met this guy. It was Dave Harden."

Harris and Harden had met once before—one night in Tempe nearly two years earlier. According to Harris, one of Harden's friends had punched out a waitress in a restaurant where Harris ate. When Harris found out about the beating, he and a friend took off after Harden and his friends—who had left on foot just moments before Harris arrived. When Harris found them, he pulled out a revolver and asked them who beat up the waitress. He took a shot at the man, who started running. Both Harris and Harden vividly remembered the incident, and it served as the basis for a discussion about the old days and the old gang. The two men drank and talked late into the night.

Harris claimed that he could not go back to Arizona without finishing his job in Ohio. "And I didn't have the nerve to do it myself," he insisted. So, capitalizing on this chance meeting with Harden, he offered him the $2,000 contract he had offered

Jones. Because Harden was broke and desperate for some crystal, he accepted.

Heading north in Jones's Oldsmobile, Harris and Harden arrived in Cleveland in early August and spent several nights hotel-hopping and partying. "Harden was driving me crazy," Harris added. "He was so goddamn nervous, and all he wanted to do was get drunk, get high, and get pussy."

Throughout this period of time, Harris alleges that he remained in constant touch with Piccirilli.

Then, early Sunday morning, August 10th, "We had heard that Milo was in town, so I called him at his house to see if he was there. When he answered and said he was the guy, I hung up. Then I told Harden, 'Let's go.' We drove over to his neighborhood in Bath and stopped at the bottom of the cul-de-sac. Harden was shaking; he was that scared. Then he took the gun and walked up the hill. . . ."

"And who gave you the gun?" I asked.

"The gun? Frank Piccirilli. Frank gave it to me—a .32 automatic, with a homemade silencer, stuffed with cotton."

Harris's insistence that Piccirilli, not Harry Knott, had orchestrated the murder of Dean Milo proved to be another unexpected twist for those investigating the crime. For months, they had been operating under the assumption that Knott had been the pivotal figure in the conspiracy. Now, with Piccirilli and Bobby O'Brian allegedly implicated in the plot, there was more work to be done.

Because the public and the press were never really privy to the actual mechanics of the police investigation, most news about the Milo murder after Fred's conviction was considered anticlimactic. For Momchilov and company, it was anything but. However, there were major obstacles to proceeding with the probe.

Although all of the investigators remained in touch with each other—now more out of personal friendship than actual duty—everyone had gone his own way. Rich Craven in Arizona and Bill Dear in Texas were working on other cases, and were only peripherally involved in the continuing investigation of the Milo murder. In Summit County, because of a serious budget crunch and cutbacks in the sheriff's department, Lieutenant Momchilov was reluctantly demoted to sergeant by his superiors. Lieutenant Bill Lewis retained his rank but was taken out of the detective bureau and assigned jail detail, which is considered by most officers to be the equivalent of Siberia. In addition, to help make ends meet at home, both officers had to accept part-time work. Rich Munsey was still a detective-sergeant at the Bath Township Police, but he was now concentrating on receiving his undergraduate degree while working nights as a guard at a nearby McDonald's.

The second problem was with John Harris. He simply refused to testify or speak officially on the record against his co-conspirators—unless he was given a reduced sentence. Although most of the investigators wanted Harris given special consideration, Zuch remained firm, convinced he could eventually convict Knott, Piccirilli, and O'Brian with or without Harris's testimony. However, because the sheriff's money problems had also impacted upon the department's travel budget, the likelihood of quick apprehensions of Knott and the others became more remote. It was now up to the FBI—which was looking for Harry Knott.

On March 2, 1982, just after noon, FBI agents moved in on the Mining Camp Restaurant in Deming, New Mexico. After distributing thousands of wanted posters throughout the Southwest, federal agents received a tip that the manager of the restaurant, Harry Martin, was really Harry Knott. Knott, who had grown a beard, did not resist. He was arrested and taken to the Dona Ana County Jail.

Two days later, Momchilov, Dear, and Summit County sheriff deputy John Rege flew to New Mexico to speak with Knott. Clad in a blue, short-sleeve shirt, blue pants, and a pair of beat-up cowboy boots, Knott refused to admit or deny anything. However, he did insist that he had nothing to do with Dean Milo's murder.

"When did you last hear from Frank Piccirilli?" Momchilov asked.

"About a year and a half ago," Knott replied sharply.

"Eighteen months?" Momchilov asked. "Think again, Harry."

"Well, maybe it's only been a couple of months."

"What did you do for Tony Ridle?"

"Well, I worked at the Star System, cashed a few checks for him, and sold a diamond ring for $10,500. In all, I received about $1,500 while working with Tony."

"Did Tony ever mention a killing in Ohio?"

"Never!"

"Did you know that you have been wanted since early 1981?"

"Yeah. At one point, I told Detective Craven that I would turn myself in."

"Why didn't you?"

"I just got scared, so I went on the run."

"And where have you been?"

"Oh, Atlantic City, a week in Oklahoma, the Bahamas, El Paso, Las Cruces, Silver City, and I've been in Deming since August of '81."

"Where's Frank now?"

"I'd rather not answer any questions about Frank. He's not involved."

"Will you cooperate without a promise of any deals?"

"I will cooperate. . . . But I don't want my sister, Frank's wife, or Joyce Servadio dragged into this. . . ."

Then, Knott stopped in mid-sentence and glanced at Dear. "I won't say anything more unless that man, Dear, leaves the room."

"What do you have against Dear?"

"He was mean to my sister. He gave her a hard time."

Without saying a word, Dear got up and left the room.

"Where's Frank?" Momchilov asked again.

"We are no longer friends."

"Could you put Frank in the trick bag?"

"Let my silence be my answer."

"Did you furnish the weapon?"

"No."

"Did Frank furnish the weapon?"

"I won't answer that until I talk to my attorney."

Knott remained silent throughout his nine-day trial, which

began on June 22. Even without the cooperation of John Harris —who refused to testify against Knott—Knott was found guilty of aggravated murder and, like Fred Milo and Harris, sentenced to life imprisonment. The jury only needed an hour and a half to reach its verdict.

On September 9th, Momchilov arranged an interview for me with Knott in the Summit County Jail. Momchilov—who had already flipped Knott and had been questioning him along with Bill Lewis and Rich Munsey—sat in on and participated in my taped conversation with Knott.

Dressed in prison garb and still sporting his beard, Knott appeared calm and relaxed. "I have nothing to hide anymore," Knott declared.

"Okay, Harry," I replied. "Tell us how you became involved in the murder of Dean Milo."

"Tony Ridle went on my amusement machine route with me for some collections one day. At the end of the route, when we were heading back toward the Star System, he casually asked me if I could supply a couple of hit men for a contract. He had a friend in Ohio who wanted to do away with his brother, because his brother slapped his father and threw him off the board of directors. The brother was going, you know, a little bit crazy. I told him at the time that I would see what I could do. . . . I went to my brother-in-law, Frank Piccirilli. I told him that this would be a perfect opportunity to milk some money out of a guy who wanted his brother hit in Ohio. This was sometime in late May 1980.

"Frank and I agreed. We set the price at $22,000, plus expenses. The following day, I went back and told Tony this, and I contacted some people that ought to take care of it. He got back to me that same day and told me that he was going to leave for Cleveland the following day and pick up some money. At that time, he told me that the guy who was paying for it was Fred Milo, and that the guy who was going to be hit was Dean Milo. Anyway, Tony left for Cleveland and returned that same day with $11,000 cash. He supplied me with a picture of Dean Milo and told me that his brother, Fred, wanted it to look like an accident. So I contacted Frank and told him. He turned around and hired a guy, by the name of Bobby O'Brian. He was offered $2,000 for the job."

"Did Ridle deal at all with Frank?"

"No, not at all. He dealt directly with me. The only time Tony ever assumed that Frank had any involvement was the day Tony took him out to the airport to pick up $10,000 sent by Fred Milo's people. Frank took the money from Tony."

Knott insisted that he was unaware that O'Brian had been approached by Piccirilli at the time O'Brian was stalking Milo during a sales conference in Phoenix. He also denied that the conspiracy—from his perspective, at that point—was anything more than a scam—a means of shaking down Fred and Dean Milo.

"I had no idea at the time of the exact deal between Bobby and Frank. But I knew that Bobby didn't have what it takes to pull a trigger. He just wasn't a cold-blooded killer. Later, I was under the impression that Bobby knew it was a scam."

Regardless of whether O'Brian was allegedly trying to kill Milo or not, he reported back to Piccirilli that he could not isolate Milo in Phoenix, because he always had so many people around him. Piccirilli then allegedly told O'Brian to go to Ohio. "It was then that I realized that Frank was sending Bobby to Akron to actually kill Dean Milo. So I decided to come along with Bobby just to make sure that nothing happened."

Knott and O'Brian supposedly flew into Akron, rented a car, and began looking for Milo. "Bobby started talking to me that he was a little bit afraid of Frank, because he wasn't out there to kill anybody. I explained to him that it was totally a scam. And he said that Frank had told him that he was suppose to hit him. Bobby and I then went to a phone booth, and I called Dean Milo at his home; I got the number from information. And Dean answered the phone. I said, 'Is this Dean Milo?' He said, 'Yeah.' I said, 'Your family is out to kill you.' Then I hung up."

Knott then called Fred and demanded more money. Fred told him that it would be delivered to him at his hotel that night. According to Knott, there were two deliveries. The first was from Barry Boyd; and the second was from Fred Milo, whom, Knott alleged, was accompanied by a woman.* "That night, there was a knock on the door. It was Fred Milo and [the mystery woman]," Knott explained. "They brought me another envelope that contained $2,500 in twenties, fifties, and several one-hundred-dollar bills. The woman handed Fred the envelope, and he gave it to me, then all three of us talked about the murder. They repeated that they wanted it to look like an accident."

In all, Knott claims he collected $4,500 from the two payments. In addition, Fred, through Ridle, told Knott that his brother had just left for Clearwater, Florida. According to Knott, because they had to show Piccirilli that they were operating in good faith, they followed Dean Milo to Florida.

"Stepping back, there had been a pistol purchased somewhere along the line," Knott continued. "It was turned over to me with a homemade silencer on it. I, myself, had packed the silencer with a complete box of cotton balls. Also, I slipped in a small piece of cardboard with a little staple in it so that the firing pin would jam and wouldn't fire. My classification in the Marine Corps was a small arms expert. I can dismantle certain guns and repair them and reassemble them. I knew what I was doing with this gun. I was jamming it so no one could get hurt. This was the gun in Bobby's and my possession."

"How did this gun come about?" I asked.

"It was bought through some guys in Phoenix, and it was turned over to Frank. Frank turned it over to us."

"What kind of gun was it?"

"A .32 automatic."

Knott only remained in Florida for two days, returning to Arizona alone and leaving O'Brian in Florida. "When I was leaving, Bobby asked me what he was supposed to do. I told him to make up a story when he came back. You know, he couldn't

* Author's note: During my taped interview with Knott, he named and identified a woman who allegedly had accompanied Fred Milo to his hotel room in late June 1980. To date, it is important to note, this information has not been corroborated by any other source. Knott has passed several polygraph examinations on this point—and failed one other.

isolate the guy. Anyway, when Bobby came back to Arizona a day or two later, he told Frank he had made the hit. And Frank told me he had made the hit. So I told Tony he had made the hit, and on it went. I knew that no hit had been made by Bobby. So Bobby gave back the piece."

"He gave Frank the piece?"

"He gave it to Frank. Frank turned it over to me."

"Was the gun still jammed?"

"Not only was the gun still jammed, it still had the cotton there in the silencer."

"Wait a minute. Didn't Frank find that somewhat suspicious?"

"He didn't look."

"There were no bullets gone, the . . ."

"The piece was in a brown bag that was in plastic, along with two Playtex gloves. Frank just handed it to me so I could wipe off all of Bobby's prints."

" 'Here's the gun, Frank.' And then he sees the gun? He opens the bag and sees the gun?" I asked.

"He didn't open the bag."

"He doesn't want to fuck with it. And he handed you the gun?"

"He handed me the gun. I took the gun out of the bag, and the gun was still jammed, the cotton was still in the silencer, and the six bullets that I counted were in there. So there was no way anybody could've been shot in Florida. Two days later, Dean turned up in Akron. Fred called Tony direct. He told Tony that Dean was alive. Tony called me. I told Frank. Frank asked Bobby. Bobby said he must've hit the wrong guy. Also, there were two stories going around: that Bobby had shot the man and that he had run him over in a car."

"How did Frank react to all this? Was he upset?"

"No, just like we were sitting here talking. There was no . . ."

"Come on, 'the wrong guy'? 'Sorry, Frank, I hit the wrong guy'? Doesn't Frank think he's getting shaken down by this story?"

"No."

"Well, who's putting the money together? You are?"

"No, Frank is."

"In other words, all the money that you are getting is going to Frank?"

"Right, with the exception of what we take out for expenses. Anyway, I sent word back to Tony, 'The wrong guy was hit.' Tony sent the word back to Fred. Fred called Tony and said, 'I want the son-of-a-bitch killed!' After I heard this, I went to Frank and said, 'Look, it's about time to finish up this scam. Let's sell this information. Let's get ahold of Dean. Let's get some attorneys involved and show that his brother was out to kill him. See how much money we can take off him.' Frank said he found out that Fred was going to be worth a lot of money—millions! So Frank wanted to go ahead with the murder and shake down Fred for the rest of his life. I told him, 'I don't want no part of the hit! I don't want to kill the man! It's strictly a scam!' So Bobby went his way, and I went mine."

"You thought the whole thing was over?"

"The whole thing was over. Well, I thought it was. Then Frank calls me about two weeks later and says that he hired John Harris and . . ."

"Jimmy Jones?"

"Jimmy Jones. Frank said they were on their way to take care of it. I started getting worried then, because Frank was really out to make the hit. I knew that John couldn't pull the trigger himself. John is a good friend of mine, and I knew that he wasn't a cold-blooded killer either. But I didn't know that much about Jones. I'd only seen him once or twice. But, from what I'd heard, he could pull the trigger."

"I don't understand. Why didn't you come to an understanding with Frank? You know, 'You're taking this thing too seriously, Frank.' Did you say that?"

"There was an understanding. I told him I wanted no part of it. I said the best thing he could do would be to call the whole thing off."

"Did he lie to you? I mean, was he saying, 'Okay, no hit.' Was that the understanding?"

"Yes and no. When Harris and Jones split up in Cincinnati, I figured that was that. I knew John couldn't do it alone."

"But weren't you afraid that the thing was going to get out of control?"

"Yeah. But I only supplied information to the time Frank hired Harris. I didn't even know that John had been hired."

"Did Frank hire John and Jones, or did Frank hire John and did John hire Jones?"

"Well, I know that Frank hired John."

"John hired Jimmy Jones," Momchilov said. "Harris was dating Jones's daughter."

"Did Piccirilli give the gun to John?"

"Yeah, oh, yeah. John and Jimmy had the gun."

"The last time you talked about the gun, you had it. Frank had given it back to you."

"Right. . . . I had taken it out to him to show him that it did fire. So I had to pull the cardboard and staple. He took it and test-fired it with all the cotton in it. Frankly, the bullet wouldn't even penetrate a piece of plywood. See, the velocity of a .32 automatic isn't all that great. It's not like a .45 or a .38. When you put an extension of a barrel on it and pack it with cotton, the velocity becomes even less. The cotton, itself, probably stopped eighty percent of the bullet's power."

"So, in other words," I asked, "if they had tried to fire a shot at Dean from twenty feet, chances are it wouldn't have done the job? The bullet would have probably gone awry? It probably wouldn't have killed him. But, because Dave Harden put it right up to the back of his head, Milo didn't have a chance."

"That's right."

"Okay, just so I have this clear: Frank's alleged purpose in using the silencer and stuffing the metal cylinder with cotton was to muffle the sound. Your intent was to minimize the penetration of the bullet?"

"Right."

"Are Harris and Piccirilli staying in touch with each other, even after Jones backs out and returns to Arizona?"

"Yes."

"I don't understand the chain of command here. I mean, is Harris supposed to be dealing with you or is he supposed to be dealing with Piccirilli?"

"See, you've got to understand John. When John needs

money, he calls Frank. If he didn't get any action that way, he'd call me."

"He would call Frank first, because Frank was the one who hired him?"

"Yeah. But Frank never wanted to send him any money. Anytime John got ahold of Frank, Frank called me, and I sent out the money."

"Why would Frank tell you to send money if Frank was the one with the money?"

"Because he never sent any money orders. I sent all the money orders."

"That's what I'm saying. Why were you essentially willing to provide a layer of insulation for Piccirilli? You fellows were taking all the risks. Why did you give him all the protection, as well as the money?"

"Because Frank was taking a lot of the money for expenses and such out of his own pocket. The other thing is that when Harris came in—and Jones left him in Cincinnati—the scam had been revived. John ain't gonna pull the trigger. I knew that. He could come up with a million reasons why he couldn't get the guy. It's just so hard to believe that Harris met Harden in Covington. I still can't believe it. Twenty-two hundred miles from Phoenix, and this guy, Harden, is ready to go. 'Yeah, I'll go kill him. Let's go.' Then he tells you that he's drank fifteen shots of liquor and fifteen beers. This murder was never supposed to happen!"

"You see, Harry," Momchilov explained, "we thought you were the kingpin behind the whole thing. All we heard was that you were the one who made all the arrangements. You were the one who set the whole thing up."

"The telephone calls, the contacts, the weapon, and the distribution of the money," I added. "The cops did a helluva job on this case. And then, all of a sudden, it twists. . . . When did you talk to Harris? When was the last time you talked to him before the murder?"

"Before the murder? It was probably around August 1st."

"Did you ever tell John it was a scam? That it was supposed to be a scam?"

"No. See, that's what everybody doesn't understand. John was hired and on his way by the time I came back to it. John was already on the road, on his way to Ohio."

"Well, you say that you talked to him on August 1st, why didn't you just tell him, 'Hey, John, this is a scam. Don't really do it.' Why didn't you do that?"

"I firmly believed, after Jones came back to Arizona, that John couldn't do it himself. When I heard he and Jones had split up, I relaxed. There was no way John was going to kill Milo. . . . During this whole mess—you have to understand one thing—except for that time when I was out of it, I was the only direct contact between the people in Ohio and the people in Arizona. I'm the only one who knew what was going on in both places. I'm right in the middle."

"When you talked to Harris on August 1st, you didn't know that he had hired a partner?"

"No."

"He didn't tell you?"

"He probably assumed that Frank did."

"You just seem to be the victim of an incredible string of bad luck," I said with some cynicism.

"Basically, that's what it boils down to, because Frank never told me about John hiring Harden. John never told me about it. All this time, I'm under the impression that John is in Ohio by himself. When I mailed John money on August 4th, nobody said, 'Mail money to John and Dave Harden. Or mail money off to John and his partner.' All I was told by Frank was, 'John's out of money. Mail him some money.' And that's what I did. I sent him some money. And I had no more contact with him until after the murder."

"When did you hear the murder had been committed?"

"It was actually Sunday morning, August 10th. We had a big blowout at the Star System the night before."

"So who told you that the murder had occurred?"

"Frank called me on Sunday morning. He wanted me to send John $600 in Cleveland. He said that John and a partner had shot Milo twice in the head. I really thought it was going to be another scam, another mistaken identity, because, from everything I had been hearing, Milo was still in Florida. I really thought John was making the whole thing up."

"You didn't believe it had happened? You didn't believe that Dean Milo was dead?"

"No! I called Ridle, and I laughed about it. You know, 'They put two bullets in the back of his head.' Then, lo and behold, Tony called me back the next day, and he said, 'Yeah, they found the body.' "

"What was your reaction on the 11th when you heard that the murder had been committed?"

"I was scared shitless, because then I was involved."

"Describe the scene. Where were you when you heard about it?"

"I was at the Star System when Tony called. He told me they had found the body. And I said, 'What body?' And he said, 'Dean Milo's.' It was a little bit of a shock. Because, from the outset, I did not want the man killed, and I wasn't going to participate in anything that would have killed him. Harris and Harden came back to Phoenix. I saw John about two days later, but he wouldn't give me any details about the murder. Tony contacted Fred Milo, and, at that point, it was either play ball or wind up in jail."

Harry Knott's bizarre tale was greeted with skepticism by nearly every police official and prosecuting attorney who heard it. It was simply too much for everyone—after all these months—to believe that Knott was only plotting the "scam" and not the actual murder.

Because the polygraph had proven to be so reliable throughout the Milo murder investigation—helping to clear those who were innocent and cast suspicion on those who were not—Knott was subjected to *three* separate lie detector tests over a period of several weeks. Specifically asked of Knott were questions regarding his information about Piccirilli and O'Brian.

On all three occasions, Harry Knott passed.

On Wednesday, October 6th, 1982, Bobby O'Brian was captured by the FBI in Miami, Florida, and charged with conspiracy to commit aggravated murder. And, on Monday, November 22nd, the FBI arrested Frank Piccirilli at his home in Philadelphia, charging him with arranging the murder of Dean Milo. Since then, O'Brian has bargained for a reduced charge, obstruction of justice, in return for his cooperation. As of this writing, Piccirilli has pleaded innocent and is awaiting trial.

"The mystery woman," who allegedly accompanied Fred Milo to Harry Knott's hotel room, is still being investigated.

Appendix

SEVERAL CONVERSATIONS, interviews, and scenes in this book have been re-created. In the following chapter-by-chapter explanation, all re-creations, unless otherwise noted, are based upon confidential police reports, court records, and transcripts, and/or taped interviews with suspects and witnesses. These interviews were conducted by either law enforcement officers or the author. Any liberties taken in these re-creations have been for the purposes of clarity, continuity, and confidentiality. Neither the basic substance of the material nor the intent of the speakers has been altered.

All re-created conversations between and among law enforcement officials have been checked and approved by the participants; these notations are not included in the following explanation.

The "verbatim portions of taped interviews," also listed, are based solely upon tape recorded interviews with the speakers by law enforcement officials. Unless otherwise noted, all of these speakers were aware that they were being recorded.

PART ONE

Chapter 1: Georgia Tsarnas's discovery of Dean Milo's body has been re-created.

Chapter 2: Shively's conversation with Bud Eisenhart has been re-created. Kirk Shively and Richard Munsey's interviews with Mrs. Tsarnas have been re-created.

Chapter 3: David Bailey's interview with George Tsarnas has been re-created. Bill Lewis and Munsey's interview with Kathleen Milo has been re-created. Lewis and Munsey's interview with Sotir and Katina Milo and Bailey's interview with Barry Boyd have been re-created.

Chapter 4: Munsey's interview with Mrs. Teresa—whose name has been changed—has been re-created. The pathologist's remarks during the autopsy have been re-created. Lewis and Munsey's interview with Fred Milo is a verbatim portion of a taped interview conducted on September 10, 1980. Adams Restaurants is a fictitious name for an Ohio fast-food restaurant chain.

Chapter 5: Lewis and Munsey's interviews with Lonnie and Sophie Curtis are verbatim portions of taped interviews conducted on September 10 and September 11, 1980, respectively. Lewis and Munsey's interview with Bud Eisenhart has been re-created.

Chapter 6: Lewis and Munsey's interview with Angelo Gieri— whose name has been changed—has been re-created. Peter Hartmann is a composite character based on four sources. Munsey and Bailey's interview with Bruno "King Kong" Kertzmayer—whose name has been changed—has been re-created.

Chapter 7: Lewis and Munsey's interview with Phil Donner— whose name has been changed—has been re-created. Nick Terpolos is a composite character based on no less than eight sources.

Chapter 8: Munsey and Bailey's interview with Warren Tobin— whose name has been changed—is, with minor editorial changes, a verbatim portion of a taped interview. Munsey and Bailey's interview with Rod Kyriakides is, with minor editorial changes, a verbatim portion of a taped interview. Munsey and Bailey's interview with Robert Bennett—whose name has been changed—is, with minor editorial changes, a verbatim portion of a taped interview.

Chapter 9: Larry Momchilov and Lewis's interview with Louis Fisi is, with minor editorial changes, a verbatim portion of a taped interview.

Chapter 10: Munsey and Bailey's interview with Arthur Knox— whose name has been changed—has been re-created. Munsey and Bailey's interview with Eisenhart is, with minor editorial changes, a verbatim portion of a taped interview. Munsey and Bailey's interview with Ray Sesic is, with minor editorial changes, a verbatim portion of a taped interview. Momchilov and Lewis's interview with Maggie Milo is, with minor editorial changes, a verbatim portion of a taped interview.

PART TWO

Chapter 11: John Hastings is a composite character based on no less than six sources. Lewis and Munsey's interview with Boyd has been re-created. Lewis and Munsey's interview with Lonnie Curtis is a verbatim portion of a taped interview. Momchilov, Lewis, and Munsey's interview with Fred Milo is a verbatim portion of a taped interview. Lewis and Munsey's interview with Katina Milo is a verbatim portion of a taped interview. Lewis and Munsey's interview with Sotir Milo is a verbatim portion of a taped interview.

Chapter 12: Lewis and Munsey's interview with James Licata—whose name has been changed—is, with minor editorial changes, a verbatim portion of a taped interview conducted on September 25, 1980. Licata's polygraph examination has been re-created.

Chapter 13: Bill Dear's conversations with Lonnie and Sophie Curtis and Fred Milo are based solely on Dear's recollections. However, their statements are consistent with their recorded interviews. Lewis and Munsey's interview with Patricia Douglas—whose name has been changed—is, with minor editorial changes, a verbatim portion of a taped interview conducted on September 11, 1980. Ed Duvall's conversation with Jack Taylor—whose name has been changed—has been re-created.

Chapter 14: Momchilov and Lewis's interview with Taylor is, with minor editorial changes, a verbatim portion of a taped interview.

Chapter 15: Taylor's telephone conversation with Terry Lea King —which was secretly taped with Taylor's knowledge—is a verbatim portion of the taped discussion. Dear's interview with Melissa Mackey—whose name has been changed—has been re-created. Mark Martin's telephone conversations with King—which were secretly taped with Martin's knowledge—are verbatim portions of the taped discussion.

Chapter 16: Lewis and Munsey's interview with Dennis King is, with minor editorial changes, a verbatim portion of a taped interview. Richard Guster's lengthy quote is a verbatim portion of his statement in open court. Lewis and Munsey's interview with Boyd has been re-created.

Chapter 17: The exchange among the law enforcement officials investigating the Milo murder is a verbatim portion of the taped discussion. Dear's interview with William Daily—whose name has been changed—is, with minor editorial changes, a verbatim portion of the taped interview.

Chapter 18: The conversation between Daily and Tom Mitchell is—with major editorial changes, due to the poor quality of the recording—a portion of the taped discussion. The conversation between the police officers and Mitchell has been re-created. Terry Lea King's polygraph examination has been re-created.

Chapter 19: Momchilov and Dear's interview with Mitchell has been re-created, based upon his February 20, 1981, discussion with law enforcement officers. Fred Zuch, Momchilov, and Munsey's interview with Terry Lea King has been re-created.

Chapter 20: Momchilov and Dear's conversations with Boyd have been re-created.

PART THREE

Chapter 21: Duvall's interview with Boyd has been re-created.

Chapter 22: Boyd's telephone conversation with Lonnie Curtis—which was taped with Boyd's knowledge—is a verbatim portion of the taped discussion. The arrest of Fred Milo has been re-created.

Chapter 23: Lewis and Munsey's interview with Sesic has been re-created. Dear's statement to Ridle is based solely on Dear's recollection. Lewis and Munsey's interview with Ridle has been re-created.

Chapter 24: Momchilov and Rich Craven's interview with Molly Triola—whose name has been changed—has been re-created.

Chapter 25: Craven, Momchilov, and Dear's interview with Bobby "Silverman" Grey—whose name has been changed—has been re-created.

Chapter 26: Lewis and Munsey's interview with the manager of the Valley View Motel has been re-created. Craven, Momchilov, and Dear's interview with Joey Washington—whose name has been changed—has been re-created. Momchilov and Craven's interview with Jimmy Jones—whose name has been changed—has been re-created. Dear's conversations with Margaret Thompson and Mrs. Piccirilli, together and individually, are re-created, based on Dear's recollection and confirmed by Craven and Momchilov to whom the two women complained. Craven and Momchilov's interview with Frank Piccirilli has been re-created.

Chapter 27: Lewis and Munsey's interview with Juan Chavez—whose name has been changed—has been re-created. Craven's conversation with Paul McCarthy—whose name has been changed—has been re-created and is based solely on Craven's recollection.

Chapter 28: Lewis and Munsey's conversation with David Harden's father has been re-created and is based on the officers' recollections. Carl Lilly and Terry Hurley's conversations with Ray Raddock, whose name has been changed, have been re-created, based on Lilly and Hurley's recollections. Dear's conversation with Raddock has been re-created, based on Dear's recollection and confirmed by eyewitnesses. The arrest of Harden has been re-created, based on Dear and Lewis's recollections.

Chapter 29: Craven, Lewis, and Duvall's interview with Harden has been re-created.

Chapter 30: Craven, Lewis, and Duvall's continued interview with Harden has been re-created.

Epilogue: The author's interview with John Harris has been re-created and is based on his notes of the conversation and subsequent discussions with Momchilov, who had also interviewed Harris. Momchilov, Dear, and John Rege's interview with Harry Knott has been re-created and is based on Rege's notes of the conversation. The author's interview with Knott is an edited version of a taped interview.

Printed in the United States
By Bookmasters